The CONCERT

A novel about musicians who defied Hitler's Siege of Leningrad

JOHANNA NEUMAN

Also by Johanna Neuman

Gilded Suffragists: The New York Socialites who Fought for Women's Right to Vote

And Yet They Persisted: How American Women Won the Right to Vote

Lights, Camera, War: Is Media Technology Driving International Politics?

Knight & Day

Press Corpse

Death with Honors

To Jeffrey Glazer
1951-2023

The Love of My Life & The Hole in My Heart.

BakeMyBook website: http://www.bakemybook.com

FIRST EDITION

Library of Congress Cataloguing-in-Publication Data is available upon request.

ISBN: 9798856395999

August, 1992

"Whenever I walk on Nevsky Prospekt, I feel my city's drama pulsing beneath my feet. Like a Greek chorus, Leningrad always wrenched between high culture and epic cruelty, as if drunk on history.

Once it was St. Petersburg, for it was Peter the Great's city, and it was he who designed the broad avenues and imported the great Italianate architecture that centuries later I still admire. True, Catherine the Great contributed to the skyline with her stunning Winter Palace and her art collections, all of which cemented Peter's legacy of "a window to the West." But in my view it was Peter who in 1703 first saw the need to open the country to the cultural, political and economic trends of the day across the continent. In doing so, he helped Russia shed its Tatar heritage and become more European. The city flourished, becoming a cultural mecca where Tolstoy wrote, Tchaikovsky composed and Nureyev danced. A haven of intellectual thought, the city also attracted a school of Marxists whose bloody Revolution in 1917 toppled the Romanovs, promising a worker's paradise but instead delivering a Gulag. As a child, I saluted the red flag, one of Lenin's young disciples. Now, at 82, I sigh at my childish ardor, seeing behind St. Petersburg's majestic landscape the ugly scars of tyranny. I am a poet. Sometimes I think only a poet could make sense of this place.

I have also come to understand, at the end of my life, what I wish I'd known at the start. History, despite all its clashing cymbals, all its sound and fury, is mostly irony. Memory is the thing."

- Olga Berggolts, Russian Poet

ONE

The Nazi
December 1945

The bombs of World War II had only months before demolished the Old Town, so I walked the streets gingerly, stepping over debris and wondering what had happened to the people who were buried by its rubble.

I knew no one in Germany, had never left my country before. At least here, in the courtroom in Nuremberg, I was surrounded by the familiar tools of my trade—the microphone, the transmitter, the headset—all the accouterments of a broadcaster. During the war, these devices had served as my voice, even my muse. Now I hoped they would help me control my anger.

"You are Soviet?" asked the reporter next to me.

"Yes," I said, introducing myself. "Olga Berggolts, Leningrad Radio."

She reached to shake my hand.

"Martha Gellhorn, American *Colliers.*"

As we talked, I learned that Martha Gellhorn was a well-traveled war correspondent. Also that she had just divorced Ernest

Hemingway, the famous author, for going behind her back to sabotage her combat assignments.

I listened to her story with wide eyes. But the truth is, I was more taken with her appearance—the hair, curved around her face in rolling curls, the jacket, tailored to her waist, the tight skirt, skimming her calves. She was a picture of 1940s style, and I couldn't stop looking at her, imagining what I could do with my lithe figure, green eyes, and auburn hair if only I had her sartorial choices. I consoled myself with the thought that unlike this woman, who seemed lonely, I have love—a husband who adores me and cheers on my career and two kids who call me Mama.

With other reporters, we sat in a courtroom, waiting for the Nazi War Crimes Tribunal to begin. I was surprised the Kremlin had sent me. Word was that Stalin had asked the other allied leaders—Churchill, de Gaulle, and Truman—not to mention Leningrad. I have always believed he was jealous of our city's cultural heritage—a rich history of intellectual and artistic creativity. He seemed more at home within the walls of the Kremlin in Moscow, where political intrigue was honed as a fine art.

No other country had as many war casualties as the Soviet Union—some said our combined civilian and military death total in World War II topped 20 million. But somehow, Stalin lost this debate. The US side was adamant. What had happened in Leningrad, the Yanks insisted, was a war crime.

I thought so too.

When I entered the courtroom, I was taken by its majesty. Outside, Nuremberg may have been in ruins, the city its own kind of war victim. But inside, the tall ceilings, the robed judges, the panel of lawyers—all seemed like an august setting of the greatest solemnity.

Seated together in a box, wearing identical grey jackets, the 22 defendants had been stripped of their medals and ribbons. They were flanked by military police officers whose white helmets and green uniforms had plenty of both. The effect peeled away the frightful power of these men, exposing them as mere if especially heinous humans. I couldn't stop looking at them. Their very presence begged the question of how men could be so cruel to other men, of why they had come to feel such an outsized sense of entitlement to kill millions of people.

"They look smaller than I imagined," I said to Martha Gellhorn.

"Justice has that effect on some people," she replied.

In the witness chair, Ernst Ziegelmeyer looked stoic. He was not on trial himself, though I had read he was an avid supporter of the Nazi regime and had once written an article praising Adolf Hitler as a great leader who rescued Germany from the economic hardships of World War I's Versailles Treaty. I knew his testimony was crucial to the case of Nazi war crimes against Leningrad.

Telford Taylor approached the witness. Tall, with a strong jaw, the graduate of Harvard Law and General of Army Intelligence had told us he was astonished when he read Ziegelmeyer's file. Everyone knew they were all diabolical, of course, Goring and

Bormann and Speer and the rest of the defendants on trial for war crimes committed by the Third Reich. But in a press conference, Taylor had told us reporters that more than any other witness, he thought this oddly-proud professor could document the Nazis' immorality, and paint their inhumanity on an epic scale.

"You are a professor?" Taylor asked.

"I am a scientist."

"Where did you work during the war?"

"I was director of the Munich Institute of Nutrition."

"And in September 1941, were you approached by one of the defendants to work for the Third Reich?"

"Yes."

"And who was that?"

"General Wilhelm Josef Franz Ritter von Leeb."

Ziegelmeyer looked over at the general, sitting in the defendants' box. I knew that former Nazi officials no longer thrust their arms forward in greeting—the *Heil Hitler* salute had been banned almost everywhere—but he seemed to be trying to convey his loyalty by eye contact.

"And can you describe his position?"

"During the war, he had many, of course. But when I knew him, he was General of Army Group North during the invasion of the Soviet Union."

"And in that position, what did he want you to do?"

"He wanted me to calculate how long it would take to eliminate the people of Leningrad."

"What do you mean, to eliminate?"

"There were three million people living in Leningrad. The Third Reich intended to surround them. General von Leeb wanted to know how long it would take—once calories, essential proteins and fat were removed from their diet—before they would all starve to death."

Taylor stared at the witness, as if pretending not to comprehend.

"Before they would all starve to death?"

A soft murmur of anguish spread around the courtroom, in waves, as translations into various languages were completed on individual headsets to journalists, lawyers and observers alike.

"And what did you conclude?"

"Mr. Prosecutor, I am a man of science. I calculated that if the people living in Leningrad were restricted to 250 grams of bread apiece each day, they would all starve to death by the summer."

"So from the time the Germans invaded the Soviet Union on June 22, 1941, you expected it would take about a year for all the inhabitants of Leningrad to die?"

"That is correct."

"And why was that important to know?"

"Because it was not worth risking the lives of our troops to occupy the city. Shut off all land and air access to food, and the Leningraders would have died anyway. No precious Aryan blood need be shed for their defeat. I simply applied the science of nutrition to the war goal of starvation."

"And was your calculation accepted by the Third Reich?"

"Oh yes. The upper ranks thought it was a brilliant stroke. And the Fuhrer issued a declaration to the troops explaining the rationale."

"I point to Exhibit 110, Director No. 65, issued by Adolf Hitler on September 6, 1941. I ask the court to admit the exhibit into evidence. I ask the witness to read the document."

"I bet he's loving this assignment—to cement his legacy with the Fuhrer," whispered Martha.

"The real crime is that the Nazis thought this was rational!" I said, nearly spitting.

But maybe Martha was right. Ziegelmeyer seemed to sit taller as Hitler's own words echoed through the courtroom. As he read, my hands started shaking.

I kept thinking about the scientists at the Leningrad State Pediatric Institute, who had labored so hard to extract vitamins for children from pine cones and tobacco leaves. The Germans had all the resources in the world to do evil, while we did good with so little.

"After the defeat of Soviet Russia, there will not be the slightest reason for this large city to exist," he read. "Blockade it, target its food storage bins, cut off its electricity and water supply, rain down a ceaseless bombardment from the air. If any civilians—old men, women and children—seek to escape our chokehold, shoot them dead. If officials show the white flag of surrender, shoot them too. We are not interested in preserving a single life in this city—with its Marxists and Jews and Slavs and Ukrainians. It is essential not to let a single person through our front line. The more of them that stay there, the sooner they will die, and then we will enter the city without trouble, without losing a single German soldier. Make no mistake—Leningrad is doomed to die of famine."

My hands shook so violently I had to hold on to the microphone for support. I had lived through the Siege of Leningrad—872 days of relentless bombing, little food, heat or electricity. So had my listeners. Everyone in our city had lost loved ones who perished of starvation, friends who had tried to evacuate with their children only to be gunned down by the Nazis, or colleagues who had eaten their pets to survive. Everyone remembered the corpses rotting on the streets, the police arrests for cannibalism, the destruction of our most beautiful buildings. Now, as I broadcast Ziegelmeyer's words in Nuremberg to my audience listening on Radio Leningrad, I shared my rage.

"Here is the proof," I all but spat into my microphone. "What we experienced was not an accident of war. It was a deliberate policy of genocide. This man, this testimony, is evil incarnate."

Taylor had sucked in his breath at Ziegelmeyer's rendition of the directive. Even now, after all the testimony about the 'undesirables' the Germans brutalized—the inhumane treatment of children, the gas chambers that killed millions, the occupation of countries across Europe—he told us he could still be stunned by the enormity of Nazi venality. Perhaps to make sure the world felt this too, he let Hitler's words linger a bit in the courtroom, waiting out translations in four languages for the resulting ripple of understanding, and its cascade of gasps. Finally, he turned back to the witness.

"But that is not what happened, is it, Professor Ziegelmeyer?"

Ziegelmeyer looked despondent, glaring at the lawyer.

"Were your calculations wrong, Professor Ziegelmeyer?"

"No, I am a scientist. My calculations were correct!"

"But how can that be? Leningrad still stands today."

"They must have been finding food sources we did not know about."

"So that is your current calculation?"

"There is no other way to explain it. I now calculate that only one million of them were living on 250 grams of bread a day. The other two million must have stolen supplies or gone on the black market for food, or escaped. There was nothing inexact about my calculations!"

"So that is your testimony, Professor Ziegelmeyer, that your calculations were correct but that the Leningraders refused to die?"

"There is a science to starvation!" Ziegelmeyer exploded. "No one can live on 250 grams of bread a day indefinitely. It is not possible!"

"He's losing his temper," I whispered to Martha.

"He best show his remorse or they'll put him in the stock with the other prisoners."

On the witness stand, Ziegelmeyer seemed to recover his composure.

"Yes, you are right," he said, his voice softening. "The Leningraders refused to die. By my calculations, they should have all been dead by the summer of 1942."

"And they were not?"

Nothing from the witness.

"And when did you learn that your strategy had not worked?"

Ziegelmeyer wiggled in his seat, seemingly uncomfortable with the memory. He grew silent, even sullen.

"Does the date August 9, 1942 mean anything to you?" asked Taylor.

"Ja," Ziegelmeyer had reverted to German. "Ja."

"Can you explain to the court the significance of that date?"

"By then we had expected to win Leningrad. The Fuhrer had printed invitations to a celebration that evening at their famed Astoria Hotel. I was to be one of the honored guests."

"And what happened instead, in spite of your calculations?"

Ziegelmeyer was slow to respond. Finally, he said, almost under his breath, "The concert. That damned concert."

"You refer to Symphony No. 7 by Dmitri Shostakovich, performed by the Radio Orchestra of Leningrad in that city on August 9, 1942?"

"Ja, that damned concert. That's when I knew they had defied my calculations. My calculations were correct," here he scowled at Taylor. "But that's when I knew we would lose."

"How did you know?"

"The drummer."

"Explain."

"Mr. Taylor, I am a student of music. It is a lot like science—elegant, clean, with a set of rules that glide toward a conclusion."

"And have you studied Symphony No. 7 from this perspective?"

"Of course," he said.

"And what did you learn?"

"The first movement depicts the German invasion of Russia, our brilliant Operation Barbarossa. The kettledrums imitate our thunderous tanks, driving the music toward a crescendo."

"And what did the drummer's performance tell you about Leningraders?"

"The drummer played the invasion theme with such fury, such intensity, that the stage must have vibrated. That drummer sounded like some fierce ancient warrior battling for survival. The Red Army broadcast the concert to our troops, and that was a very clever and demoralizing thing to do. That's when our soldiers knew, when our commanders knew, when I knew and I suspect, when even the Fuhrer knew, that Leningrad, though starving, would never give up."

Taylor nodded.

"And do you know by any chance what became of the drummer?"

"I do not, but I imagine he died within a few days," said Ziegelmeyer. "A starving body simply cannot sustain such a vigorous performance."

"That is your calculation?"

"Yes, based on science."

"I know the drummer," I whispered to Martha. "He's very much alive."

"Were you at the concert?" she asked.

I nodded, wondering how I could possibly explain the concert's magic to someone who had not experienced hunger, or Russian history.

"I will never forget the lift it gave our city. You cannot eat music, but it can inspire you to keep hunting for food. And mostly, it can give you hope amid loss."

"May I quote you on that?"

I smiled. "Of course."

Turning from Martha, I took the microphone, addressing the audience at home.

"They heard our music! They heard our drummer! That concert, that memorable concert, helped defeat them. And you, the audience, you who came shivering from hunger in heavy jackets and shaking hands to hear that concert, you are part of this moment of vindication. Victory, *Pobeda!*"

During the ordeal of our city, many of my Radio Leningrad listeners wrote me that my inspirational words, poems and anecdotes had kept them alive. I thought of them now, wondering if the words uttered in this courtroom in Nuremberg would have similar effect, would soothe their wounds.

A few weeks before I left for Germany, my sister Maria and I visited Piskaryovskoe Memorial Cemetery to pay our respects to our mother. We went often. It was always sobering. But that day, it was particularly memorable.

So many civilians died of starvation during the Siege—some said the total was nearly a million—that they were buried not in individual plots with their own inscriptions, but in a mass grave designated by the years of their passing. Nearly 100,000 soldiers who gave their lives defending the city are buried nearby. Carved into the wrought iron gates that greet visitors to the cemetery are the words of a poem I wrote.

"Know you who gaze upon these stones. No one is forgotten. Nothing is forgotten."

When writing the poem, I wanted to add, "And nothing is forgiven." But I knew these words would inflame the authorities, introducing the question of who was to blame for the hunger. Was it only Hitler's evil plan, or had Stalin turned his back on us too? Why hadn't the Kremlin airlifted us supplies or evacuated us sooner? And why was I forbidden from describing the famine on the air?

Maria and I knelt before the plot marked '1942' and threw red rose petals on its expanse. Maria sobbed whenever we came, and did again that day. I always believed our beautiful mother, Maria Grustilina, who died after our father was imprisoned for disloyalty to the Soviet state, was crushed by grief and lack of food. Almost everyone I know in our country has first-hand knowledge of hunger or ancestral family memory of famine or persecution. I always thought that was just the effect of wars. Now I realize it was also our cultural legacy, built into our bones.

That day, Maria began singing the Soviet National Anthem. I closed my eyes, nodding at the chorus, "Long live our people, strong in friendship, tried by fire." We had been tried by fire, I thought. Why was life in this country so charred? Why was our history often buried with its victims?

By then, a crowd of mourners had joined us, singing at the chorus. All of them had relatives buried in these mounds of grief. Some came over to thank me for my wartime poetry and for the words on the cemetery gate. Maria looked at the crowd, at the gravesite, and then at me.

"Olga," she whispered, "you must tell the world what happened here."

I looked at her intently, my eyes no doubt made bigger and redder by tears spilling from them.

"No one would publish it," I said. "Or if they did, they would be exiled to Siberia. Me too."

"You must write," she said. "We who trust you as our narrator will make sure the book is eventually published. But you must write now, before the memories fade and the pain grows dull."

Once, I had been swept up by the dream that was communism—equality without fear or favor. Later I saw, only too clearly, its faults. Now Maria was asking me to open the wounds of my conflicted soul, to resolve the tension between my love of the country and my hatred for its politics, between Nazi evil and the courage of the Soviet people to survive a siege meant to eliminate them from the earth.

I closed my eyes and thought about what I would say, how I would tell the story of Leningrad's ordeal. I decided quickly that I would not write about military battles or political intrigues. There were plenty of historians who could do that, and far better than a poet could. What I could do is write about the power of the individual to triumph over the political, to persevere over evil.

I would write about an orchestra of musicians, emaciated and weakened, who were like that Phoenix bird of classic mythology, who burned itself on a funeral pyre and then rose from the ashes with renewed youth. These musicians, many malnourished, performed a symphony written about the city's nightmare, bringing a bruised people roaring to their feet, their spirits uplifted, a concert broadcast to the German front lines, crushing the troops' will to fight. Some of them collapsed afterward, the first casualties, but not the last, of a concert that taxed them all beyond measure.

I would write about the meetings of my Poets Circle, that group of women—my crazy, conflicted, traumatized, triumphant friends—who met regularly through the war to make each other laugh.

After I came home from Nuremberg, I redoubled my efforts to produce a memoir. Maria was right; someone had to speak for those, like our mother, who no longer could. History has to know.

For now, I am writing in secret. Someday, perhaps, my work will be published.

TWO

The Drummer
April 1945

I have always resonated with Leningrad's cauldron of diverse ethnicities. Maybe it was because I came from a family that traces its lineage to the tsars—I think one of my ancestors was a craftsman for the Romanovs—and it would be hard to be more Russian than that. Anyway, I had long been fascinated by the influx of Ukrainians, Slavs, Turks, Jews, and other cultures who had, in my opinion, enriched us. Soviet officials tried fiercely to stamp out all cultural ethnicity. We were all comrades, at least in the eyes of the law. But in my view, it was this cluster of cultures that really defined us.

So I was delighted, if surprised, when Dhazdat Zelensky, the Radio Orchestra's burly drummer, invited me and my husband Nikolai to his parents' house, to share a real Ukrainian feast. I had hardly noticed him when I first joined the Radio Leningrad staff. But he had noticed me. Apparently, he considered me the orchestra's unofficial chronicler. And he wanted to tell me his story.

There was a boisterous flurry of introductions—Dhazdat's father Vasyl, his mother Nataliya, and his sister Anichka. Just hearing the way they pronounced their names intrigued me—Nataliya was a slight variant of the Russian Natalie. Their Vasyl, of course, was our Vasily. Anichka was the same—I had heard it meant grace. I had no idea of the derivation of Dhazdat's name, but he said he would explain all in his story. He also said his wife was in rehearsals and would be joining us later. My husband Nikolai had been unable to make it to dinner that night. I smiled imagining his reaction to learning he had missed meeting the famous Katarina Orlova, the city's beautiful prima ballerina. As for me, I loved food but not cooking it, so was looking forward to sampling everything.

"Have some *Vareniki*," said Nataliya, offering me a delicious dumpling dish with cabbage, meat and cherries inside. I'd never had it before. "It's our favorite, though Dhazdat loves Chicken Kyiv."

"Do you want to hear my story?" Dhazdat asked, his voice impatient.

I smiled, putting down my fork to watch his face. Later, when I shared the story with Nikolai, I marveled at Dhazdat's journey, wondering at the improbable turns in life that cemented his history. Maybe it's like that for all of us. I'd read that the Danish philosopher Soren Kierkegaard once said life is lived forward but only understood backward when we view our lives with a long lens. I guess some lives seem more magical than others. Looking back, I think Dhazdat's was a movie.

At the age of five, he had looked down at the fertile, lush grasslands known as the Steppes, vowing never to leave this home of his ancestors. He knew the Ukrainian territory well, having spent long hours playing in its crevices. If he hid in the stables with the horses, he imagined, he could burrow into the straw and evade detection. He had hoped this gambit would keep the family from leaving the land of his birth. His mother had explained many times that they were moving to the city for him. Still, he hated the idea. Worse, Grandpa Stenka would not be coming with them.

It was his grandfather who had put Dhazdat on his lap when he was still a toddler and told him stories of the Cossacks, about how in battle they caught the enemy's bullets in their hands, and how when crossing rivers to escape hostile fire they made the waterbeds go dry. Stenka was upset that his son Vasyl had given Dhazdat a Muslim name—in truth, it had been passed down from Nataliya's side of the family, which claimed some blood of Islam from Turkish invaders. Stenka vowed to teach the boy about his Ukrainian heritage and its code of ethics—never to attack an innocent man, never to let slip away a guilty one, never to succumb to victimhood.

"One day, my grandpa was talking and I kept looking away, I guess distracted by some bug or something. He told me later that, in that moment, he first suspected I was deaf. To test his theory, he clapped his hands. I neither flinched nor moved, just looked at him and smiled."

I had no idea Dhazdat had been born deaf and wondered if the orchestra's conductor, Karl Ilyich Eliasberg, had any inkling. I was eager to hear how it affected him as a musician.

Vasyl picked up the narrative from there.

"My father is a remarkable man," said Vasyl, interrupting. "He taught Dhazdat to dance, to feel the thunder beneath his feet before he could hear the music. After that, he made drawings of Ukraine's history and character from the time of the Vikings. We still have them. Incredible, like he sketched our history."

"May I see them?" I asked.

Anichka went to retrieve the drawings and handed them to me. They were astonishing. Vasyl was right. Like the hieroglyphics of the ancient Egyptian burial sites, they told a story.

"These should be preserved. Someday, archeologists will find them fascinating."

"For now, they stay with us," said Vasyl. "The British Queen has her jewels, but we have these!"

I smiled. In that moment, he sounded a lot like his son—so emphatic in his happiness.

When the local healer suggested they go to St. Petersburg in Russia for an operation, Dhazdat watched as his parents argued over the idea. He could not hear their voices, but he understood their body language. He didn't mind being deaf, but they seemed to.

"What will I do in the city?" asked Vasyl. "How will we make a living without the land? We know no one there."

"Maybe I can get a job as a nurse," Nataliya offered meekly.

"You will have to nurse the boy!" screamed Vasyl. Dhazdat could not hear him but saw his father flail his arms about, as if in exasperation. "And what about Anichka?"

"I was the only one in the family who was actually excited about moving to the city," Anichka explained. "I thought people in a big city like St. Petersburg ate blinis every day. And I liked blinis!"

Dhazdat smiled at Anichka and reported that when the two of them saw St. Petersburg for the first time, it looked like a fairy tale—buildings seemingly made of cake frosting, streets so wide a cavalry of horses could ride through, well-dressed people hurrying from place to place on trams.

"We especially loved that light green building with white columns and gold fillings," said Dhazdat.

"Someone later told me it was the Winter Palace where Catherine the Great lived, and I laughed," added Anichka. "It seemed so improbable, me living in the same city where a great lady ruled. It also seemed surreal, like I could touch history."

I asked how the operation went, and they all started talking at once.

"His first words were 'Ah kod hear'," recalled Anichka.

"Surgeons put a tube in each ear to allow air to flow in," said Vasyl. "It worked."

"All I remember is the first rush of sound," said Dhazdat. "It was so magical I applauded, as if at a performance. I wished Grandpa Stenka had been there to share the moment with me."

"I cried for days," said Nataliya. "It was a miracle."

"Papa was at the munitions factory the day Dhazdat woke from the surgery," said Anichka. "By the time he came home, I had taught my brother to say, 'Papa, hilow'. We all loved it."

"As soon as I could get out of bed, the whole family went to the Neva River Park," said Dhazdat. "For the first time in my life, I heard water lapping on the shore and the giggles of little children. I was mesmerized, but everyone else was crying!"

"The waves must have sounded like a symphony," I said.

"A great description!" said Dhazdat. "See," he told his parents. "I told you she speaks in poetry!"

Within a year, after a tutor had helped him learn pronunciation and reading and adjust to the shockwaves of hearing so much noise, Nataliya asked him where he wanted to go to school.

"Muzykia."

"A music school? What will you study there?"

"Every-ting."

In fact, he took an immediate liking to the drums and all that went with them—the cymbals, chimes, bells, gongs, dulcimers, spoons, tambourines, triangles—he loved them all. He spent hours testing different drumsticks, mallets and brushes, experimenting with the nuance of sound, the difference that a few adjustments could make. Soon he developed a reputation as someone who could fix any instrument, just by listening to it. In this way, he made a few friends, including Zamir Chernykh, a singer in the school's chorus who came to him for help with his pitch.

"But I don't fix voices. I fix instruments," Dhazdat protested.

"You have a great ear, or that's what people say," said Zamir. "The teachers have categorized me as a tenor, but when I sing in the high register it hurts my vocal cords."

"Tell the teacher you are in puberty, that your voice is changing."

"I did, but they laughed at me!" said Zamir. "They say I am afraid."

"Are you?" asked Dhazdat.

Zamir nodded. Dhazdat frowned.

"Without courage, you can never be a singer," he said. "You know your body better than your teachers. Insist they respect you. Embrace your gift. That is what the ancient warriors did."

For the most part, Dhazdat was pretty much a loner.

"Once, I invited him to sign up for my soccer club," said Anichka. They all laughed as Dhazdat led them in a rendition of his response, "I'm saving my feet for dancing and my head for music."

This line had become family lore, but I was fascinated that Dhazdat considered music an intellectual pursuit. I made a note to talk to him about it at work. For now, he continued with his story.

One day, when he was walking home from school, a 12-year-old Dhazdat saw soldiers marching through the streets toward Catherine the Great's Winter Palace. He was impressed by their weapons, their discipline and excited by their demeanor. He tried to walk in lockstep alongside, puffing out his chest, pretending to be a warrior. He looked at one soldier enviously.

"You are going to start a fight!"

"We are going to start a crusade," replied Sasha Polenov, the soldier, with a smile. "You are too young yet, but when the time comes, remember we are communists. We want everyone to have work—we want no one to have more riches than the next. What do you want to be when you grow up?"

"I want to be the best drummer in the world."

Polenov smiled. "Well, the Army could use some good drummers," he said. "Run along home now. It's going to get bloody soon."

Dhazdat's eyes lit up with wonder. "You have guns! There will be blood! I want to come with you."

"Not yet," said Sasha. "In good time."

Dhazdat ran as fast as his feet could carry him. He was surprised to find his father home from work, standing in the kitchen.

"Papa, there are soldiers in the streets! They look like they want to start a fight!"

"They do," said Vasyl. "Those are the Bolsheviks. They want to topple the tsars who have ruled Russia for more than 300 years."

"They want equality for everyone!" he said.

"So they say," Vasyl said carefully, "so they say. But until then we have to store up on food and supplies in case there is trouble. I'll need your help."

"I'll help!" said Dhazdat. "I'll do anything to help the soldiers."

"Bring your wagon," said Vasyl. "We will walk to the farmland and pick some produce that your mother and Anichka can turn into jars of preserves for the winter."

Winter came violent and cold. On many a night during the Revolution, the family had little to eat except those stored pickled and sweetened treasures. Gunfire was a constant background noise, but far from being frightened, Dhazdat thought it a concerto made for the drums, just for him. He practiced at home, using his hands to thump on kitchen chairs as if they were instruments, trying to synchronize his beating to the tak-tak-tak of the guns. Food grew even rarer by year's end, when the White Army, fighting to restore Russian traditions, tried to topple the Communists. Dhazdat knew his Grandpa Stenka was a White Army sympathizer with no use for the Bolsheviks, but Vasyl insisted he tell no one this, as it would threaten his job at the munitions factory.

By the time Dhazdat graduated from the Mariinsky Music School in 1926, the fighting had ended, the communists had won, and the great Bolshevik leader, Vladimir Lenin, had died. Lenin's death cast such a veil of grief over the city that officials now changed its name from St. Petersburg to Leningrad, and the Soviet Union expanded to the farthest corners of its geographic influence. The Zelenskys had left Ukraine when it was its own country, but now they were Soviet citizens.

"What will you do now?" his mother asked at his graduation.

"I will play the drums," he said. "I will volunteer for the Army. I will marry Katarina."

"That was news to me," said Katarina Orlova, who had joined the table minutes before. As expected, she was stunning—blonde hair in a bun at the nape of her neck, blue eyes as big as hydrangeas. But there was gravitas in her smile. I liked her at once.

"Dhazdat always came back after my performances with a flower picked from a garden," she recalled. "But he never spoke, never asked me out, never inquired about my health or happiness."

"A blue flower today," she said when he greeted her at the dressing room door.

"Blue like your eyes," he said.

"Blue can also be a moody color, you know. Maybe you should not get too close."

"I'm afraid of nothing," he said.

"Ah, a mighty Cossack, eh?" she teased.

"A warrior," he smiled.

One time, he went back after one of her performances—Swan Lake, a virtuoso—and he was stunned to see another man there. From the looks of it, this man was also an admirer.

"Who are you?" he yelled.

"Danil Mitkin," said the man, reaching out to shake Dhazdat's hand.

"You leave her alone," Dhazdat yelled. "Katarina Orlova is mine!"

"Dhazdat!" she said. "How could you say such a thing? You and I are admirers from afar. You've never taken me for a walk through the park, or an ice cream in the afternoon, or to a café at night."

"Okay then, I will take you now. We will do everything you want to do. We will be together."

"But I have a date with Danil."

"A date! How is that possible. Don't you know my feelings for you?"

"No, actually, I don't. And if you want to express your feelings, you'll have to ask me for a date."

Dhazdat was not comfortable in these rituals, and knew he was making a bad first impression.

"Okay, but first, I will punch him out."

With that, Dhazdat swung at Danil and struck his jaw. Danil was no prize fighter, but he landed a punch to Dhazdat's stomach, which sent him doubling over.

"Stop it, stop it, stop it both of you!" Katarina yelled. Dhazdat had never heard her raise her voice before. He loved her even more now.

"Both of you, stop now! I'm not going out with either one of you." And with that, she changed into her street shoes, grabbed her dance bag, and slammed the door of her dressing room.

Danil looked at Dhazdat and sighed.

"I guess we both lost the girl."

"Maybe we should have a drink."

And so they had. Turned out Danil was in the orchestra that played in many of Katarina's performances. He was a violinist, much leaner than Dhazdat, but with strong upper arms.

"I guess that's why you have a strong punch," said Dhazdat, and they both laughed.

"Maybe musicians are always pining after the prima donna," said Danil.

Danil suggested they both back off, giving Katarina space to miss them, or at least miss one of them.

"I agreed to this plan, but of course, I had no intention of keeping my word," Dhazdat told us. "I had but only one passion," he said, cupping Katarina's face in his hands, "to win this winsome beauty's heart." He kissed her lips, then turned back to us at the table.

"But I liked Danil and decided we could be friends as long as I won the girl. Still, I knew my mother was right. I had made little progress in the months since, as Katarina rebuffed all interest."

"Why won't you go out with me?" he asked one night.

"Because I don't want to get involved."

"But you like me, right?" He stared at her, marveling at her perfect features. "Do you know how beautiful you are?"

She shrugged.

"I want a career, not a husband," she told him. "The institution of marriage is bourgeois. Better to flower as an individual."

He was diverted from the chase when he won a job in the Radio Orchestra of Leningrad, thrilled to be a member of a tribe of musicians, with a whole nest of drums and cymbals at his command, at least when no one else was using them. The orchestra practiced at Radio House, near the Nevsky Prospekt in the heart of the city. The building housed a choir, two orchestras, and Radio Leningrad, where I worked as a broadcaster and on-air poet laureate.

One day the orchestra's conductor approached him. Karl Ilyich Eliasberg was famous for being silent. The two had never spoken before.

"Dhazdat, I have been listening to you practice," said Eliasberg. "You are rough but insistent. Normally I would start you with an easier

piece, but we are shorthanded and I believe you have the strength to play the drums for our upcoming performance of Robert Schumann's Symphony No. 3. We perform it in two weeks. Do you think you could be ready?"

Dhazdat knew Schumann's 3rd was a crescendo of a piece, leading to a crash on the timpani drums. Literally, the piece landed on the drummer. He smiled. He was a warrior. He could play anything.

"I want to play the 3rd," he said. "Please get me your arrangement as soon as possible."

"Of course," said Eliasberg.

Dhazdat practiced insistently, so loud broadcasters complained his drumming was interfering with their on-air work. He didn't care. This was his moment, the moment when his ears, his feet, and his heart would merge on stage. He invited his parents and Anichka to the performance. His mother even wrote to Grandpa Stenka, asking him to take the train up to Leningrad to witness this triumph. He invited friends from music school, like Zamir Chernykh. And he invited Danil, who sometimes played with the Radio Orchestra of Leningrad.

"Happy to come," he said as the two of them walked from Radio House to the Nevsky Bridge. "May I bring my girlfriend?"

"Is she a ballerina?" Dhazdat's face grew cloudy.

"As a matter of fact, she is," Danil said with a smile, "but not your ballerina. Her name is Zena Fedorov, and she performs for the Musical Comedy Theater. It's very popular now."

Dhazdat nodded, thinking how much he missed Katarina.

"I'm proud of you, Dhazdat," said Danil. "This is big."

At that, Dhazdat's face broke into a wide grin. He stopped at the summit of the bridge, spread his muscular arms through the air, tilted his head back, and announced to the sky, "This is big!"

They both laughed and walked the rest of the way, arm in arm.

The day of the performance, he was too excited to eat.

"You must eat," said Nataliya. "You cannot perform without food."

"I can," he told his mother. When he saw the hurt on her face, he smiled and said, "Save the feast for afterward, okay?"

"I knew there was some kinetic energy inside my body that would propel me forward," Dhazdat recalled. "I did not want food clogging my connection to this rich, inner resource. With my family and friends in the audience, I wanted to feel the music as never before."

I marveled at his account. Grandpa Stenka had taught Dhazdat as a boy to dance, to feel the earth's vibrations before he could hear them. Once he could hear, he vowed to channel that memory into the music. The Soviet Union frowned on religion, but sometimes I wondered if there was a God. Maybe Dhazdat's story is a sign that some things really do happen for a reason.

He got to the Symphony Hall an hour early for one more practice. Afterward, he closed his eyes and felt the music, thinking of the consummate duty of the drums in this performance.

"Ready to go?" Eliasberg asked, waking him from his reverie.

"I am ready," Dhazdat smiled at him. "You?"

Eliasberg laughed.

"You know, I used to think I could practice for these events. And in a way, I can. But I've come to understand that there is something unchoreographed that happens when I lift the baton for the first time, thrilling really, as so many pairs of eyes look intently at me for direction. We can all practice for every concert, but there is a magic in the performing, a shared spontaneity that cannot be anticipated. I hope that happens tonight—a bond between 42 musicians and the score."

Dhazdat nodded. He had heard Eliasberg was a curmudgeon—moody and introspective. Now he realized that he was actually a philosopher and knew he had much to learn from him.

As soon as Eliasberg lifted his right arm, the violins came to attention, as theirs was the first sound, the most pressing sound. Soon enough the heavy horns came in, and the piano, and the light flutes. Dhazdat played throughout and did not miss a cue, but his triumph came at the symphony's close when all eyes turned to him as he played the finale on the kettledrums, called timpani. The music required Dhazdat to flip his mallets from front to back, striking the drum wrap first with the felt end and then with the wood end of his sticks. Dhazdat played the instrument as well as the audience, whipping both into a frenzy, sometimes sending his sticks into the air between beats. Afterward, Eliasberg singled him out for applause. He stood and bowed deeply. The musicians around him shuffled their feet, a sign of professional respect. The audience rose in an ovation.

"You were the best!" said Anichka afterward. "The best one!"

The rest of his family crowded around him, his mother beaming, his father giving him a bear hug of approval. Grandpa Stenka was crying as he hugged Dhazdat.

"You have made me so proud," he whispered in Dhazdat's ear. "You are a warrior of the drums!"

Over Grandpa Stenka's head he saw Danil and Zena approaching. He smiled and introduced them to his family. And the next time he looked up, he saw Katarina. She had been crying.

"Katarina, how wonderful to see you!" he said.

"And you," she said. "You were magnificent tonight. I am so happy for you."

"I am happy too," he said, "but it would make me even happier if you came to dinner with us, to be with my family, to celebrate this moment."

"First, I shielded my eyes," she recalled now. "Then I looked into his eyes, and I said yes."

Danil and Zena begged off, but everyone else went home to the Zelensky home, where Nataliya had prepared all manner of treats—borscht, kasha, chicken, and Anichka's favorite—blueberry blinis.

"Were you nervous?" asked Katarina

"No," said Dhazdat, "just wired."

She nodded. "I get that way sometimes, too, before a performance."

"My grandpa taught me that," Dhazdat said, looking with gratitude at Stenka. "He taught me that energy can fuel my body from my feet to my hands and from my heart to my head."

Stenka looked embarrassed by the attention—no one had ever credited him with wisdom, only strength. But he warmed to the glow of recognition, offering more details.

"It is always best to hold your energy tight, like an animal about to pounce," he said. "Then you will always have enough for the big moments in life." He beamed at Dhazdat, and winked at Katarina.

After dinner, Dhazdat offered to walk her home. To his delight, Katarina said yes.

"You've grown up," she said as they walked through the park. "You are the man I thought you could become."

He stopped in his tracks, took her shoulders in his hands, and stared into her beautiful face.

"May I kiss you?"

"Yes."

It was a long and passionate kiss. Dhazdat felt dizzy afterward, so they sat on a bench. There were more kisses, and laughter, and a promise that he would come to see her next performance, taking her to dinner afterward. She had missed seeing him. She said yes.

"What were you worried about?" I asked Katarina.

"From the time I was a girl, I had wanted to be part of Leningrad's cultural intelligentsia, to dance the great ballets for a sophisticated audience, so I resisted for a while," said Katarina. "When he courted me, Dhazdat seemed more Cossack warrior than Leningrad cosmopolitan. But he pursued me with a fierce devotion that touched my heart. I knew no one else would love me as he did."

For the rest of that year, they shared performances, dinners, and more. One night in her apartment, she asked him what he wanted from life.

"I have everything in life—I work as a drummer, I have a beautiful girlfriend, and I live in a city of culture. I wish only for children, so I can give them the gifts and lessons I learned from my family."

"And would you like to have those children with me?"

Dhazdat was so stunned he almost lost his words.

"W-w-with you? Katarina, are you saying you would marry me?"

"Well, are you asking me?" she said, a sultry smile on her face.

He began whooping up and down like one of those American Indians she had read about in history class.

"Shhh…," she said laughing, "you'll disturb the neighbors!"

"Yes," he bellowed, "yes, my beautiful Katarina Orlova, I am asking you to marry me! Marry me!"

Her eyes crinkled at him, and she nodded.

Grandpa Stenka insisted on a full Ukrainian wedding. So they all traveled to the Steppes for the event, with Katarina bringing her sister Mariska, her father Dmitri and mother Lara, and several people in her ballet troupe, including the director, Dima Kuzmin. Dhazdat invited Danil and Zena, by then a couple. He invited half the Radio Orchestra of Leningrad, along with Eliasberg, who, after some hesitation, agreed to come. This surprised everyone, as he was not known as a social creature.

I smiled, wishing I could have attended their wedding. But I was only 20 then, still in school, not yet a member of the staff, or even married. At the time, I knew none of the characters Dhazdat and his family were describing. But I knew them now, and I hung on every word of the account.

Grandpa Stenka had handled the preparations, renting two large homes: one for the bride's side, the other for all of Dhazdat's colleagues. The morning of the wedding, Dhazdat mounted a horse and rode to the bride's house to take Katarina to church. All the others followed in special marriage carriages. At the ceremony, there were dances, songs, and blessings. Some of the toasts drew laughs.

Anichka told of the time she taught Dhazdat to say 'Papa Hilow' and how the father and son had celebrated the moment by dancing so joyously they almost fell off the balcony. Until that moment, Eliasberg had no idea his drummer had been born deaf. Now he gave a toast about how the disclosure explained much about Dhazdat's playing—his drumming an insistence that everybody hear him whether they wanted to or not. Katarina's sister Mariska, an art student, recalled how in childhood, her sister had drawn a picture of royalty and declared she would grow up to marry a prince. Stenka chose that moment to announce that for the day, he was empowered to designate Dhazdat and Katarina, the prince and princess of the Steppes. Finally, Dmitri and Lara joined Vasyl and Nataliya as the two sets of parents lifted a loaf of bread above the new couple's head and sprinkled them with a wedding mix wheat, nuts, sweets and hops.

"This is for happiness," Nataliya explained, sending the first sprinkle toward the newlyweds.

"Much happiness," said Dmitri, tossing his portion at them.

"This is for grandchildren," said Lara.

"And especially for grandchildren," bellowed Vasyl, emptying the rest of the potion at them.

Everyone laughed.

"My next role was to unbraid Katarina's hair," Dhazdat recalled, looking at her now. "I was so proud. Everyone could see how beautiful she was. And now she was my wife!"

That night, he dreamed that he and Katarina were in a beautiful field that looked like the Steppes, except it was near the Neva River, in Leningrad. They were having a picnic when suddenly, an eagle swooped down and grabbed the bread they had brought for lunch. He chased the eagle, but he could not keep up. When he woke, he was sweating. He did not know what the dream meant, but he believed it was an omen, and not a good one. What did the eagle represent? Why did it take their bread? He wanted to protect Katarina, to keep her nurtured and happy.

"I told him in the morning not to worry, that nothing could interrupt our happiness," said Katarina.

"And I told her that worry was my job. Her job was to be happy."

I helped Nataliya clear the dishes. Dhazdat pulled me aside.

"You understand now, yes?" he said. "I loved this city from the moment I first saw it, but I will always be a child of Ukraine, and I'm glad we are now part of the cultural pulse of this magnificent city."

"Your history is in Ukraine, but your dreams are in Leningrad," I said.

He nodded.

"Yes," he said. "And my fears."

THREE

The Poet
March 1938

I will never forget the day I was led from Radio House and shoved in the backseat of a police car.

I looked up at the building and saw my colleagues standing at the windows, looking sullen. In fact, the whole building looked as if it were weeping, like that painting *The Scream* by Edvard Munch. Vadim Nemkov, our director, was gesturing for everyone to get back to work. How I longed to join them.

Dhazdat told me later he knew something was wrong as soon as he approached the building. For one thing, police cars were parked outside. For another, there was no music coming from the building, no sounds of musicians warming up or practicing, not even the annoying metronome that signaled to Radio Leningrad's listeners that the day's broadcast had ended – tick, tock, tick, tock, at almost a strike a minute, as if to announce that the city's heart was still beating. He rushed through the door and felt a chill. The quiet was unnerving.

"What's going on?" he asked Viktor Koslov, a clarinetist. The two of them often shared lunches between rehearsals, and Dhazdat told me he had come to enjoy Viktor's silly sense of humor. "Why the long faces?"

"Olga is being arrested. Vadim is trying to reason with the police—but respectfully so as not to get arrested himself. The interrogation has been going on for 45 minutes."

"But why?" Dhazdat asked.

Koslov shushed him and motioned him to a side hallway.

"Stalin's police, the NKVD, have come to arrest her for disloyalty to the Communist Party."

All eyes were on the broadcasters' meeting room. Through a glass window, Dhazdat could make out Vadim wiping his brow. Olga looked frightened, and was pleading with two police officers.

Before Viktor could stop him, Dhazdat barged into the room.

"You cannot arrest her!" he exclaimed.

"Who the hell are you?" asked the young policeman. His nameplate said 'Efren Klebanoff'.

"I am Dhazdat Zelensky, and I say that you cannot arrest her!"

Klebanoff started moving toward him, as if he was going to punch him.

"You get lost, Comrade Zelensky, before I arrest you!"

Then he whacked Dhazdat on his head. Dhazdat staggered backward, holding his left ear.

Vadim opened the door of the meeting room and yelled for Eliasberg.

"Karl, get him out of here. I think his ear has been hurt."

Eliasberg was not a large man but he somehow managed to put his arm around Dhazdat's chest and maneuver him toward the door. He also put a handkerchief at his ear to block the bleeding.

"Relax, Efren," said the older policeman, a bemused look on his face. "Let us hear what this young man has to say."

The procession toward the door stopped as all eyes turned toward our improbable drummer from the Steppes. He told me later his left ear was trembling, the surgical tube vibrating. Worse, I knew Dhazdat was uncomfortable with everyone looking at him. He had never been much of a speaker and did not know what to say. He only thought it was wrong to arrest me, and he searched his memory for a way to convince the police to let me go. Stenka had taught him about how all the animals look to a strong protector. So he loosened Karl's grip and tried to stand straight.

"Olga Berggolts is our star," he began. "She reads her poems on the air and interviews Leningrad's celebrities. Ordinary people too, really interesting people. Then she lets us listen in on her interviews. She is a master of ceremonies for orchestral performances, often writing commentary after our concerts. She is the only person so popular here that she has her own fan club. At almost any hour, young girls come by to get her autograph, and old ladies stop in to bring her soups and sweets. Sometimes I eat them. She has no shortage of male admirers, but she has a wonderful husband."

"What nonsense," said Klebanoff. "She is a dissident, disloyal to the Communist Party."

"But that's impossible," said Dhazdat. "Many of her poems are tributes to Lenin!"

"Lenin has been dead for 15 years. Apparently she didn't write any poetic tributes to Stalin."

"I...I...it's just," Dhazdat stammered. "I know nothing of politics. I know only that she is...she is the leader of our pack. If you remove our leader, we will all starve."

There was silence in the room. The older policeman looked at Efren. I felt tears in my eyes.

"Thank you, Dhazdat," said Vadim. "You are right, of course. Please return to your music."

After that, Klebanoff grabbed my arms and twisted them behind my back. I heard Vadim yelling.

"Broadcasters, you have a program to put on," he said. "And you musicians, best practice! Back to work, all of you. And Dhazdat, and you too Karl, in my office, now!"

Later, Dhazdat told me what had happened. As soon as he and Karl entered the room, Vadim closed the door and raised his voice.

"What were you thinking?" he said. "Do you realize that policeman could have arrested you?"

"Or worse," Karl added. "He could have boxed both your ears, interfering with your ability to hear. What kind of drummer could you be if you could not hear?"

Dhazdat smiled. The ringing in his left ear was receding. The bleeding had stopped. His temple no longer throbbed. He looked at them in wonder.

"I know now this is the place for me," Dhazdat said. "You care about me."

"Perhaps you should take the afternoon off," said Karl. "Let your ear recover."

"What will happen to Olga?" Dhazdat asked Vadim.

"I have appealed to higher-ups to show mercy. Apparently, some years ago, she and her first boyfriend Boris were in contact with a man who supported an overthrow of the Stalin government. It's a serious charge, but we are using every lever we have to free her."

Dhazdat nodded. "I know you will rescue her. You are good men." With that, he got up to leave.

In the police van, I closed my eyes as the whole of my life replayed in my head.

Klebanoff was right. I had published tributes to Lenin, the first while a school girl. Vladimir Lenin had suffered a stroke that left him paralyzed and mute. For the oracle of the Bolshevik Revolution to be silenced in his prime was a great national tragedy. For me, it was a personal catastrophe. Lenin once said, "Give me your four-year-old children, and I will build a socialist state." I was one of his disciples. On his death, I wrote a child's poem, *"weeping about the dear deceased great leader."*

"Papa, will you read my poem?"

Fyodor Berggolts not only read the poem but arranged for it to be published in his hospital newsletter. He was a medical surgeon of Russian and Latvian ancestry who had studied in the Imperial Military Medical Academy and served as a surgeon during World War I, what we Russians called the Great Patriotic War. Once the Bolsheviks came to power, my handsome father with the smiling mustache was recruited to serve in the Red Army, a position he again embraced. Now he was a proud father, sharing his daughter's brilliance with anyone who would listen. I was thrilled, not least because I would be joined in history's telling with my idol, the father of our country.

Even before Lenin's death, I had longed to be a writer. I wrote copiously, often poetry dripping with sentimentality and heralding the ideals of communism. I told my parents that one day I would be a renowned author and earn the Lenin Medal. Like my sister Maria, I dreamed of fame. Unlike Maria, who wanted to be a star actress on the age, I longed for political stature.

At 16, I joined *The Shift,* a group for young Bolshevik writers. I was passionate about the cause, the cult, and soon enough, about Boris Kornilov. Boris was two years older than me and already famous for penning the lyrics to music that opened radio broadcasts throughout the nation. My parents did not like him. But with the certainty of the young, I thought we would be comrades for life, marching into an egalitarian future arm in arm.

As my career took off, his stalled. He took to belittling me, comparing me to those *Matryoshka* nesting dolls—one inside the other, hiding yet another until, at the very center, there was only this very small doll. I wondered if he was right. Maybe beyond all my bravado I was an insecure little girl, hiding, as he seemed to suggest.

Two years later, on graduating from the university, I was assigned to work as a journalist for *The Soviet Steppe* in Kazakhstan, a newspaper meant to connect all of Russia's ethnic minorities to a mission of shared nationalism. Almaty was not known for Leningrad's cultural riches, but I was determined to make my way as a professional writer. Besides, this was not really a job offer, more like an order from the Communist Party. I could say no, but it would come at a price, flagging me as a dissident.

The day I departed, my parents and sister came to the station. Boris stayed home—he said he was too busy but I knew he was angry—and I cried as the train chugged away, taking me to my new home, 3,000 miles away. A week later, dirty and thirsty, I disembarked, shocked by the barrenness of the landscape that would be my home for the next few years.

It was there, in the newsroom, that I first saw Nikolai Molchanov. *God he was handsome.*

He had dark eyes and a chiseled jaw, his eyebrows all but knitted together in a perpetual look of curiosity, his nose turned up as if he was sniffing the world around him. He came from a farming family and had the brains and brawn of those who had worked the earth.

I had read about the farm famine but until I met Nikolai I didn't understand how widespread it was. In an effort to reduce the economic power of the *kulaks*, Stalin had forced peasants like Nikolai's parents to join large collectives that paid little and produced even less. Lenin and Stalin, after him, had no use for the peasants, seeing agriculture as the leading edge of capitalism.

The results were horrific. The Kremlin squeezed, many died, and the country starved. Collectivization robbed his parents of their farm. At 10, young Nikolai was sent to live with his uncle, a university teacher in Peterhof, on the outskirts of St. Petersburg. In his longing for home and purpose, Nikolai began reading in his uncle's library the great authors of Russian literature—Tolstoy, Dostoyevsky, Pushkin. He was captivated by their writing prowess, their portrayal of heroes against the odds. These writers treasured the brave among men. They would be his lodestars. They would guide him on how to live, and how to judge life.

Sometimes I thought I was drawn to our asymmetry—me the writer, he the literary critic, me the city girl, he the farm boy, me light, he dark. No matter, on seeing him I understood at once the attraction of difference, the power of love, knowing I would leave Boris behind and marry this man. It made my father cringe, but I was not shy about expressing myself in public about my feelings for the handsome Nikolai, writing in one of my poems of 'the proud and happiest load of my love's unusual thrust'.

I wrote poems to Boris too. *"Guilt has aged me,"* read one. *"But I shall not start now to ask for your forgiveness, to make useless vows. I am in love."*

We married in Leningrad, where both our families lived. Nikolai's parents had died in the famine, but his Uncle Sasha came. A surprising number of friends from the newsroom in Kazakhstan made the trek too. Nikolai told me I looked like the actress Greta Garbo—my sultry eyes smiling above a costume of silks and minks that my father had purchased from a former patient. I told Nikolai he was a portrait of male perfection, his strong torso ending in a flat stomach. Afterward, the whole wedding party took a street car on Nevsky Prospekt, with me serving as tour director.

"You know the French writer Alexandre Dumas always said he could hear the angels sing whenever he traveled on this street," I observed.

"That's funny," said my sister Maria. "The only thing I ever hear is the clanging of the street cars."

I laughed. Since the time we were little girls, we always made each other giggle. Our childhood was an emotional rollercoaster. Our mother, Maria Grustilina, was a great beauty. Our father, Fyodor Berggolts, was a surgeon suspected of bourgeois sympathies and jailed. Did someone turn him in, as part of a whisper campaign against the former middle class? I don't know. What I do know is that his persecution flattened our mother, the light in her eyes exhausted. She died shortly after he was released, by then broken by the echo of the state's whip. How I missed her at my side that day.

"I guess you didn't know you were marrying a historian," said Fyodor.

"Actually, I had some clue," replied Nikolai.

On return to work in Kazakhstan, Nikolai was promoted to chief literary critic, often writing literary essays about writings by Russians outside of Moscow and Leningrad. I also got a new job—reporting on music, dance and poetry in the region.

Soon we were blessed with a daughter, Maya, a rambunctious little girl who liked to giggle. When she was six months old, I went to check on her and found Maya sleeping on her stomach. I was alarmed. I had always placed her on her back, as my father had advised. Her breathing was shallow, her eyes closed. I yelled for Nikolai but the silence in our apartment told me he had already left for work. Since her birth, he had sometimes left quietly to give me more time to sleep.

So I wrote him a note, bundled Maya in a blanket and ran to the Almaty Clinic.

"Is something wrong with my baby?" I screamed at the nurse on duty. "Help me, please."

The nurse gathered Maya in her arms and brought us both into a waiting room. A few minutes later, a doctor walked in and introduced himself.

"I am Bolatbek Omarovo," he said. "Your baby is suffering from a loss of oxygen. Was she lying on her stomach when you found her?"

I nodded, my fingers turning cold. I sensed from the doctor's silence that Maya was in danger.

"We may be able to save her," he said. "Go home. Come in the morning."

"I'm not leaving."

"As you wish."

I waited in the room next to Maya's crib, sitting on a hard chair that had lost all its cushioning. I'm just like the chair, I thought, as if I too had lost all my cushioning. What would I be without Maya? What would Nikolai and I do without our daughter? Would we ever hear her giggles again?

Nurses came in occasionally to press on Maya's chest, and once, the doctor came with a big cone that he pushed into her mouth, blowing his air into her lungs. It was hard to watch.

Just after the doctor left, Nikolai burst through the door. He took one look at Maya's body and grabbed me in his arms. We stood like that for several minutes, softly crying. Then he walked over to the crib and stroked his daughter's stomach. Tears dripped from his face to the baby's bedding. She did not respond to his touch, nor to his coos. In fact, she did not move.

I saw Dr. Omarovo standing at the door, and I gave him a look of anguish.

"I'm sorry," he said. "They call it 'Sudden Infant Death.' We don't know why."

He left then, and I collapsed in tears.

Nikolai cradled me in his arms.

"It's my fault," I wailed. "I'm being punished."

"Punished by whom?" he asked. "So now you believe in God?"

"Of course not, certainly not now," I said between sobs. "Maybe I'm not a good mother."

"You are wonderful as a mother, as you are in everything," he said.

I knew he missed Maya too. Over the next few days, I often noticed him feeling for that spot on his shoulder where he used to burp her. My grief was mingled with guilt. His was a parent's pure pain.

We buried her at the state cemetery. It was overgrown and not well tended, but there was no choice. Our colleagues at the newspaper helped pay for her tombstone. I wrote the engraving: *'To Maya Berggolts Molchanova, who died too young, before she could even name the flowers we now leave at her side'.*

I felt empty and aggrieved. I moped a lot and ate little. Nikolai watched this with his usual intuition.

"Why don't you write a book, as if you were reading it to Maya?" he suggested one day.

A purpose, at last. *Winter-Summer Parrot* was published the following year to much applause from critics and children alike. I dedicated the book 'To Maya, the Little Girl Who Missed Her Chance to Grow Up'.

To my delight, my publisher offered to print my works of poetry as well. Among my new admirers was literary giant Maxim Gorky, who invited me to join the Union of Soviet Writers. We applied to relocate to Leningrad, surrounded by the city's drama and history. We got lucky. I was assigned to be an on-air poet and broadcaster at Radio House. Nikolai won a job as a literary critic at the city's top art magazine. We were both thrilled to be home.

One Saturday in spring, I pushed away from my desk and went to the kitchen. I was never known as a great chef, but I wanted to make something special for Nikolai before I told him my big news. As he knew I loathed kitchen duties, he was immediately suspicious.

"Why are you cooking?" he said. "I can pick up something from the grocers."

"Because we have something to celebrate."

"A new book publishing?"

"No," I said, donning a coy smile.

"A new job?"

"No," I smiled.

I turned from the oven and looked up at him.

"We are having a baby. And the way this baby is kicking, I feel sure he is a boy."

Nikolai wrapped me in his arms and whispered in my hair. "We are one again. We are family."

Now all of that was threatened. Of all people, I, who had been so loyal to the Bolshevik cause, was going to jail. I knew Joseph Stalin often saw conspiracies where there were only intellectuals. I just never expected to be one of them. I was frightened. Stalin's henchmen were known for torture.

By the time Nikolai was allowed to see me, I had already been in jail three weeks. It had taken every pull he had—along with some from Vadim at Radio House—to arrange the visit. NKVD officials didn't even like to acknowledge they were holding prisoners, let alone allow visitors. Nothing prepared him for the conditions—the place reeked of urine, and there were large straps hanging on wall hooks, caked in dried blood. He told me just the sight of them made him nauseous.

"Your wife, Nikolai Molchanov," a guard said with a taunting laugh, pushing me toward him. I was afraid to look at him. My arms were covered in scabs, my hair was matted, and I could only imagine how vacant my eyes looked. I would have understood if he had run away. "Ten minutes."

Instead, he tried to embrace me, but I pushed him away, tears running down my face. I was embarrassed for him to see me like this. I could barely look at him. We sat side by side.

"Boris was arrested too," he whispered. "Same charge. That you contacted Leopold Averbakh of the Russian Association of Proletarian Writers, an anti-Soviet Trotskyist organization."

"I didn't know Boris had been arrested, but yes I know the charge. They ask me about it constantly. I have only the dimmest memory of Averbakh, a small wiry man with intense eyes."

"Boris is scheduled to be executed next month."

I clutched my stomach and leaned over, moaning. Boris and I had split up, but he was a loyal comrade and didn't deserve death. Nikolai rubbed my back.

"How is the baby?" he asked.

I sat up and looked at him, shaking my head. I could barely breathe as I told him.

"It was a boy, after all. When the police beat my stomach, he tried to swim away, as if to evade their cruelty. But he collapsed in my womb and came out the next morning. Gone. Officially marked down as a miscarriage." I looked at him in utter grief. "I named him Grigori."

Nikolai began to cry. I almost broke down too, but something told me not to mingle my tears with his, not to diminish his. He was being punished in life for being married to me. We were both innocent, but his tears were those of a collateral victim. He had earned them. Every one of them.

The next week I was released, my membership in the Union of Soviet Writers restored. There was no apology from the Kremlin, no explanation, no contrition for killing our baby. Slowly, I settled back into a routine at home and at Radio House.

I had always loved the connection to an unseen audience, and as I readjusted to sunlight, broadcasting seemed to restore my soul.

Privately, I wrestled with the arrest. I had been raised to honor our flag. Now it was stained with the blood of my martyred son, my biological link to Nikolai. I finally concluded that the goals of the Bolshevik state were still pure, and noble, but that the people running it were not. I would stay true to the ideals, not to the distortions inflicted on the Soviet people by their leaders. And I promised Nikolai I would stay quiet about politics, never again endangering my life or those of my family or colleagues.

On my return to Radio House, I was greeted as a hero. Vadim gave me flowers. Eliasberg played a little ditty he made up for me on the piano. And the staff on both sides of the broadcast booth stood and applauded. I suspect they were stunned by my appearance, but tried not to show it.

"We have missed you," Dhazdat said.

"Thank you for everything you did."

"But I did not succeed!"

"One man, up against a machine, it's a steep hill. When I was in jail it made me smile whenever I thought of you barging into the room like that. How it must have shocked those policemen!"

"You deserved more."

"We all do."

I thought the worst was behind me. They had killed my child. They had persecuted my father, now a shell of his former vibrant personality.

What more could they do to me, to us, to our city?

FOUR

The Picnic
June 1941

The world was at war, but in the summer of 1941, Leningrad was peaceful, even serene. In years to come, I wondered whether it had been planned that way, either by the authorities or by the fates, to catch us by surprise. But on that sunny Saturday in June, there was no hint.

The city was marking the Festival of the White Nights—that summer interlude before winter set in, when the sun shone all night, and the human heart knew no limits. As I looked out our window, I saw fishermen lining the Neva River, impatient at their lines. I knew trumpeter Eddie Rozner and his jazz band would be setting up soon for an all-night session at the Café Ice Cream & Green Frog. I imagined students finished with their exams, walking arm in arm across the Republican Bridge, a cast-iron span designed in 1901 to join the Winter Palace to Vasilyevsky Island. In this spirited city, even the weather was celebrated with drama. I couldn't wait to join the throngs.

Radio House—where broadcasters and musicians both honed their skills—was marking the occasion with a company-wide picnic. It was well-known I was more interested in words than food, but I hoped my offerings would pass muster with some of our more gourmet-driven friends.

Katarina Orlova and I had become great friends since my dinner with Dhazdat's family, so I asked her what the Zelenskys were bringing. Just hearing her answer—fried falafel with yogurt sauce, cold sweet potatoes spiced with pepper and cinnamon, figs and nuts—made me hungry. It also made me realize how trite my contribution was—cold borscht in a jar and hard-boiled eggs, cheeses and fruits. If my menu were a novel, I thought, critics would decry it as a cliché of ethnic Russian fare.

I had been busy of late—preparing my latest book of poetry for publication, conducting interviews for Radio Leningrad, sprucing up the apartment Nikolai won from the Housing Department as a reward for his military service in Poland. He had been away for less than six months, and I saw few scars, relieved to find him still the handsome, vigorous man I had married.

His war stories suggested he had flourished in the Red Army, and I worried he might join the ranks permanently. After my release from prison, he had promised never to join the Army. But then, I mused, I had promised not to air my political views on the radio. Most of my poems were about the current winds of change.

"Lots of bread," Nikolai called out from the shower, "don't forget the bread."

"Maria's bringing the bread. She has a suitor at the *bulochnaya*."

My sister Maria was the beauty in the family, a big-name actress in Leningrad's musical theater. At 28, she had yet to marry. She seemed more attracted to admirers than to love. Or perhaps she was afraid of commitment. No matter, I thought, if she had a sweetheart at the bakery.

"Well she may be a musical star, but you are the whole firmament to me."

Nikolai was standing in the kitchen now, a towel tied at his waist, still dripping from the shower. As he leaned over to kiss me, smells of soap on his sensuous skin overcame any thoughts of menus.

"We have to meet Maria at the tram in an hour."

"Time is what we make of it."

Afterward, as I luxuriated in Nikolai's arms, I told him Maria was also bringing a new beau.

He rolled his eyes.

"She's got a beau at the bakery and another one on her arm? Busy lady."

"Never mind her," I teased. "You just bring your A game in chess because I intend to beat you with my small but mighty pawn." Along with our picnic basket, I had packed a chess set. This was a necessity in any Russian gathering, given the game's 1000-year history in our country, where many still believed that Ivan the Terrible had died while moving his king. High symbolism that.

"You are welcome to try my dear, but your Nikolai has powers other than those of the bedroom."

He smacked me on the rear, and left to get dressed.

Soon we were on the avenue, mingling with Leningraders of all ages and shapes, sharing love for the Sun Goddess. Swinging my skirt from side to side, hand nestled securely in Nikolai's folded arms, warmed by the sun, I felt fashionable and happy, at peace with our city. People streamed through Finland Station, many buying ice cream before departing for beaches to the south. Maria was waiting for us at the famed Lenin Statue. Nikolai found her first, by sniffing for her bread basket.

"Ah, the aroma of nourishment," he said. "And I'm starving!"

"Hello Nikolai," Maria said with air kisses on both cheeks. "This is my friend, Garegin Ananyan. He plays harp in the orchestra that performs with me at the Musical Theater."

"Those crafty harpists," quipped Nikolai. He raised an eyebrow at me, a shared surprise at Maria's new beau. He was tall and reedy, wearing thick black glasses, while his instrument was curved and feminine. I did not think he seemed Maria's usual type, but I wondered if that was a good sign.

"The harp, isn't that an odd instrument for a man?" asked Nikolai.

"I'm an Armenian," said Garegin. "The strings are in our blood. Besides, ever hear of King David?"

Nikolai smiled and reached for Garegin's hand.

As soon as the train stopped at the Neva Prospekt Station, we set off for the park. I scanned the horizon, looking for a place on an attractive hill with lots of shade and a great view of the water. Then I heard a noise—tick, tock, tick, tock—and looked up to see our pianist, Alexander Kamensky, holding aloft a metronome as if summoning all to the spot he had picked for our picnic.

Whenever normal broadcasting ended, Radio Leningrad played the metronome. It was meant to let the audience know they were off the air. Now, celebrating the sun, it beckoned us.

"Almost Freudian, isn't it? How we all respond to its call?" I observed.

I didn't know Kamensky well—I spent more time on the broadcasting side than on the philharmonic one—but whenever I passed him in the hallways I noticed he always had his head down, as if he didn't want to take his eyes off the keyboard.

"It was Vadim's idea," Alex said. "He said it was the only thing we all had in common."

Vadim once told me he loved working at Radio House because his parents were musicians, disappointed he hadn't followed their path. Now he could oversee both music and news.

"A great, rousing idea," I said to Alex. "And even more impressive, it worked!"

Kamensky smiled at that, and I introduced him to my family.

"What drew you to the piano?"

"Well it wasn't the metronome," he said. I hoped the others would arrive soon—that tick, tock, tick, tock was getting a bit annoying. "I wanted to be a conductor, but the teachers at the Conservatory told me my posture lurched between corpse and lunatic, that I was ill-suited for the job."

Just then the Zelenskys arrived, with their children. As we secured their blanket to ours, expanding the size of our picnic footprint, I made introductions again.

"Nikolai, you remember Dhazdat and Katarina of course. This is their son, Pavel. And who is this precious little one?"

I said this with more cheer than I felt. Having lost a daughter to sudden death syndrome, and a son to the NKVD, I was a bit sensitive around the subject of kids. Still, I reached for the newest Zelensky's chin and tickled her. Six-year-old Pavel helpfully explained that his three-year-old sister's name was Anastasia and that she was boring. Everyone laughed, and Nikolai changed the subject, asking Katarina about her comeback as a prima ballerina. Silently, I thanked him.

"Yes, I am in rehearsals," she said. "I told the director of the Leningrad Ballet that I was too old for a return, but he insisted." Imitating Dima Kuzmin's booming voice, she said, 'If you can dance, you can defy age; I've seen it before, too many times to doubt.'

Pavel laughed. "That was a good one, Mama!"

She smiled. "And so, I find myself rehearsing *Cinderella*."

I knew Dima's reassurance was part flattery, part panic. It was no secret around town that attendance was down since Katarina's parental leave. Without her power to draw audience, his star had dimmed too, putting his job in jeopardy. Anyway, whatever Dima's motives, I knew from our last conversation that Katarina welcomed the chance to restore her body to its pre-pregnancy form.

"There is something about the rigor of daily practice that makes me feel whole again," she said. "Russian ballet is different from the French or Italian. Ours requires more discipline."

"And you have missed it," said Nikolai.

She nodded, the blonde bun at her neck moving for emphasis.

"I thought I had given it all up," Katarina said. "But I missed that feeling of perfecting movement."

"You will bring Leningrad to her feet," said Dhazdat, "but you are perfect already!"

Katarina looked at her husband, a smile of gratitude in her eyes.

"You two are such a contrast," Maria observed. "How ever did you meet?"

"We met one night after a performance, when Dhazdat came backstage to compliment me," said Katarina. "He was so unlike my other suitors—unpolished, sort of rough at the edges."

"You had other suitors?" said Dhazdat, and they all laughed.

"When he told me he had grown up deep in Steppes of Ukraine, I was intrigued. He also told me his Grandpa Stenka first noticed Dhazdat could not hear, and helped the family move to Leningrad for an operation that repaired his hearing but left him, well, socially clumsy."

"But I am a model of fluid conversation!" protested Dhazdat.

Katarina led the laughter. I wondered how often they had told their story, punchlines and all.

"My parents both worked, so it was my grandfather who raised me," Dhazdat said. "He was determined to teach me about our Cossack heritage and its code of ethics—to never surrender. After the operation restored my hearing, the two of us would have long talks about Ukrainian history, especially the famine that took so many millions of our people."

"Is that how you won Katarina," Nikolai asked Dhazdat, "by never giving up?"

Dhazdat looked at her longingly. "I had to wait for her to decide. I'm glad I did."

Maria shook her head in wonder.

"So if I want to be happy I have to find a socially clumsy Ukrainian Cossack?" she said.

"How about an Armenian one?" said Garegin. I laughed. Maybe this Garegin would be the one.

After the story, Dhazdat asked his children if they wanted to play a game of water hide and seek. At their evident glee, he began chasing them into the water.

Katarina watched as they ran toward the shore.

"Dhazdat used to worry that they would inherit his deafness," she said. "This is the place his parents brought him after the operation, where he first heard the sound of waves splashing on the shore. He loves coming here, listening to his own children scream in delight."

"Mama come join us," yelled Pavel. She smiled, and with her long graceful legs was upon them within moments.

Even at a distance, I could hear the family's squeals. Their joy was infectious. But I wondered, as I often did, about bringing children into this world, into this country. Would their spirits be snuffed out by government decrees? Was there a way to let their imaginations run free and wild?

"Anastasia you play with me," Dhazdat called out.

"Pavel," called Katarina as she caught up with them, "we have to hide from Papa and sister, okay?"

I watched as the two of them made for land and danced behind trees and under picnic tables. Grabbing Anastasia, Dhazdat chased them as she giggled and squirmed in his arms. Finally, he put her down, and chased all three of them. After a while, they all collapsed on our blanket, breathless.

"That looked like fun," said Nikolai. He managed a smile, but the comment made me wonder about the toll of our child-traumas on his soul. I asked Katarina how the two children differed.

"Anastasia adores her father, as if they were connected by spirit, as well as blood. Pavel is more my child, I guess—lithe and sensitive—but Anastasia is brave like Dhazdat. She will try anything."

"Katarina was worried all our prancing in the water would make us late for the picnic," said Dhazdat as he arrived. "I told her not to worry. I told her Radio House is always late."

"You can set your watch by that," I quipped. "Anyway, the longer the rest of them take to get here, the more of Katarina's spicy sweets I get to sample!"

As he had predicted, many of Radio Leningrad's most famous figures were slow in arriving.

Soon up the hill came Andrei Zavetnovsky, the orchestra's first violinist—his position a great honor in musical circles—and the cellist Igor Brik. The two were an odd pair—Andrei lean and proper, a bit formal, the son of elite musicians who had taught him musical notes before the alphabet. Igor was more inclined to a jolly belly and spontaneous bursts of wit. He never spoke of his family, and I sometimes wondered if he had been born already schooled, a product of his own making. Anyway, I adored Igor, who was also a great chef, and I often insisted the two of them attend our parties.

"Come join us," I said.

"Only if there's room for Igor's picnic basket," said Andrei. Amid much hooting, Igor unveiled the day's offerings: cherry blinis, caviar and champagne.

"I think they're paying the cellists too much money," quipped Nikolai.

"No," said Andrei, "it's the violinists who make the money. The cellists eat it."

Amid more laughter, I noticed another late arrival.

"Oh my goodness," she said, "here comes the conductor."

"And he's with a woman," said Kamensky.

There was a collective gasp, as no one had ever seen the conductor with a woman before.

Eliasberg always looked a bit unkempt, his clothes ill-fitting, his eyeglasses falling off his face, his gaze tilting down as if life had stolen his vanity. But Viktoria Provnoskiya was a stunner. She looked like Katharine Hepburn, the Hollywood actress who took roles that defied gender stereotypes.

Behind her high cheeks bones and mischievous gray eyes was a fighter—tall and powerful in build, with a direct gaze for anyone who met hers. A scholar at the Hermitage Museum, with a degree in art history from the Sorbonne, she had already climbed the hierarchy over many a male administrator. I knew this because I had interviewed her for my *Lyudi V Gorode* (*People Around Town*) program, and we had become friends. She had told the audience she loved the city, positioned at the intersection of history and culture, because she appreciated both. I knew she wanted to serve as director of the museum someday, but I was shocked she was seeing our elusive conductor.

"Come sit with us," I said, calling them over.

Eliasberg bowed. "This is my friend Viktoria Provnoskiya," he said. "Viktoria, these are my colleagues." Perfect, I thought, just the bare bones, a crisp introduction. So like him.

Eliasberg was an enigma to most of his orchestra, aloof and unapproachable. He liked it that way. One time, we got drunk together, and his tongue loosened enough to tell me his story. I guess you could say I'm a collector of biographies. I sometimes think no one's story travels in a straight line.

He was born in Minsk, where his father, a tailor named Lev, started Russia's first Marxist society and named his only son after the two heroes of the Revolution—Karl Marx and Vladimir Ilyich Lenin. Unlike his father, Karl was not a revolutionary seeking to shake things up but a mechanical child, more interested in how things worked. As a boy, he planted a pile of rocks on the railroad tracks, to see what would happen. Police arrested him for endangering train travel. After whipping him, his father offered his only son the solace of a violin because, he explained, "That is what Jews play."

For three years, Karl spent Tuesday afternoons at the synagogue, taking lessons from Cantor Moshe, learning how to attach the chin rest to his violin, to use rosin to clean his bow, to tune, grip, play.

One day, after he practiced the violin solo *Chaconne*, the cantor said, "You are a fast learner."

"Am I any good?" asked young Karl.

"You are good enough," said the cantor.

Karl told me that assessment—part compliment, part insult—had followed him, in life as in music. When he was a teenager, the family left Minsk, one step ahead of the Revolution. Here in Leningrad, then called St. Petersburg, teachers at the Conservatory, the city's musical gem, decided he should take up the piano, and this he did. In due time they suggested he take up conducting, and this too he did. In the end, he sometimes lamented, he felt a performer of all, a grand master at none.

On graduating, Eliasberg was named musical director for the Radio Orchestra of Leningrad. Everyone knew this was the consolation prize, that his musicians would never be as famous as those at the rival Philharmonic Orchestra. When the charismatic Yevgeniy Mravinsky won the Philharmonic post, Karl shrugged. Even now, I knew he was always trying to tell himself that he preferred the Radio Orchestra's eclectic vibe to the stuffy elitism of the Philharmonic—and maybe he did. But the simmering resentments were clear to anyone paying attention. Kamensky had called them with the Metronome that bookended our work days, but he was a rare crossover. Most of the Philharmonic group sat elsewhere at the picnic, separate from the rest. They felt it too.

All total, I mused, there must have been 200 people milling around. There was much to celebrate. My radio show was more popular than ever, and both orchestras were performing nonstop. The war that seemed to be engulfing the world had so far not touched our shores, maybe because of Russia's military prowess in defeating foreign enemies, none more famously than Napoleon. Surveying the scene—scrambling children, piles of food, laughter and chatter—I smiled at Karl, and he returned the greeting. Not for the first time I noticed that his smile was lopsided, as if his face were undecided, still reserving judgment about life.

Garegin, Maria's new love interest, sat down next to Karl and began to pour from his supply of Medovukha, a kind of mulled wine. Nikolai and I held out our cups. Garegin said the wine reminded him of his late father, Tigran, a vintner who raised him in Armenia, near Mount Ararat.

"When I was growing up, my father taught me that wines hold God's promise," he said. "He also said that Noah's Ark was buried on Mount Ararat, and that Noah was a righteous man who walked with God in a world filled with evil. I still look at the mountain and think of all that goodness."

"I always loved the story of Noah," said Karl. "The idea of two animals of every species marching into the ark to preserve their heritage, I always thought that was so logical, so orderly."

How like Karl, I thought, to find the order in chaos. Maybe that's what he did with music too.

"What happened to your father?" I asked.

"The Turks came," said Garegin.

He looked down into his wine glass, unable to talk for a while. Sensing the gravity of the moment, Maria, and this I thought spoke volumes, moved closer to him. The Zelensky children were drawing, the only sounds their scratch marks on paper. I held my breath. Eventually Garegin looked up and began his story again, his voice cracking.

"He and dozens of my male relatives were taken to the church with other men in the village, where they were all slaughtered. One of my cousins was pregnant at the time, and they killed her by cutting the child out of her stomach and holding it up on a knife to display to cheering Turkish soldiers."

At this last news I touched my stomach. Nikolai reached for my hand.

After a long spell of quiet, I broke the silence.

"It is shocking to hear of genocide in the modern era. How did you escape?"

"I was only seven years old at the time, but my sister Ani was older, and she and my mother led. We walked, ran and walked some more, over mountains and valleys, east to Yerevan. We nearly starved. At one point we met some Russian soldiers who gave us food. But one of them raped Ani."

He choked at this memory, looking down. I noticed Kamensky was quietly crying, and wondered if he too had a family connection to Armenia.

"I had relatives," Alexander said, wiping his tears with his sleeve. "They were not able to escape."

Again there was silence, until finally Garegin looked up, as if it would help stop the memories.

"Eventually we came to St. Petersburg, where I enrolled in music school."

"Were you in the Conservatory?" asked Karl.

"Wasn't everyone?" said Garegin. They both laughed, perhaps relieved that the talk of trauma was ending. Garegin offered Karl another drink.

I watched as these two refugees from tragedy—one from rigidly ideological parents, the other from abject ethnic genocide—

shared a toast, then settled in for a debate about Beethoven's best symphony. Eliasberg chose the Ninth.

"But that's what I was going to say!" replied Garegin.

"Of course you would say that," replied Karl. "Aside from the drums, the harp is the most featured instrument in Ode to Joy!"

"And what's wrong with that?" replied Garegin, as they both clicked glasses in bemused merriment.

What a day for Garegin, I thought, debating Beethoven with one of Leningrad's premier conductors, sitting by my sister, one of the most beautiful girls in the city. I hoped he and Maria would last.

"How is your chess game?" Garegin asked Karl.

"Judge for yourself," said Karl, flashing that lopsided smile again.

The Zelenskys were back in the water, the dark hair on Dhazdat's chest glinting in the sun. I nudged Nikolai to take me on a walk. We meandered a bit, then spotted Andrei and Igor climbing toward a separate hill. As we joined them, they were arguing about where to sit. Igor wanted to put down a blanket under a birch tree because aesthetically he liked its shape—narrow at the bottom and feathered at the top. Andrei would have preferred something giving them more shade, more cover.

"Olga, will you explain to this titan of the cello that we cannot be seen like this, together in the open," said Andrei. "You know, and I know, that Stalin has made it illegal for men to associate with other men. We could face five years in the Gulag!"

"We are musicians, at a picnic for musicians, on a day of national celebration," said Igor. "If it makes you happier, we can discuss the benefits of Communism. Now that would confuse them."

I sighed. I knew the two were companionable, sharing the secrets of their souls. But the Kremlin had outlawed their attraction—even though the Revolution was grounded on equality for women, people of color and other victims of discrimination in capitalist countries, like homosexuals. Even among friends, as they were today, I knew Andrei was right. They would have to be careful.

"If only we were women," said Igor. "Apparently, the Kremlin is not threatened by lesbians."

Igor took out his sketchpad—something he always had at the ready—and used color chalk to draw the scene before them—couples, families, children, the elderly. It seemed as if Leningrad were on display. He titled it 'The Luncheon of the Leningrad Boating Party', and gave it to Andrei.

"You do Renoir proud," he said. "Now if only your art would bring in some money."

Nikolai asked to see the chalk drawing.

"How can you draw such a peaceful scene when all around you is chaos—children screaming, boat horns tooting, dogs barking?" he asked.

"The noise fuels me," said Igor. "I take it in with my ears and draw it out with my eyes."

"That is a useful skill," observed Nikolai. "I may try that the next time I'm deployed."

Igor looked stricken. Me too.

"Are you planning another sojourn with our military?" Igor asked.

"Maybe," said Nikolai.

I looked at Nikolai but he did not return my gaze. Instead, he reached for my hand and we made our way down to the promenade near the river, along a tree-lined path.

"Anastasia reminded you of Maya, didn't she?" he asked.

I nodded.

We had lost Maya when she was an infant. And we had lost Grigori, our son, when he was still in my stomach, broken by interrogators seeking a confession for disloyalty. In that moment, Stalin wrenched more than a child from me. He tore my faith in communism. Nikolai and I decided there had been two miscarriages that day—one a taking of life, the other a travesty of justice. We were left bereft, parents mourning their child and their country. We were young enough to make more children—Nikolai was 31, I was 30—but I had been reluctant to speak of it again.

Today seemed different. Something about the sunshine, the crowds, the children giggling, it all seemed so normal, and suddenly I wanted to be normal too. I wanted to spread my arms and feel the warmth of this longest day of summer. I didn't want to think about my grief at the loss of two children or my mother's broken heart at my father's persecution. I just wanted to feel alive.

We sat on the ground, his arm around my waist, as we looked out on the waves in the Neva.

"I love days like this," I said. "They remind me—just look at this crowd—they remind me that residents of this city rarely refer to themselves as Russians, Soviets or Bolsheviks or Slavs, Jews, Ukrainians or Armenians. They are Leningraders, attached to the city by heritage and pride, reveling in its difference from the gray steel of Moscow or the icy plains of Siberia. It was the best place in all of Russia, in all of the world. What a wonderful day, in this wonderful city, to be alive!"

Nikolai looked astonished that I could be so cheerful. Maybe he was stunned at my attitude after all the traumas life had delivered. Or maybe he was surprised at my vision of the country.

In a nation with eleven time zones stretching across more than 6,000 miles, from the once-refined cultures of Eastern Europe to the oil-rich lands of Kazakhstan, it seemed all but ungovernable. Perhaps that's why Stalin ruled with such a heavy hand, arresting anyone who crossed him or hinted at criticism. Maybe it was time to try again, to gamble on happiness. We were in love, stupidly and helplessly and sensually in love. It seemed natural to want to share that love, to become a family.

He kissed my neck. I knew—because he had told me—that he had always found my neck the most luscious part of my body, at least when clothed. I smiled at the intimacy.

"The decision is yours, because the greater risk is yours."

I looked up at him, still the handsomest man I had ever met. I could see tears at the corner of his eyes. I was worried about making another child. His tears made me frightened not to.

"You are the best risk I ever took."

"So that's a yes?"

"It's the patriotic thing to do," I said, and we shared a laugh, quickening our pace toward the water, better to wade in and feel the pebbles and sand at our feet. It felt like a new beginning.

Later, on the blanket with the others, the food divided on plates, the wine passed around, the sun bestowing a glow on the setting, Nikolai winked at me, raised his glass and said, "To Patriotism!"

Maria told me later she liked the drama of the toast, though marveled that Nikolai had chosen that expression, having recently lost a child to the government's goons. She always said ours was a hard country for happiness, unless it derived from fame.

Andrei looked at Igor as if wondering whether patriotism would ever extend to them, ever see their union as normal. Viktoria likely thought the toast a bit anti-intellectual, banal even, beneath the brilliance of this set. As for the Zelenskys, I knew they believed in God and country, so they happily joined the salute to patriotism. What Garegin and Karl thought, they did not say. Perhaps they were replaying Garegin's surprise victory in chess, or Karl's equally unexpected job offer. Apparently, the Radio Orchestra of Leningrad was in need of a good harpist. In any event, it was always dangerous in public to question loyalty to the state. So we all raised our glasses and said, "To Patriotism."

FIVE

The Invasion
September 1941

The first thing I remember was the shriek of air raid sirens, waking me. Next came the thud of objects hitting the ground.

"Oh my God, are those bodies?" I yelled, running to the windows. "*Bozhe*, are they bombing us?"

"Get back from there!" Nikolai shouted.

I looked stunned, immobile. He ran to the windows and buried me in his arms, dragging me to the couch. We spent twenty minutes there, huddled together in fear, listening to a cacophony of sirens, explosions and ear-splitting screams. Later, when I was in the broadcasting booth at Radio Leningrad, I would describe the sound as a dragon's squeal, with the guttural authority of grief.

But it was really more than that. It was a marker, from one era to another, from peace to war, from family to nation, from relative comfort to abject misery. It was also the day I told Nikolai we were pregnant again. I had waited a few months, to make sure I could hold a child after all the scars of my imprisonment. Now we both worried. Were we crazy to bring an infant into this mad world?

Only the day before, I announced on Radio Leningrad that German troops had encircled the city. After months of gobbling up little towns to our south and east, Nazi panzers had finally arrived at our doorstep. There was a rumor that Hitler had decided not to take our city. In my romantic myopia, I assumed it was because Leningrad was too beautiful to destroy. But no, it turned out it was not our majesty he wanted to preserve but the Aryan blood of his Wehrmacht Army soldiers. So he ordered his troops to encircle Leningrad's three million residents, to starve us to death.

"You cannot say that the city is now blockaded," Vadim told me before I went on the air that day. "You cannot say that we are encircled."

"But we are. The noose is tightening around our city."

"The Kremlin does not want to frighten people."

He sighed in exasperation, as if I were a spoiled child who didn't understand why she couldn't have any more dessert. "Olga please, if ever there was a moment to stay in Stalin's good graces, this is it."

How could I stay in Stalin's good graces, I wondered, I who had been his prisoner.

I thought back to that day I was arrested. After my release, I had asked Dhazdat what happened to his boxed ears.

"I went to see a doctor. Katarina insisted."

"Of course. And?"

"The doctor said my hearing would recover, but recommended I avoid bar fights in the future."

We had laughed about it then. Now I thought it was a good prescription for all of us. Maybe we didn't start it, but it looked like we were in the bar fight of our lives.

Nikolai was grabbing clothes.

"Where are you going?"

"I'm going to volunteer. We are at war."

"But you are a literary critic, not a soldier!"

He nodded. I was still too raw from my prison experience, he knew, from the death of our children. Most people think I'm tough, but Nikolai understood what Boris had seen too. Inside I was fragile, like broken porcelain.

"I am also a patriot," he said softly, cupping my face in his hands. "And this is the time for patriots."

I sobered and nodded my assent. I wanted to bury my head in his chest, to never let him go. I wanted my future with this man. And yet I knew, as he knew, that this was the time for patriots, and that Nikolai had always wanted to be a hero. I felt on the floor for my clothes. He waited for me and we left for work together— he to the Army Recruiting Office, me to Radio House.

"See you tonight."

"Be careful."

"I love you."

A final kiss—how many did we have left before the war intruded? I wondered—and we separated.

In just a few hours of bombing, Leningrad's skyscape had cratered. The city of my birth, the city I loved, looked like a sick theatrical set. One building's front had blown away so completely that I saw pink and blue flowers on the wallpaper of its back walls. Even more haunting, a clock stood in the living room, stopped at 8 a.m. Further on, I saw one hallway where a man's jacket was hanging next to a woman's coat on a rack, a portrait of domesticity in a home blown to smithereens. An orange lampshade hung from their ceiling, gently swaying in the wind, like the last note of a symphony.

Other buildings had been demolished completely, their steel girders like crosses on the graves of the residents buried underneath. Household possessions blown out by the bombs now littered the sidewalks. As I climbed over teapots and sofas and all the ephemera of daily life, I wondered what had happened to the people who were once comforted by them. I looked up to see one man trapped under a sofa that had fallen on his back, his cries for help echoing against the collapsed walls. I screamed for a medic, but none came. I prayed a firetruck was on its way to help him.

Just then a bomb buzzed overhead, and there was no warning, no time to get to an air raid shelter. Instead I ran to the doorway of a nearby building, crowding in with a half-dozen others.

"Astonishing," I said to a woman with grey hair and a shopping cart.

"This is the Soviet Union," the woman responded. "Nothing surprises after a while."

After the all-clear, I resumed my walk, feeling for my rosary in my coat pocket. Religion had been banned in the Soviet Union for decades, but the rosary had been a gift from my mother, who placed it in my hand years before, saying, "He will look after you." I knew I could be jailed for even possessing a rosary, so I sewed it into the lining of my coat where I could feel its weight from time to time. Now I touched the smooth contours of the rosary and thanked God silently for giving me Radio House, a second home, to escape to. Also, I asked Him to protect Nikola, and our baby.

As I stepped inside, I heard an announcement that broadcasters were to gather for a news meeting in 15 minutes. I ran to the news wire room and grabbed the latest dispatches off *Pravda*. My friend Yuri Makogonenko, Radio Leningrad's top news technician, met me at the door.

"You won't learn anything there."

"I know. Just habit. What have you heard?"

"The Nazi bombing campaign, as you might expect, has been painfully methodical. Their first squadrons dropped explosives that blew up buildings. Then came a second wave dropping incendiaries—lighting everything on fire. That's why the damage is so great."

"The streets are littered with bodies."

Yuri said Luftwaffe planes had established a pattern—they aimed for whole apartment blocks, trying to extinguish entire families, to kill masses of people quickly. At 74 Marat Street, two high-explosive bombs found their target. By the time rescue teams arrived at unit 17, they found the bodies of the Potemkin family. The grandmother, 60-year-old Vera Konenkova, had been blown to the opposite side of the apartment, killed by the explosion's force. The parents and two teenage girls lay in the ruins, still, dead. The family's youngest, Vera Potemkina, was still alive, screaming for help, but by the time rescuers freed her from the wreckage, she was gone. An entire family, obliterated.

"Like a concert of death." Yuri muttered.

"Targeting the innocents. More?"

"There's a rumor that on hearing the news, Stalin collapsed in something of a nervous breakdown—smashing furniture, frothing at the mouth, his eyes turning cold. He kept using the word betrayal."

"Do you think it's true that he and Hitler had an agreement not to attack one another?"

"It sure looks like it."

"So who is running the Kremlin?"

"No way to know. Maybe Molotov. Maybe a committee."

A son of Bolsheviks in Georgia who both beat him relentlessly in their Georgian village of Gori, Stalin had developed a bully's demeanor, and a keen mind for revenge. When Hitler was first elected as Chancellor of Germany in 1930, the Fuhrer unleashed a Night of the Long Knives against his enemies. I always wondered if Stalin had borrowed the idea for his own purge of intellectuals, military high-command, rank and file soldiers—and me—anyone who might pose a challenge to his leadership. Unwittingly, his persecution of brilliant strategists depleted the Red Army of the very expertise we needed now to defeat the Nazis. Yuri told me that foreign diplomats had a saying: 'The Reds are always too busy fighting each other to put up much of a defense.'

"And one more thing," Yuri said.

I looked up.

"You look beautiful. War agrees with you."

I slapped him. I had once indulged in a boozy flirtation with Yuri, a skinny guy with an impish smile and an insatiable appetite for women. I always regretted it, if only because he always wanted more. Despite my romantic rejection, he had remained loyal, feeding me news tips and gossip that kept my broadcasts lively. There was no one I trusted more to help me figure out what the news really meant.

"I saw a man on the second floor of a bombed-out building, trapped under a steel girder."

The image haunted me. Yuri said nothing. Really there was nothing to say. We walked together to the news meeting, where Vadim told us what he knew—and what we could not say on the airwaves.

"The Germans attacked from sea, and land, and air, by tank and bomb, incessantly," he said. "Our Red Army was caught completely unprepared. You can report the attack, because our listeners know, but not the disastrous lack of response from our military."

I lurched at the thought that Nikolai would soon be joining that Army, its ranks thinned by Stalin's purge. Talk about betrayal. As he had the day before, Vadim again ordered us to avoid using the word blockade on the air—apparently Marshal Klimt Voroshilov was trying to conceal from Stalin any news of Leningrad's isolation, for fear he might fly into another rage.

But everyone knew. Like hungry predators, they were circling.

"What if I say we are an island, cut off from the main body of the Soviet Union?"

Vadim sighed and nodded. I was surprised—surely the meaning was the same. Maybe he was tired of fighting with me over words. But fight I always would. Words were my muse, my primal scream.

"A grey mist conceals the outlines of St. Isaac's, the Admiralty, the Winter Palace, the Senate and the horses above the archway of the General Staff Building," I said on the air, disbelief in my voice. "And somewhere, just a few kilometers away, are the Germans. It's incredible, unreal, like a delirious dream. How could it have happened? The Germans are at the gates of Leningrad."

At 11 a.m. air raid sirens went off again, and a new wave of bombing began. Reports were coming in of thousands killed, including children. I stayed on the air all day, shocked when the sirens blared again at 5 p.m. Neither I nor my listeners could know that for the next year, every day at 8 a.m., 11 a.m. and 5 p.m.,

Nazis—known for their precision—would rain explosives down on the city each day, testing the nerves and mettle of a people who had already been through so much. I worked hard to understand their venom, to deduce why they hated us so much.

"The Nazis feel aggrieved by the Versailles Treaty that blamed them, and punished them, for the last war. Now they want to conquer us, to punish us, to prove their superiority. Also, Hitler says he wants to capture Europe's cities to give German citizens the *lebensraum*, the living space they crave."

At noon, as it did every day, a cannon went off at the Hermitage Museum, home to more than one million of the world's finest paintings and sculptures. This day, however, the cannon was followed by an announcement over the museum's loudspeakers. There was nothing routine about it.

"Soviet citizens," came the announcement. Later Viktoria Provnoskiya told me visitors stopped in their steps and looked toward loudspeakers. "Today, German forces have invaded our country." Foreign Affairs Minister Vyacheslav Molotov was speaking, as he often did for the Kremlin. On this day, his voice cracked. "This vicious and duplicitous action will not stand. We will repel the enemy, defend our nation, triumph over evil. Comrades, close ranks around our glorious Communist Party, defend our proud homeland, rally around our great leader Comrade Stalin. We will prevail over evil."

This I dutifully reported—so many in the audience already knew, and the announcement had already been cleared by the

Kremlin. I wondered what would happen to the art housed in the Hermitage, thinking about my favorite work by Antonio Canova, *Cupid's Kiss*, in which the sculptor used a smooth marvel for lovers in a passionate kiss and a rough material for the rock on which they sat. I always thought of Nikolai whenever I saw it. Would we ever kiss like that again?

Later in the day, poet Anna Akhmatova came by to voice her feelings. Like me, Anna had once been investigated. Neither of us had to remind the other to be careful.

"My whole life has been bound up with that of Leningrad," she said. "I became a poet in Leningrad. Leningrad is the very air my verse breathes." There was a pause then before she continued. "Like all of you, I have an unshakable faith that Leningrad will never bow down to the Nazis."

I thanked Anna, wondering if my faith was unshakable, if I could write poetry while a whole city was under attack. Would my words comfort, or even matter? I ended the broadcast by assuring my listeners that, unlike other countries Hitler had quashed, he would never vanquish Mother Russia. Because Russia never bowed to conquerors. I spoke with more confidence than I felt.

"Hitler has already silenced the guns of Czechoslovakia, Poland, Denmark, Norway, Netherlands, Belgium, Luxembourg and France. But we know what he doesn't, my friends. This is not tiny Belgium. This is the vast Soviet Union. Leningrad will devour the Nazis."

I left exhausted, not so much by the hours I had to work or the news I had to report but as always made weary by the lies I had to tell, or anyway, by the omissions. In his announcement, Molotov had used the word 'duplicitous'. Had Hitler double-crossed Stalin? I felt nauseous, and wondered if morning sickness ever happened in the evenings. Maybe during war it never stopped.

I came home to find Nikolai huddled over a desk, doing paperwork.

"How was it?" I asked tentatively, eager not to replay our morning argument.

"Crowded," he said. "Must have been thousands of men volunteering for the Army, and lots of people, men and women, volunteering for civilian duty. Made me proud."

"But you made it to the front of the line?"

He nodded.

"I probably have a week, maybe two at most."

I gave him a soft hug. We ate quietly, went to bed early. I kept wondering, between spells of sleep how this special place of art, music and literature, could withstand this onslaught of evil.

"When I deploy, maybe you should move to Radio House. It might be safer."

"How I hope they never call you up."

"In the meantime, I've volunteered for civilian duties."

I smiled.

Nikolai's father had taught him that what kills a man is not a strong enemy but a weak character. So I wasn't surprised to learn he had signed up for roof duty, charged with extinguishing German bombs that landed on buildings, bearing little but buckets of water and blankets. Also as neighborhood warden, directing people to nearby air raid shelters when sirens blasted a warning.

"You'll win the Stalin Award!" I teased.

For several weeks, we passed as roommates. At dinner and in bed, we would talk quietly of our dreams after the war, about the baby growing in my tummy, about our hopes for the child's life. Both of us yearned for another daughter, another Maya. Then the next day we would leave the apartment, into the haunting sight of a city whose buildings were being systematically destroyed, block by block. Twice Nikolai came home with minor burns from putting out roof fires. One night there was a note. He was on duty at the Badaev Food Warehouse. He might be late.

Built during the tsarist era, the Badaev Warehouse was actually a series of wooden buildings constructed on a four-acre site southwest of the city. There were hundreds of structures jammed together, with only a few feet between each. Inside, they held all of Leningrad's grain, meats, fats, butter, sugar and confectionery— almost the entire city's diet. Leningraders called Badaev the city's stomach. I envisioned Nikolai standing guard there, protecting our food and our future, my hero.

"We have no weapons," he confided one night. "All available guns and ammunition are earmarked for the front."

"Then how are you supposed to protect our supplies from thieves?"

He smiled then, and I noticed his evident pride, the very virility of his response.

"What we lack in ammunition," he said, pounding his chest, "we make up for in muscle, police gear, and will."

As I waited for Nikolai's return, I opened a bottle of wine to keep myself company. I might as well have opened a vein. In minutes, the Germans launched their fiercest attack yet. Yuri told me later that in the first wave, 27 planes dropped six thousand bombs. An hour later came a second wave, 48 bombs of an even more explosive caliber, weighing up to 1000 pounds each. Massed at a recently captured airfield in Estonia, the Luftwaffe planes and their bombs came with impunity, lighting up the skies of Leningrad for hours on end without a single answer from our planes.

I sat in the hallway, thinking it safer than our apartment. When my wine bottle was empty, I looked out at the sky, and saw what looked like a red eclipse of the sun. What on earth could that be? Had the Nazis changed the color of the sky? I felt vulnerable, lonely, desperate to be around people, to stop the shaking in my legs. So I ran to Radio House. As always, Yuri was there.

"The Germans have attacked," he said.

I looked at him with one of those sneers practiced by mothers who find their children a bit slow.

"Yes Yuri, I figured it was the Germans."

His eyes softened.

"Olga, you don't understand," he began. "They attacked the Badaev."

I felt my legs begin to shake again.

"Nooooooooo!" I growled. "Nooooooooo!"

Where was Nikolai? Had he been injured? Was he still alive? Yuri tried to hold me, to quiet my screams, but I kept wailing. Finally, he shook my shoulders, handed me a script and pushed me into the studio. Once inside, I stared at the metronome. I decided to channel its monotony, absorbing its tick, tock, tick, tock into my mind. It worked. Inside I was screaming. The rest of me kept talking.

"They are bombing like drunken madmen," I said on the air, "indiscriminately hitting buildings and people." I knew better than to mention the Badaev, or the prospects of hunger. What Yuri told me was frightening: two thousand bales of coconuts, purchased from the Americans and shipped through Vladivostok, had served as an inferno for a fire so potent it could be seen from Krestovsky Island on the city's north side. The entire warehouse complex had been wiped out.

I did not ask on the air, though likely it was the only question on anyone's mind, why authorities had not thought to disperse the city's foods to more than one location. Their warehouse had been an inviting target for Nazi venality. Everyone knew they were evil. Why hadn't we anticipated them?

After the broadcast, I ran home, smelling the char of fire everywhere, even inside our apartment building. At almost every corner there were little fires, like remnants of the Hell we were living in. I ran through our front door, and there was Nikolai, lying prone on the couch. He was covered in soot and smelled of fire, but I jumped on top of him. He brushed my hair out of my eyes. Then he shook his head, as if to disparage my hero worship.

"No Olga, it's no good," he said wearily. "I failed in my job."

"Koyla, what are you talking about? You're safe, you survived!" Just to make sure, I kissed his arms, his legs, his face, getting smudge marks on my own. At least the barrage of kisses made him smile.

"The thing is, a thief was trying to steal from one of the freezer rooms. I was chasing him off the premises when the Nazi attack started."

"Thank goodness! My valiant Nikolai, you could have been killed!"

"But I didn't arrest the thief. I let him steal, the last man to eat from our collective cupboard. I didn't arrest him." He rubbed his eyes. "And it may hurt you."

"I don't care about the thief," I said. "Koyla you are alive, you are alive!"

"Olga, you have to know about this."

So I listened for a bit. Nikolai told me he had been making his rounds when he saw a thief dart into a freezer room. When Nikolai reached the door, he watched as the thief opened one freezer and pulled out a bag of chicken, then a whole ham. The man found a sack of flour to hold his bounty.

"I figured the satchel would weigh him down, so I could tackle him on his way out the door."

"And then?"

"I stood tall in the doorframe, my legs akimbo and my arms crossed, baton at the ready. But he fooled me. He went out a crack in the wood slats on the building's side, dragging his knapsack along with him. By the time I went to whack him, he was gone.

"I chased him through the gate—goodness he was fast, like a jack rabbit—wondering if I could catch him. We had run only a few blocks when a booming noise reverberated. The thief yelled, 'Look out, the Fritzes are coming, the Fritzes are coming!'

"I thought he was trying to distract me, but when I looked up, I could see the swastikas and the spinning discs on the propellers of the Luftwaffe's planes. I saw that fierce-looking eagle on their emblem. It shook me."

"What happened next?"

"I felt an explosion rock the ground beneath my feet. It sort of woke me from my reverie. I wondered if I had been hit, but I regained my footing, and hurried away from the fire. When I finally turned and looked back, I was astonished. The Badaev warehouse was an inferno of heat."

"Yes. The Nazis used 75 bombs, most of them with 1000-pound explosives."

Nikolai shook his head. "I never forget the smell. It left a stench, like a cauldron of burnt butter."

"And then?"

"The thief also stopped to look at the fire a few yards away. Suddenly, I heard him laughing. It was an odd sound, like a man strangling on his own spit. I ran over and asked him why he was giggling."

"Because no one will arrest me now, not even you," he said. "I no longer look like a thief, escaping a crime, but like any other Leningrader seeking refuge from danger. Hitler is attacking our city. The Nazis have given me cover. Everyone will be rushing to the shelters. I will just be one more man running. Maybe God does have a sense of humor."

"He said that?" I asked. "Maybe he is a Russian Orthodox."

"More like the Apostolic Church," said Nikolai.

"You mean he was Armenian?"

Nikolai nodded. "That's what you need to know, Olga. At first I only noticed that he was tall and thin, with thick dark glasses. When the fire illuminated his face, I recognized him. It was Garegin, your sister's boyfriend."

"Are you sure?" I could feel my heart quickening.

"I introduced myself, just to make sure, and asked if he had been at the company picnic in June."

"Ah, the picnic," he said, "when the sun was shining, Maria Berggolts was on my arm and Leningrad was in its glory. Of course I remember you, the handsome husband of Maria's sister."

I gulped at this news. If it ever came out that Garegin had stolen from the Badaev, that Nikolai had failed to arrest him, we would all be suspects against the state, conspiratorialists.

"I'm not sure where this came from, but I upbraided him for stealing from the Badaev," Nikolai said with a wry smile. "I called it a sin. I guess I was channeling Dostoyevsky."

"And what did he say?"

"A sin? My friend, hunger is Darwinian. In war, there is no right and wrong, only survival."

I thought back to the company picnic, when Maria looked so happy on his arm, and Garegin told us he was a survivor of the Armenian Genocide. No wonder he thought hunger was Darwinian, I mused. Maybe he understood what the rest of us could not yet see.

"Do you think we will all turn into animals?" I asked.

"It seems the natural order of things, doesn't it?"

The next day, Nikolai got his orders. As we walked to the station, I told him how striking he looked in his uniform, as handsome as Vladimir Lenin. The last few weeks of war had strengthened my patriotism—we all had to rally around our country at a time like this—and I was proud of him.

"Promise to miss me?" he said.

"Only if you promise to return to me."

We kissed then, passion mingling on our tongues along with our fear.

He looked at me with longing. I thought I saw a tear at the corner of his eye, and it made me happy. He would always be the best part of me. I was glad he felt that way, too, about me. He touched my tummy and looked forlorn.

"Take care of her, please."

My days passed in a routine of war, no longer shocked by the destruction at my feet. Already, I felt weighted down by this war, and by loneliness. But I had life stirring in my body, and when I rubbed my tummy, it gave me comfort.

One day, I was in the newsroom when I heard bellows of pain, screams beyond description, from outside. After the Badaev fire, I had doubted anything would shock me again. But when Vadim handed me a bulletin about the screaming, the fear returned. I rushed into the studio.

"The Nazis bombed the zoo," I announced, a bit numb. "We understand they killed 70 animals, including that sweet elephant Belka, the gift from Germany many years ago. And that howling you heard? That was the dogs at Pavlov Research Institute. Apparently, the Nazis bombed them too. Ah my dear Leningraders, let us mourn our animals and resolve to avenge their deaths. This is the villainy of the Hitler regime, so heartless they target the sweetest, the most innocent among us."

Vadim came in with another news item. My legs started shaking again.

"And one more thing," I said. "We are hearing that the monkeys at the zoo are so traumatized they are sitting silently, in a sort of stupor, not even flinching at the bombs falling nearby. They are a metaphor for us, the shocked residents of Leningrad. Like them, we will recover, one day at a time."

After the broadcast, Yuri asked me to go out for a drink. I was tempted, reading the hint in his eyes, welcoming the idea of another warm body next to mine. But I was carrying Nikolai's baby. And besides, I didn't want the guilt. So I shook my head, clutched my rosary, and began the trek alone. Surrounded by the ruin of buildings and seeing fear in the faces around me, I arrived home, a war widow missing her warrior husband and disappointed by her country's leaders. I felt lonely.

SIX

The Poets Circle
September 1941

I woke from another nightmare. In the dream, my words had dissolved into liquid, then taken shape as candies in a jar, like peppermints spinning in an ice cream glass. They were white candies with swirls of color—some red, others green, others blue. I kept reaching out, trying to catch the sweets. I wanted to eat them. When I woke, I realized I had been trying to eat my words.

Frightened, I sent word to the Poets Circle that I needed to talk, summoning them to a meeting at my apartment the next night. It was dangerous to meet too often, to provoke envy or resentment from the floor monitor, or the neighbors, some only too eager to please Communist Party officials by informing on this strange band of intellectuals. But I knew they would come. They always had. They were my friends, my confidants, my sister poets, musicians, dancers and artists. They were the only ones who would understand my fear, who would know how to quiet it.

Anna was the first to arrive.

"Ah, my friend, the Muse of Sobbing," I said, using the town's nickname for Anna, known for her melodramatic musings on Leningrad's history, as she had delivered on the day of the invasion.

"You should talk," Anna quipped. "For goodness sake, Olga, the monkeys as metaphors for people? You can do better. And by the way, the British call me Tragic Queen, which I much prefer."

I smiled. On the air, I had explained the vast extent of the Nazis' villainy by reporting they were even bombing the zoo, leaving the monkeys traumatized, much like Leningrad. Apparently Anna thought that was beneath my literary standards.

At 52, Anna was twenty years older than me, but somehow we had always connected. Having both lived through Stalin's purges in the 1930s, we shared firsthand the pain of being canceled for the crime of thinking, or thinking differently. In the face of persecution, with her son imprisoned in Siberia and her poetry censored, Anna had declined repeated offers to defect to the West. She made ends meet by taking a job as a translator of Victor Hugo and a memoirist of Alexander Blok. She also found time for an affair with Boris Pasternak, while both were still married to other partners. All the while she worked on her poetry, privately. I felt sure that when it was finally published, *Requiem*, her elegy to the Soviet Union under tyranny, would become a classic.

Katarina came next, fresh from rehearsals, her cheeks flush.

"So how is it to practice amid war?" asked Anna.

"It is bittersweet," Katarina said, "to practice amid the bombs, to aspire to artistic perfection while all around people suffer. I am sweating a lot and enjoying it immensely. But I am sad too."

"Why sad?" said Anna.

A cloud passed over Katrina's eyes.

"In normal times, this would be my moment of personal redemption, a time when I could regain my professional standing. If life were normal, I might have had another decade to perform, to hone the status I've worked all my life to achieve. Especially in a Communist country, where women are held as equals to men, at least in the eyes of the law. I could have taken my maternity leave, steered my children on their way, and then returned to the stage to pursue my love of ballet. But now, because of the war, it will become my swansong, the end of my career."

"We don't know that yet," I said.

But the truth was the war had changed the trajectory of all our lives, and we all saw it in each other's eyes. Also, I knew something few others did. Katarina had not taken a parental leave. After she got pregnant with her son, Dima the Tyrant had fired her.

"Oh I think we do," said Katarina. "I am now dancing to the beat of war. The two things have merged so in my mind—the ballet and the bombs—that whenever I hear an air raid siren, my legs revert to the *Dance of the Sugar Plum Fairy* from Tchaikovsky's Nutcracker."

"That must be a treat for the German pilots," said Lyubov Shaporina as she walked in. At 72, Luby, as we called her, was the senior of our group. She had grown up during the time of the Romanovs, when intellectuals thought in Russian, spoke in French and attended cultural events *en masse*. Later, she founded the beloved St. Petersburg Puppet Theater. Married to a composer, she, like me, had lost a daughter in childhood. Since her husband's death, she had lived alone in a charming apartment—full of overstuffed furniture, whimsical paintings and family heirlooms. I always wondered how she had managed to hold on to them amid the Soviet confiscation of all things personal, but she had. Witty and expressive, Luby was like a second mother to me, soothing my fears.

"But I know what you mean," Luby said, seeing the hurt cross Katarina's face. "Sometimes I feel as if I'm living inside Vesuvius, just before it blew, witnessing volcanic eruptions from the interior."

We all pondered this for a moment. It was easy to imagine what a rumbling earth would feel like—all those bombs the Nazis were dropping on Leningrad had prepared us for that. I never really understood why, though Yuri assured me that Adolf Hitler thought all intellectuals, Communists and ethnic Slavs were beneath the Aryan race. It still made no sense to me—was the Fuhrer really intent on killing everyone he didn't like? So, world domination by mass murder?

My sister Maria arrived then, breaking these sobering thoughts with a theatrical greeting, a cheery song and an offering of some wine she had discovered on a shelf at home. "How divine," she said, "a party of women in the wake of war!" We all smiled. Maria was an actress, who loved a party, no matter what the occasion. I hoped our mother's death would not tilt her to drink too much.

"It is women who will save Leningrad from war," said Anna. "You'll see, the women will prevail."

Just then Viktoria swept in, dressed in combat gear, her face smeared with silver paint.

"Have you signed up for the Red Army?" asked Luby.

"It's been a rough day Luby, but thanks for making me laugh," said Viktoria.

At 27, Viktoria was the youngest of us. But I knew she felt comfortable in our company. We all had jobs we loved as much as she did hers, as an art scholar at the Hermitage Museum. And Katarina and I were navigating the road she hoped one day to travel—balancing work and marriage. No doubt, she was a great ambassador for Russia—professional and charming—but what I liked best about Viktoria was her mind. Most people were driven by emotion. Viktoria was a strategic thinker.

"So why the painted face?" asked Luby.

"All I am authorized to say," Viktoria began. She gazed at me with that 'not for public consumption' look. I nodded, smiling. I had already heard what I thought Viktoria was about to tell us. In Leningrad, gossip was plentiful, even when food was not.

"German bombers know the outline of the Hermitage from photos—we are Target No. 9. So today, a team climbed to the roof—led by the architect Natasha Usvolskaya—to disguise the spires, turning the domes a battleship gray and draping the turrets in black sailcloth. It is dangerous work, but they are nimble. Today I joined them, and I was not so nimble, hence the paint splatter."

"I told you the women would win the war!" said Anna. "Was this your idea?"

Viktoria smiled coyly.

"How ingenious," Anna said. "This is the best news I've had in days."

I had heard they were disguising museums so German planes would be diverted, but had no idea it was Viktoria's doing. I had great respect for the conductor of the Radio Orchestra of Leningrad, but was glad when Viktoria told me she and Karl Eliasberg were only friends, even though she had appeared with him at the company picnic. A brilliant and beautiful woman, Viktoria deserved better. I poured wine and served chocolates, an indulgence I had been saving for a special occasion.

"To women," I said, hoisting my glass, "and Soviet ingenuity."

"So, you summoned?" asked Maria.

I gave her a pained look. I thought of it as more of an invitation than a summons. Perhaps, I thought, Maria was annoyed that I hadn't told her Viktoria was joining our group. But then, Maria hadn't told me that she and Garegin were now living together.

"Since Nikolai left for the front, I've been having trouble sleeping," I began. "The other night, I had a nightmare that my words—the words I broadcast on Radio Leningrad, the words that are dipped in sugar before being broadcast—my words were melting into peppermint candies. In the dream, I kept trying to swallow them. Do you understand? I wanted to recall my words."

"The subconscious thrives on metaphor," said Anna, nodding. "Our minds are so much smarter than our conscious thoughts. Still, if I have to eat my words, I would prefer licorice."

"Be serious, Anna," I said. "The dream is so clear. I am tormented by my role. I am being asked to talk about the suffering of our people but not about why they are hurting. Bravery is acceptable, but bravery in the face of hardships is treason. We can be heroes, but we can't be hungry."

"You mean you are not allowed to speak of hunger at all?" asked Katarina.

The day after the fire that consumed the Badaev warehouse, the city established food rations. At first they were generous—a daily ration of 800 grams of bread for laborers, 600 for office workers 400 for dependents. And there was a monthly allotment of meat, cereals, macaroni, fish, sugar, candy and fat. But soon the portions were cut in half, and monthly staples all but vanished.

"They call the ration cards *smertniks* now," said Luby. From the Russian word, *smert*, for death.

"Well they may be death cards, but thieves steal them anyway," I said. "Last week, I saw thugs steal one from an old lady in the queue. And I can't even mention it on the air."

"No mention of bread lines?" Anna asked. "Goodness, no wonder you used the monkeys as props."

"I rather liked the idea of the monkeys as our stand-ins," said Viktoria. "After all, they are our ancestors. And the truth is that the bombs have silenced all of us."

"Perhaps," said Katarina, "but it will be difficult to get through this war without mentioning food, or hunger. I worry about the children. Pavel is asking for seconds, something he never did before."

"True," said Viktoria. "My youngest brother Rodion is so hungry it is painful to watch. He is 12 now, growing so fast every day, a body coursing with hormones eating every morsel I can bring home from the museum. The other day I asked him if he wanted to visit the art buried in the Gold Room, a rare invitation that normally would excite him. He just shrugged and asked, 'Is it edible?'"

There was silence for a bit. Then Katarina spoke.

"I have a friend who might be able to talk about how dire the situation is without compromising her position—or yours," Katarina said, looking at me. "Her name is Dr. Yulia Aronovna Mendeleva. She was born here but received her medical training in Germany. For a long time now, I think for more than a decade, she has been running the Leningrad State Pediatric Institute."

"What do they do?" asked Viktoria, her voice making clear she was really asking what they might do for her brother.

"At the moment, she has a team of scientists testing the contents of pine needles and tobacco remnants—both abundant— to extract vitamins. If you interview her, she will tell you that researchers believe vitamins are key to children's health and development. I've been using her supplements for Pavel and Anastasia for years."

"Maybe," I said, thoughts running through my mind faster than I could keep up with them. "If we portray it in terms of protecting the next generation, of ensuring the future of the Soviet people, that might work. Do you think she would talk about the impact of hunger on young bones?"

"I think she would," said Katarina. "She's been in power a long time. She knows the boundaries. And she must know, because they also have a hospital, that the situation is getting worse."

I nodded. It *was* getting worse to anyone willing to look. Bodies were piling up in the streets—in doorways, alleys and apartment lobbies—like abandoned garbage waiting for janitors to remove them. The corpses were blue, emaciated, cold. There were no coffins, so relatives loaded the bodies on children's sleds and pulled them to the cemetery. I was grieved; I could talk of none of it.

"I heard the police formed a special team to arrest cannibals," said Anna. "Can you talk about that?"

"Good grief, no! That would suggest defeatism. Besides, I wouldn't want to give anyone any ideas."

"What if you wrote a story for children," said Viktoria. "You could talk about the need to help one another at a time when everyone is hurting. Paint with your words. We will see behind them."

"I like that idea," said Luby. "It reminds me of a play I once wrote for children. The play concerned an Italian woman, Chiara Lubich, who asked children to hold hands and pray to God. This was back in the old days, during the last world war. With bombs falling and relatives dying, one of the children told Chiara angrily that God could not help them, or He already would have. She said, 'Children, the only reasonable response to war is love.' That is your job now Olga, to shower us with love."

"Luby, would you come on Radio Leningrad and tell that story?"

"Of course," said Luby. "Besides, it would be great publicity for the Puppet Theater. We are thinking of re-opening. People seem to be eager for a diversion, for something to think about, something to experience, that's more uplifting than the daily struggle to find food."

Katarina nodded. "Dhazdat told me the orchestra is to start performing again, I think for the same reason. They are practicing Hadyn's Symphony No. 103."

"So they are," I confirmed. I had watched the Radio Orchestra rehearsing. Some musicians were so weak from hunger I wondered if they would live to perform it. I didn't want to alarm Katarina, so said nothing. Maria was not so diplomatic.

"Hadyn No. 103, isn't that a very taxing one?" I asked.

"Well it is for Dhazdat," laughed Katarina. "It's sometimes called the Drumroll Symphony. He will be on the timpani for nearly the whole performance, with a kettledrum solo in the middle."

"Maybe you can feed him some of the children's vitamins," said Luby. Maybe you can feed him some of your strength, I thought.

"What about the staff at the museums?" Viktoria asked. "It would be dangerous to talk about the Hermitage, but the others might make good stories about preserving art for after the war."

I was surprised. When Stalin first came to power, he tried to sell off the museum's collections. Josef Orbeli, the Hermitage director, reproached him, insisting, "Without art, we have no nation." Stalin relented. But now, Vadim admonished me not to utter a word on the air about the museum's dramatic evacuation of art, except the need for volunteers. I had been careful ever since.

"Like what?"

"You could interview Georgi Knayazev," Viktoria said. "He's director of the Academy of Sciences Archives. Most of the collection—and frankly most of their staff—have already been evacuated. Knayazev is confined to a wheelchair—I'm not sure why, a genetic disease, I think—so he stayed. He's very witty—he once despaired that his security staff was better at guarding the sofa in his office than the artifacts behind it. I doubt he'd repeat that on the air, but you might get him to talk about the Sphinxes in front of the Archives. He thinks they have magical powers to protect the building."

"Wonderful idea," said Luby. "Olga, do you know the four most powerful words in any language?"

I shook my head.

"Once upon a time," she replied.

We all looked puzzled, so she continued.

"Everyone is hooked on the promise of a good story. It is the foundation of literature, of art, of anything creative. You begin any tale with 'once upon a time' and you capture the audience forever."

"I love that," said Maria. "Maybe telling stories will get us through."

"If so, I have another story for you," said Katarina. "The other night, we were in an air raid shelter. An old man was reminiscing about his work before the first war. He was a pastry cook and had helped make a remarkable piece of confectionery called the Chocolate Gospel, so good they were asked to compete at a culinary contest in Paris. Imitating his voice, she continued.

"The Chocolate Gospel won the competition, we actually won!" she mimicked. "The prize was 25,000 rubles! We were elated. The funny thing is those fancy French judges thought we had used pure cream butter. They were so sure. But we couldn't afford that—we had used margarine!"

Luby clapped. Maria laughed.

"There was laughter in the shelter too," Katarina recalled. "Most of us were spellbound. We went home dreaming of chocolate—and outwitting ignorant judges. The children were so sleepy we carried them home on our shoulders. And when he put him to bed, Pavel told his father he wanted to grow up to be a pastry chef. 'A mighty pastry chef', said Dhazdat. 'You will feed the world!'"

"That is glorious," said I. "I'll ask Yuri to see if he can track down this Chocolate Gospel Man. I bet lots of people, especially the children, would love to hear that story."

"Maybe," Viktoria said with a sigh, "but they can't survive on stories alone."

We all looked at her, waiting.

"Orbeli assigned me to look after 2000 staffers and their families who opted to live together on plank beds in Bomb Shelter No. 3, in the basement of the Hermitage," I said. "They have little heat, minimal light and not much food. We managed some light by dismantling the beeswax taper candles in the Orthodox marriage service collection. But it won't last forever. Every night they fry frozen potatoes in the linseed oil that artists use for their canvasses and call it dinner. Persian expert Nikolai Lebedev died of hunger Monday, his last words, 'How I want to live, how I want to live!'

"I stay with my family at night, but I suffer for these refugees in the basement. Maybe they are safe from Nazi bombs, but what about the psychological impact of their quarantine, especially on the children. Can human beings survive without sunshine, among corpses? And for how long?"

The room was silent, so quiet we could hear each other breathing.

"Viktoria, are you authorized to tell us what happened to the art at the Hermitage?" Luby said.

"I can here, because the artifacts have already been secured in their hiding place. But for now," she said, "we should keep the news out of our diaries, and out of our broadcasts, of course."

At this she looked pointedly at me, and I nodded. It was like a silent code of fidelity. I trusted these women. No hint would leave the room. Although I did glance at my sister, a sweet soul who liked to gossip, thinking I would have to mind her tongue.

"The first train left the Hermitage three weeks after Germany had attacked, which is a pretty amazing achievement if you think about it," Viktoria began. "We sent half a million items in more than one thousand crates. The cargo train stretched for so long—500 yards—that engineers had to design two locomotives to haul it. On either side were flatcars with anti-aircraft guns."

"Yes, but who rode in first class?" I asked. It was a joke, but I was as ever sensitive about class difference, mindful of distinctions that marred the promise and purity of the Bolshevik experiment.

"There were four Pullman cars for the most precious artifacts," said Viktoria. "The Titians, El Crecos, Rubenses, Rembrandts and Van Dykes all traveled in style, if that's what you're asking. Not to be outdone, the tsarist treasures—crowns, diamonds, Faberge eggs, gold alter pieces, and Peter I's white marble *Venus*—all received first-class treatment too."

"And what about the people?" asked Anna. "Did Orbeli leave?"

"That is a bit of a story," Viktoria began. "Orbeli had asked an archeologist named Boris Piotrovsky to come help us to pack up the treasures. Years earlier, Orbeli had been his mentor, teaching him the ways of the Hermitage. And if you ask him, Piotrovsky will credit the museum with sparking his interest in archeology. He told me he thinks of both of them as collectors, Orbeli of art, he of skeletons. In fact, when he saw the chaos at the museum, with boxes and packing tape and staffers running between the rooms, Piotrovsky said he was struck by its similarity to the archeological dig he had just come from—artifacts strewn all over, piles of sand and spades on the floor."

"Orbeli?" I prompted.

"Orbeli told Boris he wanted him to evacuate with the treasures, to guide them to safety, and then bring them home," Viktoria said. "He also suggested that after the war, Boris could lead the museum, could introduce the artifacts to a new generation."

"This sounds more like a movie than a story!" said Luby. "I can't wait for the next scene."

"I guess the next scene was more like a movie," said Viktoria. "It happened at the station."

At this, she looked to Katarina, who nodded and took up the story.

"My sister Mariska and I answered the call for volunteers and worked at the Hermitage just after the invasion, designing a labeling system for all the treasures as they were packed for evacuation. Mariska is an artist herself, and that helped a lot. We had so many problems to think about—What would happen if two paintings from different rooms were in the same crate? Was there a backup plan in case labels fell off in transit? But finally, on that last morning, we were invited to stand on the platform with Viktoria as the art was boarded on that special train. It made me feel so tall, as if we had made history. The art was fleeing war. Maybe there was a shared thrill in plotting its escape, like conspirators readying the treasures' bolt for freedom. I brought Pavel with me, so he could witness this moment of optimism amid war. I actually imagine the scene now with music."

"What did they say?" asked Luby, sounding as bubbly as a child. They were all aging quickly—hunger robs the body of essential nutrients—but the war seemed only to be making Luby younger.

"I heard Boris say to Orbeli, 'Art is the first casualty of war, then.' And then Orbeli said, 'Take care of our heritage.' At the last possible moment, Boris jumped on board and blew a kiss to Viktoria and waved until he became a small dot on the train's horizon."

As Katarina told the story, Viktoria blushed. Had their flirtation escalated? War really was changing the orbit of all our lives.

"One thing puzzles me," I said. "The bombing of our art treasures, the attempt to systemically obliterate our museum, this baffles me. In other countries, the Nazis steal the art and take it as their own. Why are they trying to destroy ours?"

"Because we are Slavs," said Anna, "because they think us too ignorant, too backward, to possess such magnificent pieces of art. And because we are strong, maybe the first nation strong enough to defy their dreams of global domination."

"And another question," I said. "Why was the art evacuated and not the people?"

There was silence in the room. Finally, Anna spoke.

"I would never leave," she said. "After the Revolution, friends begged me to emigrate with them to England. I refused. I wrote a poem about my first lover Anrep, who did leave, accusing him of betraying our country. I still feel that way. It's not just the Soviet Union but the Russian language that is my homeland. A poet can only sustain her art in her own language."

"I'm not leaving either," said Luby. "I will die where I was born."

"What about the kids?" asked Katarina. "If the Philharmonic Orchestra can be evacuated to Kuibyshev to wait out the war, why are the children of the Radio Orchestra made to stay here and go hungry?"

Her question hung in the air, without answer, for there was none. That was the problem, I thought. Most of our questions were unanswerable. They were like punctuation marks in the sky.

Each of us retreated to our thoughts. Finally, I broke the silence.

"Well, I have some news too," said I. "I am pregnant."

There was much clapping, calls for champagne, girl talk, offers to get ration cards for me.

"How far?" asked Katarina.

"I think three months."

"And I think four," said Maria.

I laughed, clutching my tummy, comforting myself that a baby takes nine months to grow, whether bombs are falling or not. Maybe I would get some of those vitamins Katarina talked about.

"Maybe the Americans can speed our rescue," said Viktoria. "I heard they will join the fight soon."

"Maybe," I said. "This little American man came to visit Radio House the other day. His name was Harry Hopkins and he was an envoy from the American President, Franklin Roosevelt, to see what we needed. How I wish I could have told him."

"What was he doing in Leningrad?" asked Luby.

"Apparently he's a classical music fan. He met with Stalin to discuss munitions in Moscow, but flew to Leningrad—at some personal risk—to hear my interview with Dmitri Shostakovich."

"Shostakovich, the composer?" asked Viktoria.

I nodded. "He's working on a new symphony about the Nazi invasion. I was surprised Stalin agreed to allow the interview. I'm sure you've heard the story. When Shostakovich was a young man, his first opera, *Lady Macbeth of the Misensk District*, enjoyed much success until Stalin came to a performance. Apparently our dear Comrade hated it, walking out. Then he instructed *Pravda* to publish a review with the damning title, 'Muddle Instead of Music', calling the opera 'a deliberately dissonant, muddled stream of sounds...[that] quacks, hoots, pants and gasps'. Audiences stopped coming, the play closed. So I was puzzled Moscow gave us permission for the interview."

"Maybe they see good publicity in his new symphony," said Anna.

"Perhaps that's why Moscow let Mr. Hopkins come too," I said. "Anyway, I must say, it was a highlight for me, one of the few bright spots of the war so far."

"Were you a good girl?" asked Maria.

"Hardly," I said. "In fact, I borrowed some of your dramatic license and put on a show for the American. I wore theatrical clothes, let my hair fall over one eye, and tried to wow Mr. Hopkins with my sophistication. I knew he had come to hear my interview with the composer, but I wanted to make sure he left understanding how charming and intelligent a Soviet woman could be."

"Did it work?" asked Maria.

"Well he kissed my hand," I said, "like some nobleman. Then he asked what our wattage was!"

There was much laughter at this, Anna chuckling so hard she almost doubled over.

"Your wattage!" she said, wiping tears from her eyes. "I suppose you told him it was none of his business!"

Even Katarina, somewhat shy in personal matters, smiled at this. "Whatever *did* you tell him?"

"I told him it had never been tested."

There was so much laughter at this I feared the hall monitor would pound on the door and shush us. My friends all knew I was something of a flirt, so the double entendre rippled through the air without need of explanation.

"Of course the big moment came after the interview," I said. "The great composer spotted our own Katarina Orlova in the audience and locked eyes with hers. It was electric."

Katarina's cheeks turn pink. It was a good color for her.

"Ooooh, doesn't he know Dhazdat has a black belt in karate?" asked Luby, to general laughter.

"I wish I had asked Shostakovich how he writes without losing his soul, how he survives in the middle of art and politics. I sometimes wonder if my artist's pulse will survive this war."

"That, my dear, is the essential question of our city," said Anna. "Leningrad has always been conflicted about that, when it was St. Petersburg during the time of the tsars and when it shortened its name to Petrograd during World War I to avoid sounding too Germanic. After my first husband was shot on false charges of disloyalty, I managed to write a poem. 'Terror fingers all things in the dark, Leads moonlight to the axe. There's an ominous knock behind the wall: A ghost, a thief or a rat.' That was in the 1920s. Two decades later, living in Leningrad, little has changed."

Viktoria nodded and rose to go. Political dissent always made her nervous.

"I have to be in by 8," I explained, "the curfew demands it."

"Me too," said Katarina, "there are children to tend, and *plies* to practice."

"Wait, we have leftovers," I said. "Both of you, take the chocolates home to the children."

Katarina teared up as she thanked me.

"Thank you for your suggestions," I said. "I especially like the idea of telling stories. Maybe that will be my offering to war, as Viktoria said, painting with words. I suppose it's better than eating them."

"To stories, then," said Maria, "and to chocolate, the only thing that everyone in Leningrad will miss, even the rats."

"To stories, chocolate and *love*," said Luby. "It's the only thing there's just too little of."

"Sounds like a painting at the Hermitage," said Viktoria.

"By Hieronymous Bosch," said Luby.

"Or an operetta at the Musical Theater," said Maria.

I smiled. The Poets Circle was talking nonsense, officially drunk. I had never heard Viktoria so chatty, or Katarina either. Maybe the wine, or the war, had loosened all of our tongues. Maybe we were all saying more than we should have. I didn't care anymore. I felt loved again.

As I opened the door to the hallway, Viktoria was the first to spot the poster, which none of us recalled seeing at evening's start.

It was a picture of a young woman, a red scarf over her head, a stern expression on her lips, an index finger to her mouth. 'Keep Your Mouth Shut', said the caption. In smaller print was a verse that said, 'Keep your eyes open. These days, the walls have ears. Chatter and gossip go hand in hand with treason.' It looked like one of the many propaganda posters the party had made. Had it been put up during the evening, directed at us, to remind us not to spread rumors?

"They have been telling us to shut up all my life," Anna said.

"Yes," said Viktoria, looking worried, "but this time, they've put ears in our walls."

SEVEN

The Children
October 1941

One morning at Radio House, Igor Brik walked into my office and closed the door. His face conveyed fear, but that emotion was so unlike him, I thought maybe he just had a hangover.

"I've done something unexpected," he said. "I've come for your help."

"Igor, you always do the unexpected. What is it this time?"

Igor was a great wit, a gourmet chef and I always forgave him, even when he upstaged me. I couldn't wait to hear what had happened to bring this dear teddy bear of a man to my office.

"Yesterday I went to the clinic. I was feeling heart palpitations."

"Igor, you are an overweight cellist who delights in food and joy, living in a time of want. Of course you felt heart palpitations!" Even as I said this, I noticed that his skin was sagging.

"Yes Olga dear, and thanks for your concern." He smirked at me. I smiled back.

"Outside the clinic was a billboard. 'Will trade luxuries for food', read one posting, listing a pair of gold cufflinks, navy blue fabric, a pair of patent leather boots, a samovar and a camera. Imagine giving up your samovar for food! Down the row, another sign said, 'Light coffin for sale'. How valuable is that! Everyone knows officials have stopped clearing dead bodies from the streets. At times like this, a light coffin would be easier for dragging a relative to the cemetery."

"Your point Igor?"

"I found it all fascinating. Man's instinct to barter is surviving the Siege. Even while hungry, the human spirit is resourceful. I wondered how much food you would have to trade for a camera."

"So you were shopping?" I asked.

"Not exactly," said Igor. "Further down on the board was another note that caught my attention. 'Bring any children left without care due to the death of their parents to Room #4', it said."

I knew that Igor had always loved children. At the picnic he had confessed he longed to adopt a child with Andrei. But as long as Stalin remained at the helm—with his homophobic policies and communist views of the family as the function of the state—such a flight of fancy seemed unlikely. Surely he knew that, but something in his body language made me wonder. I drew in my breath.

"Whatever have you done?"

He looked down at his lap, his shoulders hunched over his shrinking belly, his eyes pierced with fear.

"I walked into Room #4," he said. "Olga, I walked in, announced my name, disclosed that I played cello for the Radio Orchestra of Leningrad and declared that I was looking for my missing son."

I sat back, dumbstruck. I think I was whispering when I next spoke.

"Tell me everything."

"The clerk was a woman whose nametag said Marta Magnaya and who looked to me like a librarian, with a severe bun and big glasses. She invited me to look around but warned me that if my son had been wandering the streets for a time, I might not recognize him.

"I nodded solemnly and surveyed the room. Most of the children were looking down or curled up in a fetal position. Many had vacant stares. I felt awful, like a prospective dog owner waiting for one of the pets to make eye contact. I did not feel a connection to any of the boys and was about to leave. Suddenly there was a flutter in the corner.

"'Papa,' said one boy, who could not have been more than six years old. 'Papa, it's me, Rahil,' he said weakly. I wasn't sure if the boy was play-acting or hallucinating. If I opened my arms in greeting, and the boy joined in my hug, would this Rahil recoil at encountering someone not really his father? Would he expose me, possibly leading to my arrest for impersonating someone or worse, attempting to steal a child? There was not more than a second to decide. Sweat poured down my face. Finally I smiled, opening my arms. Rahil came running, and clung to me as if his life depended on it.

"'That's okay, my son,' I said. 'We have found each other.'"

"My God," I said. "Igor, this is epic, even for you. Then what happened?"

"Miss Marta Magnaya said it was a rare and happy occasion. She actually smiled. Then she produced a mound of documents. I looked at her through a mist of fear."

"We have to make sure you are really the father," she explained.

"Of course," I said. "But Miss Magnaya, perhaps I could take the paperwork home and return with it next week. It's been a rather emotional day for both of us," I added, smiling at Rahil and ruffling his hair. Did she suspect I was an imposter? Was I risking my job with the orchestra? I wondered."

"This is most irregular," she said. Looking at me oddly she said, "But you are with the orchestra, we know where to reach you, so maybe I can allow it, just this once."

"I reached for the wad of documents—'Name of orphaned child, name of relative claiming said child' among the categories to be filled out—and bowed, as if I had just finished performing a major symphony. I took Rahil's hand and we left together."

I looked at him, stunned. Igor had placed all of them—arguably all of Radio House—in legal jeopardy. Yet, I could not help but be astonished by the grandeur of the moment. At a time when families were being splintered by hunger and death, here was Igor trying to create a new one. At a time of cynicism, there was something sentimental about this attempt to rescue a child. After all, what was Rahil's future otherwise—to be raised in a state-run orphanage? How much better to be raised by two musicians, to be surrounded by culture rather than state dicta.

Finally I stood, as if part of an audience offering an ovation, and announced, "Igor Brik, that is one of the grandest performances you have ever given." I clapped—slow, solitary, emphatic.

"Thank you for the applause, Olga, honestly, your support matters. But, now what? Rahil told us last night that his parents and older brothers were all killed when the Germans bombed their apartment. Olga, I have no idea how I will convince the authorities this child is mine. And Andrei is beside himself with fear, despite the peace offering we brought home."

I resumed my seat.

"Peace offering?"

"I told Rahil we would stop first at the site of the Badaev Warehouse fire. I hadn't been there yet. I wanted to see the enormity of the disaster German bombing had created, and maybe to contemplate the one I was creating by abducting a child. Respectfully, as if visiting a gravesite, I showed Rahil how to scoop up handfuls of sugar-infused earth and put it in my satchel. You know you can cook the earth and strain it through muslin to squeeze out its starch and produce sugar. It looks dreadful— muddy and dirty, like the water of boiled leather—but after you cook it, you can use it to sweeten food. I guess I thought I would soften Andrei's heart, or at least postpone his questions."

"Did that work?"

"Briefly. Back in the apartment, I introduced Rahil to Andrei as the child of a family friend who was now orphaned and needed shelter. Then I deflected any more questions by explaining that Rahil and I had stopped at the Badaev to scarf up the sugar earth we could cook down to make food.

"You're getting to be quite the enterprising cook," Andrei told me, even as he was eyeing the boy.

"Yes, after the war, I plan to host a cooking show on Radio Leningrad."

"What will you call it?"

"Siege Cuisine."

"Rahil laughed, but Andrei did not. I suppose he's too smart to be taken in by a bit of sugar. After we ate something—there was not much conversation as everyone was quite hungry—I put Rahil in the big armchair—I made it up as best I could with spare linens—and we went to bed.

"Andrei was hurt and worried, pounding me with questions. 'Who is this child, really, and why is he here? Will we keep him for the rest of the war? How will we find food for all three of us? Will we come to love him only to have relatives come claim him? When he grows up, will he turn us in as homosexuals? Will we spend our last days in jail?' I kept trying to shush him, worried Rahil would overhear our conversation. But Andrei's questions kept coming. Occasionally he asked me if I had lost my mind. Once, he threatened to leave us. Neither of us slept much, contemplating a life with a child we weren't supposed to have in a world of scarcity we might not survive."

Igor looked up at me, his eyes pleading for answers. I was overwhelmed, and a bit impressed, by this impulsive, grand gesture of love in a world of calculated hate. In my cramped and admittedly disheveled office, I paced, navigating around stacks of papers on the floor as I weighed options. There weren't many. But war had a funny way of opening unexpected paths. After a few minutes, I sat down on a corner of my desk, looked at Igor with a smile and told him of my plan.

When Igor left, I turned to the mail. The staff collected it for me from the mounds of correspondence that arrived daily at Radio House. I was probably the only person reading it.

After the war started, newspapers grew rare—they were just too expensive to print, or transport—and we became the source of news for most people. Officials put Radio House on a war footing, declaring us essential employees. They installed half a million fixed-wire transmitters in apartments, factories and shops all around town, and made sure the loudspeakers on public streets were in working order. That's when I began using a new signature to begin all my broadcasts, which by then were being transmitted to much of the nation. 'This is Radio Leningrad, the city of Lenin,' I would say, 'calling the country.' Many wrote to us, pouring out their hearts. With Nikolai gone to war, reading their letters was one of my few pleasures. These were our listeners, and they cared. Even when they were hurting, and how could they not be, I delighted in the connection they felt with us.

The letter from a woman named Maia Babich was heartbreaking. We had lost electricity a few weeks earlier—I guess the Germans were bombing everything that could keep us civilized—but it never occurred to me to imagine how that single lack was affecting different lives. 'I tried to feed my dying husband in the darkness, because we had no lights,' she wrote. 'The spoon kept hitting his nose instead of his mouth. I was devastated. I knew if I did not get food into him, he would die. I kept hearing the soothing rhythm of your voice, telling me that we had to keep going, because that was the only thing that distinguished us as human beings. My husband died, Olga, but when he did, he knew, as I did, that I had done everything I could to save him, thanks to you.'

I tried not to take these accolades personally. Because of the dissonance between what I was allowed to say on the air—with its themes of defiance and courage—and the grim realities in the city, I felt no credit was due. Maia Babich may have taken heart from my words, but her courage came from her soul, not mine. My writer's block had evaporated, and maybe because Nikolai was away, I was writing constantly—in poems, in tributes, even in my journal.

"I am working furiously, writing uplifting poems and articles, and writing them from the heart, that's what's so surprising. But who will that help? Against the background of what is happening, it's just lies."

Still, the letters came. Red Army units, entire collectivized farms—all kinds of listeners—wrote me long letters about their lives, their hunger, their yearning for a human connection. 'I listen every day," wrote Elena Martilla. "The rhythm of your voice is soothing, your words memorable.' Aleksei Yevdokimov's letter stayed with me. 'Oh, you, hunger, hunger, hunger! How on earth to survive you? Whoever will live will never forget these days.'

The next letter brought me up short. First, because it was written on mimeograph paper, a mass mailing that had included Radio Leningrad. Second, because its author was very, very angry. And that was always a recipe for attracting punishment.

"Comrades. Down with a regime that lets us die of starvation! We are being robbed by scoundrels who deceive us, who stockpile food and leave us to go hungry. Let us take action. Let us go to the district authorities and demand more bread. Down with our leaders! Signed The Rebel."

I reached in the pile to feel for any other letters written on this unusual paper. There was one other.

"How dare they eat while we starve! How dare they evacuate their petty bureaucrats while our children whimper toward death! How dare they call themselves communists, preaching that we are all comrades,

while they save the best for themselves. Overthrow the leaders! Signed The Rebel."

Clearly these epistles were inflammatory, and would be grounds for prosecution of anyone who even had them in their possession. But they fascinated me, evidence of how hunger was warping the bounds of our civil society. Here was vivid testimony of hardship, an important artifact of war. Perhaps if I wrote about the Siege one day, I might need them. I stuffed them in my pocket.

As I continued reading, I was struck by how often our audience mentioned music. Maybe because I was at Radio House, where musicians were constantly tuning and practicing their instruments, but the theme resonated with me. People in pain were longing to hear the soothing sounds of melody.

"Just think, the Germans are at our gates and we sing songs," wrote a woman named Zoya. "They will all rot in the earth and our city will stand. We will work and write poetry and sing." Some of the letters were uplifting. One fighter pilot whose plane had lost a wing said he made it home only by listening to Radio Leningrad the night Klavdiya Shulzhenko—described by some as the Soviet Vera Lynn—sang *Little Blue Scarf.* "Her voice gave me the courage to keep flying," he wrote.

"Bread!" wrote Elena Kochina, struggling to keep both her infant daughter and her husband alive. "We almost never talk about it, but we think about it constantly. Bread—soft, fragrant bread, with a crunchy crust. The thought of it drives us crazy. If only we could once more plunge our teeth into its redolent warmth and tear it, chomp it, eat it whole without stopping. The Russian's strength is contained in it. No, even more—life itself is contained in it. The Russian peasant understood this. We have only now realized the full meaning of *khlebushka*. Bread sounds like music to us now."

I sat there thinking about the role of music in this city. Beyond the greats—Rimsky-Korsakov, Tchaikovsky, Mussorgsky, Rachmaninoff—I knew that on any street corner of Leningrad at almost any hour, musicians would pop up. Even amid the Siege, one listener wrote that the music played on.

"Death reigns in Leningrad," wrote Vera Kostrovitskaya. "And yet, the musicians still play."

All over the city, she said, they offered music as an antidote to bombs, hunger and a bitter cold front. One day she looked out into an apartment across the courtyard and saw a group of neighborhood musicians playing. "Huddled in their overcoats, on wooden cots, surrounded by gleaming wind instruments, they played every day. Usually the clarinet would begin, establishing the melody, then it would be repeated by the first two trumpets, and then the trombone and flute joined in. The drummer, when he was free, filled the role of the conductor." Once food rations were reduced, she said, the sounds great fainter. "First the bass fell silent, then the flute could no longer be heard, and, as if paralyzed by the cold, the tempo became slower. Then it all died." How poignant, I thought. They died in the comfort of music, perhaps the only freedom still left to them.

Another writer, Kristina Lebedev, wrote that her mother, as she was dying, wanted to hear beautiful symphonic music. So Kristina left their apartment to come to Radio House, where she found Alexander Kamensky, the only pianist who had refused to evacuate with the rest of the Philharmonic. He had stayed in Leningrad, and now played for the Radio Orchestra. She begged him to perform for her mother, and he did. He followed Kristina to her apartment, through broken glass, blocks of ice and piles of sewage.

"Mommy," she said, "Alexander Danilovich Kamensky has come. He will play for you now."

"Is this a dream?" the mother asked.

But our very own Kamensky was real. He sat at their piano and played from *Liszt's Prelude in Fugue and G Minor*. He got up to leave but the mother said, "More." So he played Ravel's *Sad Birds* and Debussy's *Moonlight and Brahms' Intermezzo Es-dur*, like a lullaby. Then he stood, closed the lid of the piano, and bowed to the woman.

"Happiness," said the mother. Then she died.

I marched across the hall and into Vadim's office. He looked up from his paperwork—piles and piles of paperwork—as if dreading my latest idea, even before he had heard it.

"We have to perform Symphony No. 7," I said. "The Orchestra has to bring Shostakovich home."

Shortly after my interview with him, party officials decided Dmitri Shostakovich should be evacuated to Kuibyshev, the government's wartime capital, where the Philharmonic had already been sent to wait out the war. Apparently the Radio Orchestra was considered more expendable, so they were ordered to stay in Leningrad, though I knew their concerts were few.

"Olga, the authorities don't want any music on the airwaves except military tunes. The only reason the Radio Orchestra is rehearsing Tchaikovsky now is that the Kremlin decided we should do a performance, a Concert for Great Britain, to be aired in London for our new military allies."

"So we like the British now?"

"Don't get me started. Eliasberg has already peppered me with his conspiracy theories."

I smiled.

These days, I knew, our conductor thought the Germans were timing their bombs to interfere with his orchestra's performances. Sometimes he thought they were doing it out of spite—maybe they knew he was Jewish, or that Tchaikovsky had been gay. Or maybe they just bombed on their own timetable, he told me, killing for their own convenience. I told him I thought that more likely.

"Do you remember what Shostakovich said when I interviewed him?" I asked Vadim. "He told me he had never felt so energized to write, even amid the bombs, and that if he finished the piece, he would dedicate Symphony No. 7 to the people of Leningrad. He said the music was born here, was about the traumatic events that took place here, and that we above all people deserved to hear it."

Vadim nearly exploded, which was rare for him.

"He also said, as I recall, that artists have no less a role to play in war than soldiers, that it is our duty to show that life is still normal. I believe there was also some nonsense about how 'in a time of hunger, culture is a kind of nourishment too.' I agree with all that. But then he deserted us and left for safety and food. I have lost 10 kilos, Olga, while he is eating."

I was stunned by the show of emotion for a man who was normally placid. I hadn't noticed, but now that he'd mentioned it, I saw that Vadim was looking unusually thin.

"We are not doing it for him," I said softly. "I doubt authorities would even let him come. We are doing it for ourselves, for the people of Leningrad, for the heritage of music that defines this city."

Vadim nodded, his signal that the conversation was over.

"And one more thing, Vadim," I said. "If we are essential employees, if we are to perform concerts for the British and broadcast news programs for the Soviets, we need more food."

He looked up at me as if wishing for the energy to smack me.

"What do you think all this paperwork is for?" he asked, before dismissing me again.

I stopped in at Eliasberg's office.

"Karl, the orchestra has to perform Symphony No. 7," I announced.

"I assume you mean the one by Shostakovich?" he said.

"Yes of course," I said, ignoring his cynicism. "It is perfect for the moment."

"Well as far as I know, he has not yet finished it. And even if he had, I doubt we have the breath to perform it." He paused then, rummaged in his desk and shoved a piece of paper in my hands.

"This is the log note from our last rehearsal," he said. "It sums up the situation perfectly."

"Rehearsal did not take place," said the log. "Violinist evacuated after toes amputated from frostbite. Trombone at death's door. French horn died on his way to work. Orchestra not working."

"Karl Ilyich Eliasberg, conducting Symphony No. 7 for an audience starving for food and music is your destiny. We need it. And so do you."

"Ask Vadim," Karl grumbled. "He is the only one who can make the call."

"I already did. He is furious that Shostakovich evacuated. And furious that the composer is eating. To tell you the truth, Vadim already looks yellow, as if he's in the first stages of starvation."

Karl nodded. "We are all starving, Olga. And there is no way we can perform a taxing symphony like No. 7. Knowing Shostakovich, it will be filled with horns and drums and all manner of sound."

"I'm sure it will, Karl. That's exactly why it needs to be performed in this city."

"Olga there is no way to transport it here, or even to make copies for the orchestra. You are a sentimentalist, but those are the hard realities."

"Karl, sentiment is the only thing that will get us through the war." I may have slammed his door on the way out.

I left the office soon after. I needed to talk to Viktoria.

The Hermitage looked like a ghost of its once proud history. The windows were boarded, against the advent of glass broken by bombs. Even to gain entrance, I had to go to a back door where Viktoria had left word that I should be admitted. Once I adjusted my eyes to the darkness inside, I saw those round and rectangular indentions everyone mentioned where paintings had once hung.

"The place looks haunted," I said.

"Yes," Viktoria said. "That's what Boris said when he saw them. 'The paintings are gone, but their souls remain.' Now they are in his care, far away."

"Have you heard from him?"

She smiled. "It is a courtship through the mails. It is so strange Olga, to be writing to someone who has plenty of food. He kills his own dinner."

Viktoria had aged much since I had last seen her. Maybe we all had. Meeting an acquaintance on the street these days was a little like looking in the mirror, seeing a reflection of one's own wrinkles, lost muscle tone and foggy eyes. Viktoria still had her high cheekbones, which helped preserve an impression of dignity. But a friend would know, and I counted myself a friend, that all was not well. And when I leaned in for a double cheek kiss, I realized she had grown very, very thin.

"Are you giving your rations to others?" I asked.

"I have no choice," she said. "My brother Rodion is dying, in agonizing fashion. The other day I caught him writing a letter to our father, who is at the front." She reached into her desk. "I asked him if I could keep it for a while. He made me promise to send it to Papa after he died."

She handed me the letter. It was heartbreaking.

"Dear Papa, I am writing to you because I am awaiting death and because it comes very quietly. I know that it will be hard for you to hear of my death, and I most definitely don't want to die, but there is nothing to be done if that is my fate. Mama and Viktoria have tried hard to keep me going. Mama took bits of her bread and a little off each of grandma and sisters and brother, but it is not enough. Dear Papa, don't get upset. Know that everyone tried as best they could."

I sat back in my chair, contemplating the sad fate of children trying to survive this battle between food and their future. How many would die? Would those who survived be traumatized forever?

"Viktoria, I've come to ask you a question."

I explained my plan to her.

"Olga, you must be out of your mind," she said. "It would endanger all of us—my mother Nina, my other siblings, even my father at the front. The authorities will never allow such a thing."

"Sometimes I think the authorities have already lost control of the situation," I said. "Too many people are dying. Have you noticed—if a family member dies, you no longer have to produce a death certificate. The coroner's office does not have time to examine every body, and the hospitals don't have room to house them. Bodies pile up on the streets and there are not enough janitors to clear them away. All that paperwork we used to do—to apply for apartments, or jobs, or assignments or schooling—it's all meaningless now. Everything we loved—the paintings on these walls, the music and dance in our concert halls—all has been taken away from us."

"But that is only temporary!" said Viktoria. "Someday the art will return, the music will sound again. Someday we will eat again. And then the authorities will want to know why Rodion is living away from his family, with another boy called Rahil, in a home of someone not a relative!"

I was surprised by her vehemence. She had a good mind—maybe she saw the future better than I. Maybe I had been wrong to confide in her. Would she turn me in? Desperation had driven people to far more extreme measures. I saw a woman's corpse on the street the other day. Her bosoms had been cut off, likely for food. We were living in a time of enormous upheaval, and some were losing their minds, desperate for normalcy, or anyway, for the way it used to be. I thought about a letter I'd received in the Radio House mailbag. Before the war, the writer suggested, people liked to put forward their best front, showing a face of fidelity or honesty. Now the Siege had stripped them of dignity. They were left only with what they were, desperate thieves, not what they wanted to seem.

I looked up from my musings to see Viktoria slumped over, crying softly.

"Of course you are right Olga," she said. "I'm sorry for my reaction. I will explain to my mother that this is the only way to save Rodion. And maybe he'll even learn something!"

I smiled and got up to leave. I had one more stop to make. I only hoped the plan would work.

"Olga, what a delightful surprise," Luby said, welcoming me to her apartment overlooking the Leningrad skyline. I loved seeing the city through this space, through her eyes, trying to imagine knowing all the history she knew, with memories of the tsars, the French and the Bolsheviks.

"You have the best view in the city," I said.

"That's what my husband used to say," she said. "He likened it to a view of the Champs-Elysees."

"Do you think of him often?" I asked.

She gave me an odd look. "He died so many years ago," she said.

"Yes," I said. "Still, I imagine there are things about him that make you feel nostalgic."

"I suppose the greatest gift he left me was his music. He loved to write songs for my puppets to sing. I remember one, 'The Little Boy Who Tried', that was a big hit with the children."

How prophetic, I thought. I drew a breath and began my appeal.

"Luby, I've come in confidence to ask you something complicated. If you want to say no, please do so. I only ask that you not turn me in."

She smiled.

"I like the sound of this so far."

She clapped her hands like a small child when I relayed the story of how Igor had acquired a child, and laughed at the part when he told Miss Marta Magnaya that he would return with the paperwork the following week. She really did love a good story.

"So now Igor has two problems," she said. "What to do with the boy. And what to do with the paperwork. And you, Igor's friend, think somehow I might have the answer to both problems."

I loved how intuitive this woman was, as if her 72 years on planet earth had given her a perspective on life that the rest of us lacked. I shook my head.

"No, Luby," I smiled. "I don't think you have answer to his problems. I think you are the solution."

She paled a bit then, I thought.

"Whatever do you mean, my dear?"

So I explained my plan. She could adopt Rahil, explaining in the paperwork that he was a relative of her late husband whose family had been obliterated. The authorities were overwhelmed right now—they just needed the paperwork, not the information it contained. And if she wanted to, she might also take in Viktoria's younger brother Rodion, who was dying of starvation, his muscles shrinking.

"You could raise them together, Luby," I said. "You could teach them all the culture this city once offered. Maybe you could even put them to work in the puppet theater. Igor and Andrei and

Viktoria will help whenever they can. Maybe Igor could even come cook for all of you."

Luby had a faraway look in her eyes, which had misted up. Maybe it was too much information to absorb at once. Maybe she thought homosexuals were disgusting. I didn't think so, as she had lived so long in France. But you never knew. She pursed her lips, and looked down at her hands in her lap. After what seemed a very long time, she met my gaze and spoke.

"This is hardly the ideal time or place—I can't imagine it will be easy to get food for such a large group," she said. "But I have always wanted to teach the young about art and music and storytelling, to inspire them. To be a mother, again, at my age," she laughed. "Ah, what a gift!"

I gave her the paperwork, relieved to pass the burden of Igor's secret from my shoulders to hers.

"Please have them come quickly," she said, "the boys and their guardians. The sooner we begin to act like a family, the better it will be. And if Rodion is already starving, I have some chicken fat I've been saving for a special occasion." I was speechless. There was nothing left to do, so I hugged her.

EIGHT

The Evacuation
November 1941

The police came for me, again, just after temperatures plummeted. It seemed an unfair cruelty that nature had chosen this year to give Russia its coldest winter on record, temperatures 30 degrees below zero, when we were already struggling against the cold of hunger. I knew families of five or six who were sleeping in one bed to keep warm. A friend burned all her furniture to stay alive. And now I had to deal with NKVD interrogators, with their cruel tactics and malicious questions about motives. I didn't know how much more I could take. I felt worn to the bone. And given that I was pregnant, as I was the last time I was arrested, my heart beat fast with the fear of their brutality.

This time there was no procession of colleagues to watch mournfully as I was ripped from their company at Radio House. This time they came for me at home, with a knock on the door.

"You will come with me for questioning," said a young agent, grabbing me roughly at the arms.

As he pushed me down the hallway, the floor monitor gave me a look of triumph. So it was her, I thought. But what had she turned me in for? Since Nikolai left for the front, it was very quiet in the apartment. I shivered without my coat, but was glad I had not asked to retrieve it. They might have found my rosary. I moved my fingers now, as if to caress it. Even absent, she gave me comfort.

The People's Commissariat for Internal Affairs was notorious. The local NKVD headquarters reeked of urine, and there were large straps hanging on wall hooks, caked in dried blood, maybe some of it mine. Just the sight of them made me nauseous. I was pushed into a cold cell—turns out there was no heat in prison either. I looked around at my sparse surroundings—a thin mattress on the floor, a spittoon and a tiny window where the wall met the ceiling. I thanked God for that light.

I sat on the mattress and clutched my stomach where our son Grigori once slumbered. Would they beat me again, cause another miscarriage? Was there no end to the venality of our leaders? I was glad Nikolai was at the front, and could not see me under threat like this again by a country that he was risking his life to defend. I wondered if we would even recognize each other after the war.

I fell asleep, and dreamt that I was on a beach, watching the waves. I woke to hear the clang of the cell door opening. I looked up to see a man in uniform, with lots of medals on his lapel. His nameplate announced he was Maxim Lermontov, Captain. A lieutenant brought him a chair. I remained on the mattress. Strange, last time they took me to a special interrogation room.

He looked at me as if I were a terrorist.

"We have evidence that you and your conspirators are plotting subversion."

"Subversion?" I asked, trying to keep my voice calm. "Captain Lermontov, I am a broadcaster for Radio Leningrad. Everything I do, everything I say, is public."

"Oh don't be coy with me," Lermontov leaned forward. "We know you are a traitor. We have reports that you recently met with other dissidents at your apartment."

I racked my brain. And then, despite the fear in my body, the scars of an earlier miscarriage caused by their interrogations, the pain of having my patriotism questioned, I laughed.

"Stop laughing!" Lermontov screamed.

"I apologize Captain, but if you are referring to my Poets Circle, we are plotting nothing, unless it is survival. We are a group of women, hoping to endure this dreadful ordeal that Hitler has imposed on Leningrad by sharing our feelings." I knew better than to call it a siege, or a blockade, or mention hunger or food, but hoped the idea of a shared enemy would take the edge off his questions.

He looked little mollified, but did lower his voice.

"What role does Anna Akhmatova play in these meetings?" he demanded.

"They are not meetings, comrade," I said. Maybe the communist familiarity might soften his tone. Or maybe he would resent the inference that he and I were equals in this country. I took the risk. "They are gatherings of women, a circle of poets, artists, dancers, performers, all eager to support each other at a difficult time for our country, and for us."

"But you are dissidents!" he exclaimed.

"Hardly," I said. "Captain Lermontov, are you married?"

He hesitated, unsure if this was a trap to send him off his mission.

"That is none of your business."

"Captain, I do not mean to pry, but I assure you it is relevant to your question."

Finally, he nodded.

"Yes, I am married."

"Then you must understand that women have the need of talk. We talk when we are happy, when we are sad, when we are frightened, when we are inspired. It is how we experience life. I know it is different for men. You believe that keeping your emotions intact protects you in a crisis. But for us, it would be impossible to get through Hitler's war without talking. Simply impossible."

"You know that talking is dangerous?" he said.

I nodded.

"We are not telling state secrets," I said, remembering the conversation at our last meeting about how the Hermitage was disguising its roofline, and wondering if this statement was perhaps less than truthful. "We are sharing recipes and amusing stories and personal anecdotes about our families. We care deeply about this city's survival, Captain, but what we talk about is our own."

There was silence in the room then, except for the drumming of his fingers on the arms of his chair. I had toyed with the idea of mentioning that my husband was a soldier in the Red Army, but dismissed the thought for fear of roping Nikolai into this web of controversy. As a chilly silence filled the room, I wondered if I should have risked it.

Finally Captain Lermontov rose and leaned in so close I could smell his breath, reeking of cigarettes.

"We will be watching you, you and your coven of subversives," he said. "One wrong move, one hint of a plot against our beloved communist government and I will haul you back here, never to leave. You may have a following on the radio, but here you are viewed as an enemy. Understand?"

I nodded. With a flurry, he and his lieutenant left the room, taking the chair with them. I let my breath out, finally.

The ending was oddly lacking in ceremony, as usual. The police had driven me to the station for an interrogation. Now that they had no more use for me, I was free to walk to work. The winds whipped my clothes. The streets were littered with corpses covered in snow, as if left for trash collection. It was but a few blocks from the police station to Radio House, but it was a daunting walk. I must have passed two dozen pedestrians. Most had their heads down, as if it was less taxing not to waste energy on smiling, or making eye contact, or anything that marks us as humans.

I arrived at Radio House in hopes of collapsing in my office, to soothe my aches in private. But I opened the door to find Dhazdat waiting. Actually, he was pacing. I toyed with the idea of telling him of my encounter with the police, if only to warn Katarina. But he looked as though he had been in my office a long time, so I pointed to a chair and sat in my own to listen. If he noticed that my skin was pale, he said nothing. He dove headfirst into his story, without preamble or context, without pacing or rhythm. Unusual for a musician, but not for our Ukrainian hunk of a drummer.

"I was queueing for bread when I saw a Christmas tree with colorfully wrapped presents at its feet," he said, barely getting the words out between labored breaths. "I went to look closer. Olga, the 'presents' were actually corpses of dead children, wrapped in colorful blankets. Corpses of little children! I am horrified, wondering how long before my own children would join them."

I am a poet, but sometimes I can summon no words. I nodded, encouraging him to continue.

"Katarina fainted yesterday. We have both been skipping meals to give our portions to the children. Anastasia screamed when she learned we were eating Inna, one of her kittens, for dinner. I can only imagine what will happen when we eat the kitty's sister Kata. We are thinking of trying to escape."

I sat back in horror. The odds of them making it out were so minimal. Maybe, I thought on reflection, about the same odds of surviving without food or heat in the city.

"They say the Germans have orders to shoot anyone who tries to leave Leningrad," I reminded him. "And to tell you the truth, I wouldn't be surprised if the Soviets did too."

Dhazdat raised an eyebrow at that. I couldn't explain, so just nodded sagely. I thought this because the day before I had asked Vadim what he knew about The Rebel.

"Olga please tell me you have had no contact with him," he replied.

"Of course not," I said. "I just saw a few of his missives in the mailbag."

"Tell no one about this," Vadim said, lowering his voice. "The police are frantic to find him. He drops mimeographed leaflets at a train station near the industrial zone. So far they have examined the handwriting of more than 18,000 factory workers trying to nab him. After the Rebel wrote a letter directly to Leningrad Communist Party Secretary Andrei Zhdanov, the police intercepted every letter using the same kind of envelope. They interrogated more than one thousand families. One thousand families, Olga! When they still could not find The Rebel, Zhdanov was so furious I'm told he suggested burning Leningrad to the ground. 'We might as well do it before Hitler does,' he told his cronies in the Kremlin. Apparently cooler heads prevailed, but I wonder by how much."

I returned my gaze to Dhazdat. He looked drawn.

"There might be one way out," I said. "There's a rumor the city is about to evacuate the women and children, like the British did during the London Blitz."

The other night Radio Leningrad broadcast a BBC show about the London Blitz, in which the Germans bombed for 57 days and 57 nights. Titled 'London Calling: Long Live Leningrad', the documentary showed that the Nazis had failed, despite ferocious attacks, to break the will of the British people. One key element was Operation Pied Piper, which evacuated millions of children to rural areas in Britain and overseas to Canada, South Africa, Australia, New Zealand and the USA.

Dhazdat nodded.

"The show gave us hope," he said. "Do you really think the Pied Piper will come here?"

If I said yes, would I be guilty of giving him false hope? I said yes, and thought I saw a flicker of a smile across his face.

Three days later, authorities announced the evacuation with their usual assurances. A poster went up all over town, showing children playing in an idyllic landscape. The news was also broadcast on Radio Leningrad. "Your children will be safe," we said on the air. "They are our future."

"Do you really think they will make it?" Dhazdat asked me one day.

I had a bad feeling about the evacuation—what had the government done right in this war, I wondered—but offered Dhazdat every hope. Another mark on my sin list.

"It has to work," I said. "It's the only way our children will survive."

The day of the departure, I walked to the station with the Zelenskys. When we arrived, Dhazdat turned Katarina to face him. From his pocket, he gave her a red kerchief, wrapped around a hard surface.

"What is this?" she asked.

"It's an old French coin. Grandpa Stenka gave it to me after our wedding. He said it was handed down from one of our ancestors who fought against the French during the Napoleonic Wars. He said never to part with it, as it would always bring me luck."

"Then you shouldn't part with it now."

"No," he said. "You are the luckiest thing in my life, you and the children. And I want you to keep this close to you during the journey. It's the only way I have to protect you."

She looked up at him with tears. They embraced with such longing I thought the sidewalk would buckle. Then I approached and gave her a piece of paper.

"Put this code on all the letters you write," I said. "It is not a family heirloom but it may be as precious. If you write this number on the envelope, your letters will have priority. And sometimes, when it's a priority letter and officials are overwhelmed with mail, they won't read it at all."

Katarina took the code and thanked me. We hugged. She and the children hugged Dhazdat and waved to me, and then they were off. "Bye Papa, bye, bye," said Anastasia. How could any of us have known those were the last words we would hear her speak for some time.

As the trains set off, I wondered why they were heading West, toward summer camps at Gatchina along the Luga River. Shouldn't they be going East to Kuibyshev, the wartime capital that had welcomed all our other evacuees? I shivered, trying to convince myself it was just a quick shortcut.

Over the next few days, there were rumors in the newsroom about what happened to the children's train, but I dismissed them. I asked Yuri to keep me posted if he heard anything official.

A week later, Dhazdat came to my office with his eyes red from crying. He'd received a letter from Katarina. I was glad to see she'd used my postal codes.

I sensed at the beginning that we were going in the wrong direction, she wrote. *But I looked at the children, so serene, and wished I had some of their positive energy. I reached in my pocket and touched your coin, Dhazdat, and it gave me strength.*

I was glad the letter had survived the censors. In normal times, questioning the authorities' decisions would be grounds for arrest. I knew from our own mailbags that now there were too many letters—too many citizens with questions about official decisions—to examine all the mail.

According to her letter, at their first transit station, Ryvatskoe, they were all taken to a nearby collective farm. Friendly families greeted them with tea and cookies.

"*Mama, it's pampushky,*" said Pavel, "*those doughnuts Grandma Nataliya used to make.*"

I smiled at the mention of Dhazdat's mother, and began to allow myself to contemplate life without bombs, and with sweets. "*The tea is so soothing, don't you think?*"

Just then, the collective farm's director rushed up and shouted, "*Nazi paratroopers ahead! Nazi paratroopers ahead!*"

I gathered the children—folding as much of our food into the valise as I could—and ran in the other direction. Officials boarded us on a fleet of cars to get us to a new destination. I noticed the cars were old, from the tsarist era, and worried they would never get us to wherever we were going.

In Lychkovo we were placed on another train. I lifted Anastasia to my breast and took Pavel's hand. He squeezed hard. Maybe he had a premonition of fear. I wondered if the authorities even had a plan. It seemed like we were just being hustled here and there, put on any conveyance available. Once on board, I put the children under a train seat and put a mattress on top of them. I had learned to do this in a hurricane preparedness class. I know it's silly—Leningrad doesn't have hurricanes—but the government insisted those traveling abroad had to get training. Once, before the ballet troupe left for Greece, I had to be certified. My sister Mariska liked to tease me about it, but now I was grateful. Maybe the mattress would protect the children, maybe it wouldn't, but it made me feel better, it gave me something to do. Then I lay my body on top of the mattress, gently, as if I was caressing them. And Dhazdat, I prayed.

As the train started to roll, I looked up and noticed a young girl on a top berth, gazing out at the sky. Most of the children were traveling unaccompanied by an adult. I'll never understand why authorities made an exception in our case, but I was grateful. I tried to offer maternal warmth to all the children.

"Look—a plane," she yelled to me, excitement in her voice. "It's dropping something—maybe it will be toys."

I looked up just as an explosion hurled her to the ground. She landed with a thud on the floor, dead. That's when I realized the train was being pounded with machine-gun fire. The Nazis were also dropping bombs—on little children! —with terrifying, methodical precision. Soon children's screams filled the carriage, along with smoke. Scattered toys littered the floor. A small chess set blew to all corners of the room. A king came to rest on my leg. I was shaking.

It was a clear day, with especially good weather. The German planes circled and came back toward us. The little kids were crying. Maybe the Nazis will say they hadn't known it was a train full of children. Maybe they will say we were just casualties of war. But if this letter ever reaches you Dhazdat, I want you to know that I looked at one Luftwaffe pilot directly in the eyes. I will never forget his chilling, impassive look. They could see perfectly. They deliberately bombed our young. And when some kids fled the train, a plane would swoop in to machine-gun them dead as they ran.

Finally the bombs stopped and the smoke cleared. I heard young sobs above the quiet. I removed the mattress and stroked the foreheads of our children.

"*Are you well?*"

"*I'm fine Mama,*" *Pavel said.* "*I can't wait until I'm old enough to fight those Nazi gangsters.*"

Anastasia nodded, and sniffled.

I wondered then if it had been a mistake to leave Leningrad. I fingered your coin, Dhazdat, hoping it would help guide me about what to do next.

Suddenly an announcement came on the loudspeaker.

"*The evacuation is being aborted,*" *said a female voice.* "*We are returning to Lychkovo. There you will stay in the station until we can arrange transport to Leningrad, to reunite you with your families.*"

I searched the floor of our railroad car, trying to avoid body parts, looking for toys that might keep the children occupied during the journey. Instead I found a leaflet, a German propaganda missive written in Russian, no doubt meant to terrorize Soviet civilians into submission. I have never read anything as diabolical.

"*Dear citizens of the Soviet Union,*" *it began.* "*You cannot win. Leningrad was once a great city, more majestic even than Berlin or Vienna. But it is also the city that gave birth to the Jewish philosophy of Bolshevism. And for this, you must be punished. We will starve you until you surrender, and then we will raze your city to rubble. Surrender or starve, those are your options.*"

I shuddered as I read the note, thinking of the Nazi pilot who had locked eyes with mine.

Once we reached the train station, I rummaged through my bag for the treats we had grabbed on having to abandon it only a day before. As the children ate, I saw truck after truck stop at the station, all full of badly wounded soldiers returning from the front. Hours later, with the children haggard and tired, another truck appeared. It was moving slowly, and it was already packed. But I was desperate—I had this overwhelming urge to get home. I ran toward the truck. One soldier onboard must have seen my desperation. He held up one finger. There was only room for one.

"Anastasia," I said, bending down to her level. "I'm going to put you on this truck. Pavel and I will get the next one, do you understand?"

The little girl nodded.

"Here is your doll. Don't let go of it, it will help you get home, ok?"

Again, she nodded.

I scribbled Dhazdat's name and address on a paper and pinned it to Anastasia's dress, now tattered and torn. I kissed her forehead and handed her up to the soldier, yelling, "Please, take her to Leningrad!" The soldier pressed his palm to his heart. He would try.

I looked up from reading Katarina's letter.

"And?" I asked.

Dhazdat shook his head.

"The letter arrived in the mail, but there was no sign of Anastasia. I am tormented with worry," he said, trying not to sob. "I go every day to City Hall, demanding that officials find my family. Every day, I am told there is nothing to search for.

"You should see the crowds there, Olga. I've never seen anything like it. Usually people are very respectful of authority figures. But now mothers openly rage at officials for sending their children in the direction of the enemy. People say that two thousand children died at Lychkovo, and that some are still wandering the countryside, abandoned. Some dare to shout at officials, 'Bring back our children! Bring back our children!' One woman told me, 'Better to have them back here with us, to die together, than have them killed God knows where.' But the authorities never acknowledge anything. And whenever asked, they insist that news of a massacre on the train is Nazi disinformation, or tell young survivors that it was all in their imagination, a bad dream."

After Dhazdat left, I sat stunned. I had worried about the evacuation but had no idea it had gone so terribly wrong. It was too much information to absorb, just too much. Reeling from Katarina's descriptions of murder, I wondered if I was bringing a child into this world only to face a similar fate. I wondered where Nikolai was, and what he was doing. Was he one of the wounded soldiers coming home on a truck? How I longed for a letter. I contemplated what would happen to me if I told the story of the botched evacuation of our children on the air, but I knew the answer only too well. I silently praised Luby and Igor, and Viktoria too, for not putting their loved ones on that train. Then I put my head in my hands and did something I had not done in a very long time. I prayed. I didn't really know the right words, but I figured if a Divinity were listening, he would hear me.

On the walk home, I lifted my face to the sky, letting the snow hide my tears. By the time I walked into my apartment, I felt almost human again. But when I arrived, Maria was there. I had completely forgotten she had asked to meet me at my apartment.

I had not even taken off my coat when she burst into tears.

"Garegin has left me," she said, letting out a sob of deep emotion. It was always difficult to know with Maria when her feelings were raw and when she was performing. This seemed genuine. I moved her toward the sofa, made drinks for both of us, and sat next to her, holding her hand.

"What happened?"

"Garegin has started ranting about how we will all starve to death, how there will not be enough food." Here she paused to wipe a tear, dropping my hand. "I try to comfort him, to tell him that I can always get bread from the *bulochnaya*. He accused me of having an affair with the baker!"

"Not an unreasonable deduction," I offered.

"What does that have to do with anything?" she yelled. "I always showered Garegin with affection."

"Sometimes people want loyalty."

I almost choked on my words. Was there no end to my hypocrisy? How much greater were my sins? Would God punish me for convincing Dhazdat and Katarina to put their children on the train? Would the state arrest me if it ever came out that Rahil was not Igor's son?

"You can't blame Garegin for flying into a panic over food. He lived through a genocide!"

"Why are you taking his side?"

"I'm not taking his side, it's just that I thought he was perfect for you, remember, from the picnic, your socially clumsy Armenian?"

She smiled at the memory, and sniffled.

"Now he is gone," she said, her stage makeup smudged with tears.

"Maria, did Garegin ever come home with a lot of food?"

She nodded.

"The night of the fire," she said. "I thought maybe he had picked it up from the earth or something. He gave me a chicken and suggested I make dried snacks that would last us through the war. Then he left, saying he had a delivery to make at Saint Catherine's Armenian Church, that one on Nevsky Prospekt. After that, he grew more and more distant. Now he is gone."

"That chicken did come from the Badaev," I said, "but it was not lying on the ground. Maria, Garegin stole it. He stole from the Badaev."

"What are you talking about? He's a good man, Olga!"

"I know, Maria, but sometimes in wartime, people do things they would not ordinarily." My God, I thought, how sanctimonious am I, to cast doubt on Garegin's character and not my own.

"Why are you making these wild accusations? You never liked my men!"

"Maria, listen to me. I like Garegin very much. But I have to tell you something, in secrecy."

She nodded, looking like a child waiting for a toy, half afraid it would bite her.

"Nikolai was guarding the Badaev the night it burned to the ground. If he hadn't chased Garegin off the premises, they would both be dead." I shivered at how close I had come to losing my Koyla.

"Garegin was there?"

"Nikolai didn't recognize him at first. He said he was very fast, like a rabbit. Then the Badaev went up in flames and by the time he recognized Garegin, I guess Nikolai thought there was no point in arresting someone who stole from a warehouse that no longer existed."

Maria looked at me with eyes brimming with tears.

"He was a good man, Olga," she said, sounding mournful. "I miss him."

"I believe you," I said. "I believe Garegin is a good man, one who is reliving a nightmare. But Maria, listen to me very carefully. We must never tell anyone that Garegin stole from the Badaev, or that Nikolai failed to arrest him. It would implicate us all in a crime against the community."

My sister blew her nose with a handkerchief. "I understand," she said. Then she looked up piteously and added, "Do you think Garegin left because he didn't want to get me in trouble?"

"Maybe," I said. "Either way, no talking!"

She nodded.

"I hate to think about him, wandering the streets."

"I'll ask around at Radio House. Maybe Eliasberg knows where he is."

"Can I touch your rosary?"

I smiled, and we huddled together inside my coat, the one with the secret pocket.

NINE

The Letters
December 1941

Two weeks later, Dhazdat was back in my office. Anastasia was holding his hand.

"*Chudo*," I said, leaping up in joy, before worrying that someone might have overheard. Miracles were not attributed to the divine in our country, only to the regime.

But here she was, and it was a miracle to me. Dhazdat was beaming. Anastasia looked emaciated, but she was alive. She ran to me—I wondered if she missed a woman's shape—and looked up, her eyes containing huge pools of questions to which I was sure I had no answers.

"When she got here, I hardly recognized her!" Dhazdat said as he began to tell their story. "She was covered in grime. She was barefoot and her clothes were in rags. But when the warden put her in my arms, I knew she was my daughter, isn't that right Anastasia?"

The child nodded.

"Olga," he said, leaning in. "Every time I ask her a question, she just shakes her head no. She is mute, as I once was. I was hoping you could get her to speak."

I looked at the child and knew this was impossible.

"She will speak when she is ready. In the meantime, we can read her stories."

I pulled from my shelves a copy of *Winter-Summer Parrot*, the book I had written for Maya, and began to read. Anastasia snuggled in my lap. She felt warm next to my baby bump. I wondered if someday the baby and the child would be friends. I was still reading when I realized she was sleeping, her thumb in her mouth. Maya had done the same thing. I handed the book to Dhazdat to take home.

"What will you do now?" I asked. I could think of nothing else to say. Hunger and cold were dousing conversation. As I knew better than most, words require energy. And most of us had none.

"My mother wants us to move in with them. My father is still working at the factory, still getting a factory worker's rations. To feed us, I only have that awful bread baked with fillers the city distributes, and a bit of gravy from a neighbor who heard about Anastasia's ordeal."

"I heard many families are huddling together," I said, thinking of the family at Luby's house. "Maybe war is redefining the meaning of family."

"It would be nice to be a family again," Dhazdat said. "I sometimes smell Katarina's clothes, remembering her smile. I wonder if I will ever see her again. I wonder if she and Pavel are still alive. Sometimes I make up little ditties on the drums, hoping Anastasia will sing along to the words. So far, she only hums. I think she is waiting for her mother. Me too."

"Dhazdat," I said. "Are you strong enough to keep playing the drums?"

"Of course. I would be dead already if I couldn't play them."

"Then play your drums. You will not live without them."

He looked at me oddly.

"So that is why you write your poems?"

I nodded. Dhazdat took Anastasia from my lap into his arms, her sleepy head on his shoulders. We hugged, a circle of affection. I was stunned at how he had shrunk. Luby liked to talk about how love would get us through, but at moments like this I wondered if calories were more important.

Katarina's next letter came two weeks later. This time it was addressed to me, written for me. Every day, I read a lot of mail, and sometimes people send me diary entries and poems, even songs. But Katarina's letter was one of the most remarkable I have ever read. She asked me to share its contents with the Poets Circle, and to tell Dhazdat that they were trying to get to Grandpa Stenka.

The letter read like a thriller. As I read, I kept trying to imagine what I would have done in her place.

Dear Olga, I write this letter to you, in part because I'm not sure Dhazdat would be able to withstand it. He is a big bear of a man, but his heart is tender. I think it would break if he knew the hardships Pavel and I have endured. Please tell him I wrote you that we arrived safely in Moscow, and that I will write to him when I have more news.

After I put Anastasia on the truck, I collapsed in tears. Pavel sat next to me on the ground.

"Don't worry Mama, we'll get the next truck."

"Oh Pavel, I'm made a dreadful mistake. I should never have let her go."

Pavel stroked my face, tenderly, as if war had robbed him of a rambunctious boyhood.

"Don't worry Mama, we'll get the next truck."

What if there were no more trucks, I thought? Even if there were more trucks, what fate awaited us at home? I wondered then why on earth I had sent Anastasia back to Leningrad, where there was no heat, no light and little food. And I wondered what fate awaited the two of us if we joined her.

I kept racking my brain, trying to think of another way. And finally I realized. Everyone in Lychkovo was trying to go north to get to Leningrad. What if we went south, to the Zelensky farm in Ukraine? It was risky. We would have to go through Moscow, where we heard the Nazis were bombing. I wondered if I was making another bad decision. I shivered for Dhazdat, left alone in Leningrad. I prayed for Anastasia, deserted by her mother. How I missed them both, and despaired about the choices I had made. But I could think of nothing else. So I clutched the family's French coin in its red bandana in my pocket. Then I took Pavel's hand and boarded the first train to Moscow.

At first, we were squeezed into steerage, finding space on the floor between passenger luggage and the train door. I made a pillow for Pavel from my valise. I tried to sleep against the wall. The stench of human waste made breathing difficult.

"Tickets," said a conductor. He had a scruffy beard and an overgrown belly. Maybe they had food in Moscow, I thought. "Tickets, everyone."

I nudged Pavel's head from the valise and reached in to get our papers. Poor little guy. He was so sleepy he didn't even wake. I offered the tickets, then sat back and rubbed the coin in my red bandana.

"Going to Moscow, heh?" said the conductor.

"Yes sir."

"A pretty lady traveling alone. That's a rare sight these days."

I felt a chill of fear then, Olga, thinking of all those conversations we've had over the years about male lechery. For the last eight years, I've been protected from that—in love with Dhazdat and our life as artists in Leningrad. It feels so long ago now—my performances at Leningrad Ballet, the majesty of the dance, the ovations of the audience, even the infighting among the staff. I guess I was in a cocoon. War has made me an orphan from that life. Now I feel vulnerable, traveling alone with my six-year-old son, thrown together with people who know only deprivation.

"Let me see how full the train is," said the conductor. "Perhaps I can do you the favor of finding you seats in a cabin."

I nodded my thanks. What was the cost of a favor? What would I be expected to do for this vile-looking man?

I looked out the window at miles and miles of countryside. Surely fruits and vegetables could grow here. I had a few rubles Dhazdat had given me. Maybe at the next stop I could buy some.

After about a half hour, the conductor came back to tell me he had found us real seats.

"My name is Ivan Fydorovich," he said. "And you are Katarina Orlova, a ballerina. I've never met a ballerina before."

I noticed my forehead was sweaty. I woke Pavel and we followed Ivan Fydorovich through cars and cars of wretched humanity. When finally we reached the cabin with two seats in it, he turned to me and said, "I will see you later."

As soon as we settled into our seats in the cabin, I fell into a deep sleep. I was so, so tired, Olga. Witnessing the killing of children during the evacuation, forced to make life-and-death decisions for my own children that could traumatize them for life, or even condemn them to death, even walking through this train of war-weary victims who were refugees from man's evil—it had all exhausted me. I woke several hours later as the loudspeaker said we were nearing Moscow. Pavel was moaning, a sign I knew that he needed some food. I reached for my valise to see if I had anything, only to find the whole suitcase was missing. I searched our seats, the floor, the compartments above, growing more panicked as each location came up empty. A lump formed in my throat. There was only one conclusion. All I owned, including our papers, what little money we had, all of it had been stolen.

"Tickets to disembark please," Ivan Fydorovich said as he entered the cabin.

"Mr. Fydorovich, my suitcase has been stolen," I said with as much dignity as I could summon. "Our tickets were in the valise."

The conductor smiled.

"So you will need another favor from me."

I looked up at him and noticed a red bandana peeking out from his shirt pocket. I reached into my own pocket, but I knew before I felt the emptiness that the charm was missing, and who had taken it.

"Thief!" I screamed as loud as I could. I was shocked at how weak my voice sounded. "You stole my goods!"

"I stole nothing," said Ivan Fydorovich, "I only took a reward for my kindness. Come with me."

"No, you give me that red bandana back! It is our family heritage!"

He fingered the coin through the red fabric. "Well how much do you want it?"

Ivan leaned in to kiss me. I was so disgusted I turned my face to the side. He was so angry he bit me on my ear. As I screamed, Pavel reached into the conductor's pocket and retrieved our lucky charm.

"Get out, get out!" Ivan screamed, "you ungrateful wench."

"But we have no papers! Where will we go? What will we do? Have you no mercy?"

The conductor shrugged and as soon as the train slowed, he pushed us roughly onto the platform. Pavel made a fist and shook it at him. I was relieved I had broken no bones—all that training at Leningrad Ballet I guess. I gathered Pavel in my coat and pushed both of us forward into the Moscow Station, looking for the military headquarters.

"I'd like to report a crime," I announced. "My son and I were robbed while on the train. Now we have no papers, no food, no tickets."

"And no husband?" said one of the soldiers, looking at me admiringly. Others laughed.

I was frightened but resolute.

"I want to see your captain," I said emphatically. Where was this gumption coming from? I did not feel as confident as I sounded, to my own ears. Anyway, the soldiers laughed. One of them circled my body, making suggestive hand motions. Others egged him on. Another went into a back room and emerged with Captain Mikhail Parfionov.

"Yes ma'am, what can I do for you?"

"My valise was stolen on the train, with our tickets and our papers and our food and our clothes, for me and my son. I would like to file a criminal complaint."

I thought this Captain Parfionov looked bemused, which I did not appreciate. At first he said nothing, staring at me. Then he invited the two of us to his office. Was he going to arrest us? I wasn't sure. He poured us tea and procured biscuits from a drawer. Pavel wolfed down the crackers so fast he began coughing.

"The train is not our jurisdiction, ma'am," the captain told me. "I'm sorry I can't help you."

"But you must help me," I said, pleading. "We are refugees, from Leningrad. We have nothing!"

"Leningrad, ah yes, I hear things are bad up there," said Parfionov. "What happened to your ear?"

Ever since the bite, I had felt a ringing in my ear, an imbalance. But after the encounter with soldiers in the station, I had forgotten all about it. So much had happened so quickly, it was as if time too was a casualty of war. I touched my ear, which seemed still to be bleeding. I hesitated. Could I trust this man? Would it get me in more trouble to accuse a railroad official? Finally I decided there was no other choice.

"The conductor bit my ear after I refused his kiss. He is the one who stole our goods, I saw our family treasure in his pocket. His name is Ivan Fydorovich. You should arrest him!"

"Mama," said Pavel.

"Just a minute, Pavel."

"Mama."

"Pavel, whatever it is can wait until I talk to the captain."

"But Mama, I stole back the coin."

I turned to Pavel, in astonishment. He placed the coin in its red bandana in my lap.

"You will make a good policeman one day," I said, smiling, ruffling his hair.

Looking at both of us, Parfionov asked what happened.

"Two weeks ago, my children and I were evacuated from Leningrad," I began, wondering how much I should tell him, whether it would be considered unpatriotic to report the details. "The Nazis bombed the children's train, so the evacuation was aborted. But we had trouble getting home. I put my daughter on a truck back to Leningrad, but there wasn't room for any more, so my son and I took the first train to Moscow."

"And your husband?"

"Men were not invited to evacuate. He is a drummer in the Radio Orchestra of Leningrad. He gave me this lucky charm, it belonged to his grandfather, who inherited it from a relative who fought against Napoleon. It would be lost now if not for the bravery of my son."

My hands felt as though they were permanently frozen, but now with the captain's warm tea, I felt the numbness begin to ease. Had I said too much? Not enough? Would he help us?

"And what did you do in Leningrad?"

I wondered at this question, but answered. "I was a ballerina. It seems a silly vocation now, amid war."

Pavel perked up then, perhaps energized by the snack. "She was beautiful!" he exclaimed.

Captain Parfionov smiled.

"She still is, you know," he said to Pavel.

To me, he said, "I cannot get your suitcase back for you, ma'm," he said. "But I was hungry once, and alone. I will put you up in the women's quarters for the night, where you can bathe and eat, while I make your new papers. Where are you trying to go?"

I was so stunned I could not speak. I felt my body sag, as if all the tensions of the last few weeks, all the worry and fear, were leaving my soul. Pavel stared, looking surprised at my silence.

"We are going to visit Grandpa Stenka," he announced proudly.

"And where does Grandpa Stenka live?" Parfionov asked him.

"I think it's called the Steppes, in a place called Ukraine. They have horses there and chickens too."

"So they do," said Parfionov. Turning to me, he said he would see what they could do. Then he called a female aide to escort us to the women's quarters.

We bathed and changed into new clothes—Pavel told me I looked just like a soldier. I begged him to eat in moderation, saying our stomachs couldn't take more, but I didn't blame him when he overdid it. Accommodations were modest—a cot with a thin mattress and a knobby blanket. But Olga I hadn't slept in a bed in so long I thought I was hallucinating. I think I was asleep as soon as I lay down.

In the morning, Pavel woke me.

"Mama, can we stay here for a while?"

"That is not up to us, sweetheart, we are guests of the captain for one night."

Later that day, word came from the captain that he would need another day to get their papers in order. Would they mind staying?

Pavel hooped and hollered. Just as they were joining the chow line that night, the captain approached.

"May I join you?" he asked.

"Of course," I said. "We are so indebted to you. I don't think either of us has felt this human—or at least so clean—in many weeks."

"And I found a mouse to play with!" said Pavel. "He squeals."

"Well, that hardly reflects well on our cleanliness," said Parfionov. "Anyway, I brought you a toy."

Pavel's eyes sparkled as the captain unwrapped a wooden toy soldier from his pocket.

"*I loved playing with toy soldiers when I was your age. I thought you might like to have one.*"

"*Yes, thank you!*" *said Pavel. "I'll make up a story about him and then shoot him if he's a Nazi.*"

Parfionov smiled.

As we all sat down to eat, I asked about his background.

"*You mentioned that you were alone once, and hungry.*"

He nodded.

"*My parents died when I was four. They were at Bloody Sunday, when the tsar's army fired on protestors. My mother was hit first, or so I was told, and as my father cradled her in his arms, he too was gunned down. They had left me and my older sister in the care of a union leader's daughter. We were sent to different orphanages. I never saw her again.*"

He looked across the room, toward the windows. "I always look for her in crowds, wondering what she looks like now, or even if she survived."

"*I have a sister too,*" *said Pavel. "I hope I get to see her again.*"

"*You will,*" *I told him, "I believe you will.*" *God, Olga, why does our history always leave mourners?*

I turned to Parfionov.

"*Why did you go into the military?*"

"*I was always drawn to it, I guess. Maybe because of the turmoil of my childhood, I thrived under rules. At the orphanage I was always the first to wash, to come to table, to attend class. There was one garrulous floor monitor who liked to talk, and I hated him for it. He often made me late for meals or delayed me on my homework. By the time I was 16,*" *the military seemed a good option—they would feed me, and train me. One of my teachers told me as I left the orphanage, 'You were born to revolutionaries, but you were made for following orders.'"*

"*Did you make my wooden soldier?*" Pavel asked, displaying his proudest, now his only, possession.

"*No, my teacher Mr. Krakov made the soldiers for me. But then something unexpected happened. As I was playing with them one day, Mr. Krakov brought out a trombone and began to serenade my soldiers as I marched them around a table. I must have been 9 or 10 at the time. I had never heard a trombone before. I was so giddy I begged him to teach me how to play. After that, I was far more interested in music than in toy soldiers.*"

"*Do you still play the trombone?*" I asked.

"*Yes, I am the leader of our military band. We play occasionally, to encourage the troops. These days, my main job is as a captain in the Red Army, fighting the Nazis and helping victims like you and your son escape the worst of war.*"

I had never been called a war victim before, and it bothered me. Am I now but a statistic?

"*I came to ask you a question,*" he said, as if reading my doubts. "*If you want to go to Ukraine, I can only get you to Smolensk. But I want you to understand that the area is under Nazi occupation, and we do not advise it. I can get you to Kuibyshev, where most evacuees are huddling, or even back to Leningrad, we have one train a day running there. It is a dangerous route, but it is running.*"

I looked off into the distance, weighing the costs of fleeing to safety and the advantages of returning home, wondering if there was any longer any home to return to, thinking of how much I missed Dhazdat and Anastasia.

"Captain Parfionov, thank you so much for your kindnesses. I hesitate to ask you for more."

"Yes?" he said.

"I cannot answer your question yet. This is a big decision."

"Consider it overnight," he said. "But let me know in the morning. I am already under pressure not to house you any longer. It is highly irregular. We will have to make a decision then."

I nodded and took Pavel by the hand. Later we sat and talked.

I asked him if he remembered the story of Dmitri Shostakovich, the famous composer writing a symphony about the war.

"The one Olga interviewed on Radio Leningrad?" Pavel asked.

I nodded.

"Shostakovich is in Kuibyshev. He knows Papa. He will take care of us."

"I want to go home," he said. I stroked his hair, and he fell asleep.

Olga, as I write now I am tortured by doubts. I have made so many bad decisions, I don't want to make another. But what is the better path? I think the captain is right that we should not try to get to Ukraine—we traveled into the teeth of a Nazi advance once before, and barely survived. Leningrad offers reunion with family and familiarity. Leningrad is our city, and it is also our tribe. But when we left there was no food, or heat, and I imagine that things have only gotten worse since. In Kuibyshev there will be food, and friends, and a chance to recover from deprivation. Still, it seems like a betrayal of those we left behind. What is the meaning of character in such a quandary? Is death with dignity more ethical than survival in a city compromised by its very cowardice?

There the letter ended. I wondered what she had decided. I also wondered what I would tell Dhazdat.

TEN

The Men
December 1941

A few days later I stopped at the *Bakaleya*, the grocers, to visit the shopkeeper. Anton Semyonov was not an attractive man—he had a crooked nose that conveyed to his customers, or at least me, a menacing person. Still, he fawned over me, calling me his little celebrity, his *znamenitost*. And when I had needed chocolates for the Poets Circle, he had not only found some but given me a good price.

"Good afternoon, Anton."

"More chocolates, pretty lady?"

"I need a piece of meat, perhaps a salami, big enough to feed five people."

There was silence, which I took to be a negotiating tactic.

"That is an expensive and rare request."

I smiled.

"Ah Anton, you have always had special skills in acquiring the impossible."

He looked at me quizzically. This time the silence dragged on. I took this as part of the haggling ritual. I waited, trying to imagine how things looked from his point of view.

People were starving, their corpses dumped on the streets. The city had little food to distribute, so anyone with money came to Anton, who still had his ways. The police gave lip service to enforcing the law against black marketeers like him, threatening all kinds of punishments, but amid mass starvation there was little they could do to stop them. Heck, they couldn't even stop cannibalism.

"Slovie," he called to his assistant. "Mind the store. I will be with Miss Berggolts in my office."

He ushered me the way through a door I had never noticed before. It led to a backroom set up like a hideaway. There was a small freezer, a file cabinet, and a small cot. Anton bolted the door, and I shivered. What had I gotten myself into? He motioned me to the bed.

"Sit my dear," he said. "We will talk."

"About salami?" I asked.

"Well not the salami but how you will pay for it," he said. "I don't think you have enough money for salami. I don't know anyone who does. I'd like to suggest an arrangement."

My face reddened.

"An arrangement?"

"You take care of me in the bed," he said, "and I take care of you in the kitchen."

I was horrified, angry at putting myself in the position to be propositioned by this rogue of a man. I saw him ogling my breasts as he removed his belt buckle. I got up to leave.

"The door is locked," he said, and grabbed my hair to wrench my head back, slobbering me with kisses all over my face. I started to scream but he clamped a dirty towel over my mouth.

"If you yell, I will call the police and tell them you were stealing from my freezer."

I knew I could not survive another encounter with the NKVD, so I quieted then, praying for the horrible incident to be over quickly. I tried not to think of Nikolai, or even of Yuri, of anyone who actually knew me and loved me for my inner warmth, not my outer fame. I closed my eyes and silently apologized to my sister. I had judged her, even belittled her, for having to get an abortion after an unwanted pregnancy from a man she refused to talk about.

Anton was a rough assailant. He thrust repeatedly, but seemed never to finish. Whenever he failed he slapped me with his hands, leaving red marks on my face. I worried they would become permanent scars. I worried about other kinds of scars too.

"You're hurting me!" I yelled. "Can't you see I'm pregnant? When he comes home from the front, my husband Nikolai will kill you."

At word of a husband serving in the Red Army, Anton stopped. How I wish I'd used the line earlier. He rolled off me, his lust unsatisfied. Then he whispered something that would haunt me forever.

"You are my *znamenitost* now."

I don't know if I was more ashamed or revolted. But I knew I didn't trust myself to talk.

"Salami is a tall order. Maybe for that I should get another poke."

I winced, and walked over to his freezer.

"Where is it?"

He lumbered off the cot and came up behind me. I ducked as he tried to sniff my neck.

"Remember my dear Olga, one word about our encounter and I will accuse you of stealing."

"And when I tell Nikolai what you've done, you will wish you were in police custody."

He handed me the meat.

After he left the back room I cleaned myself off as best I could—the grocer did not provide a sink for washing and I wondered if I would ever be able to wipe the wretched stench of his body off mine. I rushed out of the shop, salami tucked in my coat, tears breaking. The brisk December air felt good on my skin. I thought about Garegin, who survived the Armenian Genocide. About Katarina and Pavel. Of Rahil and Igor. All these wartime choices. Would any of us survive Hitler?

Soon I was knocking on Luby's front door.

There was silence, though I thought I detected the scuttle of feet. Finally she opened the door.

"Come in dear," she smiled, seeing me. She closed the door and hollered, "All clear, it's just Olga."

From all corners they came, bearing love. The boys were first, giggling and fighting, with Rahil boasting that Rodion was teaching him multiplication tables and Rodion shrugging indifference. What a role model Luby was to these youngsters, I thought, an example of how to live with gusto and purpose, even amid hardship. I needed some of her positive energy now.

"So how is it going," I asked as she offered me tea.

"We decided Andrei and Igor should move in with us," she explained. "This will give us the semblance of a family unit. I play the role of the grandmother, and if anyone asks, Igor and Andrei are the nephews of my deceased husband. And of course, Igor is the father of the two boys."

"And the chef," Igor called from the kitchen. I went to greet him. He kissed me on both cheeks and came in for a bear hug. I laughed, feeling appreciated, and gave him the salami.

"Never ask me how I got this. But know that if you use it well, I will feel better. Happy New Year."

He looked at me with an uncertain gaze, making me feel self-conscious. I wondered if my face was still red, if scars had formed. I looked away.

"Join us for dinner?"

I shook my head.

"You stretch that salami as far as you can. And besides, what I really need is a drink."

I walked home, letting the snow and cold cleanse my face and hands. By the time I walked into my apartment I felt almost human again, eager to bathe and soothe my wounds. But when I arrived, a Red Army lieutenant was waiting at the door, the kind of green, young officer the military sends to inform families their loved ones have died. Fear froze in my throat, choking a scream.

"Comrade Berggolts," the young man began. "I am here to tell you your husband has been injured. He is at the Astoria Hospital, and is anxious to see you. I can escort you if you like."

"I would," I said. "But first I would like to clean up." He agreed to wait.

I showered and put on makeup that Maria had given me from the theater. I wiggled into the polka dot dress that Nikolai liked so much—he said it reminded him of springtime—thankful it had a loose waistline. All of it made me feel more human, at least on the outside. Inside, I hovered between relief and worry, shame and nerves. If, as the lieutenant said, Nikolai was anxious to see me, then he was alive. The lieutenant dropped me at the Astoria before setting off on another errand, I imagined another call on a family fearing the worst.

The Astoria Hospital of Starvation had once housed a beautiful hotel, frequented by our most elite foreign dignitaries. In fact, I later learned, it was where Adolf Hitler planned to host a victory party after Leningrad fell. Now it was a scene of chaos—gurneys being rushed about, nurses running after them, desk sergeants without information or much sympathy either. Finally, after my repeated requests to see my husband, some delivered with utter hysteria, a nurse arrived with a clipboard.

"Your husband is in Ward C," she said. She delivered this message with the efficiency of a well-trained bureaucrat—no smile, in a monotone voice, as if my precious Nikolai was already a corpse, as if I were but a number. "The bones in his left foot are broken, but he's not as bad as many of the others. Most have already been sent to the morgue. Come with me."

I swallowed hard at the word 'morgue' but followed her down a long corridor, its once-elegant carpeting now worn thin with wheelchair tracks. I thought my lungs would explode, with happiness or worry I wasn't sure. On seeing Nikolai in a bed with his foot in a cast, I started crying.

My hand was trembling and he smiled, leaning in to kiss my fingers. "Your Nikolai is not leaving you," he whispered. "We have a new generation to raise."

I told him that I loved him, that I would always love him, and he smiled.

"You are the beloved, the *lyubimaya* of my life," he said. I cringed. That sounded a lot better than being a *znamenitost*. How I longed to blot Anton from my memory, to never think of him again.

He looked older, but ever handsome. I worried at how I must look, my skin wrinkled like an old lady's. I made my eyes smile at him, brimming with love, and asked Nikolai what had happened.

"This is all confidential of course," he began, and I could tell he was secretly elated. "We have been working on repairing inlets to Lake Ladoga," he said. "We hope eventually to build supply lines along the Gulf of Finland to move food to Leningrad from the rest of Russia."

Ah, so it was true! Lake Ladoga was the second largest body of water in Russia. There had been rumors in the city for months that as soon as the lake froze over, trucks would be able to drive food to Leningrad to rescue its residents. I was never sure if the talk was wishful thinking or a brilliant strategic plan. Now, it made me proud to learn that Nikolai was in the vanguard of the effort.

"But what happened to your leg?"

"My fault really," he said. "The Germans regularly bomb our work area. To tell you the truth, it's rather discouraging. We spend all day repairing. Then they spend all night destroying everything we did. Once, I scrambled to avoid one of the incoming bombs and twisted my leg, awkwardly. Do you think Katarina could cure me with one of her famous Persian potions?"

I smiled. Katarina had attended ballet school with a Persian student named Daria, who told her about healing potions that had been handed down from the ancients. Sometimes I tried them, mostly I dismissed them as so much superstition. Katarina insisted the flower treatment worked well on wounds. I doubted they would work on broken bones and torn muscles. But all I could think of was how much had changed since Nikolai had left Leningrad. He didn't know about the botched evacuation of children that left thousands dead and Katarina living far from her family. I could not imagine what he'd say when I told him that Igor and Andrei were parents to Luby's grandchildren. Or that Viktoria and Boris Piotrovsky, the archeologist, were conducting a courtship through the mails. Or that Garegin had left Maria, and was alone in Leningrad, perhaps wandering the streets.

No matter. Nikolai was alive, and so was I. I was so ashamed of what had happened with Anton, a humiliating assault on my dignity in bartering for food. But now, it seemed, God had given me a second chance. I would have time to heal Nikolai with my love, to atone for my bad judgment.

He reached for my hand.

"I have missed you so," he said. "The nurse told me to put pressure on the foot as soon as I can," he said. "Let me sleep a bit. Maybe after I wake, we can hobble around together?"

"I would hobble with you anywhere," I smiled. I curled up in a chair next to him, and slept.

For the next few weeks, I came every day, on my way to work, and on my way back. We talked about his childhood, and about the family we were starting. I knew little about his parents, about the baby's grandparents. All he had told me was that they were among the three or four million who had starved to death during Stalin's collectivization of agriculture, a man-made disaster which Nikolai had escaped only because he had been sent to live with his Uncle Sasha in Leningrad.

"Do you ever think of your parents, now that we are all facing starvation?"

He nodded.

"They were good people, simple people, with good hearts. You would have liked them, especially my father, Alexis. He had a wicked sense of humor, like you."

He looked at me with a smile, and a twinkle in his eye, as if to end the conversation. But I had one more question.

"Why do you never see Uncle Sasha?" I asked. "I noticed he is still teaching at Leningrad University."

Nikolai looked at me quizzically.

"So you've been checking the faculty manifest, have you? Why am I not surprised."

He turned grim then.

"I stopped speaking to my Uncle Sasha just after our wedding. When I saw him there, I realized I had resented him. Why didn't he send for all three of us, why only me? Why weren't my parents there to celebrate with us? They had a loving relationship. I wanted them to see ours too."

I said nothing then, but vowed to track down his uncle. Nikolai's question deserved an answer.

As Nikolai got better at hobbling in the halls, I could tell he was anxious to return to the front. I was having none of it. Six months pregnant, I wanted to keep him at my side as long as possible.

"Stay," I said. "You can feel the baby grow. Maybe you can play her your favorite music." Nikolai loved Rimsky-Korsakov, especially his *Scheherazade*. Maybe she would hear it and become a violinist.

A few days later, Lake Ladoga froze over. I heard some people in Leningrad actually got drunk when they heard the news. Of course they didn't hear it from me—I was banned from mentioning the opening of a venue to deliver food to a starving city on the air, because it would confirm the hunger we all knew was rampant. Still, listeners wrote me about it, because everyone knew.

"This brutal cold has saved us," wrote one man. "Same as happened with Napoleon."

One day, after he was released from the hospital, Nikolai surprised me.

"I want to go see their progress," he said. "Will you come with me?"

We walked to the dock—he was now on a cane—only to find many other Leningraders gathering to watch the building of what came to be called the Ice Road, this new avenue that promised to bring in supplies or evacuate people on trucks or by skis. While we were watching, Nazi soldiers on the Finnish side of the lake began shooting potholes in the ice, and we had to take cover.

"That will slow us," Nikolai said, "but not deter us. The military has just brought in Major General Georgy Shilov, a logistics specialist. You would have liked the speech he gave us when work began."

Weeks before, Shilov ordered teams to clear snow and monitor the surface for any open water, rough ice or bomb craters, and to lay prefabricated wooden bridges across the ice in places where passage was rough. He ordered divers to lay a fuel pipeline and a cable to the Volkhov Power Station to bring in electricity. Then he had gathered his team together, truck drivers and snow plow operators, traffic controllers and soldiers loading boxes onto trucks, medics and divers, to remind them of the heroic nature of their mission. That was Nikolai's favorite part of the story. Mine too.

"Leningrad is hanging by a thread," Shilov told his teams. "We are the only thing standing between the people of this proud city and mass starvation. Make as many trips as you can—try for two or three round trips a day—to bring food in, and bring evacuees out. Remember that the people of Leningrad have undergone a traumatic experience, and they have the right to demand that you do your jobs with selfless honor. We will make sure you have plenty to eat and drink—meat, bread, vodka—but no stealing off their share. Feed the starving, save the weak!"

"What was the reaction?"

"Whoops," Nikolai said, smiling as he recalled the scene. "We hooted and hollered and whooped."

Within that first week, freight trains ran right up to the lake, delivering cereals, flour and grain. Food rations were raised. I felt so proud—we were no longer an island, no longer blockaded, and my Koyla had helped open this path to our salvation. Before the war's end, the Nazis would sink 300 of our trucks. But still, in the months ahead, the Ice Road brought 360,000 tons of cargo to Leningrad, much of it food. And an estimated 500,000 people, most on the verge of death, were evacuated.

One of those evacuated was Lidiya Okhapkina, who left home in a snowstorm with her two children. Weak from hunger, she walked gingerly to the assembly point on Tchaikovsky Street. They just made it before their truck departed. Weeks later, I got a letter from her, describing the ordeal.

The truck began crossing the lake, then halted. The driver had protected his truck with plywood—I guess he was worried about German artillery—but this allowed exhaust fumes to permeate the interior. I vomited several times, then passed out. At the convoy's first stop, I came to. Looking up, I saw good, kind-hearted people tending to me. They helped me out and laid me on a bench. They fed my two children semolina and condensed milk. They offered me beef broth but I had trouble swallowing it.

After we were transported to the base camp where my husband was stationed, a captain directed him to our truck, with other evacuees, saying, 'Lt. Novikov, your wife and children have been evacuated. They are thin and frail. Don't be too shocked when you see them.' But when my Vasili leaped into the truck we were on, he did not recognize us, so he jumped off and told the captain that his family wasn't there. This captain held my husband's shoulder and said, 'Soldier, hunger changes people, it ages them. They become emaciated. They no longer look themselves. They lose their music. But I promise you, Lidiya and the children are on that truck.' So my Vasili leaped back into the truck.

'Is it you? Is it you?' he called to the children. They scurried toward him, wrapping their thin arms around his legs. They pointed me out. I hid my face in shame. When the war began, I had a thick mane of hair and a full body. Now I was only skin and bones, especially thin at the ribs, my hair thin and grey, my skin wrinkled. Vasili looked at me and blinked his eyes. 'Never mind,' he said softly. 'The bones are in good shape. Surely, the body will follow.'

He was right, Comrade Berggolts. In the weeks since, I have regained strength, and there is color in my cheeks. I hope it will be like that too for our long-suffering city of Leningrad. Once we are rescued, I hope the bones will heal the body.

I tried to imagine her feelings in writing about such intimate musings to a stranger. I decided it was a testament to the way Radio Leningrad bound listeners to our broadcast, especially at a time of war.

One night, there was a knock on the door. I started to freeze but caught myself in time. There was no telling what was on the other side of that door. Time to face life without fear.

"Garegin!" I exclaimed on opening the door. "Nikolai, it's Maria and Garegin."

I kissed my sister, and welcomed them inside the apartment. Ever since my interrogation by Captain Lermontov at NKVD headquarters, I had been careful to avoid hallway conversations. No doubt the hall monitor was annoyed that my earlier questioning had not resulted in my arrest, giving her a chance to offer our apartment to someone else. Nikolai was a man in uniform, serving our nation, so I knew she would keep her distance for now. At the first chance, she would report me again.

Nikolai was a bit distant to Garegin but hugged Maria.

Once I encouraged everyone inside, we all sat down to recover our shared history. I rummaged through the cupboards for wine—alcohol was easier to find these days than food—and poured.

"Welcome back from the front," Garegin said to Nikolai. "I hear you have been doing great work."

"Well yes, between spells of clumsiness. So you two are back together I see."

Garegin lowered his head, as if to avoid meeting Nikolai's eyes. Then he looked up.

"Nikolai I came to apologize to you. You were right. It was wrong to steal. On reflection, guilt got to me. I couldn't face Maria, so I left to live in the church. There was no heat and little food, but the nuns there did not judge me, they do not judge anyone, they just accept."

"I never judged you!" Maria protested.

Garegin looked at her fondly.

"Nikolai, you were right. I sinned, not just against my own conscience but against our whole community. I'm sorry, Nikolai, I put you at risk. I understand that now. I put all of us at risk."

"No," said Nikolai. "Olga convinced me that you were right, that as a survivor of genocide, you understood hunger better than we did. You saw what was coming."

The room grew silent. I imagined each of us lost in our angst over decisions made in wartime. I thought about how much I had paid for a salami, and the great cost to my soul.

"We all make difficult choices during war," Nikolai said, looking at me.

Had Nikolai seen something on my body, some red scar? Did he suspect something unsavory? God, what had I done! I looked up as he began to speak again, looking at me.

"It's the choice we make to come home that's the most important."

I looked at him in wonder. I didn't know if he knew. But I knew he still loved me.

"I want to share a poem," I said, looking back at him.

"Did you write it?" asked Garegin.

"No, but that doesn't make it unworthy."

We all laughed.

"To love someone deeply gives you strength," I read, looking up at my Koyla. "But being loved by someone deeply gives you courage."

Nikolai smiled at me and opened his arms wide. I fell into them, forgetting we had company.

"Don't you want to hear our news?" Maria asked, breaking the spell. "We're getting married!"

We were all smiling. I capped the wine and brought out champagne.

In December, we watched the marriage of Maria Berggolts to Garegin Ananyan. Our mother had died at the start of the war, a casualty of the bombs, and our father was in jail, being interrogated for disloyalty. I ached for him, fearing that my behavior had cast suspicion on him. Without parents, Nikolai and I served as witnesses for the marriage. Eliasberg came, as did Maria's boss. Igor found a way to make blinis—Maria's favorite—and Garegin's sister sent wine from Armenia. Maria robbed the wardrobe department at the comedy theater for an appropriate gown. It wasn't exactly traditional, but I have to admit she looked radiant. And so did Garegin, in formal gear Maria had also borrowed for him for the occasion. There was something affirming about love, I thought, something that transcended transgressions, spats of anger, misunderstandings and even war. No outsider could understand the interior of a love story. But all of us knew it was the essential thing.

Nikolai was still with me during the holidays. One night, there was a knock on our door. I sighed, stilling my panic, and opened it to find a distinguished-looking man standing there, holding a cake.

"I am Mikhail Molchanov," he said. "I am Nikolai's uncle. Sasha."

I had written him asking about the cause of his rift with Nikolai, and cried when I read his response. Now he stood in our home. I felt Nikolai's breath on my shoulder before I could see his face.

"Please come in," I said, rushing him into the room, before Nikolai could send him away.

I took the cake—wondering how on earth he could have found such an indulgence amid the Siege. I also wondered if they would be able to forgive each other. Nikolai had been 14 when he left the farm to live with his uncle here in the city. Five years later, Uncle Sasha told him his parents had died, victims of the disaster caused by the Communist takeover of farming. I don't think Nikolai ever forgave Sasha, but his fury erupted after our wedding. He missed having his parents there.

I cut the cake and found some wine. Nikolai was eyeing me suspiciously. I guess he figured out I had reached out to his uncle, now an emeritus in literature at Leningrad University.

"This is all very nice," said Nikolai, looking at me with daggers.

There was an uncomfortable silence, so I asked Sasha about his duties at the university.

"An emeritus is really an extra hand," he said. "Lately I have been particularly busy, as the younger professors go off to war. Of course some of the students do too, so…"

"Enough!" screamed Nikolai. "Enough chatter! What are you doing in my home? My wife may have invited you here but I didn't. You are a traitor to the Molchanov name."

Uncle Sasha looked chagrined, and began to weep. There was no other sound in the apartment except the drip of the sink until finally, this elegant old gentleman wiped his eyes and began to speak.

"Oh Nikolai, have you thought all this time that I didn't invite your parents to escape that hell? Of course I did! My brother was stubborn. He insisted on staying on the farm."

"But you deserted my parents."

"You are right. I should have rescued all of you. Your father did not want to leave. I think he was afraid he would be lost in such a city as big as ours. But it was my obligation to find a way to compel him. I was his brother. I should have forced him to come. If only for your happiness."

At this, Nikolai looked stunned, though it surprised me it hadn't occurred to him before now.

"Is that really true?" he said. "My Papa did not want to leave the farm?"

"Don't you remember how he resisted Soviet authority? You were a teenager when he was arrested for insubordination for rotating the crops. Have you no memory of that?"

"Of course I remember, but he was released!"

There was another silence then. I saw Nikolai's face grow mottled with memory.

"Alexis Molchanov was a proud man," said Sasha. "You remind me of him."

Nikolai softened then, almost crumbled. Then he reached for his uncle and they embraced.

I retreated to the kitchen with the cake. These two survivors deserved quiet time to remember, and cry, and make each other whole. By the time I returned, the tears had stopped. They were talking.

"You're in the military?" Sasha asked.

Nikolai nodded. "I leave after the holidays for the front."

Sasha looked ashen.

"Please come home soon so we will have time together," he said.

"I'll drink to that," I said, raising a glass.

We passed the rest of the evening in memories. I listened to stories of the two of them as they reminisced about Nikolai's early girlfriends, trying to imagine him as a young teenager.

"I'm so glad you didn't end up with that Polina girl," said Sasha.

"A piece of work that one!" agreed Nikolai.

On New Year's Eve, temperatures plummeted beyond imagining. A woman named Natasha Medvedeva wrote me about how she had celebrated the holiday. With the weather registering at -25 degrees, she started a fire burning in their *burzhuika*, a makeshift stove with pipes sending exhaust out the windows. She used coffee grinds to make scones, and had used her ration coupons to purchase champagne. She wrote that she didn't mind, since there was no bread left to buy anyway. She woke her daughter, an artist and musician, who woke to those wonderful sights and smells.

"Thank you, Mama," she said. She said they ate and drank and listened to the radio, hearing my report on how Leningraders were persevering. I interviewed Konstantin Siminov, who summed up our shared ordeal. "In order that we understand things fully," he said, "this winter has given us a measure." Maybe the worst was over, I thought as I read her letter and heard his words. Maybe we would survive after all.

The Germans were still trying to jam our broadcasts. In response, Vadim ordered us to vary our schedule, airing the broadcasts at different times of the day. So it was that on New Year's Day, at 2:15 p.m., I read my latest poem. I dedicated it to Luby Shaporina, founder of the Leningrad Puppet Theater. I did not mention on the air that she had voluntarily become surrogate grandmother to two boys named Rahil and Rodion. But the thought was in my heart.

"I want to talk to you during the artillery fire, as you are lit by its glow," I read. "It seems a part of the landscape now, embedded in our city's history. The Hitlerites have great power to destroy. But it is only a sign of weakness. What can the enemy do? Destroy, kill, that's it. We can love. It is not possible to count the depth of my soul. I will love and I will live. *We* will live because *we* will love."

On January 2nd, I walked into the bedroom to see Nikolai packing. I smiled, and we rubbed the baby bump together, cooing and smiling. I wondered if it was folly to bring a child into such a world, but I was comforted by the thought that at least this baby would arrive surrounded by people who knew first-hand what it was to sacrifice everything for love, even when they had little of anything else.

Nikolai hugged us both as if he might never let go. But he did, and we were apart again.

ELEVEN

The Poets Circle 2
February 1942

Starvation was a form of premature aging. In a space of months, one traveled the distance of decades—losing balance and bone, feeling blinding headaches, needing a cane to walk.

Viktoria was the first to arrive, and I'm not sure I would have recognized her on the street. She was only 26, but she looked like a *babushka*, a grandmother.

"It's shocking, I know," she said, seeing the look on my face. "I'm grateful we have no mirrors at home."

Once she had such a robust, healthy look about her. Now, with temperatures dipping 40 degrees below zero, she looked wilted. As if to confirm the diagnosis, she pulled a sweater closer around her middle, shivering.

"People say women are surviving more than the men because of our body fat," she said. "But you wouldn't know it by me. I am so cold, all the time."

"Men do seem to be dropping in greater numbers," said Anna, who had arrived wearing a serious fur coat and boots. "Funny. I remember when I was younger and I worried about the extra weight around my hips. If I gained a fraction, I panicked. How I would long for all those extra kilos now!"

By then, Luby and Maria had arrived too, completing our circle except for Katarina. An expert on all things mystical, Luby had plenty to say about women's fat content.

"Women are better in a crisis because the female fat contains melatonin, a special hormone released by the pineal gland that calms people, like lavender," she said. "That's the science."

"For goodness sake Luby," said Anna, "you sound like the fortune teller in a Persian souk."

"Hmm," said Luby, as if to taunt Anna. "Maybe I'll make a Persian seer as my next puppet."

I looked over at my sister. Ever since her marriage to Garegin, she seemed to be thriving.

"I think we do better because we like to talk," Maria said. "Maybe we are just dreadful gossips, but anyway it keeps our blood flowing. Just the other night Garegin pleaded for silence."

There was more laughter at this. I worried, as always, about the hall monitor hearing us.

"Have you heard from Boris?" I asked Viktoria.

"Just today, a letter." She smiled, which softened her face. She called him her "pen pal, in a *pochta* relationship." Luby wanted to know how they met.

"We were packing the art for its exodus when he leaned over and whispered that he thought I looked like Empress Alexandra, the wife of Tsar Nicholas II, and a favorite of her grandmother, Britain's Queen Victoria. I thought he was being a bit melodramatic, but still, it flattered me. No one had ever talked to me like that. And then he told me he had always thought Alexandra was the most beautiful of the Romanovs—tall, dark, mysterious."

"Oh Viktoria, did he really say that?" asked Luby, clapping her hands. "A love story."

"Men are always given to lines of mush when they are interested in a woman," sneered Anna.

"Perhaps," said Luby, "but I've always believed they resort to clichés because they are in heat."

Another round of knowing clucks from the Poets Circle.

Viktoria seemed overwhelmed by all the questions about Boris, and asked Maria, the dramatist among us, to read his letter.

"Well he's not in heat in the Urals," Maria said, delighting in her new role.

We've had record snows, and the temperature is far below zero. I keep busy photographing wildlife—there are wolverines and polecats and foxes here—I notice the frigid air less. My favorite creature is the owl. Because they are nocturnal, I have to sleep during the day and venture out at night to capture them in photographs. I don't mind. It keeps my mind off Leningrad, though I cannot stop thinking of you, my dear Viktoria.

We all cooed at that. Except for Anna, who rolled her eyes.

"New topic," said Luby. "Did I tell you Rodion has gained three kilos?"

"You're kidding!" Viktoria said. "Oh Luby, that's wonderful news, thank you!"

"Oh don't thank me, thank Igor. He is a master at making delicious food from my bare cupboards."

She reached into her satchel and pulled out a sketchbook.

"And you know Igor's other great talent, don't you Olga?" she asked.

I nodded and we all gathered round and peeked over her shoulder. On his sketchpad, Igor had done a colored chalk drawing of his new family. He had seated Luby in an overstuffed chair, with the two boys perched on either arm and Andrei and him standing behind them.

"All you need is a Stalin portrait and some patriotic flags in the background, and the drawing would make an excellent propaganda poster about the strength of a Soviet family," I said.

There were few smiles.

"Luby is this an accurate portrayal?" said Viktoria. "Rodion really does look better. I wish I could show it to my mother. It would make her feel better about parting ways with him."

"Take it darling," Luby said, ripping a sheet from the sketchbook. "Igor makes them all the time. And tell her to come visit whenever she wants, even if she has nothing to bring."

I doubted that would happen. I noticed that people had stopped making social calls. It was traditional to arrive with a gift. None of us had anything to share, as if we had been robbed.

"And how is Rahil doing?" I asked.

"That's complicated," said Luby, her face darkening. "I think he looks up to Rodion, but recently he started acting aloof around him. He told me he wants to learn to play the violin, so he can amuse himself when no one else is around. So I wonder if maybe he's afraid to get too close to Rodion because he does not want to be disloyal to his own kin, the three brothers he lost to the bombs."

"Or maybe because he does not want to lose another brother," said Maria.

"How sad," I said. "Here this child is brought into a home that offers him the promise of love, but he feels he can't return the emotion for fear of insulting his dead relatives. Maybe there is a lesson in there for all of us, a reminder to grab what we can of life, when we can." Maybe it was a lesson to me to worry less about police hovering over my shoulder and enjoy more the life I had.

I noticed Viktoria was nodding emphatically. And Anna had taken out her notebook and was jotting down something. When she looked up, I stared at her.

"Every so often you inspire the muse in me," she said. "One poet to another." When I beamed, she added, "Not often, mind you, just on occasion."

I smiled and turned back to Luby. "And the Puppet Theater?"

Luby sighed. "I wish I had better news on that front. The puppets are ready, but the stage is not. I've asked the city for help in restoring the building. Understandably, they have other priorities at the moment. So we are planning to take the puppets on a tour of the children's hospitals. At least they can make the little ones smile." She looked at me. "What about the orchestra? Will they play soon?"

"I hope so," I said. "There was a good turnout for the Hadyn performance, and Dhazdat was phenomenal. The violinists were all ailing, so Eliasberg rewrote the string score for the harp."

"It was Garegin's finest moment," said Maria, beaming. "But how it fatigued him!"

"It exhausted all of them," I said. "I've been lobbying Vadim to have them play the Shostakovich symphony, but he insists, as he put it, that the piece is 'beyond our breath.'"

"Breath is sometimes overrated," observed Anna. I looked at her with concern.

"Does he have a point?" asked Viktoria. "It's true that we all long for the soothing sounds of music, but have we a right to ask that of our artists—to perform on empty stomachs?"

"I told Vadim the orchestra needs more food. So too the broadcasters."

"Which reminds me, how are you feeling Olga?" Luby asked. "Is the baby kicking?"

I smiled, thinking of the baby growing inside my tummy. I was hungry often, and nauseous the rest of the time. Amazingly, I was enjoying the process, even amid a siege. Sometimes I saw women looking at me with disapproval. Probably they wondered why I thought it a good idea to bring a child into the world when bombs were falling and food was lacking. Sometimes I wondered too.

Now I motioned them to gather around, even the famously ill-tempered Anna, to touch my stomach. I've always thought it sweet that women make cooing sounds at the sight of other women's pregnancies. Now more than ever, I welcomed this intimacy among friends.

"This is your family," I announced to my unborn child, rubbing my stomach. "If ever you're in trouble, come to them."

Anna raised her glass in salute to this idea, and we all drank.

"What my sister is not telling you is that she collapsed on the streets recently," said Maria. "She tripped over a dead body in front of the Philharmonia and did not have the energy to get up."

I sent a look of annoyance her way, then tried to make light of the incident.

"You'll never guess what revived me," I said. "The sound of my own voice, coming from street speakers. At first I thought I was hallucinating, but then I heard the words of a poem I had recorded a few days ago, and recognized it. You'll be proud Anna, it was a paean to the Motherland, offering Russia her love in this moment of challenge, despite all the country's past harshness."

"Shouldn't you go get checked by a doctor?" asked Viktoria.

"No point," I said. "The doctor would only tell me that I need more food, for me and my baby."

There was silence then. I started crying.

"Olga surely you can take time to recover. The nation can do without your sermons for just a few days." It was Anna, surly Anna.

"It's not that, it's my father," I said, looking at Maria. "Our father." Authorities were investigating Fyodor Berggolts for disloyalty again. He had already been in prison once, and been released, maybe because of pressure from me. Now he was being hounded again. A medical surgeon of Russian and Latvian ancestry, he had been caught between countries, between ethnicities, a victim of Stalin's paranoid obsession with nationalism. Or maybe the authorities were grilling him to keep me in line.

"For goodness sake," said Viktoria. "Why all these investigations? We are in the middle of a war for our very existence. Shouldn't the authorities focus their energies elsewhere?"

"Yes, Igor is worried too," said Luby. "He thinks the police are investigating him and Andrei for 'unnatural and seditious acts.' He says Stalin thinks the homosexuals are all meeting to foment a rebellion against him. Igor says it is more likely they are meeting to discuss dinner."

"Why are they targeting your father?" asked Viktoria.

"Because he refused to inform on colleagues, because he is part Jewish, because he is related to me."

"But you are the star of Radio Leningrad," she said. "By the end of the war, you will be famous."

"That is the problem," I said. "I think they are holding him hostage to make sure I don't veer from the script—all pro-Soviet courage, all Nazi perfidy, nothing about hunger or death."

"Did you try pulling strings?" asked Anna.

I nodded.

"I managed to win his release from jail, at least for now. But I am aware of how tenuous is his situation—and mine. One slip at the microphone about hunger, one errant note musing about the fire at the Badaev or the botched evacuation of children, and we will both be sent to Siberia."

"Have you heard from Katarina?" asked Viktoria.

I nodded.

"She is thriving. Wait until you hear."

Luby clapped her hands. You could always count on her to applaud any story.

"Maybe Maria should do the honors," I said, handing the letter to my sister.

"Delighted," my sister said, summoning her best theatrical air. Ever the stage actress, she began.

Dear Olga,

Pavel and I arrived in this city several weeks ago. At first we were packed in with a group of refugees, living in a former Monastery, repurposed as communal housing. The building was cold, crowded and dirty. The food was little better than the crumbs we ate on our journey to Moscow, and I wondered again if I had made the wrong decision.

Pavel misses his father intensely. I suppose he is just coming to that age when a father is more important than a mother. But he is also angry at me I think, for coming to Kuibyshev. We rarely talk about Dhazdat or Anastasia. He used to be proud that his mother was beautiful, but now he bristles whenever anyone compliments me. I wonder if this journey has made him realize that striking looks can attract danger. Anyway I feel I have broken Pavel's heart, and maybe Dhazdat's too, by choosing safety over family. We both mope a lot, navigating around each other.

"When do we get to the part about her thriving?" asked Luby.

"Now Luby, you know better than any of us that a good story takes time to build," my sister upbraided, before resuming her reading.

Before we left Moscow, I wrote Dmitri Shostakovich to tell him we were coming. But the composer never responded to my letter so I figured he had just been polite when I met him at Radio House. Then, after a few weeks, he came to the Monastery, and told me he had arranged an apartment for us in the complex where he lives. I see him often for coffee. He is pressing for more, but I am not interested. He is famous—and no doubt talented—but I am weary of getting close to men and their false promises. To tell you the truth, I am also still shaken by my encounter with that vile man on the train. Every so often I wake up with chills, and I think I have vertigo in my ear at the place where he drew blood. I keep trying to remember why we left Dhazdat, who would never hurt me. Meanwhile Dmitri's wife—Nina Vassilyevna—has been cold and distant. Perhaps she resents her husband's interest in us. But his children—Galina and Maxim—have been a gift for Pavel. They are older but include him in their sports, and it lifts him.

I also got in touch with Daria, my Persian friend from ballet class, who I heard was already living in Kuibyshev. We often visit her family. It is difficult for Pavel to adjust to their customs—he doesn't like all the praying to Allah—but Daria's Uncle Arham makes him laugh. Plus the Rahmanis are wonderful cooks, their food restoring us to health.

Daria and I talk a lot about what we want to do at the Leningrad Ballet after the war. Mostly, to rid it of politics. At her suggestion, I have taken up yoga, which one teacher told me is 'the practice of dealing with the consequences of being yourself.' It's been so long since I felt I was being authentic. If this war ever ends, I hope to teach ballet instead of performing it. I have started here—Kuibyshev is bursting with refugees—many from Moscow's government circles. Daria's neighbors are from the Foreign Ministry, and their daughters are my first students.

"She does sound upbeat," said Viktoria. "Maybe we should all take up yoga."

"I believe that would require food," said Anna. Another mocking comment, I thought.

"How odd that Shostakovich found them shelter," said Viktoria. "I thought from what you said about the interview, Olga, that he was something of a recluse."

"He was!" said Anna. "He was always such a nervous man. He always fidgets with his eyeglasses, and bites his nails. He is so obsessed with time, he once synchronized all the clocks in his apartment. Also he sent himself mail to test the efficiency of the postal system."

"That's what I heard too," I said. "But he is also known to have an eye for a beautiful lady."

Maria resumed reading.

Dmitri said to tell you how much he enjoyed the interview he did with you, Olga. And, I'm embarrassed to tell you, he said he had not stopped thinking of me since. And when he told me this, his wife and children—and more of a worry, Pavel—were but a few feet away!

"There is no end to their hubris," said Anna. "Honestly Luby, maybe that is why they are dying faster than we are. Now she is calling him 'Dmitri.' They are so oily!"

"The letter is almost done," said Maria. I could tell she was keen to finish her assignment.

Dmitri said he is almost done composing, and is eager to get the score into Vadim's hands to be performed in Leningrad. We are to have dinner next week to discuss how to make that happen. I will let you know. Until then, I send strength to all the poets in our circle. With love, Katarina.

When Maria finished, there was silence.

"It's like we're living in a divergent universe," said Viktoria. "Russia is freezing, and frightened, but they go out to dinner! We are cold and frightened too, but also we are starving. The only thing we still have in common is our music, our literature and our art."

"The food will come soon," I pointed out, thinking of Nikolai. "The Ice Road is starting to function. It can't be much longer before we have bread again, and maybe cheese."

"The very definition of Soviet history," said Anna, "waiting for bread, and maybe cheese."

"Anna, my dear, I have never seen a better demonstration of a curmudgeon than you have displayed here tonight," said Luby. "I think perhaps you could use a project."

"Oh, you want me to help clean up the Puppet Theater?"

Suddenly I sat up straighter. "Maybe not the Puppet Theater, but how about the city?"

"Whatever do you mean?" asked Maria.

"Spring will be here soon. The snow will melt, and we will see skeletons where corpses used to be, silent witnesses to cruelty and cannibalism. We will see human waste and contaminated river water, a result of the dysentery inevitable since the breakdown of the sewage system months ago. But if we lead a cleanup of the city, we can restore a community craving for normalcy, and ourselves. I can talk about it on the radio. Volunteers will come."

"I love this idea!" said Luby. "I will ask my tribe of boys to help."

"Maybe we can ask the military—and all the Grannies—to help clear the square in front of the museum," said Viktoria. "I think I know just the man for the job!"

"Remember early on, when the Communist Party asked for volunteers to help build trenches, to deter the Germans from capturing the city?" I asked. "I had a letter from a woman who participated. She was so excited. She thought she was finally doing something to win the war."

"I heard bad things about that," said Anna. "I had one friend who told me the ground was hard as a rock, and most of the time they had only picks. She said there were young girls in sundresses and sandals, young boys in shorts and sports shirts, old women like her. She said they slept under the open sky, next to their shovels, and many caught colds. And still they were not excused, not even allowed to go home to change clothes. Plus I heard from a friend in the military that it was all a waste of time anyway. There was no way our hand-made trenches would deter the Germans."

I mused at how people experience history differently, making it an imperfect field of inquiry.

"Perhaps," I said. "But another shoveler wrote me that she felt part of a mighty tribe of women. She said as they applied their picks to the ground, their colorful kerchiefs made them look like a giant flower bed sprouting in the city. We can feel that again. We can cleanse the city of its traumas."

"Too early," said Anna. "The ground is too hard, and it's still too cold."

"Maybe," I said. "But with the first sign of daffodils, we will launch the cleanup campaign."

"I like that idea," said Anna, "the daffodil as a metaphor for our future."

Proposing one last toast, I said, "To Leningrad's future. And to ours."

"And to our friends in faraway places," Viktoria said, "the artists, ballerinas and musicians."

"And to their homecoming," I said.

TWELVE

The Capital
March 1942

As I was readying for bed one night, I heard someone slide a letter under the front door. At first I worried Nikolai might be wounded again, but this dispatch was not from the military. The envelope declared itself from the Department of Culture, and the note summoned me to Moscow.

"I'm not leaving," I told Vadim the next morning. "My place is here, with my fellow Leningraders."

"Olga, when the star of Radio Leningrad collapses on the streets, I guess even the Kremlin wakes up. The rest of us have been hungry for some time, but when you fainted, my phone rang."

I looked at him then, taking in the signs—the sagging skin, the yellow face, the emaciated body. I longed to get him some food. I longed to get the orchestra food. Eliasberg was already in the hospital. The last time I saw him, Dhazdat looked extremely weak, as if he too were on the verge of starving to death. These people were my friends, my colleagues. How could I leave them?

"You fly out tomorrow and they want you to stay in the hospital for a few weeks to recover your strength," he said. "Then you will stay in Moscow to broadcast the debut there of Symphony No. 7, and to give speeches to our fellow Soviets about conditions in Leningrad."

"The symphony is making its debut in Moscow? Why not Leningrad?"

"Olga, we have discussed this before. It is not safe to fly Shostakovich into Leningrad, nor do we have the wind to perform it. Please Olga, go to Moscow. Restore your health. Protect your child."

My eyebrows went up then. So it's not safe to fly Shostakovich here, but it was safe to send me out? And now, after killing my son, the Soviet Union suddenly cares about the welfare of my child? And what about the muzzle on what I could say to the public—had hunger suddenly cleared the agenda?

Vadim recognized that rebellious look in my eyes and shook his head.

"Don't even think about it," he said. "In these speeches, make no mention of starvation—none, none. Offer tributes to the courage, the heroism of Leningraders, but not a word about hunger."

"So Stalin wants me to whitewash the truth so no one will hear that we are starving."

Vadim walked to his office door and closed it, so no one would hear our conversation.

"Olga, I know how you feel. Some days I even wonder if you are right. But last week I heard about a Red Army soldier who was transferred from the front at Lake Ladoga to a unit in Moscow. He started telling people about what he had seen in our city, about how people were starving to death, about how they were dropping dead on the streets. He was arrested. You must avoid the topic."

It was true, I thought. People were perishing in a most public way. They would be walking along, and topple over dead. For those who heard of these deaths, there was a measure of utter disbelief. One man wrote me, "Recently I heard of an acquaintance of mine who died. And I thought, 'Could this be the one I knew? In broad daylight? Can this really be true? In Leningrad? With a master's degree? From starvation?' Such is our shock at the events before our very eyes."

The Kremlin insisted I be hospitalized, to recover from starvation, even as they officially denied that we were starving. I wondered if Vadim saw the same contradiction I did. I could not be sure, but I noticed his voice softened then.

"Olga, I would love to keep you here, even if only for us to die together, but the authorities are insistent, and I have no leverage. Last week, I begged for kerosene for heating and lighting the broadcast studios and the editorial rooms, and the Party said no. This week I asked for fruits and vegetables and barrels for storing drinking water. Again, *nyet*, always *nyet*. Just go. Do us proud."

The next day, I boarded a plane captained by 20-year-old Lenin Litvinov. Nikolai was already onboard, cleared by the military to accompany me to Moscow. I had no inkling he was joining me, and I was thrilled, leaping into his arms, barely listening as Commander Litvinov told us it would be a perilous route, over Nazi lines, in a light plane that German artillery could easily bomb out of the sky. No matter the risks, I was overjoyed, imagining Nikolai would be with me for the birth.

"My commander told me to keep alert to the Fritzes," said Commander Litvinov. Looking at me, he added, "He told me I would be carrying precious cargo."

I smiled and nuzzled myself into Nikolai's arm, in that comfortable corner where the shoulder meets the body. Funny how life sometimes offers reprieves. I had tried to hide my feelings at work, but I had been lonely, grieving over the letters of death and hardship from my readers, anxious about my pregnancy. Now here I was in Nikolai's arms, feeling warmed and reassured. I quickly fell asleep, as contented as I had been in a long time. Nikolai told me later that during the flight, there was one scuffle in the sky. When a German bomber came into view, Litvinov banked left and climbed, forcing the Nazi explosive to miss its target. Wiping sweat from his brow, he managed to resume a level course and land before running out of fuel. Nikolai told me he was glad I slept through it.

"We are here," he whispered, caressing my stomach, "the whole family is here."

We both teared up at that. Sometimes I wondered if this birth would actually happen. It seemed like so many things could intervene to douse our dreams. Nikolai could be killed in combat. I could be too weak to push. Maybe the scars from my miscarriage would prevent a healthy birth. And even if the baby survived, we were living in a time of constant hunger. How much time we would have together as a family? How much time would we have together as a country?

Hospitalized at the Evangelical Hospital in Moscow, I slowly regained my strength. Founded by the Lutheran community in the early 20th Century, the hospital had survived the early Nazi bombing of the Kurskaya Railway Station less than a kilometer away, though bomb splinters remained in its exterior red brick walls. The hospital never closed its doors, and the staff never stopped serving.

Now, nurses fed me glucose and gradually added solid foods. I made friends with Vladimir—everyone called him Volodya—who controlled food supplies in the hospital kitchens. By month's end, my skin looked better and my eyes lost that glassy look of indifference that some said was the price of hunger. I hadn't realized how close I had been to starvation. Silently, I thanked Vadim for insisting I come. I wrote the Poets Circle that the baby had gained weight too, looking more like a bowling ball and less like a kangaroo's sagging pouch. Mostly, I knew hope again, so I did not mind writing speeches for Moscow audiences, to share the story of how Leningraders were persevering.

"We are resilient, we are brave," I told one audience. "The fascists will never own our hearts." I talked of the horrors committed by Germans. I described the wailing of Belka the elephant and the pedestrians murdered in front of Lenin's Statue at Finland Station. I talked about how the Nazis, methodical in all things, bombed on a schedule—at 8 a.m., 11 a.m. and 5 p.m.—to maximize terror. I talked about the valiant work of the Leningrad State Pediatric Institute in extracting vitamins for children from tobacco and pine needles. I did not mention the bombing of the Badaev Warehouse, which compromised our food supply, or the eating of family pets by Leningraders hoping to stay alive. Sometimes I advertised my pregnant condition as proof that Leningraders envisioned a future. "Just look," I would say, pointing to my stomach. "We are even planning for the next generation."

Audiences laughed and reacted warmly, but I could tell their empathy extended only as far as our shared experiences of air raid sirens and wartime deaths. One night I was so exasperated by the incongruity between what I could say and what I knew to be true that I wrote a letter to Maria, asking her to share it with the Poets Circle, and no one else.

I am convinced that they know nothing about Leningrad here. No one seems to have the remotest idea of what the city has gone through. They say that Leningraders are heroes, but they don't really know why. They don't know that we are starving, that there is no electricity or water, that people are dying of dystrophy, dropping dead in the streets.

Maria responded with a letter of her own, urging me to stay away. "Trust me it is better you stay there, better that you eat. It is so bad here Garegin asks me if he can rob the Badaev again!"

Two nights later, Nikolai and I arrived for the debut of Shostakovich's Symphony No. 7 at the Hall of Commons. I was extremely pregnant—hospital officials were not keen to let me check out, but they were overridden by my political minders. In this country, politics always triumphs over health, or happiness. I was still sad the symphony had not debuted in Leningrad, the city of its birth, but delighted that I would be behind the microphone for the Radio Moscow broadcast. The Hall of Commons, a magnificent building erected before the Revolution, ironically by the Moscow Assembly of the Nobility, had great acoustics and even more historical provenance—Lenin had lain in state there before his burial in Red Square.

"It's like a party in here," Nikolai observed.

"I guess a coming out party, for our survival."

"Or a celebration of our new child."

He kissed me then, and my heart surged with hope. He was right, magic was in the air, as if Muscovites wanted to celebrate the end of the war even knowing there was still more fighting to come. I tried to convey that sense of moment over the airwaves. I guess I succeeded, because after listening to the concert on our airwaves, *The London Times* waxed lyrical about the symphony, calling it 'a victory of light over darkness, of humanity over barbarism'.

As far as I was concerned, this was the symphony of and by Leningrad, birthplace of the country's arts, and my thrill at its completion was saddened by its debut here in Moscow, home of the country's political machinery. Before the concert began, Dmitri Shostakovich strode to the front of the stage and spoke. Listening to the spaces between his words, I thought he felt the same way.

"I dedicate my Seventh Symphony to our fight against fascism," he proclaimed to the cheering audience. "To our coming victory over the enemy. And especially to my native city Leningrad."

Once the music began, I was transfixed. The tap-tap-tap of the invading army, delivered by drums and trumpets, the weeping of the strings, the mournful sounds of an ending we did not yet know. Listening to the first part, I wept inside, and was so exhausted from the music's epic tension that I think I missed the middle section altogether. All I could remember was seeing Shostakovich, so tiny on the stage, soaking in the applause. I couldn't wait to get to the microphones.

"When I saw that magnificent stage, the overflow crowd, the people huddled in their coats against the cold room, when I saw Shostakovich rise and take a bow, I realized why the moment mattered," I told our Radio Moscow listeners. "I looked at this frail man in big glasses, and I thought, 'This man is more powerful than Hitler.' In this one magnificent piece of music, he has captured the evil of the Nazi invasion and the proud resistance of the Soviet nation. He has defined our generation."

The applause was thunderous. There were chorus calls for the orchestra and an ovation for the composer. I was happy Nikolai was at my side. At concert's end, Nikolai and I went downstairs and approached Shostakovich to congratulate him. He looked at my condition, and smiled at Nikolai, inviting us to sit with him in his dressing room.

"How are you Olga?" he asked.

"As you can see," I quipped, "about as wide as I am tall!"

"It was a wonderful night, wasn't it?" he said, smoking nervously. "And yet I still long to hear that this symphony finds its home in the city of its birth."

"I agree," I said. "What have the authorities said?"

"They say it would be too difficult to transport the score—it is thousands of pages long," he said. "I wonder if there are other reasons."

He looked at me sheepishly, but I understood. We had both experienced the whip of Stalin's anger, knew the dangers of being canceled for speaking too openly. Listening to the first movement, so descriptive of an invasion, I had actually wondered if the composer was channeling hatred of fascists, or of all totalitarians. If so, he was walking a tightrope even thinner than mine.

He began pacing, biting his nails.

"You know I almost lost the score once. If it is not performed in Leningrad, it will feel like I have lost it again."

"You're kidding! What happened?"

"It happened when we evacuated from Leningrad. First they flew us to Moscow. We stayed in a hostel. There were complaints and we had to leave."

"Complaints?" Nikolai asked.

"Once during a bombing raid, Nina claims she found me pacing in the basement, screaming, 'Wright Brothers, Wright Brothers, What Have You Wrought?' I have no memory of this, but other residents heard me and complained, and authorities insisted we move to Kuibyshev."

"You blamed the Wright Brothers for the Nazi bombs?" Nikolai laughed. "Isn't that like blaming artists for creating the paintings that Hitler stole?"

"Yes, I suppose you're right, though that didn't occur to me then. All I knew was that I was furious at the Germans. Every time I tried to work on this symphony, to think through its movements, it seemed their bombs interrupted. It was as if they were deliberately trying to thwart its completion."

"So that's when you were evacuated to Kuibyshev?" I asked.

He nodded. "After we boarded the train, I couldn't find the score. Nina had carefully bundled it in a quilt. I roamed the train whenever we stopped, looked in cupboards and crannies, hoping to find it."

"And?"

"During one of the train's final stops, Nina found it. It was still wrapped in the blanket, but it was sitting in a puddle on the bathroom floor, soaked in dirty water and urine."

I cringed at the image. This magnificent symphony, soaked in urine? Was this Hitler's latest insult—or Shostakovich's latest folly? He insisted the score had not been stained. I wondered.

"Dmitri I have a favor to ask," I began. "I have written a letter to Katarina Orlova. Can you deliver it for me?" The letter was short. 'Dhazdat is dying,' I had written. 'Come home.' I shoved the envelope in his hands, imploring him to deliver it.

I saw his face flash with heat, whether guilt or pleasure I wasn't sure. He eyed me inquisitively.

"When are you returning to Leningrad?" he asked.

"The plan is to deliver the baby here and then recuperate for a bit," I said. "Why?"

"Will you be flying?"

"Yes, well, I don't know really. I imagine so. That is how I got here."

"I believe we are flying home," said Nikolai. Clearly he knew more than me.

Shostakovich nodded. "I may ask you to deliver a package."

"Only if you deliver my letter to Katarina."

He smiled, and nodded.

I wondered why he was being so jocular. Surely he could guess at the content of the message for Katarina. His reaction angered me. But I soothed my temper with thoughts that sometimes, great genius is wrapped in human folly. The great composer was a flawed human.

That night I had trouble sleeping. Partly it was my tummy—so big by then, it was hard to know where to put it. But mostly, it was my mind keeping me awake. My thoughts kept drifting back to my earlier pregnancies, as if reliving the earlier tragedies could presage trouble during this one.

Sometimes I wondered if the authorities were treating this pregnancy differently out of a sense of atonement, for their crime of killing our son Grigori. I doubted it. The regime was not known for being plagued by fits of conscience. But it consoled me to think that maybe, just maybe, it was now. There was one sweet intervention just before our daughter's birth. It was a note from Uncle Sasha, wishing me and the baby good health. How he found me I never learned, but as my own father was far away, I was touched. Maybe this figure from long ago in Nikolai's life would now return to ours.

Two days later, I gave birth to our daughter. It was a long, exhausting delivery, but when I heard her cry, I felt energized beyond measure. I named her Abigail, which meant 'my father's delight'. When Nikolai looked at her, he must have seen himself. She had dark eyes and his upturned nose. This made both of us happy.

A few days later, I went down to the hospital kitchen to show her off to Volodya.

"Greetings Comrade," I said, as I took a seat at the bar in front of his stove, holding the baby so he could look at her. "I have come on a mission of health."

"You are both the picture of health!" he exclaimed. "I remember when you first were admitted, I thought both of you would perish. Is it from all my good cooking, yes?"

I smiled.

"Of course, it was your cooking. I even thought of naming the baby after you in gratitude, but Vladimir is a lot of name for a little girl, don't you think?"

He cracked a smile, though I doubted it was any more sincere than mine had been. I guess he sensed I was about to ask for a favor.

"Vladimir, I have come to tell you something, in confidence."

He nodded, listening as he cooked vegetables on the stove.

Half an hour later, I left the kitchens. I hoped I had not endangered my family by telling Vladimir that Leningrad was starving. I was cheered by his suggestion that he would discreetly take a bit of food from each day's portion, and assemble some boxes for me to take back home. But I added this transgression to the list of sins that could get me in trouble—disclosing to this Muscovite that Leningrad was starving would have to wait in line behind The Rebel's missives and the Poets Circle's wartime chatter. I finally decided I had to stop looking behind me, worrying about things that had already happened. I had to keep looking forward. After all, the Radio Orchestra had a concert to perform!

When we were released one week later, the hospital gave me enough baby supplies for a month—and Vladimir had surreptitiously mixed some food parcels in with the mass of boxes in my room.

Thank goodness Litvinov had been in the pilot's seat for our return to Leningrad. Again German bombers flashed their weapons at our aircraft, but this time we had a bigger plane, and again he outmaneuvered them. For some reason, I was calm. I was surrounded by love—my husband, my daughter and by the 55 boxes of Symphony No. 7. Hospital officials were horrified when these documents first arrived in my room, and tried to refuse delivery. But again, their health concerns were vetoed by political considerations. Seeing the public's joyous reaction to the performance of the No. 7 in Moscow, the Kremlin had decided to help us deliver the Shostakovich symphony to Leningrad. With the Army's help, Nikolai arranged a truck to meet us on arrival in Leningrad. We drove directly to Radio House.

As soon as we walked in, everyone gathered round, cooing after Abigail, congratulating Nikolai.

"She will be a violinist, I can tell from her fingers," said Andrei.

"No, no," said Dhazdat, "she will be Leningrad's first great female drummer."

I was shocked at how thin everyone looked, like shadows. Again I was plagued by questions. If there was food for me in Moscow, why was there none in Leningrad? Was Hitler the one who was starving us—or Stalin? I found Vadim and gave him the boxes Volodya had assembled.

"Feed these to the orchestra," I said. "And never ask me how I got them."

He hugged me.

As military personnel piled box after box in Vadim's office, I turned to Eliasberg.

"Here is the score," I said. "A gift from the composer. Now you must play it."

"Olga, I sleep at the Astoria Hotel Hospital," he said. "I don't know from day to day if I will even live to breakfast. And you want me to summon a great orchestra to perform a great symphony?"

"Yes," I said, "that's exactly what I want."

He smiled at me, lopsided of course.

THIRTEEN

The Clean-up
April 1942

That spring, I saw a yellow daffodil blooming. I was overcome with emotion. I left Abigail with my sister Maria, and convinced Viktoria to join me on a walk to the Summer Garden, created by Peter the Great as a refuge for the nobles living in his city. It was located where the Fontanka River met the Neva, and filled with marble statues, enormous fountains and a profusion of plants. I had come seeking the comfort of nature, although the promise of adult company was equally appealing.

"Look!" I exclaimed. "The daffodil has returned. Like a proud trumpet."

Viktoria laughed. "Maybe the flowers will sprout new hope."

"You look stunning," I said. "You have lost decades since I last saw you!"

Viktoria smiled, making her look even more beautiful.

"I am eating again," she said. "The Ice Road trucks are delivering foodstuffs directly to the Hermitage, which is a miracle for those thousands of people living in our basement, but also for me," she said. "I have enough to feed those we are sheltering, and I bring food to my mother's house, and to Luby's. What a joy finally to be able to give back. These people were part of my experience of war. I saw them suffer, as they did me. Now I can help us all recover."

As we strolled the sand paths next to the curated gardens, I imagined we looked like two young, carefree women out for a walk. True, bombs still fell, and hunger was always one missed delivery away. But honestly, all we needed were blossoming skirts and parasols and we would look like one of those Claude Monet paintings that used to hang on the walls of the great Hermitage Museum.

"And how is Orbeli?"

"He is still the director, in name, but unofficially he has taken a back seat, handing me the reins."

"How wonderful!" I exclaimed. "Are you enjoying it as much as you imagined?"

"More," she said, smiling. "I am bursting with ideas on what we can do after the war, how we can attract a younger crowd and make the art relevant to a new generation. Just thinking about these things makes me feel more certain of my love for Boris. Our letters are now bursting with energy and hope. Maybe because I feel his equal, or anyway less intimidated in conversation with him."

She asked how Abigail was doing and I was off on a romantic account of breast milk, bottles and poop. Something about looking at an infant, a child of your own making, made the everyday chores of mothering seem idyllic. Whenever I held Abigail, I couldn't stop staring at her.

I asked how everyone was doing at Luby's house and Viktoria bubbled over. No longer worried about this unusual arrangement, she gushed at Luby's ability to make sweet juice from sour lemons.

"Luby is a marvel," Viktoria began. "For months, before the food supply improved, she gave the boys a token whenever they helped with a household chore, to be cashed in whenever the war ends. Rahil delights in beating Rodion at the game, piling up tokens. And apparently he is also earning points as Igor's sous chef. Igor thanks me mightily for my contributions, saying they have little otherwise. Rodion is their grumpy child, but I am so grateful he is still alive. Sometimes I look at that letter he wrote our father when he felt near death. I can't wait to tear it up someday."

"Don't do that," I said. "It is a memento of what we went through. History will want to see it."

"Maybe you're right," she said. "Maybe both Rodion and Papa will want to see it."

"You should see the letters that arrive in my mailbag at Radio Leningrad. All of them churn with a quiet dignity. There is so much emotion seeping through these thawing snows."

"Like what?"

"Some of them say the improved food rations mean they have more time to think about loved ones they lost during the Siege. One woman named Anna Likhacheva wrote that the more nature comes to life, the brighter the sun, the greener the ground, the worse she feels. Because it reminds her of the death of her son. She thinks spring is cruel. She cries day and night."

"There are so many little tragedies inside this big one. Every daffodil comes at a price, I suppose. Some flowers never leave the ground."

After that we meandered, indulging our private thoughts.

"What do you imagine after the war?" I asked.

"A lot of rebuilding," said Viktoria. "We will have to restore the museum—not just welcome home the art but piece back together the sense of place. And then we will have to reimagine it, to position in a postwar world where onetime friends had become onetime enemies, and vice versa. I don't see us ever returning to the isolation of the Soviet era. Maybe we'll have more visitors from abroad."

"And personally?"

Ah, that beaming smile again.

"If Boris loves me as I think he does, I hope for the richest kind of happiness, the kind that flows from the heart," she said. "And what about you Olga? What do you hope for after the war?"

"I have always been a creature of Leningrad, a poet nurtured by its history. But Nikolai was raised in the countryside, and sometimes I daydream about what it would be like to live and write poetry amid lush grounds filled with nature and animals and the people I love. Of course we would be close enough to visit, to replenish our cultural instincts sometimes. But the dream tickles my imagination."

"That is so unlike you Olga!" Viktoria said. "Promise you won't wander far, and never for too long."

I smiled and we hugged. We had indulged our need for fresh air and a few minutes of reprieve from the war. Now, I was eager to return home. I knew Maria would want to leave soon for the hospital.

A few weeks before, Garegin was diagnosed with starvation, and we rushed him to Astoria Hospital for treatment. No matter how often I witnessed the process, it was a frightening thing to watch—the wasting of the body in an agonizingly slow dance of death. Maria was quietly hysterical, but filled with purpose. She visited twice a day, often with food, determined that her love would spur him back to health. I sometimes went with her, shocked at how quickly he was sinking.

His hospitalization made me think back to that night of the Badaev bombing, when life for Leningrad became insufferable, and Nikolai's fate mingled with Garegin's. I kept these thoughts to myself—the fewer people who knew, the better. But I wondered often how much trauma one person, or even one country, could take. While in the hospital, Garegin survived one bout of pneumonia, which was a miracle. But Maria and I often speculated about whether his early traumas, the genocide and the frightening evacuation from Armenia, had weakened his immune system.

Once when Nikolai was on home leave, we visited Garegin together. Their conversation made me smile. It also confirmed my hunch that men talk in riddles.

"Ah," Garegin said, on seeing Nikolai, "you have come to finally arrest me?"

"I think the famine has forgiven all debts," smiled Nikolai. "How long have you been here?"

"Two weeks, feels like four," Garegin said. "How is the war?"

"I can't say much," Nikolai said, "except that we are practicing to surprise them."

Garegin nodded. He showed me a letter had been writing to his sister Ani.

"All I want is food," Garegin had written. "I wait for your parcels like manna from heaven. Let it be just black dry bead or a crust, a potato, cheap flour, or fat—anything like that is happiness for me and Maria, a dream. I have to confess that in all my life, I have never known such terrible days."

I teared up as I read the letter. How did we get to this point of deprivation? I handed the letter to Nikolai, who grew visibly angry. In the weeks to come, care packages arrived for Garegin, some from Ani but most from the front. I smiled when Maria told me. I always believed those packages would save Garegin, so that he would be able to perform at the concert. One of the things I loved about Nikolai is that he was not afraid to act from emotion—quietly, but from the heart.

Local authorities kept warning that any expression of emotion amid the Siege could lead to defeatism, or anti-Communist sentiment. Party officials preferred a narrative of stoicism, what I thought of as a kind of heroism of the Soviet heart, full of sacrifice and character. But I knew that to most women, calling Leningrad 'a city of heroes' or bestowing awards on those who displayed 'utter selflessness and iron will' were signs not of bravery but of fear. Authorities may have seen displays of emotion as unpatriotic, a crime against the state. But to me, and to the dozens who wrote to me, emotion was the only defense against the hardships of daily life. As I wrote in my diary,

Singed and icy, the triumphant Leningrad tragedy breathes from the many pages of their letters, where they write with total candor about everyday sorrows and joys. In their words, history suddenly speaks with a simple human voice.

Sometimes I mused about how much hardship my generation had endured. Anyone 30 years old or older had already lived through four wars, three famines and two major waves of political terror. Every household, especially those with ethnic minorities, had known a relative who died, was jailed or impoverished. For me, with my father still under investigation for unnamed crimes against the state, emotion was the *terra firma* beneath my feet. This I told no one. Only my diary.

My generation measured time by the intervals between one suicide
and the next. Victory was saving a child.

Abigail was flourishing, feeding, burping and smiling. She
seemed happy to be here, I thought. She giggled whenever Nikolai
managed a visit. Sometimes when she was sleeping, she even wore
a smile, as if she were having sweet dreams. Hopefully the Nazis
would be defeated before she had much memory of anything else.
The Poets Circle doted on her, especially Viktoria. Perhaps she
was longing for a child herself. Anna remained the profile of a
curmudgeon. But I had a plan.

"My dear fellow Leningraders," I announced one day on the
air. "It is a joy to be home, to be returned to our community. Our
frozen ground is melting, exposing the trauma of our winter—
decomposing bodies, as if the dead are telling the story of our
winter." Out of the corner of my eye I saw Vadim, glaring. "But I
have an idea, to heal our city and our souls. Let us clean the streets,
clear away the debris, ready our world for springtime and the
promise of an end to our ordeal."

Response was immediate. Even skeptical Anna offered to come
read one of her poems on the air.

"I have been called the Muse of Sobbing," she began, "but now
I understand that we have all been sobbing. Spring is the time for
drying our tears, for seeing less of the past and more of the future."

I put her in charge of making posters heralding the clean-up
drive. She reconnected with a talented artist she had met after the
Revolution, Isaak Brodsky, and together they crafted beautiful

designs. This meant she had to fight officious party bureaucrats who believed that all posters were their purview. I laughed when she told me the stories. Maybe the Party had finally met its match.

My mailbag grew even larger. Apparently Leningraders were eager to do something—no doubt, the massive cleanup of our streets offered a distraction. But they also wanted to talk about it, to explain their delight. Maybe, I thought, the letters were a signal that our city was coming alive again.

"All around me were women and children, weak and malnourished, who moved slowly," wrote Elena Martilla, an 18-year-old listener to Radio Leningrad. "But there is strength in numbers. There are tens of thousands of people like us, chopping, digging, scarping, clearing tiny patches in the overall mosaic of snow and ice. Every so often a fat, well-fed city official comes over to egg us on. It is demoralizing, as we wish he would help instead of hector, but we keep picking away at the ice-encrusted refuse. We have declared war on dirt, and by this declaration, we the people of Leningrad, who had been isolated and inactive for months, are regaining a sense of purpose."

I had a friend at Leningrad's Public Library, Ludmila Lourie, who had shared stories of how they survived the Siege. Even after the building no longer had water, electricity or heat, the library stayed open. Reading rooms were closed but patrons could come to the director's office—which had a small stove and a kerosene lamp—to request books and information. Staffers searched the library stacks by using burning pieces of wood as candles. Popular topics for requests included unjust wars, Germans in literature and—everyone's favorite—a recipe for making candles. To the patron's surprise, the staff found one, in an 18th century manuscript. Some readers died sitting in their chairs, their corpses carried outside by the staff for pick up by city officials who rarely came. Now Ludmila and her staff cleared the pile of bodies outside, to announce their doors were cleared again.

To tackle cleanup at the Hermitage, Viktoria told me she brought in the museum's security chief and told him to do whatever it took to clear the square in front of the museum, key to our psyche.

"You can have any staff you need, and all the crowbars, shovels and brooms you can find," she instructed him. "Your primary job is to uncover pavement and clear away the refuse. If you do that, you will restore this historic site to its glory, and lift the spirits of this city."

A former soldier who had been discharged because of a genetic heart ailment, Pavel Gubchevsky assembled a staff of 30 women, all 55 years or older, who for months had been guarding the building. Under his command, the Grannies moved into the streets like soldiers, clearing mounds of snow and dirt. Blocks of ice, frozen mounds of trash, stalactites of sewage—all fell to their shovels.

Their progress inspired others to join the effort.

"Nobody ordered us to clean the courtyard, we did it of our own free will," wrote 11-year-old Fima Ozerkin. "The snow mound is gone because Toyla and I cleared it. Tomorrow we will do more."

I took to the airwaves to herald the effort.

"Leningrad is turning out—housewives, school children, professors, doctors, musicians, old women and men. One appears with a broom, another with a crowbar, a third with a sled. Many hardly have the strength to drag their legs, yet five people harness themselves to one tiny sled, and pull and pull, trying to clear mountains of accumulated waste. As they work, people pass on their strength to each other. And through this strength comes an affirmation of common cause. We will defy Hitler's cruel order that our city should be erased from the earth. We are proud Leningraders."

Sometimes I worried about what we would find under all the snow and slush. So many Leningraders had died—perhaps half a million in just the first few months, up to 30,000 a day. One day I decided to research the police files to investigate the depravity of what might be uncovered underneath our shovels. It was always a challenge for me to visit police headquarters, fear rising in my throat. But on this day, officials seemed more than happy to help a journalist dig through the rubble of their files.

It was grim reading. Police had created a special division to combat cannibalism, and by spring, had arrested more than 1,000 people. The Russian language had two words for it: *trupoyedstvo* (corpse-eating) and *lyudoyedstvo* (person-eating). Eating from corpses seemed the most reported crime. But the most heartbreaking, to both police and parents, was the killing of small children for food. In the files was a case of one mother who went to City Hall to find her missing child. A police officer directed her to crates of clothing marked by numbers. If she found her child's clothes, she should report to them the number on the crate, and they would tell her the district where her child was eaten. Would the evidence of this heinous child-eating crime be found under the snow? Were there children's bodies to be unearthed, or would their bones already be disintegrated into dust?

The police files were like a guide to the depths of our hunger. Police who found people with stolen ration cards shot them on the spot. For stealing food, the Military Court sentenced 2,104 during the Siege, more than the combat strength of most divisions at the front, and 435 of them were executed. Often thieves targeted the vulnerable. One teenager tore a piece of bread from the hands of a weakened old woman, shoved it into his face and chewed so vigorously it quickly disappeared. "No matter how much witnesses hit and kicked him, he chewed and swallowed it all," said the police report. Also in the files was news of a thriving black market—this year alone, police had seized more than 23 million rubles from racketeers, plus gold, diamonds, silver, antiques and even $40,628 in U.S. money. I searched the files for Anton's name, half-hoping the authorities had finally nabbed him.

One story caught my attention. A man named Dmitri went to a flea market one day to haggle for a pair of boots, *valenki*, for his girlfriend. A vendor showed him a boot, and they negotiated a price—Dmitri's 600 grams of bread. The man, named Ivan, said the other boot was at his apartment. They left together, meandering through stalls and alleys until they came to a door up a flight of stairs.

"It's me. I've brought you a live one," said Ivan, knocking on the door. Dmitri froze. When the door flung open, he saw hunks of white meat swinging from hooks on the ceiling, one still attached to a human hand, with long fingers and blue veins. Running down the stairs as fast as he could, he saw soldiers and pointed to the apartment shouting, "Cannibals!" Later Dmitri wrote to thank them for saving his life, though he said he would always regret the loss of his bread.

Most horrifying were lists of the dead. The Leningrad Funeral Trust recorded burial of 102,497 bodies in March alone. How many bodies, how many untold stories, would we find below the snow?

If the police files depressed me, Viktoria energized me. She asked me to visit one day as Gubchevsky's crew was working.

"Look at this miracle! Soon, the beautiful pavers on the Palace Square will be liberated from their burdens, freed from the Nazis. And look, the Alexander Column still stands."

I trained my eyes upward and marveled that, indeed, the 155-foot red granite statue commemorating Russia's defeat of Napoleon was still standing. Maybe after the war, we could build another one celebrating the defeat of Hitler by the Soviet people.

Spring brought other signs of hope. Authorities distributed seeds, and many planted corn and potatoes in vegetable gardens with help from their children, who enjoyed the new game. On Leningrad's Field of Mars, they planted cabbages and potatoes. Everywhere, the laughter of children could be heard, helping their parents, enjoying this new adventure of waiting for vegetables to sprout. While they waited, many ate weeds and wild grasses, anything to satisfy the yearning for greens. The Party even launched a campaign urging people to collect maple leaves in place of tobacco. 'Grass, grass, grass,' went the new saying. I heard that so many searched for spring's first offering of dandelions and nettles in the city's parks—good for making soups—that they were forced further and further into the city's outskirts, always dangerous since the Nazis had orders to kill anyone trying to leave the city.

Inna Bityugova was one of the children who worked on the city gardens. Inspired by the growth around her, she asked her mother for a writing book so she could draw the vegetables she was planting—turnips, radishes, beetroots. In her drawings, she gave the vegetables smiling happy faces, and little arms and legs. Her mother was charmed, and suggested she make up stories about them. And thus was born The Vegetable Man, soon published. In one tale, The Vegetable Man encountered a little girl whose arms were thin, and eyes sad. She was very hungry. So all the vegetables fed themselves to her, and she got stronger. In another story, Germans surrounded The Vegetable Man. They dropped bombs and fired at him, but he hid in a trench where an exhausted Soviet soldier sat, looking at a map. The soldier faced a long walk, but The Vegetable Man offered him some greens and he felt strong again, with the courage to march toward victory. The book of sketches and stories was passed around to her fellow gardeners, and was soon the talk of the town. After I heard about her stories, I invited Inna to come talk about them on Radio Leningrad.

"Why did you write these stories about The Vegetable Man?" I asked her.

"My Mama told me that the greens would make us strong again," said Inna. "I was very thin when we started eating the vegetables, but I am stronger now. So I wanted to write stories about it."

As I had feared, there were still disturbing images, many revealed by the now cleaned sidewalks. One woman wrote me about a pamphlet she found underneath the rubble. Dropped by the Germans, it said, "Finish your bread," it said. "Soon you'll be dead."

Still, spring made its inevitable journey, bolstering all of us. Lime trees in the Botanical Gardens by the river began to bloom and their scent deadened the smell of decay from the rubbish and corpses not yet cleared. "Could it be," I wondered aloud on the air, "that happiness will return?"

For others, the signs of hope came in unannounced returns to normalcy, popping up like unexpected spring flowers. Dhazdat's mother Nataliya was a nurse at the Leningrad State Pediatric

Institute, where she cared for hospitalized children. Suddenly one day, she heard the sound of the trams. At first she wondered if she was hallucinating. The tram had been silenced for months, killed by German bombs, buried in deep piles of snow, a train system stilled by war, forcing Leningraders to walk for so many miles for the barest necessities. Many of her smallest patients were near death, suffering from starvation, diarrhea, physically depleted. Suddenly there was a collective gasp. Patients who could move went to the windows. Others crawled on hands and knees to join them.

I heard about the incident from Dhazdat and asked if Nataliya would come tell the story on the air. "What a joyous moment," she told our audience. "It was as if the children came back to life. One little boy, perhaps 10 years old, kept yelling, 'Victory, Victory.' One girl began singing the *Internationale*. The tram that was immobile on Bolshoi Prospekt all winter was now roaring past us. It revived the children. Funny how a tram—so ordinary, so commonplace—became our little miracle."

And then there was the return of cats and dogs—their population decimated by starving Leningraders desperate for meat. The cats were especially needed to curtail a growing population of rats, feasting on debris. Moscow arranged to send us a train with boxes of cats. During their journey, the cats became spooked by German shelling. Evidently, they busted out of their boxes for more comfortable quarters on passenger seats. When the train pulled into Finland Station in Leningrad, railroad employees ready to unload the boxes were instead treated to the sight of feline faces looking back at them through train windows. "We didn't have to unload the boxes," one worker joked in an on-air interview at Radio House. "We just opened the doors and let them find their way home."

No sign of restored health was more uplifting than the return of the city's menu of cultural offerings. Leningraders queued for newly opened cinemas and theaters. At the Young Pioneer Palace, they stood in line for jazz concerts. The Radio Orchestra of Leningrad was performing classical concerts at the Philharmonia, with those musicians still able to play. Maria was more popular than ever at the Musical Theater—audiences loved the menu of escape. The work, and the applause, put a smile on her face that could have melted even a Nazi.

Throughout the Siege, Leningraders had seized on music as a tonic. To Viktoria's cleanup commander, the rebirth of the city's cultural touchstones had awakened in him a new appreciation.

"Before the war, I hardly ever went to concerts at the Philharmonia, or enjoyed plays at the Kirov Theater," Gubchevsky told me. "I took them all for granted. What a fool I was. Now I understand the work that goes into making these performances— there are a thousand pieces of the puzzle. I never appreciated the wonder of what was around me. Now I will never forget it."

I thought often about Shostakovich, wondering if his music would find favor in Leningrad. Maybe survivors of this ordeal were too hardened to enjoy its themes. We were the victims of Hitler's invasion. Would we even want to relive its cruelties in music?

By this time, London and New York had performed Symphony No. 7 to packed audiences. With much of the world fighting Nazi Germany, the All-Union Society for Cultural Relations with Foreign Countries—an organization I had never heard of before—sensed a rare opportunity to promote the Soviet Union as a country with a pedigree. Yuri told me they persuaded friends in the Kremlin for permission to fly copies of the score to Tehran. From Iran, the microfilms were transported by car over what diplomats called the Persian Corridor, through Iran's vast countryside to Iraq, Palestine and the Suez Canal, to Cairo. From there, they flew west across Casablanca on the West African Coast, where they were put on a plane either to Britain, or to Brazil. Those in Brazil turned north to Florida, then New York. It sounded like a movie to me. Maybe someday it would be.

The London Philharmonic performed the symphony at the sold-out Albert Hall, broadcast on the BBC. "It was listened to with profound attention by an immense audience," reported *The Times*. *The Times* and other critics saw the music as unworthy, and dismissed Shostakovich as little more than a heroic fireman who thought up the music as he was 'waiting for the next moment of action in his duties as an air-raid warden, watching for incendiaries on the roof of the Leningrad Conservatory.' Vadim told me that if critics were haughty, the public was enthralled, hearing in the music the heroism and sacrifice of their new Russian allies. "You can hear the march of the invader, the noise of his panzer tanks and Heil-Hitler saluting armies sweeping forward," one listener told the BBC. "In depicting the resistance of the Russian people to the German boot, it was triumph."

In New York, the score arrived in a small tin, about the size of an Olympic medal. Thomas Belsivo, head of the music department at NBC, had to find printers who could replicate the score for the conductor and 110 instruments—2,038 separate prints in all. As Belsivo contended with this logistical nightmare, *Time Magazine* reported the symphony had created a buzz of anticipation, making it the season's must-see event. Putting a picture of Shostakovich on its cover, in a fireman's helmet and uniform, the magazine said in its caption, "Fireman Shostakovich—Amid bombs bursting in Leningrad, he heard the chords of victory."

"So hungry was the world for a Soviet hero," wrote the 64-year-old poet Carl Sandburg, "that it looks on and holds its breath. In Berlin, in Paris, Brussels, Amsterdam, Copenhagen, Oslo, Prague, Warsaw, wherever the Nazis have mopped up, we hear no new symphonies. This one, this song, tells us of a great people beyond defeat or conquest who are contributing new meaning to the ideas of human freedom and discipline."

Arturo Toscanini, the famed conductor, led the NBC Orchestra in a performance of the symphony heard by an estimated 20 million people. Yuri told me that one of them was First Lady Eleanor Roosevelt. He'd heard that Toscanini set the tone by opening with a rendition of 'The Star-Spangled Banner,' the

USA's anthem. Predictably, there were some nasty reviews from elitists. American critic and composer Virgil Thomson called the work 'written for the slow-witted, the not very musical and the distracted.' Still, the symphony was so popular with the public it was performed sixty times in the USA in its first year. The symphony was more than music now, I thought, it was a symbol of the world's determination to defeat Adolf Hitler. Yuri kept me posted on all of this—he had a friend at the BBC, and lots of international sources. But I heard nothing in all these hoorays from abroad that this was our symphony—of, by and for the people of this remarkable city, which had carried the war against the Nazis on its back.

We had the score. We had a conductor. We had some musicians, and could summon more. We had paved the streets and cleaned the walkways. And there was no shortage of patrons who were frequenting the theaters, risking their lives even as they devoured artistic performances.

The time had come for us to perform Symphony No. 7 in Leningrad, where it all began.

FOURTEEN

The Rehearsals
May 1942

One day in spring, I walked into Eliasberg's office as he was studying the score with the orchestra's coordinator, Yasha Babushkin.

"How does it look?" Babushkin was asking. "When can I schedule No. 7?"

"Impossible," said Eliasberg, looking up from all the musical notes on paper. "We'll never play this."

"Why not?" I asked, plopping down beside Babushkin. "It has been a year since the Nazis invaded our country, and we need to kick them out with our music."

Eliasberg looked at me as if I were a romantic who had lost her mind.

"Olga, this is a colossal work, requiring dozens of strings, and lengthy arrangements for woodwind and brass. A city short of breath cannot perform a piece of music demanding so much of its lungs."

"Karl," said Babushkin, "we have orders to play this symphony. The Party thinks it will lift morale."

"They should have thought of that earlier and delivered us food!"

Eliasberg paused then. I imagine he knew such outspoken opinions could bring as much danger to his life as a case of dystrophy. Karl looked at us, his eyes dripping with sentiment like those on a cocker spaniel, although hidden behind eyeglasses, as always falling off his face.

"This symphony requires an abnormally large orchestra," he said more quietly, as if he were patiently explaining something difficult to musical novices. "For the brass it requires eight French horns, six trumpets, six trombones. For the woodwinds, three flutes, two oboes, three clarinets, a bass clarinet, two bassoons and a contrabassoon. As for the strings," he said, reading from his notes. "It's 16 first violins, 14 second violins, 12 violas, ten cellos, eight double basses and two harps, 62 in total."

Admittedly, it was a daunting number. I tried to think of ways to minimize the weight of it.

"I saw that in the last box Shostakovich sent you a note," I said. "Did he have any suggestions?"

"Oh yes," Eliasberg nodded. "The great composer was audacious enough to warn me that we must not cut corners. 'All instruments must play their parts!' he wrote. As if he has no idea that we do not have the strength to play all of these parts. As if he has no idea we are starving."

"I think he knows we are starving," I said. They both looked at me. "When he was evacuated with his wife and children in the fall, authorities promised to transport his mother Sofiya, sister Mariya and nephew Vasily soon after. By the time they arrived in Kuibyshev months later, they were emaciated beyond recognition. On seeing them, he told me in Moscow, he felt guilty for leaving."

"Well he has a funny way of showing it," said Eliasberg. "He embodies arrogance."

"Perhaps," I said. "But maybe arrogance in the cause of talent is a virtue?"

Karl sneered. I knew he was right. For Eliasberg, getting the band together again would take a triumph of will over reality. Weeks earlier, the orchestra had given a radio concert—performing Mozart, Tchaikovsky, Schubert—and most musicians collapsed afterward. He reminded me of this now.

"Olga, most of the Radio Orchestra of Leningrad is already dead—27 died last month alone—and the rest are at the front. We have, at best, a dozen fit to play, and many are dystopic, including me. And I am expected to check back into the hospital again by nightfall." He looked at me glumly.

"I know it is difficult. But honestly, don't you think it is your destiny to conduct this symphony? Your musicians are starving, for both food and comfort. So are the people of this proud city. This is the chance of a lifetime, Karl, to bring Leningrad to its feet."

"I don't know where to begin," Karl despaired. I felt the momentum shift then. Our conductor was no longer saying no.

Now he was asking for help. Without conferring, or even making eye contact, Yasha and I became a Committee of Ideas. For every objection Karl raised, we offered a suggestion.

"When the score landed in New York, it was sent to a printer to make copies for all the 120 musicians, for each of the instruments," Karl said. "We don't have the printers for that."

It was Babushkin who came up with the idea of finding elderly musicians who were too old or too weak to play but still able to copy music. With help from the orchestra's onetime pianist, Nina Bronnikova, these older copyists would spend hours leaning over their desks, drawing note heads, treble clefs, accidentals and tails. By the time rehearsals started, they had produced copies of the score for each musician and his or her instrument. Unlike printed scores in New York, these were all done by hand. It was an unheralded, stunning achievement. I imagine they are collectors' items now.

As for performers, Babushkin instructed Vadim to put out a call on the radio, soliciting musicians to play in the orchestra in return for increased food rations, and so he did.

"All musicians remaining in Leningrad must report to the Radio Orchestra for registration," Vadim announced on the air. "With your help, the Radio Orchestra of Leningrad will perform again."

Soon Radio House looked like the lobby for a casting call. I interviewed several applicants, for in addition to helping Yasha with the paperwork, I was doing a documentary on the concert.

Basically, I hijacked anyone coming to register, in hopes their stories might enliven the broadcast.

Galina Yershova came from the Kirov plant in Petrograd Side, where she worked making shells.

"The radio was on in the factory, and a broadcaster said that all the musicians should report here," she told me. "Before the war I had taken flute classes at the Mussorgsky College of Music. So I took my flute and came to register."

I noticed she had trouble walking straight. She told me she had scurvy, and hoped we would give her Vitamin C pills. I doubted it would be that easy, but her enthusiasm brought a smile to my face.

"I was registered!" she said, sounding as if she had just won admission to a great theater production. "I was told to come back when the scores for individual instruments are ready. Imagine that, me, in the orchestra!" Not for the first time, I thought hope was the most powerful vitamin of all.

Posters also went up around the city too, with the same request—that all musicians report at once to Radio House. Another early interviewee was Katya Medvedeva, the woman whose mother had written of their New Year's Eve scones made of coffee grinds. She told me when she saw one of the posters, she hurried home to find her oboe.

"Mama, they are re-forming the Radio Orchestra of Leningrad. They are looking for volunteers."

"But Katya, you haven't played your oboe in years."

"The main question now is whether I can find it."

She told me the two searched the apartment, finally locating the instrument under some blankets in a closet. It had withered from neglect, its valves green, its pads coming off. It no longer could make any noises. How fitting, Katya recalled thinking, the oboe has dystrophy, like me.

Eliasberg had told her about a repairman he knew on the far side of town.

"He told me this repairman could fix anything," Katya said, "even people."

She said during the hour it took her to walk to Mikhail Dernov's apartment, she pondered Eliasberg's remark. Did he see some lapse in her? As Dernov opened the door, she recoiled.

"All the chairs, couches, desks, every surface was covered in the skins of cats and dogs," Katya told me. "I started to ask him whether he had eaten all the animals that once lived in these pelts, but stifled the question. The answer seemed obvious, and I figured he might resent the inquiry."

"Do you want the instrument fixed?"

"Yes. My oboe is missing some of its pads. How much would you charge to fix them?"

"Oh I don't charge. No one has any money anyway. Me, I barter."

"And what do you want?"

"A small cat. I haven't had a good meal for weeks."

Katya looked askance. She had heard on the radio that the cats had returned, but had no idea where to catch one. Besides, she was not sure she wanted to abet such inhumane behavior.

"Could you do it as a gift? We are re-forming the Radio Orchestra of Leningrad. This oboe will be part of history."

"Nothing is free, my pretty lady, especially history. For a price, I will fix your oboe."

She didn't tell me what she 'paid' for the repair, but having survived an unpleasant encounter with the grocer, I could only imagine. Katya did tell me that when she arrived back at Radio House with her repaired oboe, she went into the rehearsal hall to wait for the other musicians. As they came in, she was shocked at their sight. Each one seemed weaker than the one before.

"I didn't recognize them," she told me. "I knew many of them before, from school, some as friends, one as a lover, but now they were like skeletons. The orchestra used to be this mighty thing— a company of one hundred musicians capable of grand performances. Now they had shrunk, many barely able to stand on their feet. During rehearsal, one man, a flautist, fell over dead."

I nodded. I had sat in on their first rehearsal. Eliasberg arrived from the hospital, on a sled.

"Dear friends," he said while seated, "we are weak, but we must force ourselves to start work."

He raised his arms. I imagine it was the first time in his long career he had raised his arms and heard no sound. The musicians seemed distracted. Igor was looking down at his sketchpad, drawing a caricature of a hollow-cheeked Eliasberg conducting his orchestra from a chair. Dhazdat was too weak to drum, his hands trembling. Garegin, who had joined the orchestra amid the first guns of war, held the sticks for him. The rehearsal, scheduled for three hours, lasted 20 minutes.

Afterward, I joined Babushkin in Eliasberg's office.

"They are like the dead—empty eyes, their only thoughts of bread," I said. "How hard, how painful, it must be for them to play music when all they want is food, and warmth."

"We will get them more bread," Babushkin said. "The heat may be harder to arrange. I will talk to party officials today. If they want the No. 7 performed here, they have to feed the musicians."

I don't know what Babushkin said, but it seemed to help. Soon after, food rations improved a bit for the musicians, and officials moved Eliasberg to an apartment closer to the Pushkin Theater, where rehearsals would now be held, and gave him a bicycle for transportation. They also gave him more food. He was still complaining, but at least he was back to his usual curmudgeon-like persona.

He kept insisting that he had a third of the musicians he needed. So, when he was strong enough, he and I went door to door, seeking out players he knew who had not responded to the call. We walked the city streets, two misfits from Radio House, with a simple request: The Radio Orchestra of Leningrad, and the Communist Party, needed anyone who could play an instrument.

"My God, how thin he was," he said as we left one apartment. "Did you see how that man livened up when I enticed him out of his dark rooms?"

"I know, it was like the lights were restored," I said. "All our visits have been like that. All these musicians, living in darkness and hunger. I will never forget the sight of them bringing you their concert clothes, their violins and cellos and flutes. It was very moving, like the *magi* bringing gifts to the newborn king. You will see Karl. This concert will save us yet."

Karl said we were still short. Babushkin suggested reaching out to the military. Karl was dubious.

"They are not so much musicians as marching band performers," he said. "I doubt any of them has even heard a symphony, much less played one."

"Maybe so," said Babushkin, "but they are soldiers, willing to serve."

The senior officer in the Red Army's 45th Division band was Mikhail Parfionov. I remember hearing the name when Katarina wrote us of her harrowing escape from danger with Pavel after the botched evacuation of the children. Now I welcomed him to Radio House with a smile, telling him that many of us, including our drummer, wanted to thank him in person for rescuing Katarina.

"We all do for each other what we can. It was so long ago I had almost forgotten!"

"Come, our conductor is eager to see you."

Much as Eliasberg had predicted, Parfionov protested at first.

"Mr. Conductor, as you know, this is a very complex, daunting piece of work."

"I am aware of that, Captain."

"But we are not accustomed to playing symphonic music. Our last performance was a song called *Greetings, Russian Machine Gun*, meant to rouse the troops."

"I am aware of that, too, Captain. But in these times, life has been reduced to the basics. You play the trombone. I need trombone players. I hope you will become accustomed to it."

Hunger was affecting them too. It was affecting all of us. Parfionov told me he once saw Eliasberg walking by the military canteen of his division and asked him what he was doing there.

"He asked if I had a spare ticket to get bread, he was so hungry," Parfionov recalled. "I said I didn't and, besides, it was against regulations for him to come in. We saw him every day, but it was impossible to get to know him. He wasn't interested in personal contact."

Now, I thought, they would come to know him, whether the conductor wanted them to or not.

The military men fascinated me, perhaps because my husband was one of them, but also because they adhered to a work ethic I admired. We called them 'The Crew'. They rehearsed the symphony in the mornings and then went straight to the front in the afternoons. They were issued special ID cards saying 'Eliasberg's Orchestra', so they would be allowed through at checkpoints and not shot as deserters. I shuddered just thinking about it. Parfionov always stood erect when he lined up the military men in the rehearsal hall and later when he marched them out to their Army duties. He told me that nothing ever prepared him for the contrast between the two assignments.

One day, the military men went directly from rehearsal to the Piskaryovskoe Cemetery, to bury corpses. As they dug graves, Parfionov told me he turned to Pavel Orekhov, an intelligence officer and French horn player whose favorite assignment was to perform marching band music.

"A terrible sight," Parfionov said as they dug, corpses lined up nearby, almost like witnesses to their own burials. "I look forward to returning to rehearsal in the morning. At least the music is alive."

"For me it's almost easier to dig a grave," said Orekhov. "Trying to play the French horn, I get dizzy. My head starts spinning as soon as I blow with my lungs. My lips can scarcely touch the horn. It is so cold. I feel I am disappointing the conductor, who always has to wait for me to blow."

Everyone knew Karl was a perfectionist. Before the war, he had once clocked the precise time it took to walk from the music store on Nevsky Prospekt to Philharmonia Hall. Now, of course, his calculations were irrelevant, as it took much longer.

One day I watched rehearsals. When the first trumpeter's solo arrived, there was silence.

"Trumpet, play your music!"

"Sorry sir, I just don't have the strength in my lungs."

"I think you do have the strength. No complaining."

Often, Eliasberg had to repeat instructions two or three times before people could understand. With most players weakened by the trauma of the last few months, he had to review the same passage of music over and over simply to help them retain it. Always he tried to temper his emotions.

"I try to inspire, to win their hearts, without yelling to get their attention, but I don't want to pamper them," he told us one day. "One of my teachers drilled me on how to use discipline."

Babushkin nodded.

"Have you tried appeals to patriotism?"

"In my experience, Yasha, those work best on a full stomach," Karl said, his face in a snarl. "But yes, I am trying everything."

Eventually, the orchestra rehearsed every day except Sunday, sometimes twice a day. Eliasberg often rehearsed by section, so as not to tax the strength of everyone.

And then a miracle happened. Suddenly, toward the end of the month, the bread rations were doubled. Slowly the food situation improved, though never to the comfort level of the musicians.

"They gave us extra food in the canteen at the Pushkin Theater," Katya Medvedeva told me one day. "The soup had more beans—and some wheat germ. Plus, they had beets!"

Still, hunger and cold haunted their efforts. One day, pianist Alexander Kamensky tried to warm his hands by putting two hot bricks on either side of the piano to generate some heat. The result was to deaden the sounds coming from his instrument. Eliasberg had trouble containing his anger.

"Comrades, we are not here to serenade death!" he exclaimed. "We are here to defy it. Put some energy into this. Show the world what we are made of! This symphony is about us."

To my surprise, he then asked me to address the orchestra, to explain the symphony. Having seen the symphony's performance in Moscow, I recalled a speech I gave then, and reprised it now.

"This music is about those days full of rage, our sorrow, and our tears. It is about defenders of Leningrad killed in combat outside the city, and those who fell on its streets and died in its houses. It is music played in their memory, in tribute and in sorrow, and in determination to win."

Eliasberg looked up at me, a crooked smile on his face. He addressed the orchestra.

"Now play!"

Often, long after most of the staff had left Radio House, I would see Eliasberg in his office, studying the score again. I imagined him thinking about new ways to get them to perform. Exacting, he wanted the notes played crisply, with attention to the rhythm. He wanted the wind instruments to breathe together, and the strings to play in uniform strokes. He told me he was frustrated the orchestra sounded so ragtag, so sloppy.

"One day, the cellos were so discordant I pulled Brik aside and asked for his help," Eliasberg told me. "I asked him if there was any way to get them to play together."

"And what did he say?"

Eliasberg gave me one of his lopsided smiles.

"Apparently the cellists like to play with their coats on, to stay warm. He hinted that I might get a better sound if I make sure their instruments are out in the open, not smothered with wool."

Out of the blue one day, he asked me how I thought we could get the oboes to play as one.

"That section has one woman. Katya Medvedeva is new to the oboe but wise to human nature. Ask her to smile between sets. Even when they are hungry, men will follow a woman's smile."

"Seriously? You think the smile of a woman who has no philharmonic experience will energize this orchestra to play a masterpiece?"

"Try me if you don't."

Throughout rehearsals, Eliasberg kept pushing the musicians for perfection, even as earlier concerts had exhausted them. Garegin told me of one encounter he had with the conductor after rehearsal.

"We must have a break from music," Garegin said. "It is too much."

"The only break from music," replied Eliasberg, "is death."

A low point came when Arseny Petrov, a 63-year-old drummer who had played for the tsar's orchestra as a young man, was late for rehearsal. I was there that day. Petrov apologized, saying he missed the morning rehearsal to bury his wife. Karl was unmoved, or anyway pretended to be.

"This must not happen again," he said. "Arseny will lose his extra bread rations today."

I was stunned. I imagine everyone was. I could see on their faces that they were judging him.

"All of you, listen," he said. "We have a symphony to prepare. Yes, it is complex and difficult. Yes, we are working in harsh conditions, with no heat and little light or food. Yes, sometimes your wife or husband or child will die. But if we don't practice, we won't be able to perform. And if we are unable to perform, we will rob the people of Leningrad of this great moment of triumph. It is on our shoulders, it is our mission and our destiny, to lift this city to victory, no matter our hardships."

On the day when Dhazdat failed to report to rehearsal, Eliasberg nearly exploded in a rage that in no way looked healthy. He asked me to gather a search party, and this I did, asking Yuri and other broadcasters to participate. We fanned out across the city, each taking different routes, trying to find the big Ukrainian who had warmed all of our hearts.

"He left yesterday—he said he was going to sleep at the Radio House—and we have not seen him since," his panicked father told me when I went to the Zelensky apartment. "Now you tell us he did not come to rehearsal. Praise God, please find him." Beside him, Nataliya cried quietly to herself.

"We will look for him," I said. I ran to find Eliasberg and we retraced the steps that Dhazdat might have taken the night before. Soon we came to a church awning piled high with corpses. I guess families had dropped relatives there, believing the bodies would be blessed by religion. We were just about to turn away when Karl saw what looked like Dhazdat's broad chest.

"Soldier, here, help me move this body," Eliasberg yelled to a nearby military man.

Two soldiers came to help, and we watched as they moved corpses out of the way and unearthed Dhazdat's body. They placed it gently on the ground. Eliasberg began to cry at the loss of this great drummer. I was too shocked to cry. All I could think about was that day when he burst into the radio room to tell the NKVD that they could not arrest the head of our tribe. I bowed my head as tears rolled down my face, looking at the body. Suddenly, it seemed to twitch.

"Karl, look!" I yelled. "Look, Dhazdat is moving his finger, as if he wants to play the drums."

"He's alive!" he screamed. "We must get him to the Astoria. Soldiers, please help me."

One soldier made a harness out of his belt and lifted Dhazdat's head on his shoulder. The other wrapped his feet in a sweater and lifted from the back. Eliasberg and I tried to hold up his sagging back in the middle. Even though he had lost so much weight, he was still a big man. By the time we got to the hospital, Dhazdat's finger was no longer moving. Perhaps it had been a spasm, I thought. Please show us again, I prayed.

"You must admit this man," Karl said to the nurse on duty, with the nameplate Svetlana Magareva.

"I'm sorry, but we are full," she said. "We have no more beds."

"You must make an accommodation. You cured me—I am the musical director of the Radio Orchestra of Leningrad and we are to perform Shostakovich's Symphony No. 7 in three months' time. I was a patient here. You saved me. I know you can save him. He is my drummer. We cannot perform without him. Please let me talk to the director."

Svetlana rolled her eyes. She told me later that she thought Dhazdat was beyond saving, but never ruled out miracles. Once, an emaciated mother and her infant were brought in. They had been found in a deserted apartment. The mother had run out of milk so she had opened a vein, and the baby sucked greedily of her blood. By the time they were found, the mother was all but dead. Eventually, mother and baby survived. Now, Svetlana left to find the hospital director as the two soldiers lowered Dhazdat onto one of the gurneys stacked in a hallway. Eliasberg bit his fingernails. We sat and waited.

"Thank you," he told the soldiers. "We could not have carried him without you. Come by Radio House. I will give you tickets to the concert. You will see the character of the man you saved."

The two soldiers looked at each other with doubt, probably dubious this corpse could come to life again. He was heavy, and they had carried him halfway across town. Politely, they thanked Eliasberg for the offer. They left just as Hospital Director Anna Petrova approached.

"Conductor Eliasberg, how good to see you up and about," she said. "You are a living example of what medicine can accomplish, against the odds."

"Director Petrova, you must help me," he said. "This man is my drummer. We are preparing a concert of Shostakovich's Symphony No. 7, about the Nazi invasion of Leningrad."

"I've heard of the symphony," she said. Looking at Dhazdat, she asked, "He is that important?"

"It is hard to imagine how we could perform without him."
She nodded.

"We will find room," she said. "We will give him all the vitamin cocktail and glucose and heat and food we can find." She looked doubtful he would breathe again. So was I.

"We will try, Mr. Eliasberg," she said. "For you, and for Leningrad, we will try."

In early summer they moved rehearsals from Pushkin to the Philharmonia, where they would perform. The windows broken by bomb blasts were still in need of repair. The temperature outside was still bitter cold, especially for those suffering from chronic hunger. The reed of Viktor Kozlov's clarinet froze, and his lips were cracking, and he told me it made it difficult to grip the mouthpiece.

News from the military front was not good. One of Germany's top generals, Erich von Manstein, was rolling forward with a massive military might, on the brink of taking the port at

Sevastopol in Ukraine, home of the Black Sea Fleet. Leningraders felt a special kinship for the port city.

"There is great alarm in my heart," Georgi Knyazev wrote me. "There is bitter fighting at Sevastopol." Three days later, the port fell. Some feared the Nazis would now move north, toward Moscow. Eliasberg worried they would unleash a new assault on Leningrad, just before the concert.

"Soon, the enemy will start another offensive against us," he told me. "You'll see. They do not want this concert to play." I wondered where Nikolai was, what he was doing.

Dhazdat was in intensive care. He was still unconscious, but alive. Nurses had to clean him daily, to turn him in his bed, to attend to his toilet needs. Nataliya told me she visited every day. She always held his hand. She wondered if he felt her touch, but she doubted it. He never moved.

"I cannot think what more to do," she told me, her voice cracking. "He never responds."

"Bring Anastasia," I said. "Maybe he will wake for her."

The next day, Nataliya brought four-year-old Anastasia with her to the hospital. Dhazdat's daughter still had not spoken since the bombing of the children's evacuation train, but she made lots of sounds, and with the addition of some wheatgerm Nataliya brought home from the Leningrad State Pediatric Institute, she seemed to be able to keep her eyes open longer and was sleeping less.

"This is where Papa is," Nataliya had explained as they walked up the steps of the Astoria. "He may be sleeping when we get there, okay?"

Anastasia nodded. When they arrived in his room, and she saw her father sleeping on a bed, tears slid down her face. Nataliya told me she pulled up a chair and placed Anastasia on her lap. She told her to be a good girl while they tried to help Papa wake up. The child nodded. Then she placed Anastasia's hand in Dhazdat's palm and prayed. Anastasia made giggly noises and they both waited.

Within a half hour, Nataliya noticed Anastasia had fallen asleep. She also noticed Dhazdat had opened his eyes. Mother and son smiled at each other as Dhazdat squeezed Anastasia's hand, and she woke. Nataliya told me she had never seen such wonder spread over a child's face, like the sun rising.

"Papa!" she squeaked. "Papa, you are awake!"

"And you can speak," he said, his voice a raspy whisper.

Nataliya said Dhazdat tousled Anastasia's hair as tears slid down his face.

"God kept me alive for this moment. We will recover together."

Anastasia leaped into his arms.

Nataliya left father and daughter in an embrace, and went to find a nurse. When she returned, Anastasia had curled up next to Dhazdat in the bed, her little body warming his side.

"Well look who's awake," said Director Petrova. "I imagine you are hungry."

Dhazdat nodded, and Dr. Petrova turned to a nurse and ordered the usual post-recovery meal.

"You will have to start slowly, eating soft foods, to restart your engines," she warned. "But I think now we can move you to a regular room, and put you on a path to recovery. I'm glad you made it," she said. "Conductor Eliasberg would have never forgiven me if we had failed you."

"Thank you," was all he could say.

That day, and for the next few weeks, Nataliya told me, Dhazdat ate three meals a day and learned to manage his own toilet. Nataliya came every day, as before, sometimes with Anastasia, sometimes with Vasily. One day Dhazdat asked if they had heard from Katarina. Vasily looked at Nataliya, who nodded her approval. He gave Dhazdat her latest letter, which he had been carrying in his pocket.

My dearest Dhazdat, we are on our way.

When I heard this story, I wondered if Shostakovich had delivered my note to Katarina, or if she had decided on her own to come home. At any rate, after six weeks in the hospital, Dhazdat returned to Radio House to a hero's welcome. He was still weak, and might have stayed longer, but the hospital needed his bed. Pretending the worst was behind him, we put up a big sign on the front of the building saying, '*Dobro Pozhalovat Domoy*, Welcome Home'. I gave Dhazdat greens from my young friend, author of the Vegetable Man. And Vadim even managed to find some cheese and crackers for a little celebration. Dhazdat thanked us all, but I could tell he had no energy for socializing. All he really wanted to do was to be reunited with his family, and his drums.

"Good to start practicing," Eliasberg said as he and I made the rounds. "Rehearsals tomorrow start at 10 a.m. We perform on August 9."

"August 9?" said Dhazdat, looking at Karl with incredulity. "That's only a few weeks from now!"

"True. Here is your copy of the score."

Dhazdat smiled weakly at me as if to say, Karl Eliasberg, ever the taskmaster.

"Karl, Director Petrova said you never would have forgiven her if the hospital had failed to revive me. Whatever did you say to her?"

"You mean no one's told you?" he said.

Dhazdat shook his head. Eliasberg looked at me, and I nodded. Dhazdat deserved to know.

"I found you on a pile of corpses, left for dead. But Olga saw your fingers moving. And she thought you were trying to tell us that you could still play the drums. And so, in a few weeks, you will."

FIFTEEN

The Poets Circle 3
June 1942

Katarina looked radiant. I looked around the room and decided the rest of us looked bruised, as if we'd survived a heavyweight prize fight. I knew she had suffered, had been tested and challenged. But for several months, she had eaten regularly and lived without bombs. And it showed on her face.

For her part, Katarina looked around the room, her smile of reunion guarded. I remember having a similar feeling, on returning from Moscow with the baby. I couldn't wait to embrace the familiar. But I was shocked at the physical state of deterioration. Sometimes I think that's why I started the cleanup campaign. It had sickened me to walk the streets, seeing landmarks in disrepair, sidewalks pockmarked by corpses, a city without its soul. Once the public squares were cleared, I was happier.

"Tell us everything," said Luby. "How was the trip home?"

"We came by rail. There is only one a day, and it creeps along. Quite a few times we had to stop for repairs after Germans bombed our train. Once, during a bomb attack, Pavel started to shake, as if he were reliving that traumatic ride out of Leningrad when the Germans strafed that train of escaping children. He was so brave then. Now, he is skittish. I put my hand on his forehead and felt fever."

"Why don't you bring him over to play with Rahil?" Luby suggested. "Might be good for both of them. Two little boys who are surviving war."

"Rahil?" Katarina said, a blank look on her face.

Luby and I looked at each other and started laughing.

"It's a long story," I said. "Basically Igor Brik, the cellist, rescued a six-year-old child named Rahil whose parents were killed by German bombs. I asked Luby to become the child's grandmother."

"They all live with me now," said Luby. "Andrei too. Also Viktoria's brother Rodion. If called on, I tell people Igor and Andrei were my late husband's nephews. It's surprising how few have asked."

"I sometimes think war has overwhelmed the bureaucrats," I said. "Blissfully, they have no time to keep records. Perhaps that's why they haven't noticed how much is missing from our lives."

"I guess the concept of family has changed too fast for them," Viktoria said. "Especially with Olga orchestrating living arrangements. We are all orphans now, in some sense, with pieces missing from our genealogy."

Katarina nodded.

"When our train pulled into Leningrad, I was shocked at how different the city looked. So many of its trees had been cut down, maybe for firewood? And it's so quiet. There is none of the hustle and bustle, none of the energy of a major metropolis going about its day. And few smile. People seem all hunched over, as if it is less taxing to walk closer to the ground."

"In many ways the city has moved underground," Viktoria agreed. "At the Hermitage, we are still housing more than 1,000 people in the vaults, along with artifacts too large to be evacuated. Some are taking up poetry or dabbling in sketches, trying to keep their creative minds afire. I imagine it will take time for them to adjust to the sunlight once we are freed from quarantine. But I believe these underground creators will emerge the most resilient, with life preserved and projects renewed."

"How very interesting," said Anna. "It makes me wonder if art is best done away from the sun. Maybe there is something private about the need to create, which at its core is the merging of talent and materials. The poet gives voice to feelings, which are but fleeting impressions, kept inside."

"Anna that is brilliant," I said. "I've been struck lately at the power of words to combat evil. Maybe because they are authentic representations of our inner voices."

"I am afraid of my words," said Luby. "I suppose that is why I use puppets. They can speak for me. They can tell stories and make silly jokes that prompt the audience to laugh and make them nostalgic for happy times. If I speak, well, I might say the wrong thing."

"I feel the same way about my comedy shows," said Maria. "Better to play the fool than be one."

We were silent then, musing about the dangers in our country of speaking too candidly.

"What was it like living in Kuibyshev?" Luby finally asked, perhaps to change the subject.

"Sometimes I felt like I was on a stage set," she said, directing her comments to Luby and Maria. "It was as if we were living with props for furniture and other actors for relatives. It didn't feel real, somehow. And there was no sense of home. Everyone you met was an evacuee from somewhere else—Moscow, Leningrad, even Ukraine—so no one belonged to the place."

"That's funny," said Maria, "it sometimes feels like a stage set here too, except the backdrop is barren and the scenery stark."

"Seeing you makes me leap with hope," said Viktoria. "You look so beautiful."

I agreed.

"How was the reunion with family?"

"My mother Lara died just days before we arrived home," Katarina said. "I had hoped to get back in time to say goodbye. Yesterday I asked to visit her grave. My sister Mariska said that was out of the question, that the Nazis bomb the cemetery regularly. She called it a psychological weapon against those of us grieving, to remind us of our impotence. What words could combat that kind of evil?"

"Words of hope," said Luby. "We are here, we are fighting to survive, we are optimistic about the future. And when we win the war, the Hitlerites will stop bombing our cemeteries and we can go honor our dead. But enough of war. What I want to hear about was the reunion with Dhazdat!"

I watched as the wonder spread across Katarina's face. Then she choked up a bit, with a spray of tears behind her smile, before she told us the story.

"That was like a movie too," she began.

"Pavel suggested he and I hold hands as we stood on the doorstep of the Zelensky home. His gesture touched me, as he had spoken to me so little since my decision to move us to Kuibyshev. Anichka, Dhazdat's sister, opened the door and screamed. Then the rest of the family, all except Dhazdat, came out to see what had occasioned all the fuss. There were lots of hugs and tears. I looked into the apartment and saw Dhazdat asleep on a chair. He looked so shrunken to me, so unexpectedly small. I was shocked when they told me the Hospital of Starvation had released him. I shuddered to think what he looked like when he was admitted."

I gave Maria a look that said, 'Better she never saw that'.

"Once inside, Pavel started tickling Anastasia, but their grandfather shushed them. I think he wanted the reunion of husband and wife to be sacred. Nataliya pushed me toward him. I knelt down and put my face next to his, slowing my breathing to match his. And when Dhazdat finally woke, and looked at me, it was like watching the sun rising in the West. Radiance spread over his eyes and into his mouth. He kissed me with the tenderness of a wounded animal. And when I kissed back, he responded like an old lion."

Luby was clapping. She was a sucker for a beautiful story, I thought.

My sister was dabbing at her wet tears.

"That is so beautiful!" she said. "It is almost worth having a war for that moment."

"A bunch of sentimentalists," said Anna disparagingly. But I could tell she was moved.

As for Viktoria, she went over and hugged Katarina.

"Thank you for bringing me hope," she said. "I now believe in the power of reunion."

"Katarina, you would love these letters Viktoria has been getting from Boris," I said.

"Boris! You mean you two...I mean I knew you were attracted but...so you blossomed?"

"If you can describe a pen-pal correspondence as a courtship, I guess that is ours," Viktoria said, blushing. "His magnetism comes through so clearly in the writing—his deep reverence for the history of human beings and the things they leave behind is so appealing. I adore his ideas. But I can hardly remember him in person. Will I find him charming when I see him after the war?"

"I seem to recall he was pretty charming in person too," Katarina said, and she reminded Viktoria about those days just after the invasion when volunteers were cataloging all the artifacts, in an atmosphere of frenzy and shared hope that one day there would be a reunion of art and patron.

"Gosh that seems so long ago," Viktoria said. Her face darkened. "Did I tell you, Olga, that Orbeli has been admitted to a sanitarium? He'll be examined and perhaps treated for dementia."

"So does that mean you will be ascending to the top post?" Even as I spoke, I wondered if this was too ghoulish, like dancing on the grave of a dear colleague whose post you covet.

"How marvelous," said Maria. "I'll get the champagne."

"That would be premature," said Viktoria. "In fact, the board of directors has cooked up charges against me for losing the list of treasures sent to their hiding place. I fear there will be a trial."

"A trial!" said Katarina. "But you didn't lose the list. Don't you remember, you gave it to Orbeli, who gave it to Boris."

"I do, of course I do, but I'm not sure it matters," said Viktoria. "The board seems keen to prosecute me."

Anna was the first to speak.

"I think we'll need something stronger than champagne," she said.

I nodded.

"I think there's some vodka somewhere."

After that, we grew pensive, and quiet.

"I never told you something," Katarina said, turning to look at Viktoria. "Olga knows but no one else does. Now maybe it's time everyone did." She paused, looking down at her drink. "I was never on parental leave from the Leningrad Ballet. Dima fired me. For getting pregnant."

"Bastards, bastards, all of them!" said Anna. "There is no sense of style in the male heart."

"Do you want to return to the ballet?" asked Maria.

"Not as a dancer, but as a teacher," she said. "Someone asked me recently if I knew the difference between a master and a novice. The answer is that the master has failed at a task—dance, or art, or music—more times than the novice has even tried. I want to impart what I've learned to a new generation. And I want to loosen the bounds of Russian ballet, to make it more fun, more joyous."

"How on earth will you do that?" asked Viktoria.

"After the war, Daria plans to return to Leningrad. We are plotting a campaign to replace Dima at the Ballet. We need a director who feels passion for both the dance and the dancers. And I tell you this Viktoria. Don't wait as long as I did. Fight for what you have earned. I will help you."

I looked around and considered this circle of artists, surviving Leningrad's ordeal.

"Anna, you are the only one of us who has lived through this war alone," I said. "Does it change your perspective?"

"I was better alone," she said. "Maybe artists need solitude for their thoughts, their music, their art. People need each other, I know, but marriage is a demanding queen. During my first marriage, I wrote a poem about my husband. 'He loved three things in life: evening prayers, white peacocks and old maps of America. He hated it when children cried, and I was his wife.' Now I am married to my country, under attack by our enemy, living in this terrible ghost that used to be our city."

"It's true, some days I am grateful that Boris is not here," said Viktoria. "It is too much weight, too much of an obligation, to be responsible for one more person's happiness."

"I love caring for someone else," said Maria. "It makes me happy."

"But Anna, living alone for a lifetime is such a dark vision!" said Viktoria. "You are always the one that urges us as women to overcome barriers. Katarina has already volunteered to help me to climb the ladder to the top of the Hermitage. Won't you help me too?"

"I know nothing of ladders, dear, nor of corporate governance or hierarchical executives," said Anna. "But I know much about human nature. So if that is of use to you, yes, count me in."

After that, it seemed like everyone was talking all at once.

"Wait!" I exclaimed, laughing. "Let's take one injustice at a time. Katarina, go."

"For a long time I chafed under Dima's control," she said. "He is dictatorial, and sometimes unreasoning. There are many generations of ballerinas who feel the same way. I know that Russian ballet is exceptionally demanding, but his style leaves scars,

scars of the mind and soul. And I am excited to heal them for the coming artists, to give them space and history to create anew."

I thought about my own scars, wondering if they would ever heal.

"I have something to confess too," I said. "I never told you this, Luby, but remember that salami I brought for your new family?" She nodded. I looked down, unsure if I could continue.

"I got it by bargaining myself to the grocer, a vile man who was very rough. Months later, when I was in the hospital, a nurse's assistant offered me a slice of salami, and I was so revolted I exploded in rage. The poor nurse, he was just trying to feed me. But it just came out in a torrent. I was filled with shame. Nikolai was fighting for our country, and I was negotiating for food."

There was a long silence.

"If it helps," Luby said, "that salami saved us from starvation. Igor said it made all the difference."

I looked up in wonder.

"Really?" I asked.

"Really," she said. "You can ask him."

"We all did what we had to do," said Maria. "It was war. I guess it still is."

I had one more confession to make.

"Oh Maria, I'm so sorry I teased you about your relationship with the baker."

"Olga, I never offered myself to him, did you really think I had? I just flirted."

I nodded. "Do you forgive me?"

She smiled—and when Maria smiles it is a radiant thing to behold—and came to my side for a hug. It felt nice to be caressed. The baby's coos are a wonder, so reaffirming, but it was nice to have flesh on flesh, or as one of my friends once said, wrinkles on wrinkles. Soon all of them joined our circle, offering hugs, kisses and an occasional finger-wagging.

"If you ever again avoid coming to visit us because you have no food to offer, I will have to box you around the ears. Or maybe I'll have Rodion do it. He's very strong now, you know."

"Thanks to you," Viktoria said to Luby. Looking at me, she added, "Olga, if you hadn't done what you did, Rodion might not be alive now. Try to forgive yourself."

I felt tears forming then. Was it possible to get past a trauma? Nikolai had forgiven me for whatever he saw in my eyes that day before he returned to the front. Now my circle had as well. Maybe my guilt could end now. Maybe the war would end soon too.

With that, we dove in, talking about Viktoria's upcoming trial, divvying up the work to be done.

Katarina volunteered to testify about how she and her sister made the list of treasures.

"I don't want to pledge Mariska until I talk to her, but I imagine she would as well," said Katarina. "We could talk about how instrumental you were in spearheading that Herculean effort to preserve our national heritage, how you would never do anything to bring dishonor on the institution."

"I have been a friend to Joseph Orbeli for more than twenty years," said Anna. "Find out what sanitarium he's in, and I can visit him."

Viktoria smiled. "Good idea. Maybe I'll go with you. I actually miss the old guy."

"I can't imagine the charges will stick," said Luby, "but the larger task will be to win the directorship. In my experience, men never relinquish power unless they are cornered."

Viktoria nodded.

"Any ideas?"

"First, I'm not sure it's a good idea to embarrass Orbeli publicly. He has a much-deserved reputation in this town for protecting the museum from political interference, and many, many friends. Better not to testify against him but to work quietly behind the scenes to have the charges dropped."

"I like that idea," I said. "But who do we know who would be willing to talk to the NKVD about the injustice of these charges against Viktoria? And don't look at me. I tried that once."

There was quiet for a time, and then my sister spoke up. She rarely did during these gatherings, I had noticed, but when she did, it was usually of import.

"Someone who is dying," said Maria. "Someone who knows they will not live long, and is willing to risk whatever torture or imprisonment the police throw at them, to go out a hero."

We all looked at her with astonishment.

"Do you have anyone in mind?" I asked.

"I do," said Maria. "You interviewed him once on your program. The guy in the wheelchair, who runs the Academy of Sciences, I forget his name."

"Georgi Knayazev," I said, amazed at this information. "But what makes you think he is dying?"

Maria dropped her eyes at first, then looked up.

"When Garegin first took ill, I took him to the clinic to see if they could give him some vitamins. Knayazev was there. I heard the doctor tell Georgi that there was nothing more they could do."

"That could mean anything," I said.

"Olga, he looked so thin and weak. I'm not sure what else it could have meant."

"Let me reach out to him," I said. "He is a cultural treasure. How awful it would be to lose him."

"In the meantime," said Luby, "let's talk about how to get Viktoria the dictatorship, I mean the directorship."

Everyone laughed at that, especially Katarina.

"It seems to me that networking is the key," said Luby. "During this war, Viktoria, you have in essence assembled your own team. You hired that architect, what was her name, Natasha something, and a group of nimble climbers to disguise the Heritage roofline to prevent Nazi bombs. You hired that old soldier to do cleanup in the square outside the museum, and he commandeered a platoon of Grannies to remove ice, frozen mounts of trash, even sewage and corpses."

"Pavel Gubchevsky," Viktoria said, looking at Luby in wonder. Probably she thinks 72-year-olds lose their memory, I thought, but Luby was different than most.

"These are your people," said Luby. "They are your network. Go to them, talk to them. I promise you, if they feel about your abilities as we do, they will summon an army for you. And never forget that you have Boris in your corner. He is not just a romantic interest. He is an enormously influential figure at the museum. He may even be the presumptive new director."

"My goodness Luby, you are so inspirational," I said. "I have to have you on the show again. Perhaps you can tell another puppet story."

"Maybe we can perform a radio show," she said. "It would be telling a story but without the puppets, for radio. I can ask the boys to help me with the voices."

"Do you have a story in mind?"

"Not yet, but I bet Katarina might," said Luby.

"Me?" she said. "The only stories I know are of *Cinderella* and *Romeo and Juliet*."

"What about the story you wrote us about, about how you and your son were stranded in Moscow, without papers or food, and were rescued by a kind captain in the Red Army?"

"Do you think it would get Captain Parfionov in trouble?" Katarina asked. "He put us up in the women's quarters for several nights. He called it 'highly irregular.' Apparently some in the military were unhappy with him over that. I'd hate to cause him any more trouble."

"All the more reason to tell the story," I said. "Besides, Parfionov and others in the military band have been recruited to play with the Radio Leningrad Orchestra. They are heroes twice— once for protecting our homeland, and again for helping bring the Shostakovich Symphony to life."

Katarina smiled. "Luby, how about if I bring Pavel with me, and he can play with the boys while you and I work on a script?"

"And I can go talk to General Govorov," I said. "I think a gentle reminder that our soldiers sometimes depart from the rules to rescue Soviet citizens might win his permission."

"Well then I better go with you," said Maria. "Olga, I've never known you to be gentle with anyone!"

I laughed out loud. "I suppose subtlety is not my strongest chess piece."

"Is the baby sleeping?" asked Katarina. "I'd love a chance to meet her."

I went into the bedroom and cradled Abigail in my arms. She woke at my touch, smiled and giggled.

"Another of your family has come home," I whispered to her. "I'd like you to meet her."

I walked with her in my arms back to the couches where my friends sat, and let them coo over her again. She actually linked eyes with Katarina—sometimes, I think babies are drawn to beauty.

"She's so much bigger than when I last saw her," said Viktoria.

"And she looks so much more like Nikolai," said Maria.

"You have no idea," I said, "how happy that makes me."

SIXTEEN

The Trial
July 1942

The trial of Viktoria Provnoskiya began two weeks later. We were all shocked, none more than Orbeli, that authorities were accusing her of stealing from the Hermitage to feed her brother Rodion. Everyone at Luby's house—and at Viktoria's—was terrified the blame would settle on their heads as well. I felt guilty, for roping all these people in on a conspiracy to feed Rodion. I missed Nikolai, wondering what he would say, how he would handle the situation. Plus I noticed that my pride was wounded. I had felt such hope after our cleanup campaign. Now my feelings were smothered in despair over this charge of larceny. So often the way with Russian history, I thought, like a roller coaster of emotion, followed by a crash landing.

I reached out to Anna, who of all my friends best understood the cruel logic of the Stalin regime. We took a walk along the Neva River.

"It puzzles me that they arranged a public trial," I said. "Usually they just send people away."

"Yes, it is odd," she said. "Maybe they want to make an example of her. Or maybe it's Orbeli they want to incriminate. Or maybe they want to tarnish the reputation of the whole Hermitage."

"That does not really narrow it down."

She gave me a smile of irony that suited her demeanor.

"Have you reached out to Boris?"

I nodded.

"I am waiting to hear back. But I'm not sure what he could do without damaging his own position. Orbeli thinks we should all attend, like a Greek chorus of defenders, rallying to her side."

"That would be amusing. Also dangerous. Viktoria thinks Orbeli is losing his mind."

She paused, deep in thought, only the waves and our shoe soles interrupting the quiet.

"I have an idea," she said, finally. "Stalin is motivated by vindictive passion. He will wait ten, twenty, thirty years, as long as it takes, secretly plotting to bring an enemy down in an exquisitely appropriate revenge. When the moment is right, he will pounce. But there is one flaw in his modus operandi."

"You must be kidding," I said, incredulously. "He has already killed so many at a whim, abused so many others. He killed my son. He tortured yours. What leverage could we possibly have?"

"His vanity," she said. "Stalin wants to be remembered as the man who won this war, who finally vanquished the evil Adolf Hitler after years of the Nazis terrorizing all of Europe. And there is only one group of people who can cement his victorious reputation in the eyes of history."

"The Nazis?"

"Hardly," she said. "No, only the Americans."

"The Americans?"

Anna nodded. "History will say that they were the ones who came to Europe's rescue, all those Yanks in their clean uniforms, fresh-faced and free from tribal rivalries, coming in ignorance to save the Western world. And if they sing Stalin's praises, everyone else will nod their heads in agreement."

"But how could that possibly affect Viktoria's trial?" I asked. Even as I said it, I realized what Anna was suggesting. I had a connection to the American president's top aide. And so did Viktoria.

"You can't mean that little Mr. Hopkins?" I asked.

"I know it's a long shot," she said, looking pensive. "But it's the only shot we have."

And with that, we divvied up the work. Anna would contact everyone she knew in Leningrad who knew an American, and that turned out to be a surprising number. And I would write letters. At the beginning of the war, Viktoria had led a guided tour of the Hermitage for a visiting American delegation. I would write them now, especially Hopkins, who seemed to take a shine to her. I would also write to Arturo Toscanini and Eleanor Roosevelt and anyone else I could remember from the story of Symphony No. 7's travels around the world, including Winston Churchill. Then we would wait.

I also decided to pray. Before the Revolution, our city boasted nearly 800 churches, a dozen monasteries, 1700 clergy and almost as many monks. Now there were only 21 churches left and none taught religion to children. Most of the famous churches had been closed. After the Revolution, the Church of the Savior had become Police Precinct No. 28. The Church of Spilled Blood was being used, ironically, as a morgue. The instruments of God were being turned into vessels of war. But something about the Siege was pushing me towards religion. With Nikolai still on the front, and Viktoria facing a show trial, it seemed a good time to seek God's blessings, even if I had to just pray by myself, at home. I just hoped that after all these years, God still spoke Russian.

On the morning of the trial, a large crowd gathered at the courthouse. Orbeli had insisted that we all mobilize, and after initially fighting him on it, Anna relented. What difference did it make, she told me, if the Kremlin already had all our names and addresses anyway. And so the friends and family of Viktoria Provnoskiya gathered to watch as the Kremlin prosecuted her for a burglary that never took place, and which she never would have committed anyway. Her mother Nina sat on an aisle, looking for all the world like Madame Defarge in Charles Dickens' *A Tale of Two Cities*. In the novel, Defarge sat knitting into the wool the names of all the enemies of the state she thought should be executed. I wondered if Nina, like Defarge, was compiling a mental list of those who had wronged her daughter.

For the first few days, prosecutors laid out their case. This was highly unusual in the Soviet Union, where trials were more often conducted in secret, the better to convict the defendant. Maybe Anna was right, I thought, maybe Stalin was hoping to curry favor with an American audience.

Whatever the motive, they alleged that Viktoria had overseen the evacuation of the art treasures, and had kept her brother Rodion alive during the war by selling some of the art to black marketeers. The prosecutors made no mention of Rodion's whereabouts at Luby's house, and for this I was grateful, though guarded. How long before they threw this into the mix? As I sat listening, I had to marvel at the literary genius of the Kremlin's masterminds. Like Dostoevsky, these agents of propaganda wove together a tale that was at once improbable, yet psychologically compelling.

Viktoria's defense was allowed a modest rebuttal, though hampered by strict rules against claiming innocence. This, of course, was the most maddening part of the whole process. Orbeli testified that he had personally overseen the removal of the art from the walls of the Hermitage, and that none of it had gone missing. Georgi Knayazev, the wheelchair-ridden director of the National Archives, backed him up, testifying that Orbeli had deliberately sent the list of boxed-up artifacts into exile with the art, the better to keep it out of the hands of the Nazis, should they capture Leningrad.

"So the only list you know of is in hiding, with the art?" sneered the lead prosecutor, Gavriil Chaika. "And you know of nothing that was stolen for the black market?"

"There was no burglary."

"That is not for you to assert!" said the prosecutor. "That is a judgment for the court."

Knayazev put his hands on the arms of his wheelchair, obviously straining to rise. He pushed himself up, his weakened legs wobbling, until he was standing.

"As I stand on these crippled legs, I swear that nothing was taken. Nothing is missing."

A frightened hush fell over the courtroom. In all my years in the Soviet Union, I had never seen such a public display of bravery against the state. I looked over at Maria, who had tears in her eyes. Viktoria looked about to burst, with worry or gratitude I could not tell. Orbeli looked morose, as if he had messed up. Knayazev crashed back down into his wheelchair.

The prosecutor looked as if he was going to assail the witness, contesting his version of history. But a voice from the bench stopped him in his tracks.

"The court will adjourn for the day," announced the judge, a Communist Party functionary named Panas Golubev. "You will be notified when we resume."

Luby looked as if she were about to faint, but steadied herself on Anna's sleeve. Maybe it was a good thing, I thought, that Andrei and Igor had decided to stay home. In a courtroom where accusations of actions against the state were flying, open attendance by two friends suspected of being homosexual lovers—and child kidnappers too—was hardly a smart strategy. Viktoria looked drawn as she was marched out of the courtroom, likely back to her prison cell. I hoped she would not be beaten into making a confession, but I was not overly confident. I remembered how it felt to be jailed in a confined space, trapped with neither hope nor a future, fearing menace. Now, I felt stale air choking the courtroom, as if we were all exhaling at once. I couldn't get outside fast enough.

"Messy," I said to Anna.

"But interesting," she replied. "Let's walk. Tell me who you've heard back from."

"Hopkins telegrammed first. He said he would work with the U.S. embassy in Moscow and Winston Churchill's people in London to see what they could do."

"Was he optimistic?"

"Not overly. He said President Roosevelt was not well, and without his vigor, not much was getting done. But he remembered Viktoria from the tour and of course he remembered me, and said he would try. From Eleanor Roosevelt's office I got a form letter, thanking me for writing. Somehow I do not think it will be the diplomats who can save her. I wonder if they have ever saved anyone."

"Have you heard from Boris?"

"Not at all. Not from Boris, nor Toscanini. How about your contacts, did any respond?"

"I have a friend whose mother was an American. She came here in the 1910s, part of the Greenwich Village free love movement so enamored with the Communist Party. Unlike most, who grew disillusioned, she stayed, married and produced what the Americans call red-diaper babies. Anyway, my friend said he still writes to his American cousins, one of whom works for the Smithsonian Institution, a museum. His cousin said he'd be happy to 'push from my end', as he put it. Plus I reached out to the Sorbonne, where Viktoria took her art history degree. I'm hoping they will help."

"Anna, what do you think the judge's interjection meant?"

"I have no idea. I only hope that remarkable performance by Knayazev prompted a big conversation among the prosecutors. Of course, it could make it worse—they could expand the charges to all of them, or more if they include Orbeli, making conspiracy more plausible."

"The only conspiracy is by the Kremlin and the Communist Party, in accusing Leningrad's young cultural talents of heresy."

"Stalin has always been very adept at destroying the best of each generation."

Court resumed two days later. Yuri had heard that the prosecutors were going to proceed as if nothing had happened. I guess they would just ignore the evidence offered by Knayazev, who sat in the back of the courtroom, a witness to travesty, dying of hunger.

"There is a new witness in the case," said Judge Golubev. "We will hear from him now."

There was a buzz of anticipation. I craned my neck toward the front, eager to see this new witness. When I saw him, I smiled with genuine happiness, more than was appropriate for a show trial.

"State your name please," said the prosecutor.

"My name is Boris Alexander Piotrovsky," said the witness, who seemed to be trying not to look at the accused. Viktoria, however, seemed unable to stop staring at him.

"And your job title?"

"Until the war began, I was the senior archeologist at the ruins in Yerevan, where we are studying the ancient civilizations of the Caucasus. Now I am assigned to the Hermitage Museum."

"And what is your assignment with the Museum?"

"I am guarding the treasures, in their secret hiding place."

"Can you tell us where that is?"

"I am not at liberty to say," Boris replied. "No one who cares about these artifacts will ever disclose their hiding place."

The prosecutor looked like he'd been snubbed. But he carried on.

"You returned to Leningrad for this trial?"

"Yes sir."

"And you left the treasures behind?"

"They are being guarded by officers of the Red Army."

How interesting, I thought, so Boris' trip to Leningrad had been sanctioned. Someone in the Kremlin wanted this trial to end. I looked over at Anna, and she seemed to nod.

"And why did you return?"

Boris looked at Viktoria then, with such conviction, I thought, as sometimes afflicts the smitten. If a look could define a relationship, his said that he loved this woman and would protect her, even if it cost him everything. Viktoria gasped, as if understanding the enormity of the risk he was taking.

In the witness chair, Boris seemed to sit up straighter then, staring at Chaika. Perhaps he felt a certain pride in what he was doing, surmising that if the state decided to ruin him, he would go down with valor. Or maybe his stare was simply meant to intimidate the prosecutor.

"Because I know the defendant to be innocent of these charges," he said. "Here," he said, raising his voice and thrusting a paper through the air. "Here is the list of all the treasures still in their hiding place, the list that Joseph Orbeli handed me just before I boarded the train with them." I thought I saw Luby gasp for air. Really, watching this trial might be one drama too many for her.

"Nice try," sneered the prosecutor, "but how do we know they are still there?"

Boris drew a breath and reached into his pocket, bringing out a fat envelope. He looked at the judge for guidance. Had the two of them conferred? Golubev nodded at the witness to continue.

"Because for the last month, ever since I heard of these unfounded charges against Miss Provnoskiya, I have been photographing the museum's treasures, and developing them in a dark room I set up on the property. It was an arduous process, as I had to unpack every item, then repack it, and I can assure you they had been packaged with meticulous care. But now it is done, and as you will see if you compare them to the list, there is nothing missing. Not one thing."

There was much buzz in the courtroom. What a neat trick, I thought. I hoped it would work.

The prosecutor walked over to the table to confer with the other prosecutors.

"Why should we believe you?" he all but shouted.

"Why shouldn't you?" Boris asked. "I have exhausted myself gathering the evidence. I have risked body and limb to get here. Trying to get into Leningrad while enemy artillery is raining down is not an idle adventure. I have come because I know Viktoria Provnoskiya to be innocent.

"If you want to fault someone for mishandling the treasures, blame me. I'm the one who rode off with them. But don't compound the ordeal of this war—the relentless evil of the Nazis, the cruelties visited on our beloved Leningrad, the sacrifices of a brave people enduring unbelievable hardships—by blaming

upstanding Soviet citizens like Miss Provnoskiya." Here his voice
rose, as if the strength of his vocal cords could free Viktoria from
danger. "She is a great ambassador for our country, and for our
culture. And if you don't believe me, I have testimonials—from the
White House, from 10 Downing Street, from the Louvre and the
Smithsonian and museums around the world. These are our allies,
and they are rooting for us, and Comrade Provnoskiya, to restore
this city to its grandeur after the war ends. With our culture and
our music, our ballet and mostly our art, we will."

He sat back then, looking depleted, even shy. He handed the
letters—the ones Anna and I had solicited from sympathetic
Westerners—to the judge. There was a stunned silence in the
courtroom. And then, one by one, people began to stand up. No
one dared clap or demonstrate, still fearing the retaliation of the
state against an outburst of emotion. But we stood in silent
admiration for what we had just witnessed – an assertion of
principle in the face of politics. How I wished Nikolai had been
with me to watch this. He would have cherished all of it, especially
the valor. I caught Anna's eyes and we smiled. Funny how private
hopes can sometimes turn into public displays. I couldn't wait to
explain to my daughter one day that this was our Leningrad, where
people stood for courage.

"Sit down!" bellowed the judge. "This is a most unusual
display. Most unusual."

He sighed then, as if it took effort to address such a quandary.
He glanced at the letters from our friends abroad, and at the

photographs Boris had taken. He motioned to the prosecutor to approach the bench. There was much nodding and finger-pointing between them. I tried to imagine how they would appease both the people and the politicians, sort of like Solomon choosing between warring parents. Finally the bench conference ended, and Gavriil Chaika announced his next witness.

"We call Joseph Orbeli to the stand again," he said.

I caught Anna's eye in disbelief. I doubted this had been planned. As Orbeli stumbled toward the witness stand, he seemed in a trance.

"Comrade Orbeli, when you evacuated the treasures from the museum into hiding, how many lists of their contents did you make?"

"I'm not sure," he said. "Why do you need to know?"

I had to suppress a laugh at that, though it was no laughing matter. It was clear that our esteemed director was not himself, perhaps even in the early stages of dementia. I was fascinated to watch the intersection between his mental illness and the relentless interrogation of the Soviet state. How would prosecutors deal with answers from a confused mind? Would they even notice—or simply plow ahead with a pre-established narrative, badgering an old man into the confession they needed?

"It's not for you to know why I need this information," said Prosecutor Chaika, his voice rising. "It's a very simple question, Mr. Director, how many lists are there?"

Orbeli's lower lip was trembling, and he started tearing up.

"What kind of lists?" he asked.

"Stop pretending you don't know!" Chaika shouted. "You are the director of the Hermitage Museum, and you oversaw the evacuation of the art treasures. Don't pretend you are too old or feeble to know what I am talking about. Tell this court how many lists you ordered to be kept."

Orbeli was shaking his head violently. In his lap, his hands were shaking. I didn't think it was an act. It was painful to watch. I caught Anna's eye. I'm pretty sure she was horrified too.

"How many?" asked Orbeli, spitting out the two words slowly, separated by long silences.

At this, Chaika looked at the judge, who summoned him to the bench. After an animated conference in hushed tones that excluded the rest of us, Chaika returned to his table and stood up.

"We ask that the charges against Viktoria Provnoskiya be dropped," he said. "We are convinced that she committed no crime, nor Georgi Knayazev who testified here. We make no apology for our actions—we were only pursuing justice for the people—but we see no point in continuing the trial. We will interrogate Comrade Orbeli separately for his contradictions. As for Mr. Piotrovsky, we ask that he return to guarding the treasures as soon as possible, as he is an admirable sentinel."

Judge Golubev nodded, as if the script had been written in advance. He rose and left the room.

I felt a sigh of relief course through my body as I had not known since Abigail's birth. I remember feeling a tremendous relief, that the scars I carried from earlier traumas had not tainted her life. I felt that same kind of emotional release now. Before I realized what was happening, I held my face in my hands, weeping, silently thanking God.

I saw Viktoria released from her handcuffs, but then she disappeared with her jailers, I surmised to process the paperwork for her release. I hoped she did not sign anything incriminating.

Boris still looked as if he had used every ounce of strength in testifying for the woman he loved. Now, he sat in the courtroom, seemingly unable to move. I saw Nina walk over and lead him over to where she was sitting. The two of them sat holding hands, waiting. When Viktoria finally appeared, she hugged first one and then the other, a circle of love that began the process of recovery. I watched from a distance, remembering my own release and the long journey to health that followed. It would take time to recover, I knew, hoping the effort would restore Viktoria to the vibrant, ambitious woman I had admired before the war.

Maybe that was the task for all of us, to heal from these twin wounds of war and accusation. For now, I hoped she and Boris would have time to nurture their love. That night, I wrote a letter to Nikolai, telling him all about the trial, its moments of fear and glory and its surprise ending. Only months later did I learn that Nikolai already knew all about it. Now, I begged him to apply for home leave. I stamped the letter with my secret priority code— hoping to get it by the censors. And I waited, feeling a desperate longing to hold the brains and brawn that was my husband.

SEVENTEEN

The Concert
August 1942

A deep and reverent silence fell on the theater audience as Karl Ilyich Eliasberg emerged from stage left. As he approached the podium, I wondered if our listening audience could sense the hushed gravity of the moment. Later I heard that there was even quiet on the German front, where Colonel Leonid Govorov's plan had worked—he had pounded their lines the night before with such ferocity that on the night of the concert, the Nazis were still too busy counting their losses to launch any new offensives. Thanks to this bit of clever Soviet psychological warfare, and the wizardry of our radio technologists, the Nazis had no choice but to listen to the defiance of Symphony No. 7.

Eliasberg wore a tailcoat, as befits the conductor of a major orchestra. He told me he had been hoarding potato paste for months so he could starch his coat properly. The effort was mostly symbolic, as he hardly cut an elegant figure. The conductor had lost so much weight during the Siege that the outfit hung down from his emaciated frame as it would from a coat hanger. Katya Medvedeva said he looked like 'a wounded bird with wings about to drop at any moment'.

Eliasberg had told me he was worried.

"Shostakovich envisioned this as a piece performed by at least one hundred musicians, maybe 110. When the Americans performed it, they had 120. We have 83. We are short in every section—three in the woodwinds section, seven brass and five strings. We are also down one piano and one percussionist. I'm most worried about the woodwinds and the brass. They are so critical to the invasion theme. The audience has to hear the thunder. And Dhazdat loves the drums, but I wonder if he will have the energy to pound them into submission."

There were question marks among the musicians, about whether we would even make 83.

"Dmitri Chudyenko has tuberculosis," Karl had told me. "Sometimes when he puts his trumpet to his lips, blood drools out. And Igor Brik told me he could be arrested at any moment, for homosexuality. Apparently his talents as a cellist matter not at all to the NKVD."

I knew the orchestra had only gotten through the entire score once, during the final rehearsal three days earlier. Now, perhaps stunned by the crowds and the lights, alone with their fears, would they have the will, the strength, to summon their breath?

One surprise was the lights. After months without electricity, Nikolai Baranov, the city's chief architect, was determined to relight the Philharmonia's chandeliers, once the most dazzling in Europe. He decided to run a cable from Tsar Nicholas's yacht, the *Polar Star*, which was still moored on the Neva. It is hard to express how astonishing this was, for the musicians and their audience. We still had no heat, and most patrons shivered in their quilted jackets or minks. But the reflection of glass and the prisms of light suggested we would soon, surely we would be restored soon.

"I will never forget seeing those sparkling lights," Viktoria told me as she arrived with her mother Nina, looking stunning in a velvet gown Nina had sewn from old curtains. "I'd almost forgotten the beauty of electric light. It's breathtaking. Surely it will lift the city."

Outside the concert hall, people were sharing listening stations or staring at the sky, as if the stars would any minute explode in music. Inside it was jammed, buzzing with conversation and even laughter. I started interviewing anyone who would talk to me for our documentary on the concert. Later I thought it was some of my most memorable reporting from the war.

"When I saw this mighty crowd, I felt their energy and was determined to play with as much strength as I could muster," Parfionov told me, his trombone at his side. "I also apologized in my mind to Eliasberg for resenting him. He was so relentless about missed rehearsals and weak playing. Now I understand why. He understood what most of us couldn't see—that Leningrad was counting on us."

Once Eliasberg raised his hands, the din of anticipation quieted. Musicians locked eyes with his and waited for his downbeat. There was this shivering silence, both on the stage and in the audience.

I knew, from hearing the symphony in Moscow, that the first movement was the most important. A musical rendition of the German invasion, *War*, begins with violins, depicting life at peace, echoed by the woodwinds, in octave-long runs. There is a slower, more tranquil section of flutes and softer strings. And then, the pounding of percussion crashes through, a 22-bar *ostinato* led by the snare drum, as if the Nazi tanks were again blitzing their way to conquest. The march is repeated twelve times, always with greater and greater foreboding. Then, a trumpet solo interjects a new, more frantic sound, the arrival of the invaders. I imagined those who heard it remembered where they were when the Nazis circled Leningrad, and how that event had changed the trajectory of their lives.

Dhazdat had told me he viewed the first movement as a depiction of brute force—the kind without conscience, like the cruel blasting of trains filled with children. He thought of his drums as the sounds of the Nazi boots invading his country— boom, boom, boom. And he meant to deliver it with the utter outrage it deserved. But despite the music's almost crude, repetitive pulse, he also knew that it required discipline from his snare drums. Like Ravel's Bolero, the themes built to a crescendo. But this symphony was not written for a poetic ballet. This was a symphony

written for a sinister war of hate. He had to be measured if he
wanted the world to feel it.

A few days before the concert, I had been in Eliasberg's office
when Dhazdat walked in.

*"Sit, my friend," Karl pointed to a chair. "You want to talk about
the first movement, I imagine?"*

Dhazdat nodded.

*"How did you know? Yes, I want to talk about how to express
outrage, but not so much that I overwhelm the music."*

Eliasberg looked at his drummer, and smiled.

*"You have learned much, my son. Now I will teach you one more
thing. Do you know the purpose of a conductor's two hands?"*

Dhazdat shook his head no.

*"The conductor's right hand is for pacing and poise. Watch my right
hand for tempo, for when to speed up and when to slow down. It's what
I use to cue in an instrument, or temper it down."*

"And the left hand?" Dhazdat asked.

*"You know this intuitively, I think," Karl said. "But there's a
proverb I learned at the Conservatory. They say that a conductor's right
hand is steady, but his left hand has 100 different expressions. That is
where I keep my emotions. If you follow my left hand, we can all finish
together, in harmony."*

Dhazdat smiled.

"Now I know what to do."

Eliasberg nodded.

"Just follow my fingers, as I once did yours."

I thought back to that day when I noticed Dhazdat's fingers moving among the dead. How remarkable he was alive to play in this concert. How remarkable it was, really, that any of us were alive to hear it.

The concert began at an *allegretto* pace, upbeat and brisk, full of violins, flutes, French horns, oboes, cellos and clarinets. Then they grew softer, almost pastoral. Dhazdat told me later he was nervous, but with a kind of kinetic energy, anticipating the great vitality that could course through his body toward the drums. Grandpa Stenka had taught that his own orb of inner energy would give him the strength, like an animal about to leap. He was still weak—Dr. Petrova had estimated he was getting about 1100 calories a day, hardly enough for a man of his size. But he knew he would be fueled by his pride in his country and his fury at the Germans for the traumas they had inflicted on his family.

As I watched Eliasberg, I noticed the conductor's left hand tremble. Was it a sign of nerves? A signal to Dhazdat to get ready? I was glad I didn't have to read our elusive conductor's signals.

On the next chord, Eliasberg cued him in, and Dhazdat began with a soft tap on his snare drums. He told me later he felt like the whole orchestra was following his lead—the violins and the cellos were tapping their bows and plucking their strings in time with his drumming. When Eliasberg wiggled his left fingers and raised his left hand, he began pounding the drums with ferocity. He said he felt like a warrior pummeling an opponent, relentless in his anger. The orchestra again came with him—this time adding the sounds of the bassoons, trumpets and trombones, always with his insistent drumbeat beneath them. Karl cued in Arseny Petrov at the cymbals. The clash shook the room.

Next, Dhazdat picked up the sticks with the larger poms, brandishing them like weapons against the animal skin pulled tight over his drum frame. I thought I saw him look at Eliasberg for a cue to slow down, but the conductor had closed his eyes, and was communicating only through his fingers. He kept raising his left hand—give me more, it seemed to say—and so Dhazdat did, harder than he had ever pounded before. I imagined his body was throbbing, maybe the tubes in his ears too. But still he beat, and beat, and beat—and it was hard in the incessant beating not to think about the way the Nazis had destroyed the Badaev warehouses, had attacked innocent children, had demoralized a grieving city by bombing its cemeteries. Dhazdat looked like he was channeling anger for all of us, sweat pouring from his body. Soon people in the audience started crying, perhaps releasing tears they had held in all winter. It was if they were weeping in concert with his fury.

Then the most remarkable thing happened, throwing the whole orchestra into uncertainty. The score called for a slowdown, but Eliasberg kept Dhazdat pounding in sync with his left hand, as if he was possessed. As long as those fingers pulsed, Dhazdat pulsed with him, relentless. The rest of the orchestra sat stunned, waiting for the signal to come back in. It was as if the two of them were locked in messianic frenzy, under a spotlight, alone on the stage, as audience and orchestra looked on. Finally, Eliasberg slowed his drummer down, quieting him, and cued in the mournful flute, backed by the piano and Dhazdat's now softer beats on the snare, all of it suggesting the counting of deaths after the smoke had cleared. I was mesmerized. Nothing like that had happened at the Moscow debut. It was so emotional, validating the decision to perform in Leningrad.

A few minutes later, the conductor brought both hands down emphatically at the same time. The first movement was over. The applause was thunderous. Many in the audience, and also in the orchestra, were crying. The event was an emotional ordeal for everyone who had outlived the Siege, I thought, everyone who had buried loved ones and suffered from soul-crushing hunger.

Dhazdat looked drenched, utterly depleted. He told me later that when he finally picked up his head and looked into the audience, he was relieved to see people had not been frightened by his ferocious playing. Amid the glaring lights of the chandeliers, he saw in the eyes of strangers not despair but a determination to fight on. He may have been drained, but he was proud of giving them strength.

Seated nearby, I saw Parfionov salute Dhazdat. He told me he was so moved by Dhazdat's rendition of the invasion that he felt weak. The ordeal of military duty, the rehearsals under Eliasberg's strict rules, the exhaustion and horror at what he had seen, suddenly the accumulation of a year's sorrows surfaced. "Dhazdat was so loud, so powerful, so insistent, I thought the chandeliers would crack," he told me later. "And then I thought, oh my goodness, we're going to win the war!"

After the first movement, I sat behind a microphone and described the reaction of the audience.

"When Conductor Eliasberg lifted his right hand, there was almost a gasp of anticipation," I said. "And when the symphony began, from its very first bars, we heard ourselves in its music, the ruthless enemy bearing down on us, our defiant resistance, our grief.

"Our first drummer, Dhazdat Zelensky, played with such rage during the invasion theme that it seemed he held a warrior's horned helmet instead of a musical instrument," I added. "His drumming was frightful in its stupidity—ruthless and senseless—and it matched our mood."

The second movement, *Memories*, brightened the atmosphere. A renaissance, like beauty born out of ashes, it starred Viktor Kozlov on the clarinet and Katya Medvedeva on the oboe. Theirs was a bittersweet passage that seemed to cry over the despair and melancholy of life under the German boot. Katya said she was drenched with sweat afterward, but happy. Viktor puffed out his chest and winked at Dhazdat, as if to say, "Look at us, we are playing this better than we ever have before."

The third movement, *Wide Expanses of Our Land*, depicted the ordeal of the Soviets people against the backdrop of Russia's great natural beauty. The set featured a chorus of singers and an answer from the violins, featuring Dhazdat's friend Danil Mitkin, who had joined the orchestra on hearing the call for volunteers. He had never found his wife Zena or their daughter Lara, who left the city during the evacuation. He told me the violin was his only solace, and he played it with the desperation of a man tested by trauma. In the movement's middle, the flute was to play a touching song. All eyes turned to Galina Yershova. In rehearsals, she had doubted her ability to move her scurvy-plagued arms. She was young, not yet 21, and complained that the music was too melodramatic. Eliasberg told me she had come to his office seeking advice.

"It's too complex," she told Eliasberg. "It's difficult for me to understand."

Eliasberg nodded.

"And how are you finding the war?" he said.

"The war?"

"Do you find it melancholy?"

"Of course."

"Do you have enough to eat?"

"Of course not."

"Do you ever get angry, or frustrated, because of the Nazi blockade?"

She started to answer and stopped. She stared at him.

"So this is a symphony about our frustrations?" she asked.

"In a way it is, and by the third movement, when you are in the star's position, it is about our hopes and dreams. Your role is to play us a

*touching song, pure and consoling, to soothe our wartime wounds. The
strings and the piano will back you up. But it is you who must carry the
emotion of the moment. Remember when you could barely move your
arms to play the flute?"*

She nodded.

*"Channel that frustration into this meditative piece, tell us of your
earlier despair and your hopes for the future. Tell us that you are
determined to walk again, to move your arms without pain again."*

The hint of a smile broke on her face.

The night of the performance, she told me she listened to
Dhazdat's solo in awe, knowing that he had been given up for dead
in the outdoor morgue. When her turn came, she looked at him,
and he nodded, as if to affirm, "You can do this." And so she had.
Afterward she smiled at him and at Eliasberg, though she was not
sure the conductor noticed.

Shostakovich had told me the fourth and final movement,
Victory, had been the most difficult—how to convey victory when
it had not yet happened, how to telegraph redemption without
glossing over the horrible history they had all lived through and
most of all, how to write it in exile in Kuibyshev while pining to
know what it felt like to be in Leningrad. In some ways, Eliasberg
had a similar dilemma—to make sure the ending was hopeful, but
not sugarcoated.

As he usually did, Shostakovich had begun the final movement
with a musical intake of breath, a quiet interlude before the

clamorous sounds of agony. Chudnenko had suffered a pulmonary edema and was unable to play. So a very nervous backup, Nikolai Nosov, came in on the trumpet, paced by the steady beat of the drums. Again, Dhazdat was called on to reprise the sound of the German tanks blitzing Leningrad. He began with the timpani roll and thundered toward a conclusion as the music climaxed with brass fanfares, violin frenzies and cymbal crashes. The symphony was set in C major—usually an upbeat key. But for this symphony, the orchestra had to play it tempered by sorrowful sounds depicting the unimaginable suffering of war, and of loss. It required an act of subtlety only possible by watching Eliasberg's left hand, the hand of one hundred expressions.

Toward the end of the 80-minute performance, many of the musicians were utterly spent. But the audience seemed to hold them up. When Igor Brik faltered, falling forward onto his cello, there was a gasp. Then many stood and applauded him on, staying on their feet until he could recover. They did the same for Alexander Kamensky, one of the pianists. I was so moved by this display of mutual affection that I went on the air and proclaimed it like a shared bond—the musicians came to play for the people of Leningrad, and the people of Leningrad came to shore them up.

When the piece ended, I took to the airwaves.

"After the symphony ended, there was not a sound in the hall," I announced. "Then someone in the back started clapping, and then there was a thunder, a storm of applause. For over an hour, the audience stood and applauded. It's as if they could not stop saying thank you."

Eliasberg was called for a bow several times, and a little girl whose family had a farm in the countryside brought flowers on the stage for him, a rare sight in Leningrad.

Elena Kochina was one of those who stood and clapped, even as tears poured down her face. "I cried for my father, who did not live to see or hear this concert. I cried for my brother, still at the front. I cried for our city," she told me. "This concert was a beginning, and that drummer was a confirmation that Leningrad is alive, and will not be defeated by the soulless Nazi machine."

"People stood and cried," Eliasberg told me later. "They knew this was not a passing episode but the beginning of something. The whole city was one human being, seizing this victory. We had done it, in the music. We had played out our souls." What he did not say, what it would take him many years to understand, is that the concert had shattered him.

For now, he and the orchestra absorbed the waves of applause. At one point during the ovations, Eliasberg singled out Dhazdat, who stood. The audience erupted in applause again. And then, to everyone's surprise, a little girl ran on stage toward him, shouting, "Papa, that's my Papa, that's my Papa!" Dhazdat lifted Anastasia in his arms, kissed her and smiled through his tears.

Katarina was crying too. On impulse, she grabbed Pavel's hand and bounded toward the stage, and Dhazdat saw them just as he bowed to the crowd. He screamed in joy, almost falling over.

Parfionov told me he had spotted Katarina out of the corner of his eye and caught Dhazdat before he fell. When Katarina joined him on stage, the two embraced in a hug of such longing that many in the audience rose to their feet. I thought it was beautiful—an affirmation of love, but also of survival. How I wished Nikolai could have been here. Waves of applause seemed to go on and on and on.

Most of us declined the invitation to a post-concert dinner at the Pushkin Canteen organized by Andrei Zhdanov, the Communist Party's great cultural icon. It was a bribe of food, wrapped in an intrusion of politics into an evening of pure musical magic. Where was the food during practice?

"Oh, everything was delicious," Viktor Kozlov told me later. "Everyone was hugging and kissing. We ate and ate—they had beef!—but most of us had to throw it up. It was too rich for our bodies."

There was a concert playbill, and it became one of the most sought-after souvenirs of the war. Possession was an assertion that 'I was there, I saw, I heard, I felt that concert'. On its cover was a quote from Shostakovich's interview with me on Radio Leningrad, in which he said, "Even in a time of hunger, culture is a kind of nourishment too." There was also a quote from Alexei Tolstoy, second cousin of the late writer Leo Tolstoy. "The No. 7 Symphony arose from Russia's fight against the dark forces," he wrote. "Written in Leningrad, it has become a work for the world,

understood on all meridians, because it is about human beings at a
time of trial and struggle."

The other prized souvenir of the concert, rarely found in
Russia, was an invitation to Hitler's victory party scheduled that
same night at the Astoria. "They never had their party," Katya
Medvedeva told me for our documentary. "The Germans were not
singing the *Horst Wessel Song* at Leningrad's Astoria Hotel. We
played our symphony, and the spirit of our people was lifted. We
will yet win."

After the concert, there was a feeling of pride, which I thought
came through in the documentary. One soldier talked about
listening to the concert while lying down on the ground with his
eyes closed. "It seemed as if the sky was bursting not with lightning
but with music," he said. "The city was listening to the symphony
of heroes and for a brief time forgot about the war."

"I think the concert gave everyone a shock, a good shock,"
Elena Kochina told me. "Everyone thought we were a dead city.
And now, Russians and Germans alike, they hear our performance
and they wonder how we did it. To tell you the truth, I wonder
how we did it too."

Galina Babinskaya came to the concert with her sister Marisha.
She wrote me that music had always sustained Leningraders, and
had again on this magical night. I arranged to interview them.

"Those who have not spent the winter here, who have not
endured what we have endured, cannot understand our happiness
when we see the rebirth of our beloved city," wrote Galina. "It is

as if we have been lifted to a victory stand by the relentless playing of our drummer. I promise you, he understood, he spent the winter here, he knew hunger, cold and fear. Now we are whole."

Her sister Marisha echoed the thought.

"We, who had suffered a frightful famine and a bitter winter, sat here in our fur coats and caps. As the musicians played, their breath steamed in cold air. The thrill I felt was not simply the pleasure of the performance—though it was mighty—it was pride in my resurrected people, in the great art which compelled those human shadows—the emaciated musicians, the audience—to come together in that great house of music, daring the shells and sirens to interrupt. Truly, it was a heroic assertion that man does not live by bread alone."

Josef Raskin came to the Philharmonia with his mother. He was eight years old.

"What do you remember about the concert?" I asked him.

"I remember that everyone kept telling me to keep quiet."

I laughed.

"Anything else?"

"Yes," Josef answered. "When the drummer played, I saw people smiling while they were crying. I never saw that before. I decided that is what music is for. It helps people feel things in their heart."

For Olga Kvade, the event reminded her of her father, who died during the Siege.

"For some reason, I immediately thought of Papa. He loved good music. He himself played, and he'd been teaching me. And I remembered how he would take me to the Philharmonia, and it seemed to me that, somehow, he was listening. I had a sense of peace, feeling him there with us."

She had buried her Papa on Christmas, and her grandfather, *dedushka*, three weeks later.

"I took him on a sled to the morgue," she told me. "It is difficult to forgive these things—he was head of family, and everyone loved him." Now she was alone. But in the strings of the orchestra and the pounding of its drummer, she heard the call of resistance, and it made her proud.

"We will persevere," she told our Radio Leningrad audience. "It doesn't matter how many people the Nazis kill here. The people of Leningrad will never give up. The lesson of this concert is that we have music in our souls. And now, we have this memory—of a beleaguered drummer delivering hope amid our own deprivation. Who can say whether wars are won by guns or by soul? Take note, Heir Hitler, we will bury you with the ammunition of our music."

She was relieved the Nazis had not bombed during the concert. "That made me proud too," she told me. "I kept thinking, 'God, let us listen to the end.' They were always shelling us, but this time there was this feeling we had finally bested them. No bombs. The orchestra played to the end."

Garegin, our harpist and my brother-in-law, played with special gusto. Afterward he held Maria's hand as he heard two women in the audience speaking in Armenian. He and Maria went down into the audience to sit with them, to talk about Armenia.

"How homesick I was on hearing you speak our language," he told them. "I sometimes imagine the peak of Mount Ararat shining in the August sun, with the valley below covered in vineyards."

"How romantic," said Sofia Lalayan, a military surgeon. She and her sister Ruzanna, also a doctor, were taking a short break from the operating theater to hear the concert, a reward from their hospital for their work. "I will ask our parents to send you a delicious wine from Armenia."

"Thank you," said Garegin, "but there is no need. I have played with the last of my strength. Say goodbye to Armenia for me. Long may her mountain shine."

He and Maria left the Philharmonia. She told me later she cried all the way home. She knew that he had played with all of his strength, that he had given all to the music, that he had nothing left. He died that night, the first casualty of a concert so intense it had depleted his reserves.

After Garegin's death, Eliasberg had raged at Babushkin.

"He yelled at Babushkin that he should have gotten the musicians more food," Maria told me. "Karl said there is something rotten in the system if party officials are so well fed they eat beef and the rest of us were left to starve. Of course Yasha needed food too."

I nodded.

"Olga, he wanted to be buried in Armenia, beneath Mount Ararat, among his people. Can you help me?"

I tried, God how I tried, but it was difficult to transport bodies amid warfare. Like so many others in Leningrad, we put his depleted body on a sled and dragged him to the cemetery where the military would later bury him, with our mother, in a huge grave called 1942.

I thought back to the first time I had met Garegin, at the picnic, as Maria's date, and as the surprise winner at a chess game with Eliasberg. And later when he married my sister, and when he was hospitalized for starvation. Garegin had always seemed vulnerable, even when winning. He was the first musician to expire after the concert, the first who gave his all to the music. He would have liked that, I think. Finally his life had served a purpose, making him no longer a victim but a hero.

I wrote Nikolai about Garegin, and he wrote back that he and his troops had listened to the concert.

"He played out his heart," he wrote. "And when his heart was empty, he left us."

EIGHTEEN

The Aftermath
September 1942

After the concert, messages of congratulations had poured into Radio House. Winston Churchill was effusive, especially about Dhazdat—"I should have said, 'We shall fight on the beaches, in the concert halls and on our drums!'" he wrote—and there was a warm note from Franklin Roosevelt, about how fear had met its match in the Radio Orchestra of Leningrad. I wondered if Harry Hopkins had helped write the message. There were reports that Hitler had screamed at General Erich von Manstein for not stopping the Red Army from installing loudspeakers the night of the concert. Three Aryan soldiers of the Third Reich had surrendered, their pride sundered.

But as always, Stalin managed to turn triumph into pain. Anna had told me once that just before his death, Lenin had written a letter to Stalin, cutting off all 'comradely relations', and another to the Communist Party. The missive to the party warned that Stalin had a tyrant's demeanor, and would push their country toward a totalitarian nightmare. I always thought Lenin was the smartest of them.

"Did you hear what happened at the Kremlin?" Yuri asked me soon after the concert.

"No Yuri," I said, a bit churlishly. I guess I was angry that Nikolai was still at the front, and taking it out on my best friend in the office. "Sorry, Yuri. Tell me, what happened at the Kremlin?"

Yuri looked a bit hurt, as if I no longer trusted him. But he plowed ahead.

"Foreign Minister Molotov was so excited by the worldwide reaction, he proposed a grand tour," Yuri said. "As you know, No. 7 had already debuted in London, New York and Moscow, so Molotov figured they should plan more stops around the world to help finish the fight."

"And what did our great leader think?" I asked, humoring him.

"He exploded," said Yuri, proceeding to act out the scene, as if he had been there.

"Have you lost your mind!" Yuri as Stalin railed, pounding his palm on the desk. "We have a war to win! I am outlawing that bourgeois composer's Symphony No. 7. Banned. Canceled. Eliminated."

I laughed. Yuri could always make me laugh. "You should audition for Maria's Musical Comedy Theater," I said. "I will recommend you, based on that acting performance alone."

After we stopped carrying on, I sobered. "Stalin does not want the rest of the country to know how Leningrad suffered," I concluded. "He doesn't want anyone to ask why he evacuated our art and our children but left our people to starve to death. The concert is a reminder."

Yuri looked at me with an odd expression.

"You never heard me say this," he said, "but actually, that's a good point."

Dhazdat took the banning of No. 7 as a personal insult.

"I don't understand," he asked me one day. "But why?"

"It's part of his attempt to cleanse the record of any indication that Leningrad went through special hell during the war," I explained, thinking back on those speeches I was forced to give in Moscow, praising Leningraders as heroes without mentioning their hunger. "Stalin has denounced Shostakovich for favoring bourgeois values, the crime of choosing the West over the East. *Leningrad Pravda* urged residents not to mention the concert publicly, for fear it will douse Soviet patriotism."

Dhazdat was dumbfounded. "I thought they liked the symphony," he said.

"Maybe too much," I said. "It's always dangerous to be more popular than the Supreme Comrade."

In truth, I agreed with Dhazdat. Whatever the rest of the Soviet Union was feeling, grief was at the heart of Leningrad's war. To ban the playing of Symphony No. 7 was to deny our shared experience. I was still getting letters from women who took solace from the concert. I showed him one of them.

"I stayed warm during the Siege by burning everything in sight—first my big wooden kitchen table, then my mahogany chest, paper, books, anything that would feed a blaze," wrote Tamara Korolkevich. "By the night of the concert, there was little left. But as I listened to that drummer, and his rendition of the savage march of Nazi boots, I finally warmed. He was the ray that gave me light, at a time when I had already fallen in spirit. After the concert, I felt recharged."

Dhazdat smiled up at me. "Has the recording been preserved?" he asked.

"Of course," I said. "It's in a separate cabinet that Vadim keeps of banned concerts."

"After we win the war," he said, standing tall, "we will resurrect our history."

I looked at him, a bit surprised. I had never known Dhazdat to be a political person. He was a proud Ukrainian, loyal and fierce, protective of his clan. Somewhere along the line he had also become a Russian, believing that our history was a heritage never to be forgotten. I opened my arms for a hug.

"You lifted us when we most needed it," I whispered. "That memory can never be erased. My children and yours, and their children after them, and kids all over the world, will hear the story."

After the concert, Leningraders ventured out more, daring the Germans to strike. Maria was again performing at the Musical Comedy Theater, and I thought it was a good thing. Her smile was back, as if Garegin's death were part of her story, but not its ending.

When her theater performed a comedy about the Soviet Baltic Fleet, a silly thing called *The Wide, Wide Sea,* it sold out quickly. I invited Luby to attend the premiere with me. She brought all her boys. In the middle of the make-believe, the Nazis launched a real-life aerial and artillery attack on the theater district. I noticed Rahil grab for Igor's hand. The curtains came down and Maria walked to the front of the stage. "I ask you, our dear audience, shall we take shelter or shall we continue the performance?" she asked. From all corners of the theater came the response, "Continue!" I turned to Igor and searched his face, wondering what the war had meant to him.

"Why?" I asked. "Why are people risking death to see a farce?"

"People are tired of waiting," he said. "The hunger pains are receding—and the need for cultural sustenance is burgeoning. It's like that American slogan, 'Give me death or give me music!'"

I laughed. "I think the American slogan was 'Give me death or give me liberty.' But I take your point—we want our customs back." Someone behind shushed us.

One day, as quickly as they had been extinguished, the lights came back on. Leningrad was back on the grid, and to all of us who had survived the Siege, it was a thing of utter joy. I could hear voices raised in laughter all up and down my street. That same week, Radio Hall came to life with excitement, as if the metronome had increased its tempo. Yuri brought me a news bulletin. I stared at it in astonishment, unable to move. Vadim frantically waved me to the microphone.

"My fellow citizens of Leningrad," I said, "I am happy to announce that we are no longer an island. We are no longer cut off from the mainland. We share their pulse. What happiness, what joy! Hitler's evil chokehold has been broken. We have waited a long time for this day, yet we always knew it would come. During our darkest months, when our friends and relatives perished, when we were turned to stone by our sorrows—always we believed. And now, we are unshackled."

The war was not over—the Nazis would continue shelling the city for more than a year, like the drip of oil from a leaky engine. Starvation was not banished. But the blockade bottleneck was cracked—food and supplies could now reach the city through a land corridor. And Leningraders had no intention of waiting for the official armistice. Giddy with relief, they broke out the vodka at once.

At St. Peter's School, one class celebrated early, though not with vodka. Inna Bityugova, the 12-year-old author of the *Vegetable Man* series, wrote me that she told her mother the day before it happened that soldiers would break the blockade, and 'bring us ginger biscuits'. She knew this because she was a pen-pal to an army officer serving in Shlisselburg, who had read her book to his daughter back home. Now this officer wrote to her that the Red Army would liberate them soon.

As soon as the blockade ended in June, almost a year after the concert, Nikolai retired from the military. He told me his commanding officer had begged him to stay, reminding him that the Nazis were not yet defeated. But Nikolai told him he no longer had the fire for combat.

"My work here is done," he telegrammed. "Can't wait to see you both."

I was overjoyed. I took time off from work and we often went to the park to delight in each other's company, celebrating our reunion. I had forgotten how much I liked simply looking at him, seeing the muscles ripple through his shirt, the upturn of his nose putting a smile on my face. It also inspired me to see him with Abigail, her little fingers resting in his big palms, as if he were inviting her to come explore the world with him. It felt like we had the future. Sometimes they came to Radio House, where Abigail liked to play with the metronome, and Nikolai beamed at seeing how respected I was there, though he did comment about my office, suggesting a cleanup might be in order. I laughed and told him it was messy, just the way I liked it.

A few days after his return, as a new Sunday dawned, people ran into the streets. There was no public announcement, no official call to celebrate the end of the Siege. We all just knew.

Few got any sleep as the public square became the site of a spontaneous and gargantuan celebration. No passes were needed. There was music, speeches, dancing. Many were crying, others were kissing, and everyone was telling the story, over and over, of where they were when they heard that famous concert that marked the beginning of the end. Soon enough, trains of supplies would roll into Finland Station, greeted by local officials, bunting, a brass band and a banner proclaiming, 'Death to the Fascist German Usurpers'. For now, it was a street party.

I grabbed Nikolai and we went to join the masses. I saw Dhazdat dancing with Katarina. Sitting on the sidelines—Koyla and I have never been much for dancing—I looked up just in time to see Dhazdat bend Katharina backward as he kissed her, her hair trailing on the ground. Someone snapped a photograph, and it became the iconic image of Leningrad celebrating its liberation.

I mused with Nikolai about this unlikely pairing of a prima ballerina and a wild country drummer.

"Think of it. The Zelenskys survived the Siege of Leningrad. They can tell their grandchildren the awful tale of how the Germans bombed Katarina and the children when they tried to evacuate from Leningrad. Or how they were forced by hunger to eat their own cats. Or how Dhazdat had been given up for dead, left on a pile of corpses, until I saw his fingers move."

"And we can tell Abigail about how her mother was evacuated so she could be born," he said.

"And how her father almost lost his leg building an Ice Road that could bring a starving people some food."

We kissed through our smiles.

The truth is I didn't think anyone would remember much of anything except the concert, that magical night when Dhazdat almost single-handedly put the city on his shoulders and drummed their anger at the German invasion onto his snares. The music pulsed with the sound of his fury, and it revitalized a city, rekindling Leningrad's hopes for a future again.

We decided to stroll through our city. Down the street, we saw Viktoria, overseeing a vast feast at the Hermitage for all who survived the war in its basement. "*Ura, na zdorovye*, cheers to your health!" she shouted. She looked exuberant.

"Any news from the Urals?" Nikolai asked, with a wink in his smile.

She smiled back. "I cabled Boris to bring the treasures home," she said, reaching in her pocket for his telegrammed response. I smiled too as I read it aloud. "We are all coming. Stop. Plan for delivery 2 weeks. Stop. Meet me at the station. Stop. Only accept payment in kisses. Stop."

"Two weeks!" she exclaimed. "Do you have any idea how much we have to do?"

"Tell me," I smiled, knowing Viktoria to be one of the best organizers I've ever known.

"We have to clean the place first," said Viktoria, clearly flush with excitement. "But Luby was right. We have a wonderful team. The Grannies have already volunteered to wash the walls and floors, we have painters coming—not the paint-splatting but professional ones—to repair damage from bombs. Of course the greatest task of all will be after the treasures come home, when we have to put all of them back in their place. I've asked Katarina and her sister Mariska to spearhead the effort."

"And after all that, perhaps you'll have to plan a wedding," said Nikolai.

"Maybe," she said, blushing again. "Ever since Orbeli returned from the sanitorium, he's seemed a gentler soul. He's left me in command—he calls himself 'Viktoria's *sous docent*'—and yesterday he asked me if he could officiate at my wedding!"

I had heard that the NKVD interrogated Orbeli for a long time over his confused handling of lists of the art evacuated to the Urals, before concluding that he was a senile old man, incapable of either command or memory. Orders came down that Viktoria would run the museum, though it was not clear if this was only a temporary wartime measure.

"Orbeli thinks we should have the wedding here," Viktoria added. "What do you think?"

"At the Hermitage?" I asked.

"Well, at the Winter Palace across the street," she said.

"A marvelous plan," said Nikolai.

That," I said, "will make your wedding the most coveted invitation of the post-war era."

Four weeks later, the Hermitage Museum reopened. Crowds were enormous. Viktoria told me she stood proudly at the first salon, ready to guide guests through the collections. Katya Medvedeva and her mother Natasha, who had been at the

Hermitage the day of the invasion and heard Molotov's announcement of the invasion, arrived in great anticipation.

"I want to retrace our steps," Katya told Viktoria. "I want to make sure Antonio Canova's *The Three Graces* and Henri Matisse's *Dance* have made it home."

"I don't care which pieces survived, or have been moved, or even nicked," said her mother. "Just seeing the art on the walls will affirm that they, and we, survived."

"I think we can make you both happy," said Viktoria.

As they walked away, Viktoria told me she overheard Katya say how proud she was that they had survived. "And against all odds," she added, "I performed at that magical concert that lifted Leningrad to its feet." To which her mother replied, "He who doesn't take risks, doesn't drink champagne." They had both laughed at that, their giggles bouncing off the walls.

Outside on the plaza, architects were designing a grand outdoor event, envisioning where rows of chairs would go and how to position the platform in front of the Winter Palace. Viktoria told me she loved the setting, loved the idea that Catherine the Great would look on and bless her marriage. Of course we both hoped Viktoria's love life would be a lot more monogamous than Catherine's, but I suppose it was always nice to be celebrated against the backdrop of a historical frame.

One month later, on a brisk fall day, after a long wartime correspondence, Viktoria married Boris Piotrovsky. Nikolai and I sat in the front row for the ceremony. I held Abigail on my lap.

The audience was mostly family, if you count the Poets Circle as kin. Katarina was there with Dhazdat. Luby came with Andrei, Igor and Rahil. Maria made sure Anna found a place. Eliasberg and half of Radio House were on hand, as we had more or less adopted Viktoria as one of our own. Anastasia served as flower girl, and Pavel as the ring bearer. Nina sat in the front row, beaming, next to the large Piotrovksy family, who came up from Moscow, each seemingly smarter than the one before. Captain Parfionov had arranged for a dramatic military flyover before the processional. He looked tall and dapper, despite his cane. He was sitting next to Katya Medvedeva. Maybe these two wartime musicians, I thought, had found a song in their hearts. I loved the symmetry of that. My father Fyodor had died in the camps, a victim of my fame I suppose. At my invitation, Uncle Sasha came to the wedding, dotting on the baby, giving me a sense of family again.

The only important person missing from the family tableau was the bride's father, who had died in combat, one of an estimated one million Leningraders who did not survive the war. With their father gone, Rodion walked Viktoria down the aisle. It was the first time I had seen a resemblance between them—both tall, radiant and charismatic. How close we came to losing them both, I thought, how resilient was the human spirit. I squeezed Nikolai's hand, thinking about how one day he would walk his own daughter down the aisle. I was roused from my daydreams by Orbeli's voice.

He sounded stronger and more like himself than he had during Viktoria's trial.

"The reassembling of this museum would not have been possible without these two people," he said as he officiated. "They are now joined as husband and wife, and their union is ours, for the collection housed in this impressive building would not have survived without them." Their wedding, he said, marks 'a rebirth for the city, and for us'.

"They look so in love," Katarina whispered to me.

"The greatest gift life offers, don't you think?" I replied. We held hands and smiled.

During the ceremony, Boris paid a ransom to Nina, Viktoria's mother, an old Russian tradition that recognized the bride's value to both families. Then, the couple released balloons—Anastasia Zelensky was thrilled to catch one—and climbed into a car lent by the museum for a tour of the city. This too was a traditional part of the Russian wedding ceremony, but now it had taken on special meaning. How could a tour of war-ravaged Leningrad, with the war still going on, do otherwise?

"We hope to heal the city with our love," Viktoria announced to us all.

"What do you think," Boris said, addressing the crowd next. "Perhaps we already have?" We roared.

To my surprise, Boris came over to Nikolai and gave him a big bear hug.

"Thank you for everything you did," Boris said. "We would not be here without you."

"What was that all about?" I asked.

"Did you ever wonder how Boris got back to Leningrad for Viktoria's trial?" he asked, a smile playing on his face. "Or who guarded the treasures while he was gone?"

I'm sure my face reflected the shock I felt.

"But how," I sputtered, "how?"

"A story for another day," he said, kissing me. I would have to wait for this delicious morsel of news to unwind itself. For now, we joined in waves of farewell to the newlyweds.

A few weeks later, I asked again my husband what he had to do with Boris's escape from the Urals.

"It was because of you," Nikolai said. "When you wrote to Boris about Viktoria's arrest, he was despondent, unsure how to help. Once he devised a plan, he knew he could not carry it out without help from the military. It was risky—he might have been arrested just for seeking permission to make a brief return to the city. Viktoria's father had already died, and I was the only person Boris knew in the military. So he contacted me, and I convinced my commander to approve this plan."

I looked at Nikolai in absolute wonder.

"You mean you…?"

"I set off from Lake Ladoga, heading away from Leningrad," he said. "It was difficult on my leg but I kept hearing the nurse say that hobbling was good for me. Remember her?"

I nodded.

"Anyway I caught trains and took rides on trucks and finally arrived in Yekaterinburg, where Boris said he would meet me. It felt like the place was deserted, so quiet you could not only see your breath but hear it. For several days, I stayed at a hostel. To tell you the truth, it was so devoid of people there, I kept thinking about whether my childhood in the countryside had made me a more introspective person, at least until you came along. Anyway, finally Boris found me."

I was so moved I couldn't wait any longer, not even to hear the end of the story. I jumped up and kissed him, and pulled him toward me in an embrace that announced my amorous intentions. Although perhaps that was also clear by my suggestion that we make another baby. We romped and wrestled, lunged and loved. I had never felt more united with another soul. And sure enough, a few weeks later I learned I was pregnant with our son, Fyodor.

Later, he told me the rest of the story. He gave Boris a lot of military passes he had secured before leaving his base, and told him the best routes to take to avoid danger. Boris gave him the keys to the Safe Haven for Art, the room where the tsar was secluded before his assassination. They exchanged uniforms—Boris outfitted as a soldier—and shared one last dinner, musing about the risks they were taking. Koyla said it was the best food he'd had in years—freshly killed red deer meat from the forest and good cognac from a stash hidden by Bolsheviks when they guarded the Romanovs.

With that, they shook hands.

"Men," I said. "You are so much better than we are at keeping secrets! Were you not planning to tell me this story?"

"Someday," Nikolai said, in a teasing voice. "If you had asked nicely. But of course you know you can tell no one. If the winds shift in Army circles, we could still be punished as examples to others."

I have been musing a lot lately about patriotism. Nikolai had risked much for his country, and so had Boris. But when country is controlled by a monopoly of opinion, when all dissent is suppressed, when the government is in thrall to one political party, then what is the point of loyalty to flag?

Loyalty to Leningrad, in my eyes, was different, and I was convinced it had made us victorious. We had survived because of our own grit, and our own culture. We had defied Berlin, and Moscow.

One day I walked into Radio House to find Eliasberg waiting in my office. He had been traveling a lot for work, leading orchestras with local musicians in places that rarely heard quality music. I told him he was welcome to use my office whenever he was in Leningrad.

"You will never guess what happened."

"Can't imagine."

"I was walking through the Senate Square, near the Bronze Horseman."

"Hardly unusual," I said dryly. The Bronze Horsemen, which celebrated Peter the Great, was the starting point for many a Soviet story.

"Suddenly I was approached by a group of German tourists. At least, I thought they were German, from the way they pronounced my name. But one of them spoke Russian."

I waited. Maybe Karl was slowing down. I had always delighted in his stories for their quick wit.

"They were veterans of the war," he said. "They had served here in Leningrad. The spokesman told me they had come to Leningrad expressly to see me. They wanted to tell me how the Radio Orchestra's performance of Symphony No. 7 had convinced them they would lose."

"You must be kidding," I said.

"I am not," he said. "This soldier told me the concert had a slow but powerful effect on them. He said it convinced them they would never take Leningrad. He even mentioned Dhazdat's drumming!"

"This is incredible," I said. "Have you told Dhazdat?"

"Yes," said Karl. "He was as disbelieving as you are. I think the soldier's quote was, 'We heard the will of musicians to play even as they were starving, and we knew we would lose.' Trust me, I didn't believe it at first either. It seemed improbable they had come to Leningrad just to see me, unfathomable that they attributed their defeat to a concert. I thought they were just mocking us."

"So what convinced you that they meant what they said?"

"One of them dug in his pocket and asked for my autograph on the playbill."

I sat back, stunned. Maybe Dhazdat was right. Maybe allegiance was not to nation but to culture. And if any two peoples were born to understand the arts, it was Russians and Germans. The nation that produced Bach, Brahms, Liszt, Schumann and Wagner had tried to silence the country that gave the world Mussorgsky, Rachmaninoff, Shostakovich, Stravinsky and Tchaikovsky. Could our victory have really come down to endurance? Did it mean we had a longer, deeper acquaintance with pain?

Yuri thought it did. He told me about a strange encounter he had heard about, a debate between a German and a Russian, at a professional conference in post-war Stockholm.

The Russian was Dr. Alexei Bezzubov, who had worked at the Leningrad State Pediatric Institute, trying to find sources of vitamins and minerals for starving Leningraders during the war. The other was Dr. Ernst Ziegelmeyer, deputy quartermaster of Hitler's army, former head of the Munich Nutrition Institute, who had calculated how long it would take for Leningraders to starve to death.

"What a pleasure to meet you," Ziegelmeyer said on being introduced to the Russian. "I have been wanting to ask you a question for a long time."

"Proceed," said Bezzubov.

"I am a scientist. The Third Reich asked me to calculate how long it would take—once calories, essential proteins and fat were removed from their diet—before all three million residents of Leningrad would starve to death," Ziegelmeyer said. "Restricted to 250 grams of bread apiece each day, I said they would all starve to death within a year."

"Ah," said Bezzubov, "so you are the famous Ziegelmeyer who predicted our demise?"

"Ja," said Ziegelmeyer, "but tell me how I erred."

"It's very simple, Heir Ziegelmeyer. You forgot to calculate the human instinct to live. Leningraders tried to stand, no matter how hungry. We saw that over and over at the clinic. They would come in yellow with jaundice and weak from dystrophy and when we told them of our attempts to extract vitamins from pine needles, they rallied with dreams. People came to the Philharmonia in tatters, freezing from hunger even in the August warmth, suffering the loss of loved ones. But they burst into tears and applause when they heard the Shostakovich symphony performed by musicians themselves worn down by hunger and cold. Of course, many hundreds of thousands died. But hope is a very powerful emotion, Heir Ziegelmeyer, and it can disrupt the rigid dictates of the numbers."

"As I thought," said Ziegelmeyer, "it was *das konzert*."

NINETEEN

The Poets Circle 4
September 1946

W e had not met in a while, everyone busy rebuilding or coming to terms with what the war had done to their lives. I imagined we were all healing our bruises, or finding new ones. When I had suggested a reunion, I heard a chorus of longing. Katarina asked to bring Anastasia. I was delighted. She and Abigail could form a new generational brigade. They would live on. Viktoria was the first to arrive, and there was a lot of her.

"Look at you!" I exclaimed, pointing at her stomach. "So pregnant, so quickly!"

She gave me a warm hug, the joy clear in the twinkle of her eyes. "Isn't it wonderful?" she said. "But hardly quick, Olga. You may have lost count, but it's three years since Boris and I married."

"Three years?" I asked, stunned. "Has it really been that long since we saw the end of the Siege?"

Anna came next, surprisingly spry.

"Don't look at me like that," she said. "I have taken up calisthenics. It's an ancient Greek system for keeping muscles fit as the body ages. Soon I will be able to beat you in an Olympics race!"

I laughed. They all came in a group then—Katarina and her daughter Anastasia, my sister Maria followed by Luby, looking bubbly as ever. Everyone oohed over Viktoria's evident news.

Anastasia and Abigail went off to play games. Now 10, Anastasia had become quite the little chess master, and wanted to teach Abby. I nodded my approval. I figured that even if she got bored, she could play with her Matryoshka nesting dolls. I had hesitated to buy them for her. They always reminded me of Boris, his belittling me for resembling the tiniest one, hidden behind layers of outer cover. But there were few other toys for children in our country, so I finally relented. A month earlier, I had given birth to our son, but I expected him to sleep through the evening. Luby of course insisted on visiting the bedroom. She always doted on him, and he always giggled on seeing her.

Maria and I had grown closer since the war. Our father had died in the work camps, one more victim of a brutal system that robbed people of life and dignity. Maria was navigating a postwar world without the man she loved—Garegin was gone and along with his death, my sister's *joie de vivre* had also disappeared. I kept telling her how nice it was to have her help raise Abigail and Fyodor, especially at a time when Nikolai was so engrossed in his work, at the crossroads of international relations. For tonight, she helped me with the menu—squares of pumpernickel bread topped with herring, olives and capers. I had wine and champagne—and juice for the children.

"Well this is quite an improvement on the so-called food we endured during the war," said Anna.

"I see the calisthenics have not improved your temperament," I said.

"Speaking of food, you'll never guess what happened!" said Luby. "You know how Igor was always talking about doing a show about cooking after the war?"

"I always thought that was a fanciful dream," said Katarina. "We had nothing to cook with then!"

"Well now it has happened!" said Luby.

"On the radio?" asked Katarina, sounding surprised not to have heard of it.

"No," said Luby, "it's on television."

"What is television?" asked Anna, to general smiles. I explained it was radio with pictures.

Few Soviets had access to TV but among the elite class in the Kremlin, apparently the show was a wild success. Andrei served as Igor's 'waiter', and their interactions were the talk of Moscow. Yuri told me that in one bit, Andrei presented an empty plate to Igor, who looked up and said dryly, "What, you expect me to fill this?" Stalin himself had reportedly laughed out loud at this, calling the pair 'the Abbott and Costello of Russian TV'. I had no idea who Abbott and Costello were, but I hoped this newfound celebrity would protect Igor and Andrei from further harassment.

"Maybe we should go around the room," I suggested. "We could play a conversational game of 'you'll never guess what happened next.' And the most outrageous story wins extra champagne."

"Well I think we can all imagine what happened next to Viktoria," said Luby.

Viktoria blushed. "Actually much has happened," she said. "I'm sure you have all heard that Boris and I were named co-directors of the museum. But it's working out better than I had dared hope. He is the liaison to other cultural institutions in the world, and deals with all delicate political issues that I have no talent for, or patience with. Meanwhile I run the day-to-day operations. I have offered jobs to most of the Grannies, and our famous climbers too. Basically anyone who helped protect the Hermitage during the war became part of its official family. And I'm trying to curate exhibits from our collections that will appeal to a younger generation."

I noticed as she said this, she caressed her stomach. How I remembered that feeling of connection with the not-yet born.

"And what will you do after the baby comes?" Katarina asked.

"I guess times have changed," said Viktoria. Looking at Katarina, she added. "It's not like it was when Dima fired you from the Ballet for getting pregnant. Now, he would be dismissed for such an act. The museum directors agreed to set up a nursing room for me. That way I can check up on the baby during the day. Boris likes the idea that he can also stop in to see our son during the day, though my mother of course has volunteered to mind him at home as often as we consent."

"So you know it's a boy?" I asked.

Viktoria looked at me.

"We don't know for sure, but we both believe it will be a boy. And if so, we'll name him Nikolai."

I was stunned at first, then touched. I was sure he would be flattered.

"As Nikolai is not here to give his blessings, I will," I said. "But what if the baby is a girl?"

"Much the same," said Viktoria. "If the baby is a girl, she would be Nikola."

I was overcome, really, and held my fist to my heart. I have no idea where this came from, but from my lips came this sentence, "May we serve as the baby's godparents?"

"What is it with you and religion lately?" asked Anna. "Have you gone full priest on us?"

"Not exactly," I smiled. "But religion seems to comfort me. Nikolai is so busy with work now, it helps. I want to bring that soothing to Viktoria's baby, to show him—or her—how to balance life's challenges with conviction in a Supreme Being bigger than ourselves."

"I like that," said Viktoria. "Boris will be thrilled too. He always talks about what Nikolai stands for—honor, loyalty, valor. For the same reason, Katarina, we briefly considered the name Dhazdat. His performance at the concert was so magnificent, so much an example of excellence amid deprivation. But honestly, that is a lot of ethnic complications to place on a little baby's head."

Katarina smiled and nodded. Viktoria asked her how the Zelensky family was faring.

"I think Dhazdat has had the most trouble adjusting," said Katarina, lowering her voice so the girls wouldn't overhear from the next room. "After the war, Anastasia became a chatterbox—this girl who spent months without speaking—and nearly drove her father crazy with requests to play chess. I remember once Dhazdat teased, 'What would a five-year-old child know about chess?' and she replied, 'More than you do!' We all laughed. But I always thought there was something poignant about it, as if in that moment, the baton had passed to a new generation.

"Since Stalin banned the playing of No. 7, Dhazdat seems less interested in his drums. He was so mesmerized by that picture of the two of us dancing at the victory celebration in the streets that he took up photography. Pavel is smitten too, and the two of them are taking classes. Sometimes I hear them talking about opening a father-son business—Photos for the People."

"Has Pavel forgiven you for the trek to Moscow and Kuibyshev?" asked Luby. "I always thought that was one of the most poignant parts of your letter, your sensitivity to his feelings."

Katarina nodded. "I'm not sure he'll ever forgive me, but I think he understands me better now. And anyway, he is a happier child, much closer to his father than he would have been otherwise."

"And what about you?" I ventured. "Are you back at the ballet?"

"I was fascinated by Viktoria's story because it's similar to ours," Katarina said. "Once I got the children settled, I worked with Daria on a plan for us to take over the Ballet from Dima Kuzmin. He protested some, but not strongly. I think the war robbed him of this earlier boom. Anyway, the authorities were surprisingly open to our suggestions—Daria runs the performances, I operate the school. Teaching has become my passion, a way to convey what I also wanted ballet to be—an expression of self. Both of us have expanded the look of the place—we are adding courses for children, broadening the performance menu, like Viktoria, in hopes of attracting a younger audience. Maybe I'm flattering myself, but I sense a burst of energy, and I love it."

"Do you need any young male students?" asked Luby. "I suspect Rahil would be good at that."

"We are always short of boys!" said Katarina. "Send him for an audition. I will look after him."

She turned to Luby and asked, "What happened after the war? Did Andrei and Igor stay with you?"

"At first they did, but then they decided to get their own apartment," Luby said. "I was sad when all three of them left, and of course Rodion went home to Nina's house, and suddenly I was alone again, as I had been at the war's beginning. But I knew that they had been a wartime gift, largely from you Olga, and that I should not complain. Then one day, Igor came by and told me that they all missed me, that Rahil kept asking about his grandmother.

Now they come to Sunday dinner every week, and we listen to music, play with puppets and reminisce about the war. You threw us together to solve a bureaucratic problem, Olga, to convince the state we were really a family. But it's funny, that's what we have become in reality, a family, and I am thrilled. I think maybe they are too."

I smiled. Maybe sometimes necessity really was the mother of invention. The girls rejoined us then.

"And what about you Olga?"

"As you know I am still on the radio, but there are younger stars now, competing for the microphone. And it's hard to recreate the high drama of the war years. Sometimes I think my poetry is suffering from too much contentedness. And maybe with Nikolai navigating diplomacy in Asia, I feel less certain of anything. I can barely find Korea on a map, let alone reason why we are there."

There were nods at this.

"The truth is I am also at odds with the requirements of the job," I said, looking at Maria. "I am plagued by the death of our father. Why had this valiant and honorable man, so loyal to country, had to suffer so at its hands? Why is the state so keen to destroy our happiness?"

Maria started crying, her chin in her chest. For some reason, we all gathered round.

"What's wrong, Aunt Maria?" asked Abigail. "If you have *la plaie* I can kiss it." Abigail was becoming quite the little linguist, and I wasn't sure if Maria would know that *la plaie* was French for a booboo.

Either way, it made Maria cry even harder. If only her woes could be kissed away by a child's sympathy, I thought. Actresses rarely age well, and Maria was no exception. I had noticed lately that her waist was thicker, her skin more wrinkled. She was still pretty, and I knew she still drew admiring looks from men on the street. But there were fewer parts at the Comedy Theater for a performer of her years. And I knew she was drinking, a lot. Really, who could blame her?

"Garegin's sister has invited me to visit Armenia, to see the haunts of his childhood," she said. "I could meet his relatives. And maybe it would make me forget the traumas of the war."

I doubted such a visit would help heal wounds, but who was I to say? Maybe travel would be a tonic.

"Have you ever left Leningrad?" asked Anna. "You'll be shocked at how primitive it is elsewhere."

Maria looked at me, and we smiled.

"Once when we were children—I think I was 8 and Maria was 6—the Civil War broke out in St. Petersburg," I said. "There were White Russian soldiers battling Red Army troops in the streets, and it was dangerous. One day our father announced he was sending us, with our mother, to Uglich, a small town along the Volga River that the Bolsheviks had already won. I begged him to let me stay, to witness the revolution. 'It will inform my life's work!' I exclaimed, but Papa insisted."

"It was awful," said Maria. "We lived in the Bogoyavlensky Monastery, which authorities had turned into a big dormitory. The building was cold, crowded and dirty, the Volga River had no beautiful parks, the city had no theaters or concert halls, and we thought the people seemed sad."

"Exactly my point my dear," said Anna. "Your people are here, not in Armenia. This city is more than where we live. It informs who we are."

"That may be true Anna, but I think travel does heal, or anyway it distracts," said Katarina. "Pavel and I still laugh over our memories on the road—in Moscow, of his dressing and sleeping in the women's barracks, of Captain Parfionov's gift of a toy soldier, and in Kuibyshev, of eating all that delicious Persian food with Daria's family and watching them pray five times a day. We even laugh now about the traumas, like that evil man on the train who stole our Napoleonic coin and how Pavel stole it back. Dhazdat didn't travel with us but he knows these stories as if they were his own, as we know the story of Anastasia and her inability to talk after the Nazis bombed our train and she became a refugee from war. Sometimes I think travel is a way for people to cement their memories, even when they are far away from family and friends. Maybe it would be good for you, Maria."

Maria smiled, and nodded, and drew little Abby closer, as she wiped her tears.

"I'm sure you're right, Anna, Armenia offers none of our cultural offerings. But in the theater I was taught to always befriend the stage manager because they know where all the bodies are going to be buried." We all laughed, obligingly. "I think maybe travel is when you *don't* know what will happen next. And maybe that's a good thing for someone so rooted to schedule as I have been."

I looked up and noticed Anastasia whispering in her mother's ear. They both looked at me.

"Olga, my daughter thinks that Abigail has great promise as a chess player," Katarina announced.

"Of course she does," I replied, "she's Russian, on both sides."

Everyone laughed at that, even Anna.

"Listen children," said Anna. "A few years ago I was invited to attend a famous chess match between two writers. Boris Pasternak, my friend, played against another famous writer, Alexander Bek. It was an epic battle, lasting more than six hours. Afterward, I asked Boris what it felt like. 'It was like a war without the blood,' he said. 'And no war ends simply by white winning over black. Victory, or defeat, both change a person.' Do you understand? He was saying that any experience, in chess or in life, and Maria maybe even in travel, teaches us something new about ourselves."

"Speaking of change, what got you into calisthenics?"

"My doctor suggested it, and I have to say it has given me a new approach to life," she said. She stood up to demonstrate, and the girls joined in, imitating her, and giggling. Soon we were all participating, even Luby, doing jumping jacks and pushups.

Within a few minutes, we were chuckling and gasping for breath. Maria insisted we eat something. I couldn't stop laughing.

"What a brilliant way to punctuate the war, the concert, the hunger," I said. "It seems like my laughter has been bottled up, waiting for a chance at release."

"Nonsense," said Luby, a bit breathless. "I remember in this apartment, in our Poets Circle, why we practically laughed all through the war."

"True," said Viktoria. "I'll never forget that time I came with silver paint all over my face and body and Luby accused me of signing up for combat, and I had to confess we were disguising the rooftops of the Hermitage skyline to confuse the German pilots."

"The Hermitage," said Anastasia. "That's where Mama and Aunt Mariska worked during the war, right?"

"Yes they did," said Viktoria.

She smiled at Katarina, who nodded. "I'll never forget that time after I returned from Kuibyshev, when Luby suggested I bring Pavel over for a play date with Rahil, and I had to ask who that was."

"I'll never forget, Katarina, when you told us about the Chocolate Gospel Man you met in the bomb shelter," said Luby. "I loved that story. Anastasia, do you remember him?"

"Not really," she said, "but Mama has told me and Pavel the story a lot, so I think I remember the story more than the man."

"Well I'll never forget that little American man touring Radio House and then asking Olga what her wattage was," said Maria.

"I loved her answer," said Anna, looking at me, "how brilliant that you responded with, 'It's never been tested.'"

We laughed anew, as if it were still 1941 and the war was still unfamiliar, an inconvenience before it was a tragedy. It made me glad that we had retreated into the comfort of the company of women. How I loved my father, and Garegin, and all the other men we had lost. But I was anchored here, to this tribe, with all our foibles, sentimentality and even body fat.

"But why Anna?" I asked. "Why did the doctor recommend exercise?"

Anna looked at me sternly then, and I knew I should not have asked.

"My time is soon," she said. "Apparently I drank some contaminated water during the war, tainted with sewage, and it has compromised my kidneys. There is little they can do, but the doctor told me that exercise would make my remaining days happier. And that is a bargain I am willing to make."

"Have you finished your meditation on Soviet history?" I asked. For years, Anna Akhmatova had been writing her 'Poem Without a Hero', an elegy to the Soviet Union's twisted history. I suppose it would have to await publication until after Stalin's death, but for years I had longed to read it.

"Very close," she said.

"Could we hear a bit of it?" I suggested.

"It's very long," said Anna, with a heavy sigh, "and I've not committed it all to memory. But there are some passages that I remember, that you might enjoy."

I nodded. She closed her eyes and recited.

"From childhood I have been afraid of those mimes, those creatures who wear white faces," she said. "I always saw an extra shadow without name who had slipped among them. And I wondered, 'Is this the visitor from the wrong side of the mirror? Is it the new moon playing tricks, or is someone really standing there again between the stove and the cupboard? And if it is a new moon, why must it haunt my dreams, never letting me enjoy a peaceful sleep?

"And now that I am old, I contemplate how fragile gravestones are, and wonder if that too is a metaphor for our history," she continued. "Were we ever destined to live under the fickle injustices of dicta? It is as if we followed pebbles down a path paved with power-craved rulers who dashed our freedoms. I wonder why the mime beckons me now with his hand. And I think, maybe this is the moment of peace I have longed for, the peace of the tomb. Maybe there I will breathe."

She opened her eyes to a stunned audience.

"You are the bravest of us," I said. "At great personal cost, you told the truth. And you survived the war alone, with only your poetry to bolster you."

"Don't be silly," she said. "I always had this circle. I will never forget my friends."

"We will make sure your poem is published," I said. "And honored," said Luby. "It deserves to be remembered, and honored."

Fyodor had fallen asleep on my lap, and I could see Anastasia was pulling on her mother's sweater. It was time to say goodbye. So, after refreshing glasses, I proposed a toast.

"To the Poets Circle," I said, "may we always treasure our connections, and our adventures. And to our new generation, who will continue our tradition of friendship."

Just then, there was a knock on the door. I gasped, ever fearful of what an unwanted interruption could bring. I opened the door to find the hall monitor standing there, her frizzy hair unkempt and her ample waistline giving her the appearance of a square.

"I brought you a cake," she said, ringing her chubby hands. "I do this for my best tenants."

So it had been her, all along, the one who turned us in for sedition. I had told the circle about how the hall monitor had given me a snide smile on my arrest. I had told them about my trip to the police station, and how I wiggled out of prison by convincing interrogator Maxim Lermontov that women needed to talk more than men, that we were not planning rebellion but survival.

I thought about inviting the hall monitor in, to ask her to join our feast, but worried she was just coming to compromise us. I looked at Anna, whose eyes warned me away.

"Thank you," I said. "We appreciate your grace."

The floor monitor nodded. I smiled.

As I shut the door, Katarina said she had never seen anything so remarkable.

"What times we are living in," she said, "when survivors come to make peace with their enemies."

"They say that truth is the first casualty of war," I said. "But maybe it's more accurate to say that humility is the first obligation of those who survive war."

"I like that," said Luby. "Maybe I will design a new puppet show along those lines."

"Just don't use the floor monitor as a character," I said. "I doubt her tolerance extends that far."

One by one, everyone gathered up their belongings. I wondered when we would next share each other's company, when we would again be a support system at a time of trauma.

During the war, when I had opened my apartment door to the hallway, I had encountered that frightening poster warning us to be silent because the walls had ears. Now, in its place, I saw a poster of a man and a woman, looking skyward, with the inscription, "Now it is our turn. Now our country will become the greatest force for peace in the world."

"Inshallah," said Katarina.

"What does that mean?" asked Luby.

"It's Arabic," she said. "I learned it from Daria's family. It means, 'God Willing.'"

"I like that," I said, "I think God is more than willing to fight for the cause of peace."

Luby smiled. Actually, everyone but Anna did. She grimaced, no doubt thinking my concept of God something of a cliché. And then they left, some for the last time.

TWENTY

The Passing
February 1953

Ever since Fyodor had started school, it has been our tradition to leave the house each morning together, a family on our morning walk. He was our postwar baby, and he made Nikolai and I feel complete, as he rounded out our family circle. This day was no different.

"Come children," I sang from the front door, "the sun is out and your teachers are waiting."

We dropped Abigail first at the Leningrad Language School for Children, housed in the historic Kunstkammer, a neoclassical mansion across from the Neva, built in 1783. Early on, she had shown a natural gift for languages, and we wanted to nurture her talents. Now 10, she already spoke some English and French, along with Russian. How I envied her.

"*Bonne journee,*" I said, wishing her a good day in French. She winced at my accent, rolled her eyes and gave us all a big smile, waving as she skipped up the steps.

As Radio House was nearby, the boys dropped me off next. I never stopped marveling at the building's majesty, so grateful I did not work in one of those hideous tower blocks of architecture the Kremlin was starting to build all over our city. For a long time, even approaching the building made me queasy, thinking of the traumas I had experienced there. But now those memories had softened. How could I toil in pain, with the warm embrace of my men to remind me of life's bounties? Fyodor was only 6, so he still accepted hugs. And of course Nikolai squeezed me goodbye as if we might never see each other again. Such was the bond of war or trauma, I suppose.

I watched as they left together, holding hands. After long talks, we had enrolled Fyodor in the Leningrad Nikolaevsky Military Engineering School. As a child, he was fascinated with how things were made, and we thought engineering would appeal to him. I was less sanguine about the military part of the school's curriculum, but Fyodor, ever eager to imitate his father, was thrilled. During his first year there, he actually thought the school was named for his father. We all laughed later when he mentioned this, embarrassing him a bit, but I always thought it was sweet.

One of the school's great advantages was that it was right next to where Nikolai worked, at the Smolny Institute. What charm and history that yellow baroque building held. Catherine the Great had founded it in 1764 as the Smolny Institute of Noble Maidens, extending education for girls of the upper classes. During the Revolution in 1917, Lenin devised the Bolshevik military campaign in its offices, and a statue of him still stands in front, his right arm thrust forward, as if urging the troops forward. These days, the building houses Communist Party officials and military strategists like Nikolai. How he loves walking in dressed in his military uniform.

Nikolai served on the Korean taskforce, and he told me early that he would not be able to talk much about his work. He explained that since American and United Nations soldiers were already on the ground in South Korea, Stalin wanted to keep Soviet military involvement a secret, to avoid stirring another World War. So most of our military's involvement was covert, or at least private. Many top Korean Communists were in our country, studying Soviet military strategy. Now the Kremlin wanted them to return home, to fight from within. One of them was known by his *nom de guerre*, Kim Il-sung. Years later Nikolai told me he was assigned to arrange Kim's travel. And safe passage.

One night, Nikolai burst into the apartment. He seemed a bit breathless. The children ran toward him, as they always did. He kissed Abigail and Fyodor, delighting in their coos.

"Wait until I show you what I did at school today!" said Fyodor.

"I can't wait to see that," said Nikolai. "But first I have to talk to Mama. Why don't you get everything set up for me and I will be in as soon as I can."

Fyodor looked disappointed but marched off to his desk, following Abigail, whom he adored. I looked up at Nikolai expectantly.

"Have you been in the office lately?" he asked.

I shook my head.

"No, I've been working on my memoir. Sometimes it's easier to write here, where no one will interrupt me with bulletins to read on the air. Has something happened?"

He sat close next to me, and lowered his voice.

"Stalin is ill," he said. "It's not public information yet. No one seems to know if he is alive or dead."

Part of me wanted to leap up and run to the office. Yuri would no doubt have some juicy gossip. And as we only had two Supreme Leaders in our entire history, it would be a huge story. During the war, I would not have hesitated. But now, surrounded by family, it seemed less urgent. Funny how age softens ambition, its call to action tempered by a renewed sense of perspective.

As Nikolai applauded the children's school work, I made dinner. My efforts in that department were still modest, though I had learned some helpful culinary tips over the years from Katarina and Igor. As I busied myself in the kitchen, I thought back to the time our first Soviet leader had died.

In 1924, Vladimir Lenin suffered a stroke, his once eloquent voice made mute by illness. Soon after, he died. Then, I had mourned with the purity of a child, wounded beyond description by the tragedy. Now, nearly three decades later, I felt only resentment, simmering below the surface of my heart. Stalin had haunted my dreams. My father and my unborn son were both dead, because of his cruelty. I had heard from one of my father's old friends that only a few months earlier, Stalin had started a purge of Jewish doctors. Claiming to have uncovered a conspiracy of physicians in league with Zionist forces, the Kremlin leaked reports to *Pravda* that there was a doctors' plot afoot to murder leading Soviet officials while pretending to treat them. My father had already perished in Stalin's Gulag work camps. At least he didn't have to go through another witch hunt, I thought.

Yuri had told me Stalin was pursuing a scientific research project to extend human existence. This rumor was no doubt fueled by the fact that he spared Dr. Lina Stern—convicted of treason and espionage amid the purge of Jewish doctors—from the death penalty because he thought she could prolong his life. But I had little faith in what might come after Stalin. True, there was a younger generation of patriots, like Nikolai, who might steer the country away from its bloody past. But they would have to fight their way to the top, I knew, brushing past hardcore Communists as brutal as Stalin. And what real patriot, I wondered, would even want to endure that kind of peril?

I looked at Nikolai and saw only goodness. And goodness, I figured, was incompatible with power.

The next day I went to work. Almost as soon as I arrived, Vadim rushed into my office and handed me a bulletin to read on the air. I was surprised the Kremlin had sanctioned the announcement.

"Friends and listeners," I began, "the man who has led our nation through war and hardship, who has defeated our foreign enemies, Our Great Comrade Joseph Stalin, has suffered a stroke. We are told that he was in his Kremlin apartments four nights ago when he was stricken by a cerebral hemorrhage causing loss of speech, and paralysis on his right side. He is receiving medical treatment under the constant supervision of the Communist Party, and despite his grave state of health, doctors are applying a series of therapeutic measures to restore important functions."

I looked up at Vadim, unsure of how much more he wanted me to read. There was a list of 21 doctors who were said to be tending to Stalin's care—some reporting to the Communist Party, others to the Minister of Public Health. It was almost comical to believe that a committee of two dozen could tend to a patient's needs, at least well. None of these doctors, of course, were Jewish. Vadim nodded. Maybe he thought, as I did, that no one would believe such a fairytale anyway. But the announcement had come from the Kremlin. There was peril if we did not read it in its entirety.

How odd, I mused, that the only two leaders of the Soviet Union were both felled by strokes. I wondered if Stalin's campaign against Jewish doctors had compromised the care he was getting. I also wondered if he had even been at the Kremlin, as Yuri had heard Stalin was spending more and more time at his southern dacha, revived by the warm Caucus weather of his childhood.

Two days later, when we again left the house as a family, heavy black-bordered red Soviet flags hung from many a government building, and there were huge portraits of Stalin in his gray generalissimo uniform, draped in black. Later that day, I reported on the air the official arrangements for the funeral: Stalin's body would lie in state in the House of Unions, within a few hundred yards of Red Square, for three days. I didn't mention this was one day fewer than what Lenin had, but imagined the father of our country would be relieved. If Anna was right, and she usually was, Lenin had no love lost for Stalin. In fact, he would no doubt have preferred his brutal successor be buried elsewhere.

Even before Stalin was laid to rest, a power struggle began. Yuri told me a troika of officials—Georgi Malenkov, first secretary of the Communist Party, Laventi Beria, feared Minister of Internal Affairs and Nikita Khrushchev, a close Stalin ally who had overseen Soviet affairs in Ukraine—were vying for the top position. Most of Leningrad's inner circles were engrossed in the fight. I was suddenly disinterested, and turned my broadcast duties over to a young colleague, who of course, was thrilled. But the crisis in Moscow meant little to me compared to the trauma in my own home.

For the first time in our marriage, Nikolai and I were fighting.

"I have to go," he announced one night. "The command has asked me to serve abroad."

"But you promised!" I exclaimed. "You promised you would serve at your desk, here in Leningrad, with your family at your side."

"I never promised," he replied. "I said I would try."

"Nikolai, I went through most of the war without you. I felt the loss intently. It's not a feeling I want to repeat."

"Olga, for goodness sake, during the war, we all served where we were needed, you more than most of us. How could you say I wasn't here for you—I came home when I could, and the rest of the time, I tried to save our city from the enemy! Is that the same as being absent?"

I nodded weakly.

"Of course not. Sorry. I just can't bring myself to say goodbye again."

Nikolai still looked wounded.

"I understand that you are a patriot, who answers when your nation calls," I said. Even my apology sounded feeble, I thought. "It's just that, just that…"

I started crying then, and he came to embrace me. We held each other tight. Perhaps he was as alarmed as I was that we were fighting.

"*Dover'te mne*," he said, whispering in my ear, "trust me."

And so, even as military brigades were marching in tribute to Joseph Stalin and throngs of mourners were memorializing him in Moscow, Abigail, Fyodor and I walked Nikolai to the train station in Leningrad. I am glad we were not in the capital—a friend in

Moscow wrote me that the crowds were so thick, and the planning so poor, that big military trucks stood in the streets and mourners were crushed to death. No one knew how many, but it haunted me that when asked to move their vehicles, the soldiers refused, as they had no orders to do so. Here is the final legacy of Stalin, I thought. All of us were vulnerable to suffering in the cause of his reputation. I remembered how Anna had told me that Stalin would only cede to the Americans, as they could write his legacy as the man who had finally defeated Hitler. But we were in a Cold War with them, and Stalin was gone.

"You look as handsome as Lenin," I said. We both laughed, to quizzical looks from the children. I explained that I told him that years before, the first time he went off to war. I was relieved when he told me he was going to East Germany—so much closer than Korea!—but alarmed when he told me why. He was part of a brigade being sent to put down an uprising of dissidents who wanted to be free from the Soviet arc of power. He would be fighting another war.

Three weeks later, we got his first letter. I smiled when I noticed Nikolai had used my secret postal code on the envelope, meant to bypass censors. It had worked well during the war. I guess it still had. After reading the letter, I prayed it had not been opened by officials. If anyone in the Ministry of Interior Affairs had seen this letter, I cringed to think what they might do to Nikolai.

"We are battling comrades in the streets," he wrote. "Our foreign language specialists are trying to make them understand the benefits of living in a Communist world. I asked one of them, my friend Simeon Savin, to tell me about those conversations.

"I talk about a society where everyone is taken care of, their food, shelter, medicine," Simeon told me. "I talk about a culture where everyone is equal, no one is better than anyone else."

"And what do they say?" I asked.

"They say they want free speech and free will."

"So what do you tell them?"

Simeon paused before finishing the story.

"Once, I made the mistake of telling one man if he wants that he should go to America," he said.

"And what did he say to that?"

"He said, 'Can you get me an exit visa?'"

I knew then that Nikolai was in danger, that our country's great experiment in Bolshevism was in peril. If our comrades in other countries no longer wanted to live under our influence, if they were willing to rebel at great personal risk, Communism would only survive by brute force. By writing me about Simeon Savin's story, Nikolai was suggesting that he shared those concerns. I prayed no one else had seen the letter, or read between its lines.

Two weeks later came another letter. Nikolai was coming home. I left the children with Luby and met him at the station. When he saw me, he held me as if he would never let go again.

"I pray I have not compromised you or the children," he said.

"What happened?"

"I questioned the mission," he said. "After listening to Simeon's reports, I started thinking that maybe we should not be there, should not be imposing on will on people dictatorially. So one day, I asked my commander if he agreed with the mission. I might as well have spit on Stalin's grave."

He was discharged, a man left without an identity. I was grateful he had not been arrested. The children sensed something was wrong—Fyodor kept asking why Papa wasn't going to his office, and Abigail wondered why he was always in his night clothes. Nikolai retreated, as he always had, to literature, offering to read the children from his favorite Dostoyevsky passages.

What do I care for a hell for oppressors? What good can hell do, since those children have already been tortured? And what becomes of harmony, if there is hell? I want to forgive. I want to embrace. I don't want more suffering.

One day, he came home from a visit to Uncle Sasha's library. He was coughing.

"It's nothing," he said, reading my face. "You worry too much."

"Tomorrow we will go to the doctor."

God how I hate Soviet medicine. It's so cold, so dehumanizing. A doctor in a white coat takes blood samples and leaves us to wait. Then—after what seems like hours—he returns to tell us that the patient's loss of food and vitamins during the war has weakened his heart, like an unexpected consequence of survival. Doctors suggest food, glucose, anything to sustain him.

In the end, it was too late. This time there was no mistaking the symptoms—the yellow skin, the dystrophy, the loss of muscle. For me, it was like reliving a nightmare. I could only imagine how it must have seemed to him, like a soldier dying after the armistice had been signed. We held hands often, and pondered such questions of whether and how to tell the children. Probably they already knew.

I was bitter. We had survived the war, and now, almost a decade later, after the Nazis had been defeated and new enemies rose to take their place, the cruelty of illness crossed our journey. I was preoccupied with how to ensure Nikolai's dignity as he faded from our company.

I took to prayer—Saint Catherine's Armenian Church on Nevsky Prospekt had reopened after the war—and asked God to cleanse my heart. Before long I came to appreciate that none of us could write our final chapter, none of us could write the script for that moment when we had to say goodbye. I tried to take comfort from what we had, and what we had created. Nikolai Molchanov had been the greatest blessing in my life. I was lucky to share his love for as long as I did.

Eventually he was hospitalized, my big strong Nikolai now too weak to lift a fork. I took the children to visit as often as I could, hoping they would cement a memory of their father. My own had died in Siberia. I had been unable to save him from the Gulag. Or maybe he never recovered from my mother's death years earlier.

Anyway, I wanted Abigail and Fyodor to have a lasting memory of what a wonder it was to have a great father.

"Gosh she looks like me," he said one day after Abigail's visit. "What a thrill that is." He caressed my chin, stroked my neck, and locked into my eyes. "Isn't it funny that Fyodor looks like you?"

I smiled, but inside, I was crying. Nikolai was only 49 years old. His children were not yet teenagers. He deserved more time. We all deserved more time.

"I remember when you told me I was the best risk you ever took," he said one day, taking my face in his hands, the way he always did. "But you were wrong. You were *my* treasure. You brought me spirit and love, sunshine and laughter, drama and contentment. Life would have been far less exciting without you." He kissed me then, softly on the lips, through both our tears.

I clung to him as long as I could, and he to me. I look back and think we were like two bears preparing for winter's hibernation — eager to devour every moment we could before we retreated.

"You look so beautiful," he said one day when I visited the hospital.

"And you so handsome," I said.

We smiled, and gazed into each other's eyes, willfully refusing to see the inevitable.

How cruel it was to lose a soldier to wars after they had ended, after he had escaped the battlefields but not its wounds. My tears were of love, mingled with grievance. Why us? Why was this happening to us? We who had given so much to win. I grew melancholy then, but tried not to show it.

As the weeks went on, his condition worsened. The end came swiftly, inevitable and terrible. He was delirious, and in lucid moments did his best to comfort me, before again relapsing into delirium, groaning softly. Nikolai Molchanov died in February, on St. Valentine's Day, a statistic among so many others. There was no funeral, only a procession. Maria, Dhazdat, Sasha and Eliasberg led our caravan to the cemetery. I held Nikolai's hand, cold now, in a glove, for the last time, and cried. The children walked behind. Later, I took to the airways, my refuge, to read a poem.

"During the war, a friend of mine called around," I began. "Without a tear she told me she's just buried her one true friend. Then, I had sat in silence with her until the morning. Now I know why we said nothing. What words were there to say to her? How could I comfort her? I couldn't know then, but I know now. I, too, am a widow now, dear Leningrad. Like all of us, I too, am grieved."

Dhazdat told me he cried on hearing that poem. He knew how much I loved Nikolai. And he reminded me of the Radio House picnic, the day before the invasion, when the sun shone brightly, food was plentiful, and we all sat on a blanket contemplating our futures, toasting patriotism.

"Do you think we had an inkling that our loyalty would be so tested?" I asked him.

He shook his head. "I had no idea," he said. "I only know the ordeal has changed me. I'm not sure I would toast to patriotism so mindlessly again. Or anyway, I will toast family first."

After Nikolai's death, I spent months crying into my pillow, cursing the fates. Maria roused me from my bed, reminding me of my obligation to history. I had to tell the story of Leningrad's ordeal. I had to remember, before I could forget. And so I have.

TWENTY-ONE

The Reunion
August 1992

When I walked in, I heard Katya Medvedeva and Mikhail Parfionov reading off the names of all the musicians who had performed at that famous concert during the war, taking turns, first a feminine voice, then masculine. It sounded like the metronome, *tick, tock, tick, tock,* the one that played on Radio Leningrad during the war, simulating the city's heartbeat, haunting my dreams.

I teared up as I looked at the stage, recalling the remarkable concert that took place there exactly fifty years before. Of the 83 musicians who had originally played amid the mass starvation of the Nazi blockade on August 9, 1942, fourteen survivors appeared for this reprise in 1992. They tried to sit in the same seats with the same instruments as they had done a half-century before, though some had trouble remembering and had to be reminded by their colleagues. Then, they played Symphony No. 7, which Dmitri Shostakovich had dedicated to his native city of Leningrad. Now, they came as witnesses to that time, when a symphony uplifted a city weighed down by bombs, hunger and cold. So few were still alive, I thought, and they all looked so old! I sat in my same seat too, ready to provide commentary and maybe a bit of poetry.

The world had changed much in the intervening half-century, our world in particular. After the war, the Soviet government awarded a Defense of Leningrad medal to 1.5 million people, almost the same number who survived here. As ever a character in its own story, Leningrad itself was declared a 'hero city', with statues erected to the city's bravery, some of them featured these days in a network of new metro stations. Local officials even created a Museum of the Defense of Leningrad, with a display of the guns and ordnance confiscated from the Germans, and a mock-up of a wartime ration station and, of course, two thin slices of tampered bread on which so many managed to survive.

The museum's most popular section featured the diaries kept by so many of my listeners. The one most often quoted, and most often photographed, was by a 12-year-old girl named Tanya Savicheva. I always thought it was the most precious artifact of all. Its stark objectivity, its bloodless description of death, its simple writing on the pages of a pocket address book, will always speak to me about the legacy of this haunting Siege. I always grow rueful when I see her diary, as it makes me reminisce about Nikolai, of our happy times, and of the heartbreak of losing someone before their time.

"28 December 1941 at 12:30 a.m., Zhenya died. 25 January 1942 at 3 p.m., Granny died. 17 March at 5 a.m., Lyoka died. 13

April at 2 a.m., Uncle Vasya died. 10 May at 4 p.m., Uncle Lyosha died. 13 May at 7:30 a.m., Mama died. The Savichevas are dead. Everyone is dead. Only Tanya is left."

Before his death, a paranoid Stalin reneged on these symbols of healing. I imagine he thought that telling the story of how Leningraders survived the Siege would diminish his own role in winning the war, that boosting Leningrad's fame would curb his own. So he closed the museum and, not content with control, added cruelty, sentencing its director to 25 years in the Gulag for 'amassing ammunition in preparation for terrorist acts'. Then he commenced a purge of Leningrad's military and party leadership—anyone with the memory of acts of bravery to save Leningrad—and an array of academics and professionals deemed too cosmopolitan, too Jewish, too Western. I felt lucky to escape this round of suspicion. I thought maybe God was looking after me after all. Peter the Great had opened his 'window on the West' to take the Tatar out of the Russian. Stalin, born in poverty in Georgia, seemed to want to return the country's view East.

I was more and more turning to my diary, sharing confidences with no one.

"How is my heart to grabble with this attempt to erase history? How is my mind to understand that Stalin is just another word for Hitler, just another dictator who wants to rid the world of Jews. Shostakovich. Eliasberg. My father. Are these icons of the past to fall from memory? If so, Hitler will have succeeded, with Stalin's consent."

Though awarded a Hero of Leningrad Medal for his role in willing the orchestra to perform, Karl Eliasberg proved expendable. One day, as unceremoniously as when he had arrived 32 years before, he walked into Vadim's office for the final dressing down of his career. The director had told me what he planned to say to Eliasberg, and I was worried. I asked if I could sit in on the meeting.

"Karl, we thank you for your service during the war," Vadim began. *"Now we would like you to travel, to bring music to Soviet citizens outside our great cities."*

"You want me to become a vagabond conductor?" Eliasberg asked, unable to curb his sarcasm.

Vadim looked down at his hands, uncomfortable at having to choose between his two conductors, between the prestigious Philharmonic and the more working-class Radio Orchestra of Leningrad. On a professional basis, I knew, the decision wasn't close.

Unlike Eliasberg, Yevgeny Mravinsky had been blessed with pedigree. He could trace his musical heritage to his aunt Yevgeniya Mravina, principal opera soloist at the Mariinsky Theater in the late 1880s. As for his political credentials, those he owed to her half-sister, his other aunt, Alexandra Kollontai, a Marxist theoretician who served as People's Commissar for Welfare, the first woman in Lenin's first revolutionary government. Mravinsky once quipped that the combination protected him from the Gulag—and the critics. I often thought those were the same. Now he sat in Vadim's office, waiting to bring the ax down on Eliasberg's head. It was hard for me to watch.

"You are not good enough for Leningrad," scoffed Mravinsky, in a judgment that was part resentment at Eliasberg's reputation and part determination to restore his own. "Yes, you were here during the war, and you led the reserve orchestra in a performance that made people feel better. But musically, that concert was pathetic, and unworthy of a great city."

"It was valiant," said Eliasberg, raising his voice in defense of his musicians. "You were too important to stay in Leningrad during the war, Yevgeny. You fled with your acclaimed orchestra to Siberia of all places, that great mecca of cultural sophistication." I smiled at this. You had to credit Karl for his wit. The slight seemed lost on Yevgeny, who maintained a smirk throughout.

"We did the work that you abandoned—it wasn't just No. 7," Karl continued. "We performed 400 concerts during the Siege—and many of the musicians played through pain, hunger and weakness."

I looked away then. Karl was too straightforward, too intellectually honorable, to offer false flattery, I thought. Perhaps it wouldn't have mattered anyway.

"You old Jew fool," Mravinsky sneered. "Did you really think you and they will be remembered? History is written by those who are powerful, not those who are weak. You are from Minsk, not from Leningrad. You are nothing. History will remember you as nothing."

"Stalin didn't think I was nothing when he named me Meritorious Artist of Russia."

"That was during the war. That was for morale. Now you are nothing, and you will die forgotten."

Karl told me he always understood that Mravinsky was the favored one. He had a star's charisma, a magnetism, that drove audiences to exuberant ovations. Behind the scenes, he was a despot. But on stage, he was a charmer. Eliasberg looked the part of the plodder, the one who had to work harder to reach a similar result. But I knew from our talks he truly believed his work ethic would catapult him, would give him equal standing with those who came to the task with a store of entitlement.

"You can keep me out of Leningrad," he said, *"but you cannot keep me out of history."*

In some sense, I always thought Karl had the last laugh. Soon after the war, he was invited to conduct Symphony No. 7 in Britain, with the London Symphonic Orchestra. While there, King George VI awarded him the King's Medal for Courage in the Cause of Freedom. The medal was awarded to citizens of allied countries who helped win the war. Some recipients were members of Resistance groups in various countries in German-occupied Europe. Others helped British servicemen evade the enemy or escape from occupied areas. Karl was the only musician to win.

"For meritorious service in furtherance of the interests of the British Commonwealth in the allied cause," King George read at the medal ceremony, "I hereby award this medal to Karl Eliasberg of the Soviet Union. His heroic conducting of the famous concert of Shostakovich's Symphony No. 7 was an inspiration to the people of Leningrad, and to their allies here in Britain and throughout the world, at a time when we were fighting annihilation by Adolf Hitler's Third Reich."

I smiled when Yuri told me about the medal. He'd heard about it from a colleague at the BBC. Take that, Yevgeny Mravinsky, I thought. A few weeks later, word circulated that Karl Ilyich Eliasberg, only son of the founder of Russia's first Marxist club, named for the two great icons of Soviet history, Karl Marx and Vladimir Ilyich Lenin, had defected to Britain. All mentions of his name were quickly expunged from public records, as if erased from memory. A movie made about the concert after the war made no mention of his name, nor of his role in directing musicians in pain.

At this reunion, Nina Bronnikova, who led the team that transcribed all those scores for the musicians, talked about Eliasberg with great bitterness. I sometimes thought she had been in love with him, but she had not followed him to England, where the conductor died 14 years ago. All his life, she said, people kept telling him he was 'good enough but not special', 'the second fiddle', 'undeserving of fame and honor'. She was very blunt—more than the occasion merited, I thought—about Eliasberg's showdown with Mravinsky and how it left him stooped over.

"He always believed that he and his musicians were the equal of any, and he would have wished history to record that on August

9, 1942, they proved all the naysayers—Hitler, Stalin, Mravinsky and even Shostakovich—wrong," she said. She quoted something that Eliasberg had said after the concert: "Moments like that do not come often. I cannot explain the feeling I had. The glory of fame and the grief of loss, and the thought that maybe the brightest moment of your life is gone. I imagine the city lives a peaceful life now, but it does not have the right to forget the past."

As I looked around the concert hall, all I could think about were its chandeliers. They were the first thing people noticed when they arrived for the concert, their brilliant light casting a sense of magic on the scene. Electricity had been out in Leningrad for months, and I thought the chandeliers would cheer the audience. But Captain Parfionov told me the lights would inspire the musicians more than the audience. He was right. Now he was here, with Katya. Their three grown children watched as both parents took their seats, he with trombone, she with oboe.

"Wonderful to see you, Olga," he said. "Tell me, as a writer, do you know where the years went?"

"To memories, and emotion," I said, smiling. "How are you two doing?"

"Well," he said. "We have a wonderful family. And last December, I met my sister for the first time since we were sent to separate orphanages as children."

"How wonderful!" I said, remembering the story of how their parents had been killed during the revolutionary riots during Bloody Sunday, when the tsar's army fired on protestors.

"Yes it was," he said with a rare smile. "She is three years older than I am and had memories of our parents that I never knew. At first I didn't recognize her at all, but the longer we talked, the more I saw in her some resemblance to me. Katya saw the likeness immediately and teased me for being slow. But honestly, Olga, I like being methodical. I sometimes think it's what got me through the war. One foot in front of the other, like a soldier on duty. Like your Nikolai too."

I paused then, and contemplated my Koyla. After his death, Yuri had tried to woo me but he knew, as I did, that Nikolai would always be my only love. Sometimes when I look in the mirror, I'm glad Nikolai is not here to see how I've aged. But other times when I look at our daughter—Abigail is her own woman now, who with her husband has given me two grandchildren—and our son Fyodor, who is about to marry his lovely Sonya and who is thriving as an engineer—I hurt for him that Nikolai did not survive to enjoy their company. My granddaughter Svetlana has just made me a great-grandmother. Her newborn, Aleksei, looks like Abby, who looks like Nikolai. Every time I see the baby, I marvel at the connection between genetics and memory. What a legacy Koyla has left us.

As I sat waiting for the pared-down concert to begin, alone in my thoughts, an old man approached. I would not have recognized him in any event—he had entered my life, and exited, so long before—but he introduced himself as Efren Klebanoff, the policeman whose interrogation led to my imprisonment, and the miscarriage of our son Grigori. He asked to sit next to me.

"I came here to apologize to you," he said. "It was wrong to accuse you of disloyalty to the party."

"Wasn't that your job?" I said, with more kindness than I felt.

He nodded. "Yes, but I might have done it with less enthusiasm." He looked off into the distance. "It shames me now, to think of the things I did to stay alive then."

"Did you know I was tortured in prison, and lost a pregnancy?"

He bowed his head and nodded.

"Yes, I heard rumors. I was ashamed then, but said nothing. Now I want to say I am. I'm sorry."

"Are you a man of religion, Efren Klebanoff?"

He shook his head.

"You might consider it. There are saints there, and priests, who will forgive you."

By the time of the reunion concert, Mikhail Gorbachev had almost single-handedly closed the record on a Communist regime that had purged, tortured and slaughtered many of its citizens, often on flimsy evidence of disloyalty. Breathing now in a world where freedom at least had a competitive chance against repression, I found I was less angry at things that had happened during that era when individual independence was often confused with treason.

"We all played our roles, I suppose," I said. "I only wished you had not played yours so well!"

We both smiled at that.

"Is that drummer here?" he said. "I'd like to apologize to him too."

I directed him to where Dhazdat and Katarina were sitting. Dhazdat's dark hair had turned white, and his gait was slower. He stood to greet Klebanoff, and I saw the two shake hands. Maybe it's age, I thought, maybe being older conferred a certain forgiveness. Later, when he picked up the drumsticks and beat on the timpani, Dhazdat's face broke out into a smile as wide as our country, and I could see the young man again. I remembered that frightful day during the Siege when he was given up as a corpse, until I saw his fingers move. Maybe God meant for him to survive. It's hard to imagine how the Radio Orchestra could have performed this concert without him. I always loved what Winston Churchill wrote to the Kremlin afterward, saying he wished he'd changed his famous Dunkirk speech to say, 'We shall fight on the beaches, in the concert halls and on our drums!'

Katarina was all smiles. She was walking on a cane now, but somehow had managed to retain the look of a ballerina. There was something regal in her appearance, no doubt an inspiration to generations of students, but to me, an emblem of character. She was a beauty who radiated grace. Maybe it was the yoga. Anyway, I envied her for that. I sometimes marveled that our friendship, forged over a warm family Ukrainian meal, had lasted through war, famine and heartbreak. I suspect she will be remembered longer than any of us. She was the greatest ballerina of her day in a country that reveres the ballet. Then she reinvigorated the art form. But no one in this city will ever think of the Siege without envisioning that photograph of Dhazdat and Katarina, taken during the street party after the blockade was lifted and he bent her backward, her blond hair grazing the street and their lips joined in a kiss. As our mighty Cossack took his seat behind the drums, I saw tears in her eyes.

Viktoria was at the reunion too. She had taken a leave from the museum to give birth to her two children, and returned to lead a reinvention at the museum. I always suspected her organizational skills were great tools for family life, but at the museum they helped the institution flourish. These days she stayed in the background—creating new lecture series and arranging brilliant traveling exhibits where others could shine. With her energy and creative ideas, the Hermitage had become a mecca of culture and a source of pride for all Russians, even those just visiting from the countryside. On special occasions, she would personally give a tour of the museum's artifacts, which she had been so instrumental in saving during the war. Once, she and Boris traveled to Paris, where she studied art history at the Sorbonne. They were honored with a special tour of the Louvre's collections, and she gave a talk about the importance of preservation. To my knowledge, she never spoke publicly about the trial where she was falsely accused of stealing the Hermitage treasures, though in private, she often celebrated her husband's chivalry in testifying on her behalf. Boris, that great enthusiast for nature, art and family, died two years ago of a cerebral hemorrhage. It filled me with pride that their son, Nikolai, named for my Koyla, assumed his father's duties at the Hermitage.

"The lights are still here," Viktoria said as she hugged me at the reunion.

"And so are we!" I replied.

Other members of the Poet's Circle had left us. Anna died after Stalin did, and I always thought she was pleased to see him buried first. Her epic poem, *Requiem*, had been published in her lifetime, during the Khrushchev era, when the new premier opened the floodgates to memories of Stalin's wrongs even as he cemented power by aligning with the party apparatchiks who had imposed so much tyranny on so many. *Requiem* was a majestic poem, and it earned her nomination for the Nobel Peace Prize. Sometimes I muse about whether great literature requires living through adversity. After her death, her reputation grew even greater. A porcelain figurine of her—in a flowered dress and a red shawl— became a popular acquisition. I hated the icon. To me, Anna Akhmatova was a character of great height, of great sacrifice, and the figurine seemed so silly, so commonplace. But I concluded that her literary fame was its own reward, however dressed, separate from public memory.

As for Luby, she died away from the crowds, peacefully in her sleep. Andrei spoke at her funeral, as did Rahil, giving testimony to how her love had steadied their lives. My sister Maria died a few years ago, of heartbreak really, though alcohol might have contributed. She had visited Garegin's family in Armenia, but had never found comfort there. I'm glad she had met him, and brought him to that picnic, and made a life with him, the man she and I jokingly called her socially clumsy Armenian.

Sadly, Igor and Andrei had also died a few years back—Andrei of cancer, Igor of a heart attack. Their death made me feel I was at that age of longevity where friends, who had been for me a circle of family, were leaving. At the concert's reunion, their son Rahil rose to speak for them.

"I want to say how much they meant to me," he said. "Papa Igor taught me how to cook—well, he actually taught the whole country how to cook—and Andrei taught me manners and morals. I feel lucky to have grown up with them, lucky they lived long enough to dance at my wedding to my beautiful bride Sofia." At this, he stopped and blew a kiss to his wife. "And I want to say one more thing. Igor and Andrei adopted me after my family was obliterated by German bombs. They took me in, they fed me— and this was in a time when there was not a lot of food—and they loved me. And so did Lyubov Shaporina, who became my grandmother, and taught me the art of puppetry and the primacy of loyalty. In the new Russia we are building, I hope that men who enjoy each other's company will be welcomed into the fabric of our nation. I was a small boy when the two of them played on this stage in that historic concert, but I remember how proud they were of being part of this orchestra. And now it is time to say how proud I was of them—Andrei on the violin, Igor on the cello—and how proud I am still to call them my parents. If Igor was here he would think of something witty to say, but all I can say is how lucky I feel to be their son." With that, he took Igor's place on the stage, cradling his cello. How proud it made me to have been part of their story.

I rose to speak. I wanted to explain to this audience, most of them from a generation that had only heard about the Siege, who had not lived through its miseries and fears, why we were victorious.

"We gather here today as survivors of totalitarian rulers," I said, mentioning neither Hitler nor Stalin by name. "This is no small achievement. It is even more difficult, but very Russian, to do this by embracing creativity. Music is in our souls, and when we reached for its comforts in those terrible days of starvation and destruction, we were affirming not just our humanity but our culture.

"The concert that took place here fifty years ago was a work of love. Our conductor pushed his musicians through hardships—the death of loved ones, the loss of toes to frostbite, the lack of breath with which to blow into their horns—he pushed them to perform. And when they did, Leningrad stood and roared, energized to finish the fight, to win the war. Some military leaders, trained in battle planes and weapons superiority, might scoff at this idea. But ours did not. The day before the concert, General Leonid Govorov hit the enemy's batteries, their observation points, their communication center, all in an effort to keep them quiet during the performance. It worked. And everyone—from German troops to starving Soviet citizens—felt the call of the music.

"My brother-in-law, Garegin Ananyan, played the harp for this performance. He died immediately afterward, of starvation. He was the first casualty of this concert, but he considered it a triumph. As a young boy, he had escaped the Armenian Genocide, and as a young man, he felt it an honor to play in this orchestra, to fill the people of this city with hope at a time of trauma.

"There were many stories like his in this orchestra. When we met here fifty years ago, Dmitri Nagornyuk performed against the strenuous advice of his children. No one knew exactly how old he was, but Nagornyuk had played in orchestras conducted by Rimsky Korsakov in the 19th century. His son, fighting for our army, had been severely wounded in battle, and pleaded with his aging father, now thin to the bone, to be evacuated with him. 'No,' said Nagornyuk, 'I cannot leave the orchestra. It is my proudest destiny to play Shostakovich's Symphony No. 7.' And so he did.

"Scholars say history is written by the victorious, but for me, this concert was proof that history is also shaped by its victims. When Dhazdat Zelensky unleashed his ferocious zeal on the drums, it felt like we were all pounding, all purging ourselves of the many agonies of the Siege. The starvation, the constant bombardments, the friends dropping dead on the streets—it felt like Dhazdat's fingers were a defiant rebuttal, our declaration that despite it all, we intended to live.

"This is our legacy, children, not only the music, not only that we persevered against evil, but that we did so by honoring our cultural history. It is important that we remember this history, and tell it to our children, who must tell it to theirs. We put our suffering, our survival, our memories, in your hands. Because I have come to understand, at the end of my life, what I wish I'd known at the start. History, despite all its clashing cymbals, all its sound and fury, is mostly irony. Memory is the thing."

I sat down then, to polite applause. It reminded me of the applause I received from those audiences in Moscow. War-torn like us, but not starving to death, they sympathized but could not really understand our ordeal. Maybe memories of suffering belong only to those who suffered, not to their descendants or to their biographers. Would this generation be any better putting themselves in our shoes, would they ever understand how much that concert meant to us?

With Gorbachev's arrival, and the reinvention once more of Russian history, officials took down the red flag of sickle and hammer that flew over Catherine the Great's Winter Palace and replaced it with the Russian tricolors. The people of Leningrad voted to change the name of their city back to St. Petersburg. If only Maria had been here, I thought, to see Peter the Great's triumph. Maybe, like Alexandre Dumas, she would finally have heard the angels singing on Nevsky Prospekt. Kuibyshev, where we sent more of our evacuees during the war, was renamed Samara. I hear it's booming.

Another man approached. He was tall and very fit, with a muscular handshake. I figured him to be about 40 years old, born after the war, not a witness to the events I described.

"I found your talk interesting," he said. "My parents were survivors of the Siege, and I know from them of the depressing hardships."

I nodded at him to continue.

"My father was a sailor. His legs were shattered by shrapnel during the war. A friend in the Navy saved his life by carrying him on his back across the frozen Neva River to the Astoria Hospital. There he encountered my mother Maria, who had been given up for dead, a victim of starvation, and my brother Viktor, then 10, who was suffering from diphtheria. Viktor succumbed to his illness. That my parents survived is a miracle, that I am here is a miracle, but it has nothing to do with music, or culture. It has to do with the will to live."

I nodded weakly, thinking of Nikolai.

"We all have a will to live," I said. "Sometimes the body fails us. But I believe, I will always believe, that hope gives us more of a fighting chance."

The man shook his head.

"Hope is the mischief of losers. It is strength that saves us, strength of character, but also of nation. The lesson I took from the Siege is that we must never let anyone invade our nation again."

"That is an admirable goal," I said, cautiously, "but I suppose I am more spiritual about the role of hope in our lives. We will have to disagree, I suppose. But thank you for talking to me."

"I am not done talking," the man said. "I want to write the forward to your book about the Siege."

"And you are?" I asked.

"My name is Vladimir Putin," he said. "For 16 years, I have been in foreign intelligence for the KGB. I recently resigned, to join political circles here in St. Petersburg. I would welcome this opportunity to put my own memories down, to interpret the Siege from a different view."

I was taken aback. Why would I want a military man, an intelligence agent at that, to put his mark on my memories? Maybe it was a sign from God. Finally I said, "I would agree on two conditions.

"First, I insist that you read the whole book. Second, I ask that, in your comments, you acknowledge the role of culture in easing our pain. Even if you think raw power was more determinative in our ultimate victory, I insist that you acknowledge the role of art, music, theater, ballet, literature and poetry in our survival."

A smile broke out on his face, and it made him look less menacing. He reached to shake my hand.

"We will be joined in history, you and I," he said. "My father would be overjoyed."

I watched as he walked away, wondering if the Era of Gorbachev would prove a temporary peak in Russian history, a brief interlude when truth is no longer hostage to government propaganda, to be replaced again by totalitarianism, led by former intelligence officers. It made me shudder.

Dhazdat came up then, as he had many times before in my life, pulling me from my reveries.

"Come," he said. "Katarina has made you spicy treats. She says delicious foods and daily yoga are the only paths out of sadness."

"That and memories," I said, thinking back to Katarina's spread at the picnic before the war began.

With that, I looped my hand through his arm and together, we left the stage.

ACKNOWLEDGMENTS

They were key in launching this project—Rhys Williams for giving me the idea, Sloane Hagenstad for serving as an early sounding board, Shelley Greif for remarking on its promise as a book about women. There are several non-fiction accounts of the Siege of Leningrad—Harrison Salisbury's *900 Days*, Anna Reid's *Leningrad: The Epic Siege of World War II*, Michael Jones' *Leningrad: State of Siege*. About the concert there are others—Brian Moynihan's *Leningrad Siege and Symphony*, M.T. Anderson's *Symphony for the City of the Dead*. To these authors, thank you for the research that inspired this book.

But in its soul, *The Concert* is a work of fiction.

I had a long career as a journalist—covering the White House and State Department for *USA Today* and the *Los Angeles Times* in Washington. Then I enrolled in American University to earn a PhD in history, writing two books about the history of the women's suffrage movement, *Gilded Suffragists: The New York Socialites Who Fought for Women's Right to Vote* as well as *And Yet*

They Persisted: How American Women Won the Right to Vote. With this book, I have reinvented again, as a novelist.

Book doctor David Groff helped me transition from a historian to an author of fiction, though he expressed surprise when I told him I had decided to tell the story through Olga's eyes. "A radical and exciting approach," he wrote. He suggested a huge whiteboard. A shout-out to Sean Sullivan, who painted with care and aesthetic sensibility a huge easel I bought on which to put the whiteboard, the better to reimagine the characters and the plot. All kinds of scribbles, in all kinds of colors, dot the board. I have not yet erased them, so memorable was the book's evolution.

I am indebted to several who know Russia well, who provided insights on language and culture, though any errors remain mine alone. John-Thor Dahlburg was a colleague from the *Los Angeles Times*, who was posted in Moscow for many years. He provided help with character names and valued institutions. Eugene Poltoratsy advised me on place names, and his friend Victor Smirnoff, whose grandfather, Alexander Kamensky, played in this concert, sent me the diary that Kamensky's wife kept. It was a thrill to read, and I think its insights added immensely to the fabric of this story.

I thank the talented team at BakeMyBook Inc., which guided the book through proofreading, copyright and production. A special thank you to team captain Theo Madden, his talented proofreaders, Felton Nichols and Francesca McCullough, the head of the design team, Hugh Aarons, and the entire marketing team.

Namaste to my yoga world of teachers and practitioners—I could not do this work without our daily practice. And, as usual, thank you to Jeffrey Glazer, as always my greatest fan, and dearest love. All through the pandemic and beyond, even when he was fighting leukemia, he pushed me to keep writing.

I no longer remember how often I rewrote this book. I know that two dozen agents turned it down.

But through the process, I often recalled an anecdote Jeffrey had told me about a tennis player named Vitas Gerulaitis, who beat Jimmy Connors in the semi-finals of the 1980 Masters. Asked by a reporter how he finally managed to defeat the reigning king of tennis after 16 tries, he said, "And let that be a lesson to you all. Nobody beats Vitas Gerulaitis 17 times in a row."

As *The Concert* finally neared its publication date, I thought of Gerulaitis often. He has convinced me it is never too late to produce a win. I hope readers agree.

ABOUT THE AUTHOR

Johanna Neuman is an author, historian and blogger who delights in the power of words. Her newest book, *The Concert*, traces the ordeal of the people of Leningrad during World War II after the Nazis invaded the Soviet Union and food, heat and electricity vanished. *The Concert* tracks a group of musicians, many starving, who triumphed over the twin evils of Adolf Hitler and Joseph Stalin by embracing their creativity, performing at a rousing concert that lifted the city to victory. An award-winning historian, Johanna is also one of the nation's leading experts on the history of women's suffrage, with two books, *Gilded Suffragists* and *And Yet They Persisted*. A former journalist who covered the White House, State Department and Congress for *USA Today* and the *Los Angeles Times*, she also writes a blog on substack.com, *Make Orwell Fiction Again*, about the decline of American democratic values in favor of authoritarianism.

Made in United States
Orlando, FL
12 August 2023